ROYAL ICING

MADISON SCORE

That's What She Said Publishing, Inc.

Royal Icing

ISBN: 979-8-88643-886-4 (ebook)

ISBN: 979-8-88643-887-1 (paperback)

madisonscore.com

111125

To Dan and Tim (mostly for being an excellent brother and brother-in-law, but also because they can't possibly be mad at me for writing a holiday book if I dedicate it to them).

CHAPTER ONE

LEO

"Okay, crank the burner." Leo stepped back from the stove and wiped his hands on a rag.

Christmas music played in the background as volunteers bustled around the community kitchen, already preparing for the evening meal ahead. The scent of chopped onion made his eyes water, but even uncooked bulb vegetables were better than another stuffy dinner at the castle with his parents.

Flames burst forth from the newly installed burner. He sniffed, but there was no hint of sulfur in the air. Another town catastrophe saved by YouTube.

"You did it again." Gus, a grizzled bear of a man and the soup kitchen's head chef, wrapped him in a tight hug. "Thank you. Truly. This is plenty of time for me to make tonight's minestrone."

"Happy to help. Anything else going on?" Leo cast a glance over the kitchen and the dining area beyond. It had certainly seen better days. While the staff had attempted to bring some holiday cheer to the space with lights and a fake tree, the tables were scrubby, the chairs were mismatched and wobbly, and the equipment was on its last legs. With any luck, that would all change by the end of next year.

"Nothing catastrophic," Gus said.

A light bulb over his head popped, leaving part of the kitchen in darkness. He sighed.

"I'll get the ladder," Leo called out.

It was always something.

Minutes later, he stowed the ladder in the closet and stepped out into the serving room. Someone shoved the creaky door open, bringing a burst of frigid air into the room. He really needed to grease those hinges.

Kat, a local architect, bustled in with a smile. "Your Highness." She curtsied and banged into one of the wooden chairs.

He grimaced. "It's Leo."

She faltered, and a pink tinge crept into her cheeks. "Are you sure?"

"Positive." It was an empty, outdated title. "Are you finished already?" he asked.

"Oh, yes." Kat looked like she was about to curtsy again, but instead she pulled a long tube from her messenger bag. "I stayed up all night working on these. I love your ideas for the lot. This would be life-changing for our community."

The plans unfurled, covering one of the dining tables in a dream. A future for his country that he could be proud of. His love letter to the hardworking citizens of Lynoria.

"I did add some things. I couldn't help myself. This is just a rough sketch until we get the library's input, but it deserves to be the biggest library in the kingdom. There's also space for a new playground and duck pond." She pointed to a green space. "An outdoor amphitheater for music or plays. I thought it would bring some peace to the women and children staying at the shelter."

Leo pored over the plans. He wasn't an architect, but he could practically see it in front of him. "And you were able to figure out space for a store? Storage for donations?" He squinted at the depiction of the new shelter, which was sorely needed as the shelters in the city were in a shameful state of disrepair.

"Yes, though I'd really like to chat with the other shelters in the city before finalizing any plans, Your High—Leo," she corrected herself with a cringe.

He smiled. "These are excellent. Thank you, Kat."

The flush was back in her cheeks. People were frequently nervous in his presence.

"I understand you have some architects on staff," she said in a low voice, "but if your bid is approved, I'd be honored to head up this project."

"You have my word." Leo's phone buzzed, and he pulled it out of his pocket. Great. An SOS from his mother. Had John royally messed something up again, or had another incredibly low-stakes problem arisen during the planning for the kingdom's 500th anniversary party? If he didn't return to the castle now, she would send a member of the royal guard to drag him home. And that was the last thing he needed.

"I have to go. Thank you for these. I look forward to working together."

"Oh, thank—" Kat's voice was cut off by the door swinging closed behind him.

———

WHEN HE ARRIVED AT THE DRAWING ROOM, THE REST OF HIS family was already there. A gold-trimmed table runner had appeared, and garland adorned the mantel even though Christmas wasn't for another four weeks. The staff must have decorated today.

John languished in an armchair by the fire, whiskey glass dangling from one hand as he gazed at the flames. Leo squinted. Was he imagining things, or did John have a black eye?

Ruby sat across from him, feet tucked underneath her and scrolling on the phone she never seemed to put down. Leo was about to scold her when his mother's voice interrupted.

"There you are," Queen Eleanor said. Her voice was sharp, like he had personally inconvenienced all of them. She started to say something else but stopped. "What are you wearing? Did anyone see you?"

Leo raised an eyebrow and glanced down. He had on jeans and steel-toed boots. It wasn't like he had wandered in sporting sequined nipple pasties and assless chaps.

She threw her hands up like he was a hopeless cause. And maybe he was. "Never mind. We have a problem."

"What is it this time? The kingdom is entirely out of cloth napkins? There's an international shortage of holly and mistletoe?" He plucked a snifter from the bar cart and poured a finger of bourbon.

"Your brother has had an affair with the royal baker."

"Oh." For once, a scandal worthy of an SOS.

Ruby looked up from her phone. "Dude," she said with a glance at John.

"Don't say 'dude,'" their mother snapped.

"It wasn't my fault." John threw a hand up. "She came on to me."

Ruby leaned forward. "I'm sorry—isn't the royal baker married?"

"Yes," John muttered. He touched his swollen eye.

"Silence." His mother's voice cut through the din like a siren. "The problem has been dealt with. The royal baker has found a lovely new position in Switzerland and will not be returning to Lynoria. A nondisclosure agreement was signed this afternoon, and they have been compensated for their silence."

Leo stifled a grunt. Typical. They seemed to have no end of money for bribes, but apparently they couldn't scrounge up anything but the bare minimum for improvements in the kingdom.

The queen strode over to the fire and stared at it. "Do you have anything to add, Beatrice?"

Beatrice, the royal publicist, perched at a table under a portrait of King Frederick. The real king hadn't looked up from his newspaper once since Leo had entered.

"Well, in the unlikely event that this does leak, we'll need to present a united front," Beatrice said hurriedly. There was nothing on this earth she was more afraid of than Queen Eleanor. The white-knuckle grip on her clipboard suggested she was waiting for a bomb to go off. "The only comment is 'no comment.' It wouldn't hurt to do some proactive public outreach. Some warm fuzzies. Leo, what have you been up to?"

He shook his head sharply. There was no way in hell they were going to use his public outreach for good press. What he did for his community was none of their business.

"Okay." Beatrice pivoted. "Princess? The people love you. There's a ribbon-cutting this week at the new ski apparel store."

Ruby looked up from her phone. "No, that's boring. I'll

read a book to the children at the library on Thursday after my harp lesson."

Leo smiled. Roo might be a tech zombie and angsty teen, but she was a good kid.

"Uh, great." Beatrice shuffled some papers and made a note. "So that leaves us with one more problem."

"Which is?" The queen shot her a look that would stop a rampaging bull in its tracks.

"No royal baker for the ball. I know you had high expectations for the dessert this year, Your Majesty."

The queen muttered something under her breath.

Ruby gasped and straightened up. "Oh, Mom. You remember that place that I told you about in New York? With the espresso croissant that changed my life? Please, can we hire them?"

The queen sighed. "A New York bakery? On this short of notice? I don't know, sweetheart."

"Please? No offense to Sarah, but they really were the best pastries I've ever had. And they're very prestigious. Look at their Instagram." The princess handed over her phone.

Eleanor scrolled for a while, seeming to be in deep thought. After a minute, she handed it back to Ruby. "Beatrice, can you have someone reach out to this bakery? The princess will send you the details."

"Thank you, Mama." Ruby threw herself on the queen for a quick hug. His mother wore a smile when she pulled back.

"Shouldn't we be hiring a local bakery to handle the dessert?" Leo asked. "There must be sixty in Lynoria."

"Maybe, but do they have espresso croissants? No," Ruby said with a look that was startlingly similar to their mother.

"Besides, look at them." She showed him a short video of complicated-looking fruit tarts sliding into a display case.

"Social media is not real life," he said flatly. They had way more important things to worry about than a damn dessert.

CHAPTER TWO

EMMA

"W̲HAT THE HELL IS THIS?"

Emma Clark cringed as something solid landed on the stainless steel countertop behind her. There was no mistaking that voice, even over the Christmas music crooning in her earbuds.

She pulled her hands out of the dough and took a deep, cleansing breath before swiveling to face the intruder.

Maya, her boss and a canker sore of a human being, tapped an impatient foot on the tile floor. Her astonishingly long ponytail brushed over a rolled-up mat slung over her back. Must have been on her way to Pilates.

She didn't have time for whatever this was. It was six a.m., they were opening in less than an hour, she'd only had two sips of coffee, and her mother had fallen while trying to get to the bathroom in the middle of the night.

Emma's gaze slid from Maya's monogrammed chef's coat —that had never seen a teaspoon of flour—to the muffin on the countertop. Shit.

"Looks like a muffin to me."

Maya's manicured finger pointed in Emma's face. "Don't play coy with me. This was found at the farmer's market in Williamsburg."

Emma pressed her lips together. Who had ratted her out? She had gone through great pains to cover her steps. She had given the muffins to a trusted friend to sell at her alpaca scarf booth. She'd done everything short of leaving them in a shipping container at a dock in the middle of the night. But what Maya lacked in baking ability and common decency, she made up for in snooping prowess.

"You think I can't spot your crumble topping from a mile away?" Maya grabbed a pinch off the top and ground it between her fingers. Great, now the floor was going to be crunchy.

"I know it's yours," Maya continued. "And you know this is a violation of the noncompete. You can't sell anything outside of these four walls. Not. A. Single. Macaron." She stabbed the counter with each word.

Emma turned back to her dough and rolled her eyes. Maya could never prove it. Besides, now that the insurance was dropping coverage on one of her mother's medications in the new year, she didn't have a choice. She couldn't maintain her savings percentage and afford the medication without supplemental income, and the freelance social media work she did on the side wasn't cutting it.

"I don't know what you're talking about," she said, but there was a tremor in her voice. "Do you mind? I have a lot of work to do."

Two more years and she would be free of this overhyped hellhole. She would be her own boss, and no nepo baby with a skull full of termites and glitter would ever take credit for her hard work again.

The timer on the oven dinged, and Emma hurriedly washed her hands.

Maya's expression instantly changed from one of suspicion to delight. "Let me." She tossed her phone to Emma and shrugged off her yoga mat. "Tooth check?"

Stress coursed through every vein in Emma's body. Would there be no end to the interruptions today? The Fulton Foundation had placed an order for five hundred assorted croissants to serve at their fundraising brunch the next day, and she had only made two hundred of them. Gaby had called out sick and Isaiah was working the counter, so she was making everything herself. And that didn't even address the mountain of administrative tasks that waited. The sooner she got Maya out of the kitchen, the better.

She turned to her boss and barely kept herself from reaching over to strangle her. She pulled up the camera app and lifted the phone. "You're good."

She would have given the all clear even if Maya had a California redwood between her front teeth.

Maya smoothed a hair back and slid her hands into hot mitts.

Emma took three different videos of Maya removing croissants from the oven. After Maya approved one, she stood there watching until Emma edited it, added some festive music, and posted it to the bakery's Instagram.

"Thanks. Anyway, don't let the muffin thing happen again. I'm not—"

"Maya?" Isaiah's head popped through the double doors. His hairnet barely contained his black ringlets, and he looked flustered. A candy cane pin on his apron flashed red and white.

"What is it?" Maya asked.

He jerked his head toward the counter. "There's some European lady knocking on the front door claiming to be representing the kingdom of Longoria? Something like that."

The kingdom of what?

"She wants to talk to you about a job. Said she couldn't get through on the email."

An alarm bell went off in Emma's head. She had definitely deleted a couple scammy-sounding messages from someone claiming to be a royal publicist last night. People were in their DMs all the time pretending to be celebrities to jump the waitlist for personalized creations. But she'd never had a scammer visit in person.

"Can you deal with her? I'm still loading the case," he added.

Maya smoothed her ponytail and disappeared through the double doors.

If Emma remembered correctly, the messages had mentioned something about procuring their services for the country's 500th anniversary celebration.

She straightened. In the incredibly unlikely event that this was legitimate, would Maya go there and leave the country for two weeks? There would be no greater gift on earth.

Even better, Maya had zero baking knowledge. None. Her father owned the business and had placed the day-to-day operations in her hands, which of course meant that everything fell on Emma and the other staff members. If this country was planning to hire her, she'd be turning in nothing. Unless she somehow ordered the bakery staff to FedEx cupcakes across an ocean.

Cheered by the thought of a Maya-less holiday season, Emma cranked up the Christmas music and returned to the croissant problem.

———

"Mom? I'm home," Emma called.

The front door swung shut behind her, and it didn't feel much warmer inside than it did outside. The apartment seemed extra dingy today in the gray New York winter. One of the light bulbs in the entryway had burnt out, and paint was starting to peel off the wall.

A maelstrom of stress swirled inside her, but there was nothing she could do about the derelict apartment. It was a great location—in Greenpoint, close to the G train, on the first floor, and it even had a tiny garden in the back to let the dogs out. But even if it had been on the fortieth floor of a mega apartment building next to the airport, they could never leave. It was one of the last rent-controlled apartments left in the city, a gift from her great-aunt, whom they had cared for in her last years. They couldn't afford to live anywhere else.

All the damage was cosmetic, and her mom had told her time and again that her savings and future business were the only priorities. But her heart ached at the thought of her mom trapped between these shabby walls all day. Someday, she would fix everything. Better physical and occupational therapy, fresh vegetables, name-brand peanut butter. Come hell or high water, she would make life easier for the woman who raised her.

Thunderous footsteps came from down the hall, and Cooper, the Bernese mountain dog, happy-stepped toward her.

"Hi, baby," Emma crooned. She buried her face in Cooper's mound of hair. He was unbothered by the cold.

"Back here, sweetheart," her mom called.

As Emma hung her purse on a peg in her room, the collage on the wall caught her eye. Images of the Eiffel Tower, tulip fields in Amsterdam, and pigs swimming in the Bahamas stared back at her. She really needed to take the collage down. She'd never see any of those places. In fact, she'd probably never see anything outside the tri-state area.

She pushed those thoughts to the side and stepped back into the hallway, determined to put on a cheery face for her mom. A bag of rejected croissants crinkled in Emma's hand. Their Thanksgiving leftovers had finally run out, but at least they still had a dented can of green beans left in the pantry. It wouldn't be a hearty dinner, but it was better than nothing.

Her phone buzzed, and she pulled it out. Ugh, Maya. She was off duty.

She let it go to voicemail and wandered down the hall. Maya had left without a word shortly after the alleged representative of the kingdom had showed up. With any luck, she was already on a plane.

"You have to turn the heat up. You're going to freeze," Emma said as she walked into the living room.

It was like walking into a terrarium. Plants covered the far wall, crammed into every space touched by sunlight. Her mother had once been a master florist for New York's most elite weddings and fundraisers. Now she tended a tiny garden in their backyard during the warmer months.

The TV was on, set to an episode of *Blue Planet*. Her mom had an unquenchable thirst for both knowledge and mundane real-life drama.

"Heat's expensive, love." Lisa sat in her wheelchair

under a pile of blankets. Arizona, her service dog, sat on the floor next to her. "I can manage."

Emma shook her head and cranked the heat up to sixty-five. She would dip into her savings if she had to. "How's your hip?"

"I told you this morning, it's fine."

"You know you need to ring the bell if you need me in the middle of the night."

"I'm not going to wake you up every time I have to pee," her mother said sternly. "I can get to the bathroom myself with the walker."

A retort was on Emma's lips, but she swallowed it. Things hadn't been easy for her mom these past two years. Watching her transform from a 5k runner with a zest for life to a wheelchair-bound homebody had been heartbreaking in more ways than she could count. Lisa was a proud woman who had never asked for help, and she wasn't about to start now.

A change of conversation was in order before this escalated. "How was Shante today?"

She glanced at her mother's daily pill container, which was appropriately empty, thank goodness. Shante, their day nurse for the past two years, was excellent company but sometimes forgot to take her home care duties seriously.

"Oh," Lisa exclaimed, turning away from the TV. "Wait until I tell you what her boyfriend did yesterday."

Emma smiled. Her phone buzzed again—Maya. Was she still pissed about the muffin thing? Didn't she have better things to worry about?

Lisa told a tale of missing condoms and mysterious credit card charges while Emma bustled around the kitchen. She pulled out the can of green beans to reveal a forgotten can of Spam that was in date. Protein was a luxury these days. She cubed it and added her ingredients to some water with a bouillon cube. A pauper's soup, maybe, but soup nonetheless. Payday wasn't for another few days, so she would have no choice but to pull grocery money from her savings. Every dollar withdrawn took her another step away from her goal, but she wasn't about to let her mother go hungry.

Someone banged on the front door, causing them both to jump. Her heart flew into her throat, and the ladle crashed to the floor.

It couldn't be him again. He was supposed to be in prison.

Cooper let out a low growl. Emma grabbed the metal baseball bat from behind her bedroom door and approached the entrance. Her heartbeat was hummingbird-fast as she pressed her eye to the peephole. Relief hit for an instant, then was replaced immediately by annoyance. Fuck.

She yanked the door open.

"Why aren't you answering your phone?" Maya stood on the stoop, hand on a hip and irritation in her eyes.

Cooper poked his head out the door to stare accusingly at Maya. She offered him a hand to sniff, which he did not accept.

"I was making dinner. If it's about the croissants—" Emma began.

"Forget the croissants. We're leaving tomorrow."

Those words made no sense. Leaving where?

"What do you mean?" Emma asked.

"You have a passport, right? We're going to Lynoria. They need us for their anniversary party."

Emma seriously considered slamming the door shut and cranking up her mother's favorite Frank Sinatra album until Maya left. There was no way in hell she was leaving her mom alone to jaunt off to some country she'd never heard of. Tomorrow was the start of their twenty-five days of Christmas celebration. Besides, her mom couldn't be left alone, and they couldn't afford more than the six hours a day from a home health nurse that they currently had. Even if she wanted to go, she couldn't.

"Are you even sure this is legitimate? There must be a million bakeries in their own country. Why would they want us? What if this is an elaborate human trafficking scheme?"

Maya shook her head. "I FaceTimed with the queen," she said smugly. "I guess the princess had our espresso croissants last year while she was touring colleges and she was obsessed."

Emma sighed. She did not have time to get caught up in Maya's insane plans, and she certainly wasn't about to get kidnapped by some alleged royals. "I can't leave my mom. You'll have to take Gaby."

Gaby, one of the other bakers, was a little flaky but had a knack for making beautiful macarons. On the off chance that this was real, they would be fine by themselves.

Maya shook her head. "This is the big leagues. They want something amazing. Show-stopping. Something the entire kingdom will be talking about for years. It has to be you."

Great, no pressure.

A wheelchair creaked in the hallway. "What's going on?" Lisa asked.

"Maya is going to Europe tomorrow," Emma said.

"How exciting," Lisa said.

"And I need Emma to go with me for a life-changing opportunity." Maya set her sights on Lisa.

"For how long?" Lisa asked.

"Ten days. Unless the extremely eligible king-to-be falls

in love with me. Then I'll be running the bakery from Europe." She let out a haughty laugh.

Emma set her jaw. "I'm not going."

Christmas was her favorite time of year in New York. The city went all out on decorations and festivities. She wasn't going to miss the magic to bake cookies for some presumably morally questionable aristocrat. If they even existed.

"Yes, you are," Lisa said.

Emma whirled around. "Are you insane? I'm not leaving you for ten days. And besides, we can't afford it."

Maya looked up from her phone. "Oh, did I forget to mention? Everyone who's going gets 25k, plus free lodging in a fairytale castle. And they're covering all the materials, equipment, and travel. There's even a stipend for food."

She flashed her phone at Emma, revealing a picture of a gorgeous castle overlooking a lake.

Emma's hand froze on the doorknob. Her pulse thudded in her ears. Twenty-five thousand dollars? She couldn't have heard correctly.

The possibility rose in front of her like a lovingly tended sourdough. That money would be enough to cover her mother's medication for the next year. In fact, she'd have to run the numbers, but it might even cover the first few months of rent in a commissary kitchen. If this was a legitimate offer, her days of saving every spare penny and subsisting on dented canned goods would be over. She could quit, freelance social media or waitress for a year until her noncompete wore out, then start her own baking empire. And more importantly, she could start saving for better care for her mom.

But shit. She couldn't leave her mom. What if something

happened again, and this time she was thousands of miles away?

Lisa's hand closed around Emma's. "I'll be fine, sweetheart. Helen from next door will check in on me. I insist you go. You need an adventure. I'll even help you set up the nanny cams that you think I don't know about."

CHAPTER THREE

EMMA

DESPITE A VERY LONG CONVERSATION WITH HER MOTHER about why this was an insane idea, Emma had somehow agreed to get on a plane. Now she was bleary-eyed and sandwiched in a middle seat between a businessman drowned in cologne and Cooper, who she had insisted on bringing along in a last-ditch effort to avoid going. But apparently the royal family had no problem with pulling strings to arrange red-eye airfare for gigantic canine companions.

Maya, meanwhile, was just visible taking selfies behind the curtain that separated first class. They were somewhere over the Alps, preparing to touch down in Spain, then they'd travel by chauffer to a country that until yesterday she wouldn't have been able to find on a map.

Emma had never been a spontaneous person, so jetting off to a foreign country with twelve hours' notice had felt like being kicked out of an airplane with a partially assembled parachute. She had dipped into her savings to grocery shop and frantically prepare freezer meals for her mom, so there had been no time to research. She didn't know what the primary language was in Lynoria or if the SIM card she had picked up in the airport would actually work. She knew nothing about the royal family beyond the princess who liked their espresso croissant. Every part of this trip was giving her anxiety, but it had the potential to change the trajectory of her entire life.

According to the terms the royal family had sent over, half of their pay would be sent before, and the other half would be given after they assembled their dessert. She had checked her bank account before takeoff and saw a pending wire for over $12,000, so some part of this was real.

The stakes were almost insanely high. Baking for one of the Kardashians had been stressful enough, but this was *royalty*. In an unfamiliar kitchen. In a country that might not even speak English.

But if she could pull it off, everything would change. Gone would be the days of Maya taking endless advantage of her—claiming credit for her baked goods, using her for their social media, shifting the responsibility of running the entire business to her while paying her a pittance.

She would have control over her schedule, the ability to bring her mom along to keep an eye on her, the freedom to take on only the projects she wanted. Her next step was closer than ever, and she could have it if she could just make it through this trip. A better life was within her grasp, and it was as subtly sweet as her legendary buttercream.

The plane shifted, signaling their descent. Emma leaned around Cooper's floof and peered out the window. A dreamy blanket of snow covered the land. A city was in the distance. Patchwork farms bumped up against rolling hills and rocky mountains. Lights dotted the mountainside, marking ski slopes. It was a pity it wasn't a Mediterranean climate, but at least it would still feel like Christmas.

Her heart ached. Even though they were on a shoestring

budget these days, they always found a way to make the holiday season magical. She was missing their most treasured tradition—Decoration Day. Lisa promised that they could celebrate from afar, but Emma's ability to stick to the schedule was going to be limited.

The worst part was having no way of knowing how many more Decembers she would have with her mom.

———

At baggage claim, Emma's phone rang. Oh good, at least the new SIM card was working.

She looped her wrist through Cooper's leash and answered without checking the caller ID. "Hello?"

"I can't believe you're in freakin' Europe right now. What alternate universe have we stumbled into?"

Warmth spread through Emma's body at the sound of Lola's voice. They had been best friends since elementary school, and even though Lola had gotten married and moved to Chicago, they still talked every day.

"I know, right? I'm still pretty sure that we're going to show up at the castle and they'll have no idea who we are. But at least it got me out of the 5 a.m. shift for a day or two."

"Great point. How's your mom?" Lola asked.

"She claims she's fine. Our neighbor agreed to take her to her appointments this week and next. But I'm going to check the nanny cams the second I get connected to Wi-Fi."

"She'll be fine," Lola said. "She's not going to take risks while you're gone."

"Have you met my mother?"

"You have a point."

Emma glanced around the airport. It was a good thing she had taken Spanish in high school. At least she could find the bathroom. "How are things? Writing any interesting proposals this week?"

"It's festive as fuck out here," Lola said over the wind whistling in the background. "I can't walk more than three feet without getting brained by tinsel."

Emma snorted. Lola was six foot two and regularly struggled with things five-foot-two Emma had never experienced.

"But anyway, I'm working with a nonprofit to secure some funding for renovations to the playground in Humboldt Park."

"You're such a badass," Emma said as she hefted her bag off the conveyor belt.

"Me? What about you? You were personally selected by a royal freakin' family to fly to Europe and make a dessert for their anniversary party. That's insane. Whose life are you living right now?"

"They personally selected *Maya*," she clarified in a low voice.

"And of course the she-beast couldn't do jack shit without you," Lola said.

"Mm-hmm." Emma spotted Maya in line at the airport Starbucks. A prickle of irritation grew. A driver was waiting for them somewhere, and something told her the queen of Lynoria did not enjoy being kept waiting. "I better go. I have to corral Maya."

Lola snorted. "Your work is going to be cut out for you this trip. I looked up the royal family. Two princes, one princess. None of them are married. She's going to plant her lips on the eldest brother's ass the second you arrive in that castle."

"Well, at least she'll be out of my hair. Tell Mateo I said hi, okay? Love you tons."

Emma hung up, straightened her shoulders, and clicked her tongue to make Cooper fall in line. He followed her over to Maya.

"We have to go. I think that person's here for us." She gestured to the baggage claim area, where a man in an impressive uniform held a sign that read "Farrell & Clark."

"Not without an iced matcha latte," Maya said without looking up from her phone.

Emma tutted and walked over to the person holding the sign. Maybe she could convince the driver to leave without Maya.

"Miss Farrell?"

"Clark. Emma Clark." She reached over and shook the driver's hand. "It's nice to meet you. What's your name?"

He seemed surprised by the question and nearly dropped his sign. "Walter, madam. We're delighted to have you. Will Miss Farrell be joining us, or did she fly separately?"

"Oh, she's here." A prickle of irritation crawled up Emma's spine. If they got fired because they kept the queen waiting, she was going to throw Maya's phone in a storm drain.

She fought the urge to clap at Maya the way she clapped at Cooper when he was taking too long to poop. Cooper accepted redirection, but Maya believed there was no word higher than hers. Actually, she probably *would* make a great queen. Maybe the eldest prince would take Maya off their hands for good.

Maya finally strolled over with a violently green beverage and pushed her bag at the driver. "Let's get this show on the road."

Cooper rode shotgun. Emma's head was on a swivel as they drove through Spain and entered Avolis, which, according to the driver, was Lynoria's capital city. City workers atop ladders hung wreaths on lampposts. Storefronts frosted with fake snow glowed with multicolored lights and displays of miniature trees. It wasn't exactly the jaw-dropping glamour of the tree atop Radio City Music Hall or the incomparable magic of Hudson Yards, but it was charmingly festive nonetheless.

Restaurants of all kinds lined the streets. A tantalizing mix of smells invaded and left the car like spirits. It felt a little bit like New York, but cleaner and smaller.

They left the city behind and drove through deep woods before emerging onto narrow cobblestone streets.

"This is Hollybrook," their driver reported.

The sun was cresting the mountain to their left, casting golden rays over the idyllic hamlet. A lake shrouded in mist sat to their right. Someone was carrying a reindeer on the roof of what looked to be a municipal building. Christmas lights sparkled on the snow-dusted roofs of Tudor-style cottages. It was a Thomas Kincaid painting come to life, but her heart still ached for glittering six-story trees and the cozy traditions that gave her something to look forward to every day.

Even though things were significantly leaner than they used to be, Emma and Lisa didn't let that keep them from their traditions. Ugly sweater day, a holiday movie marathon, making cookies from scratch, preparing care packages for the homeless. Every day held something special. December 1 was always Decoration Day, and she had missed it for the first time in two decades.

"Almost there," the driver said. Emma leaned closer to the window. They were emerging from the mist. Spires appeared in the distance above snow-laden branches.

Thyme and rosemary perfumed the air outside a small

pub. They passed a playground in a state of disrepair, more cottages, a handful of shabby-looking businesses, and what seemed to be the edge of a farmers market, or maybe a winter carnival.

Interest prickled. Would they have time to sightsee while they were here? This might be her last trip for a decade.

They turned off and began a steep ascent.

The most magnificent castle she had ever seen stood imposingly in front of them. Turrets adorned with white Christmas lights pierced the golden sky. Endless yards of garland hung from the privacy walls. Through the security gates and into the courtyard, Emma's mouth was agape. A beautifully decorated Christmas tree that must have been thirty feet tall stood in the middle of it all.

So there really was a castle, and a royal family, and presumably the biggest job of her entire career waiting behind the impressive front door. Time to panic.

When they jerked to a stop, Maya finally looked up from her phone. "Huh. Not bad."

Understatement of the century.

They exited, and Emma snapped a quick picture to send to her mom and Lola. Cooper sat in the freshly fallen snow next to her, panting happily.

"Here." Maya handed over her phone. She struck a pose next to the Christmas tree.

Of course. She had nearly forgotten that half her job here was being Maya's professional photographer.

Emma captured a couple pictures and handed the phone back. The driver dropped off their bags and drove away, leaving them staring at the castle.

Maya marched up to the front door and knocked on it. It swung open, and they were greeted by a maid. Cooper followed Emma inside and sat on her foot.

The hall was luxurious, with mile-high ceilings and art in ornate frames lining the walls. Polished marble floors stretched into the distance, where a double staircase covered in rich garland curved gently to the second floor. Was that a suit of armor? She was definitely going to get lost here.

Heels rang down a long hallway to their left, and another woman appeared. A navy dress flattered her trim figure, which helped distract from the fact that her smile looked like it was plastered on.

"Ladies. Thank you so much for joining us. How was your journey?"

"Comfortable enough," Maya said. She leaned forward and shook the newcomer's hand. "Nice to see you again."

"I'm Beatrice, the royal publicist," the woman explained to Emma.

How had Beatrice beaten them back? The royal family must have a private plane.

"We're going to meet with Her Majesty, and then I'll show you where you're staying."

Cooper let out a low woof.

She glanced at him, then called for a maid.

"The dog—"

"Cooper," Emma clarified.

"Cooper can stay here while you have your meeting."

A knot formed in Emma's stomach as she passed his leash to the maid. She certainly had not planned to meet the queen fifteen seconds after arriving. She hadn't slept or showered, and she was in leggings and a sweatshirt covered in dog hair. Not exactly apparel for meeting a world leader. She would have to hide behind Maya, who always dressed like someone was going to leap out from behind a bush and put her on the cover of *Vogue*.

"Follow me, please." Beatrice turned and marched down the hallway. They passed room after room. Harried-looking people scurried by carrying linens, feather dusters, and candlesticks. It was hard to believe that people actually lived like this.

Eventually, they arrived at some fancy room—a parlor? A drawing room? Whatever it was, it was bigger than her entire apartment.

"Your Majesty," Beatrice said with a bow.

Emma almost tripped. Shit, what was she supposed to do? Bow? Curtsy? Handshake? Definitely not handshake. She'd end up in the dungeon. She mimicked Beatrice's bow, and her knees creaked. Maya curtsied in an exaggerated sweeping motion as though she had practiced for hours. And maybe she had.

The queen was as stately and imposing as the castle itself. Even though it was barely eight in the morning, she wore an expensive-looking dress with a cropped jacket, and her hair was gathered in an elegant chignon. Her back was ramrod-straight, and her walk was more of a glide as she left her desk and approached them. She paused to take them both in, with a lingering glance on Emma's outfit.

Emma swallowed hard.

"Ladies," the queen said. "Thank you for joining us on such short notice."

"We're honored to be here, Your Majesty," Maya said. Her voice dripped with honey. She was definitely vying to be the queen's future daughter-in-law.

"Please, sit." The queen indicated two chairs in front of a desk.

They sat, and the queen moved behind the desk. "You've been briefed on the anniversary party?"

Maya nodded enthusiastically. "We're looking forward to

hearing your ideas for the dessert. The rest of the royal family won't be joining us?"

Emma almost kicked her. Now was not the time to be shopping for a husband.

"Regrettably, no." The queen put on a pair of jewel-encrusted reading glasses. "The king tends to leave such matters to me. My direction for you is simple. I want the most magnificent dessert that's ever been served at a ball. I want people to talk about it for the next year. I want it to be delicious, opulent, artistic. An unforgettable centerpiece that celebrates the rich history of Lynoria and the strength of the monarchy."

Oh. Was that all?

"Did you have a budget in mind, Your Majesty?" Emma asked. Maya almost always forgot to ask.

"There is no budget. You'll give your shopping list to the head maid. We'll have a meeting tomorrow to discuss your ideas. Samples would be helpful. A basic version is fine. There are staples in the pantry you can use, but you'll need to wait until the dinner service has ended to use the kitchen."

"Wonderful," Maya said.

Wonderful? What, were they supposed to bake in the middle of the night while already completely jetlagged?

The queen rang a bell, and a maid hastened into the room. "Could you escort Miss Farrell and Miss Clark to their quarters?"

They both curtsied on their way out of the room.

Anxiety flared in Emma's chest, but she barely had time to register it before the maid stopped in her tracks and curtsied at a teenage girl. Shit, who was this now?

"Good day, Your Highness," the maid said.

Oh, it must be the princess who liked their croissants.

"Are you guys from Crumb and Get It?" The girl's blue eyes sparkled.

"We are," Maya said before turning her attention to the stretch of hallway behind her.

"I had *the* best espresso croissant of my life when I was in your bakery last year."

Emma glowed on the inside. Croissants and show-stopper cakes were her specialty.

"Thank you so much," Emma said. "They're a little labor-intensive, but I love making them."

"Do you guys want a tour?" the princess asked.

"That would be awesome," Emma said. "Are you sure you have time?"

The princess tilted her head. "Who's going to stop me? I'm Ruby, by the way."

"Emma." She held her hand out, then snatched it back. She was pretty sure no one was supposed to touch royalty. Instead, she administered another awkward curtsy.

"You don't need to do that," the princess said. She reached over and shook Emma's hand.

Emma turned to Maya, who was back to staring at her phone.

"Coming?" Emma asked.

"I think I'm going to take a nap and then do some exploring on my own," she said, scanning the halls again. "Don't be gone for too long. You have homework to do."

Of course Maya wasn't planning to help. It figured.

CHAPTER FOUR

LEO

Leo pumped a stream of black coffee into a cup and checked his watch. It was almost ten. He cast a glance around the town hall building. Not even a third of the creaky wooden seats were filled. It was a modest turnout, maybe twenty people. But it was necessary work.

"Catch the match last night?" Salvador Gomez, Leo's best friend and the owner of the local pub, sidled over and picked up a stale-looking donut.

Leo took a sip. "Madrid slaughtered Barcelona. You owe me twenty euros."

Sal grumbled and pulled a twenty out of his wallet. "Here. Put it toward better donuts next time."

"Our baker left," Leo explained. "This is all we have."

Sal raised his eyebrows. "Can't imagine your mother is pleased about that."

"It's John's fault," Leo muttered. "I'll explain later. Grab the mic?"

Scandal aside, he would really miss Sarah. She was always pleasant, and her crusty homemade bread slathered in Irish butter was better than sex. Well, almost.

Sal nodded and dusted his hands off before picking up a wireless microphone.

Leo walked down the center aisle. Everyone in attendance leapt to their feet, and he shook his head.

"There's no need for that," he called to the room. But no one sat.

He sat on the edge of the table at the front of the room, dragging a yellow legal pad into his lap. Finally, everyone took their seats.

"Thank you all for coming. We're going to start with a couple of community updates, and then we'll air our grievances."

A couple people chuckled.

"Captain Allard, where did we land on filling that open position for another officer?"

A beefy-looking man in uniform accepted the wireless mic from Sal. "Filled, Your Highness. Officer Trusdale joins the force next week."

"Perfect. And I trust you'll be able to dispatch an officer to patrol the high street? People have been flying down that road, and there are children trying to walk to school."

"Consider it done," the captain said.

"Excellent. Any other agenda items from the force?"

The captain mentioned some upgrades to riot gear, and Leo jotted it down. Parliament would probably balk at sending more funding to the force since they had just approved a full-time position, but it was what it was.

After a few other updates, talk turned to the winter carnival.

"Isabelle, how is setup for the carnival going?"

"Things are going well, Your Highness," said a short, brown-haired woman with rhinestone glasses.

Leo grunted. No matter how many times he requested people drop the honorific, they never did.

"The RSVPs on the event site are encouraging, but I think foot traffic would increase if the royal family were to make an appearance on opening night?" She phrased her statement as a question. There was a hesitancy in her voice.

Leo frowned. Proceeds from this year's carnival were going to support the local no-kill animal shelter. Football was on tomorrow, which meant his father would be cemented to his armchair. His mother didn't usually attend town events, and John and his blooming black eye were supposed to be lying low. Ruby probably had plans with friends.

"I'm not sure how much it will help, but I can make an appearance tomorrow night. Everyone else is...occupied."

"Thank you so much, Your Highness." She was still talking fast. "There is one other thing."

"Go on," Leo said.

"The stage in the park is a little worse for wear. One of the stagehands almost fell through it, so we've had to close it off. We've sent a work request to the parish, but they won't get to it until the new year."

Leo looked at Sal, who nodded. He jotted down the issue and starred it. "We'll take a look at it. Might be cutting it close, though."

"We're grateful for any help."

She sat, and Leo opened the floor to the public. A number of issues came up—potholes, a broken printer at the library, bike lanes that needed to be repainted in the spring. He triaged the items in his notebook and dismissed the meeting.

Sal walked up and checked his watch. "I've got an hour. Should we go check out the damage?"

Leo nodded, and they left town hall. Leo pulled his base-ball cap low over his eyes. Fortunately, as the most boring member of the royal family, the paparazzi almost always left him alone. But he wasn't in the mood to be curtsied at.

The sun was punishingly bright, glaring off the fresh blanket of snow. Cars ground the powder into slush, and irritating Christmas lights blinked incessantly at them every step of the way.

After a quick stop at Sal's pub to grab his tool bag, they walked to the park. The corner of a vacant lot was just visible beyond the park, and his mind turned back to the project.

There was no reason why his parents wouldn't approve of the plan. The lot had been vacant his whole life. It was on the edge of town and butted up against the Endless Moun-tains. It wasn't even used as a green space, so Hollybrook would lose nothing by developing it. He even had a crew and all the other pieces in place. It would be an incredible gift to the community. A new library, a domestic violence shelter, a community garden, and a playground. It would create jobs and serve the most vulnerable in their population.

If he had his way, the soup kitchen would have a new space as well, but he had to be realistic. It was already a big ask, but one of the few pieces of power left in the royal family was directing charitable giving. At least he could do something good with this empty title. He had to wait until his parents were in the right mood to broach the subject, but the project needed to be approved before the end of the year. Time was running out, and the queen hadn't been in a good mood for longer than three minutes since their holiday in the Maldives in June.

They dodged around a person constructing a roasted

nut stand and circumvented the beer tent. Christmas decorations were everywhere. Candy canes, wooden trees, strings of lights, and even errant mistletoe. It was a lot of fuss for a celebration of consumerism, but at least it raised money for local nonprofits.

At the back of the park, the hazardous stage waited.

Together, Leo and Sal tested each shabby board that made up the stage floor. Nails stuck out like jagged teeth. He grabbed a hammer and pounded them back in. The whole thing could stand to be replaced, but they could at least fix the unsafe boards before the carnival started.

"What are you and Callum doing for the holiday?" Leo asked over his shoulder.

Sal hooked his measuring tape on the edge of a board and walked to the other end. "We're headed to Belfast."

"Nice," Leo said. Getting away from the aggressive holiday bustle of Lynoria sounded amazing.

"The weather's going to be miserable. I assume you're going to the quincentennial party?"

Leo scoffed. "I'm not getting involved in that. I scheduled another town hall at the same time."

Sal raised his eyebrows. "Do you want your mother to murder you?"

"She won't even notice. This party is the only thing she's been talking about all year."

"She will definitely notice if you don't play nice and show up for the cameras. Image is everything, Leopold," Sal mimicked in an eerily accurate impression of the queen.

"She'll be too busy matchmaking for John."

Despite a decade of family discussions about the need for a royal heir, his eldest brother had left a string of broken hearts behind him and burned bridges with a number of aristocratic families around the continent. He had an insatiable taste for models and actresses and no intention of settling down, especially not with whatever eligible patrician his mother hand-selected for him.

"At least she's left you to your own devices in that department," Sal said.

Leo grunted. It was true. In fact, she rarely seemed to remember that Leo existed at all.

"You want me to set something up?" Sal asked.

"Sure, because that worked out so well last time."

"In my defense, I did not know Renee had a penchant for petty theft."

"I don't know if stealing an original Monet counts as petty theft."

"Maybe it was an accident."

Leo shot him a look.

"Art thieves aside," Sal said, "I really wish you would find someone. Cal's been on me about double-dating."

"I'm sorry that my lack of dating life has been so difficult for you."

Dating had never been easy for Leo. Even though he was an empty figurehead with no real power—doubly so since he was second in line to the throne—some women were entranced by his status as a royal. It made it impossible to tell who was interested in him as a person and who was just hoping to become a member of the royal family. The paparazzi that usually left him alone had been whipped into a frenzy when he started dating someone two years ago. They hounded her until she left the country—and the relationship. Since then, love had been on the back burner.

A low woof drew his attention to the sidewalk, where a striking woman was walking a Bernese mountain dog that was bigger than she was.

The hammer fell from his hand and clattered to the

wooden boards. She jumped at the sound and turned, drawing the dog in closer.

A knot formed in his stomach. Why had she responded so strongly to an innocuous sound?

The woman surveyed the scene, then their eyes met over a mulled wine stand. She smiled sheepishly at him but didn't curtsy. Interest flared. She didn't recognize him. Or maybe she wasn't a citizen. She definitely wasn't someone he had seen around the village before.

There was a flush in her cheeks, but it was impossible to tell if it was from the cold or from embarrassment. She was short but must have been strong to control the dog. Her blonde hair was partially obscured by a black hat with a pompom.

The intrigue was instant. Magnetic.

But that was insane. He didn't know her, and she probably didn't want the attentions of some random guy. She could be married.

Oh, shit. She was about to walk into a light pole. He straightened up to warn her, but it was too late.

Thonk. Her head smacked the pole, and she fell to the ground.

Leo left everything and ran across the park, dodging a pretzel stand and skirting a field of fake trees.

He dropped to a knee beside her. "Are you all right?"

She was even lovelier up close. Her hair was long, straight, and the color of the wheat fields he ran through as a child. Her eyes were a striking shade of green.

"I'm fine," she said.

Ah, American.

"Just incredibly mortified," she added. She pressed a hand to her forehead and squinted with one eye.

"Can I get you some ice?" he asked.

She glanced around them. Snow was everywhere. Right, idiot.

"I'll be fine," she said warmly. She was talking fast. "Thank you for checking on me. Sorry to interrupt your—Cooper, no!"

The dog, who had been sniffing the edge of Leo's jacket, had just lifted his leg. Leo's arm grew warm.

She clambered to her feet and yanked the dog away.

"Oh my god. I'm so sorry. He's never peed on anyone before." Her fingers closed over the zipper on her black coat, which had a long rip that looked to be hand-stitched with red thread. "Here, take my coat."

Leo laughed and shrugged out of his coat. The sun was shining, and he was sweaty from hammering boards anyway. "I'm fine. I don't think we're the same size."

Now that they stood next to each other, he towered over her. She couldn't have been much more than five feet tall.

Her eyebrows contracted. "You have a point. Well, I could buy you a new one or have it cleaned or—"

He raised one hand. "It's okay. I promise." He bent down until he was eye level with the dog. "Just try not to pee on anyone else, okay?"

The dog licked his cheek in response and looked thoroughly unashamed.

"I'm so sorry again. I—I'm going to go now," she stammered, then darted down the street, dragging the dog after her.

Something stirred in him. His mouth opened, ready to call after her. But she was fast and disappeared around a corner before he could snap out of it.

He turned back to Sal, who was watching with arms crossed and one eyebrow cocked.

"What?" Leo called defensively.

"You're seriously going to let her go?"

"I—" He turned to look again, even though he knew she was already gone. He was being insane. She clearly wasn't local and wouldn't be sticking around long. She was a tourist, not some divine intervention from the universe.

He went to take a step back to the park but hesitated.

It didn't make sense to chase her down. It might even scare her. But why was it that every cell in his body was screaming for him to do it? It was the strangest feeling, like he recognized her even though he'd never seen her before.

He glanced back at Sal.

"Go, you plonker," Sal called.

Without pausing to think of the consequences, Leo turned and jogged in the direction she had disappeared.

His steel-toe boots pounded the sidewalk as he scanned storefronts and side streets. A handful of citizens stopped in their tracks to bow, but she wasn't among them. How could a woman and a human-sized dog hide so effectively?

Eventually, he pulled to a stop and trudged back toward the park with a heavy heart. He searched every face on the way back, but she really was gone. It was just as well. It wasn't meant to be. He didn't need the distraction, no matter what his gut was telling him.

CHAPTER FIVE

EMMA

Emma blew a sweaty strand of hair off her forehead. She had only been in the kitchen for an hour, but already a creeping sense of panic had set in.

These were by far the highest stakes she had ever faced. And she was in an unfamiliar kitchen that ran on Celsius, trying to impress a woman who had offered her no insight. While the castle chef had kindly given her a tour, the implication was clear that the kitchen needed to be spotless before staff arrived to prepare breakfast in the morning.

But it was only for ten days. She could do this. Her apartment in the gatehouse was unexpectedly charming and had a small oven. She could bake small batches of things throughout the day. After she got some freakin' sleep.

"You're sure you're all right, sweetheart?" her mom called through the speakerphone.

"I'm fine, I just have a lot of balls in the air."

The head injury she sustained from gawking at the hot maintenance guy hadn't helped anything.

She rolled her shoulders back and took stock of her progress. The kitchen was a mess of dough. Some rising, some chilling in the industrial-sized refrigerator. The dreamy scent of vanilla emanated from the closest oven, which was hopefully not burning her famous sponge cake. Choux pastry rounded out the preparations. It was barely controlled chaos, but it was the environment she thrived in.

"So the princess herself gave you a tour?" Lisa asked.

"She did. She's honestly so lovely and funny. I didn't expect a princess to be just a regular teenage girl. She's actually going to be attending NYU next fall, so maybe I'll be able to introduce you someday."

"How exciting."

A yawn racked Emma's body.

"You sound tired," her mother said. "Did you get any rest?"

The past twenty-four hours hadn't been restful by any sense of the word. She was running on two hours of sleep and was only allowed to use the baking facilities at night. Maya had disappeared—undoubtedly on a quest to make herself the next queen of this country—and shifted the entire burden of this project onto her. And when she had ventured into the impossibly beautiful village looking for some inspiration, Cooper had *peed* on an innocent—and very handsome—maintenance worker. She would never be allowed in Lynoria again.

"I'll be fine. Have you taken all your medication today?" Emma asked.

"Yes, mother," her mom mocked.

"Good. How's the hip?"

"It's fine, sweetheart. The doctor checked it at my appointment today."

The timer on the oven dinged. That was the choux.

"Good. I better go. Please be safe."

"You too, sweetheart. Give Coop a big hug from Gigi."

"Will do. Love you."

Emma hung up and pulled the choux out of the oven. She breathed a sigh of relief. They seemed normal, so the Fahrenheit to Celsius conversion must have worked. It was hard enough to bake with minimal ingredients without having to convert everything.

She eyed the tarts. They were cool enough to top. She had rescued a bag of apples and a few quarts of raspberries from the refrigerator with the chef's permission. These tarts wouldn't be nearly as spectacular as she usually aimed for, but hopefully it would be enough to give the queen an idea. And then maybe she would provide some concrete direction.

Over the next forty-five minutes, she piped vanilla crème and intricately arranged each tart. Not her best work, but they were still beautiful in their own slapdash way. She dusted the raspberry tarts with powdered sugar and added edible gold leaf she had found in the pantry. Painstakingly assembled apple rosettes donned the other tarts.

She turned her attention to the next task, the caramel sauce for the croquembouche, but her bladder screamed at her. She definitely needed to pee before starting that task because caramel waited for *no one*.

After five solid minutes of doing a pee dance down the hallway, she finally found a powder room.

She barely recognized the person staring back at her in the elaborate gilded mirror. There was flour on her cheek, and her eyes were hollow from lack of sleep. She splashed some water on her face and took a deep, cleansing breath. Everything was going to be fine. She was a damn good pastry artist, and she was going to show this kingdom what a Brooklyn girl could do.

When she stepped back into the kitchen, panic flared in

her chest. A man stood next to the oven. One of her raspberry tarts was in his hand, and there was a dusting of powdered sugar on his cheek.

He turned to look at her, warm brown eyes regarding her over the tart. He inhaled sharply—in surprise maybe?—and his eyes widened.

"Oh, hi," she said.

Hang on a second. Was that the mega hot maintenance guy Cooper had peed on this morning? It couldn't be.

His face was growing red, and his eyes were bugging out. The tart tumbled to the floor.

"Oh my god. Are you okay?" she asked.

His hand flew to his throat. His eyes were wide in alarm.

Holy shit. He was choking.

She leapt into action, crossing the kitchen in three quick strides. Her mind ran a mile a minute. She had no idea what the local emergency number was. The staff was gone for the night. She was the only thing standing between him and death.

Her training took over. She stood behind him and draped an arm over his chest. She guided him down to a bent posture, then administered five back blows between his shoulder blades. Her hand stung, and adrenaline surged through her body. The stranger nearly collapsed, but she used every ounce of her strength to keep him up.

There were no breaths. The pastry was still lodged in his throat.

She pressed herself to his back and wound her arms around him. Her heart pounded fast and hard in her chest. His life was in her hands. If this didn't work, she needed to run screaming into the castle until someone came to help.

She found his belly button and rolled her fist up.

"It's going to be okay," she said to him, but her voice was shaking.

She thrust her fist into his abdomen, inward and upward as hard as she could. She had never given the Heimlich maneuver to someone so tall.

Five thrusts as hard as she could manage. Nothing. Her hands shook as she returned to back blows. One. Two. Three—oh, thank god.

A glob of pastry shot out of the stranger's mouth and onto the tile floor. They both collapsed to their knees in front of the oven.

She scooted in front of him, anxiously peering into his face. His color was returning to normal, but his breath was coming in ragged gasps.

"Are you okay? Here, take a deep breath. Slow." She instinctively took his hand and planted it on her chest.

Raspy breaths ripped between his lips, and she held his hand with her trembling one until they evened out.

"I'm so sorry for scaring you."

Peeing on and then choking a maintenance man all in the same day? She was definitely going to get kicked out of the country at this rate.

"Scaring me?" he asked.

Oh, that accent. Her toes curled in her shoes.

"You saved my life," he added.

"After almost killing you," she clarified.

"Where did you learn to do that?" He gestured toward his stomach.

Now that the danger had passed, she couldn't help but stare. He was even more handsome than he had appeared in the park. His eyes were the color of a cocoa ganache behind black-framed glasses. Brilliantly white teeth were framed by rosy, generous lips. His dark brown hair was mussed—as one would expect from a near-death encounter—and blended with the edges of a trimmed beard.

Her heart staggered a little. Did the province hire only panty-dropping maintenance workers? How did anyone get anything done?

Oh, shit. He had asked her a question. Focus, idiot.

"The Heimlich? My mom chokes a lot, so I get a weird amount of practice."

He turned the full force of his brown eyes on her. "I'm sorry to hear that."

"It's not my favorite family pastime." She jumped to her feet and offered her hand. He took it, and she pulled him up. A thrill ran through her body at the contact. His hands were calloused and strong.

He dusted some powdered sugar off his T-shirt. "This might be an insane question. Do you have a Bernese mountain dog?"

Shit. She was right. It was him.

"You mean Cooper, who peed on you earlier today? Yes, I do."

"So that *was* you." His look of post-near-death-experience malaise had been replaced by one of interest. "How's your head?"

Warmth rushed into her cheeks. Of course he remembered her making an idiot of herself.

"Oh, it's fine. There's supposed to be two of you, right?"

He smiled and laughed, looking almost startled by the joke. He glanced at the tarts on the counter and shifted his attention back to her. "You must be the American baker."

She bit her lip. "Oh boy, I already have a reputation?"

"No," he said quickly. "We were just expecting you."

She adjusted her apron strings. "It's not every day the royal family of a country you've never heard of hits up your bakery and asks you to fly overseas and perform a border-line-impossible task."

He smiled again, and her heart stuttered.

"I don't know about impossible. The tart that almost killed me was incredible."

Was steam rising beneath her collar? The kitchen was suddenly stifling. Maybe she should open a window.

"I'm glad you liked it. Hopefully it will be good enough for the royal family. The queen gave us basically no direction, so I'm more or less grasping at straws. Do you work here too?" she asked.

He hesitated. "I do."

Oh. Perhaps she would run into him around the castle.

"Maybe I'll see you around, then. You'll probably want to get checked out in the morning, by the way. I broke one of my mom's ribs once, giving her the Heimlich."

His expression clouded. "That's awful. Is she…disabled?"

Emma's shoulders tensed up. The story never got any easier, no matter how many times she told it.

"She had a stroke. A bad one."

His eyes softened. "I'm so sorry to hear that."

"Yeah, it sucked." The rest of the story was on the tip of her tongue, but she bit it back. She didn't need to spew a bunch of overly personal stories to a maintenance worker she'd probably never see again.

"I'm Emma, by the way." She extended her hand.

"Leo." A strange sense of peace set in at his touch.

They looked into each other's eyes for a long moment, hands still connected. Her heart was thumping again, but at least this time it wasn't because anyone was in mortal peril.

She glanced down at his other hand. No rings. But maybe people didn't wear wedding rings in Lynoria.

What was she thinking? She was only here for a week

and a half. She didn't need to get involved with some hammer-wielding stud. Her whole future was hanging in the balance. She needed to focus up.

As if it agreed, the timer on the oven chimed.

"Oh, that's my star bread." She dropped his hand and bustled over to the oven. She pulled the rack out and withdrew an imperfect pastry. Not her best work, but at least it wasn't actively on fire.

"Well, Leo," she said. The name felt like candy on her tongue. "I'm sorry for almost killing you with my baked goods."

"It was worth it," he said with another slow smile.

Another thrill ran through her. What did that mean?

"Where's your dog?" he asked, glancing around the kitchen.

"We're staying in the gatehouse," she said. "I figured it was best to not add dog hair to the croquembouche."

He smiled. "I suppose you're right."

Another massive yawn racked her whole body. Exhaustion hung from her like a winter cloak, but at this rate, she'd be up all night.

His expression changed to one of concern. "I'm distracting you. Is there anything I can do to help?"

She hesitated. Leo was intriguing, handsome, and completely unexpected. And those calloused hands certainly looked like they were capable of washing a dish or two. If it were any other place or any other time, she would have chalked this meeting up to fate. But this project demanded her full attention. Nothing and no one was more important than changing her and her mom's circumstances for good.

"Thank you, but I'm fine."

Leo eyed the dirty pile of dishes in the sink, but when his gaze shifted back to her, something softened.

"I assure you I'm quite capable of washing dishes."

She bit her lip. "I'm sure you are. But I have a lot to do, and sometimes I get irrationally angry if someone's standing in front of the drawer I need to open."

He nodded. "If you're sure. I'll leave you to it."

"Have a good night," she called at his retreating back.

He shot another glance over his shoulder before disappearing.

The silence was almost deafening in his absence. Holy shit. In another lifetime, she would have obsessed about this encounter for weeks and dissected every moment with Lola. But she wasn't the carefree and optimistic girl she once was. There was so much at stake, and she did not need any distractions. Especially ones that came in the form of hunky maintenance men named Leo who lived five thousand miles away.

CHAPTER SIX

LEO

LEO TRUDGED INTO THE BLUE ROOM, BODY FEELING AS battered as if he'd just had a session with his personal trainer. Early morning sunshine streamed in between the thick velvet curtains.

Why had his mother insisted on a family breakfast meeting? He had gone to bed entirely too late the previous night, poring over the architect's plans in his workshop until nearly dawn. As much as he wanted to bring up the project, it wasn't the right time. He could practically feel the tension simmering in the room.

His mother wouldn't be able to focus on anything until the ball was over and done with. With any luck, it would fulfill her every dream, and she would be in such a good mood the next day that she and Father would greenlight his plans. In the meantime, all he could do was prepare.

"Good morning," he said to his father, who was reading a newspaper while sipping a cup of tea.

"Leo," he said, raising his gaze from the paper. "Did you catch the match last night?"

Did all the men in this country care solely about sports?

"What, the football? No, I was working on something."

The king tutted. "Busy, busy. How is it that you're busier than the king?"

Leo smiled. He opened his mouth to say something about his near-death by pastry, but he stopped himself. His parents would probably find him weak if they knew an errant tart had almost permanently impacted the royal bloodline.

His thoughts returned to the baker. Emma. Finding her in the kitchen had felt like fate. Although it had nearly caused his death, her raspberry tart had been a vision. Maybe his sister was right to insist on this bakery, even if it meant not supporting a local business.

The odds were very good that he would run into her again. His stomach twisted. He had sort of lied to her when she asked him if he worked at the castle. Technically, he did. He just also happened to live here.

It had been a long time since he'd run into a woman who had no idea who he was—maybe even since university. It was almost intoxicating. Would she be upset when she learned the truth?

He poured a cup of coffee, and the warm, buttery scent lifted his mood. He was the only one in the family who drank it—one of his many failures of character—but the cooks always kindly brewed a pot for him. The first sip burned his throat, and he involuntarily flashed back to the night before.

He could have died in that kitchen. His throat still ached from the lodged pastry, a constant reminder of his near-death experience. But Emma had saved him. And she didn't even know who he really was.

His mother bustled into the room, followed by a bleary-eyed Ruby. John trudged in last, a pair of sunglasses hiding his eyes even though he was indoors. Apparently Leo wasn't the only one who was up late.

John collapsed into a chair. A servant descended with a plate already made up. His brother had probably never made up his own plate in his entire life.

"Why did we have to have a breakfast meeting? I was sleeping," Ruby complained.

"It's important for families to eat together," the queen said as she sat at the far end of the long, polished table. A servant pushed her chair in for her and immediately poured a cup of tea. It was almost irritating, a performative dance that went on and on for decades. Could no one in this family do anything for themselves?

"Besides," the queen added, "we're sampling the pastries from the bakery you insisted we fly across the world. I could use your help in deciding what we want featured at the ball."

Bollocks.

Ruby immediately sat up in her chair. "Fine, I forgive you. When?"

The double doors opened, and two women walked in carrying trays. The first one he didn't recognize, but if he had to guess, he would say she was American. Rail-thin, heavy makeup for eight in the morning, and blue eyes that immediately settled on John. Behind her, Emma carried a two-layer cake decorated in purple-and-gold—the colors of Lynoria. His heart rate kicked up a notch. She looked very professional in a crisp black chef's outfit, but it didn't hide the fact that she mustn't have slept at all.

Was she going to be upset?

The first woman curtsied almost comedically deep. "Good morning, Your Majesties. Your Highnesses," she said with a second curtsy and her eyes still set on John.

Emma scanned the room and stopped in her tracks when she saw Leo. Her polite smile froze.

Uh-oh. Her mouth had dropped open, and she didn't look pleased. He smiled at her, and color rushed into her cheeks. Then her jaw clenched. She averted her gaze and instead looked at his mother.

"Good morning," she mumbled with a much shallower curtsy.

"Thank you for joining us this morning, ladies. Would you like some tea?"

"Oh, thank you, Your Majesty," the first woman said with another curtsy.

Ruby let out a small snort, then clapped a hand over her mouth. The queen shot her a look. Even though they were somewhat used to people fawning over their family, some people took it to a whole new level. But Emma wasn't interested in fawning. If anything, she looked pissed off.

The other woman shot Ruby a look, then surveyed the room. "Thank you so much again for having us, Your Majesties. I don't believe we've met," she said, striding over to the king. "Maya Farrell."

The king nodded deeply at her, and she turned uncertainly in the direction of John.

He slid the sunglasses down his nose and appeared to take her in. "Prince John," he said simply.

Great, they were already careening toward another scandal.

"Would you like us to explain what we brought?" Emma's voice cut through the awkward silence.

"Please," the king said, folding up his newspaper and sitting forward to inspect the trays of baked goods that had landed in front of him. Apparently the smell of butter had shaken him from his football-induced stupor.

Leo glanced at his watch.

As lovely as it was to see Emma again, he had a long day ahead. The stage needed to be repaired before the carnival started, he had to deliver a printer to the library and replace some bulbs in the reference section, and there was a rumor that a debilitating storm would hit later in the week. That meant checking that the community kitchen and homeless shelter were well-stocked. The shelters in Avolis would be overrun, and sometimes people in need made their way to the village.

The other baker's attention shifted back to the table. Emma still refused to look at him.

"So," Maya said, "we've prepared several options for you to try."

Leo squinted at the use of the word "we." Unless Maya was out fetching ingredients, Emma had been all alone in the kitchen the night before.

"And, of course, we're open to suggestion," Maya continued. "The first is our legendary espresso croissant. It's the item that put us on the map as a must-visit pastry destination."

While she spoke, Emma donned a pair of gloves and arranged croissants on plates. She walked around behind them and passed them to each family member. She even did it correctly, so she must have done some googling in the night. Her presence was like a radiant heater as she stood behind him. She smelled like vanilla extract, and her sleeve brushed against his shoulder as she reached. The croissant landed more harshly in front of him than it had for the others.

He bit his lip. He would have to find time to make it up to her. She had saved his life, after all. He should have told her the whole truth.

It was his own fault. It had been intriguing to consort with a beautiful woman who had no idea who he was. She had been so natural and relaxed—apart from the Heimlich, anyway. A far cry from the nervous debutants he usually met.

Maya was still babbling about the croissants and their commitment to using sustainable and conflict-free ingredients as Emma walked back to her side.

Ruby let out a deep sigh from down the table. There was a smudge of espresso powder on her cheek. The queen, who was sampling her pastry with a fork and knife, cleared her throat and raised her eyebrows.

Ruby sat up straighter in her chair. "I think we're done here, right? We just need like six or seven hundred of these. Do they freeze well?"

Emma smiled, and the queen fired a warning.

"Ruby."

Oh, right. He should probably try the dessert that Emma had put so much effort into. An unexpected twinge of anxiety hit when he picked up the croissant, and his heart beat faster. He hadn't eaten anything since the choking incident. Being unable to breathe had been uniquely horrifying. All because he was an idiot who couldn't chew properly. He took a small, cautious bite and chewed for what felt like an eternity.

It was incredible. The exterior was flaky, buttery, and crispy. The ganache inside was delicately sweet and reminiscent of a cup of espresso enjoyed on the terrace in fall. How did she do it? She pulled a memory out of him that he didn't even know he had, all with one baked good.

"Ruby's right," he said, dabbing a napkin over his mouth. He would swim in that espresso ganache.

Emma's cheeks tinged pink again, but she avoided eye

contact with him. Maya's gaze was on John, while Emma was fixated on the queen.

The king nodded his approval, and the queen put her fork down.

"And the next selection?" she asked.

One by one, Emma passed out the desserts while Maya gave an explanation. A couple of times, Leo caught Emma shaking her head at Maya, who then quickly changed whatever she was talking about. The raspberry tart was even better when he wasn't choking to death on it.

Finally, Emma reached into the lowest tier of the cart and withdrew a breathtaking miniature croquembouche tower. Glistening strands of spun caramel wrapped around perfectly sized creampuffs. She gingerly set it on the table in front of the queen.

"Croquembouche is a classic showstopper," Maya intoned. "Refined, elegant, and delicious."

For once, Maya was right. Everything Emma had created was incredible. Whoever married her one day would be heartily spoiled.

His mother had withheld her opinion the whole way through. Classic Eleanor. He had been in Emma's shoes many times, bated breath while waiting for her judgment.

"Well," the queen said, sliding her plate away from her. "I don't so much care for a coffee flavor, but I know many of our guests will. You're a skilled baker," she said to Maya.

Maya looked very pleased with herself.

"But none of these desserts were magnificent enough on their own," the queen continued.

Emma's lips pinched together, and flames of anger grew in Leo's stomach. In what universe were these not good enough? They had surpassed their old royal baker's standards by kilometers, and Emma wasn't even sleeping with John.

"I'd like to see some of each of these, plus other kinds. It needs to be artistic, elegant, regal. A show-stopping display. I want the servants to cry out in displeasure at having to cut into it. It must be magnificent."

She didn't actually have a gavel in her hand, but she spoke with the authority of someone holding one.

She stood, and everyone but the king stood with her. "I'll check in with you in two days to hear your ideas. That should leave enough time to gather supplies and make preparations."

With that, she left the room. He could practically hear the anxiety sizzling off of Emma. It certainly wasn't the most helpful feedback.

"Thank you, ladies," the king said.

They both curtsied, then left the room with their cart.

The taste of caramel was still on his tongue. Emma's caramel. He shouldn't bother her. She was clearly sleep-deprived and probably angry at him for concealing his identity. But he couldn't help himself.

He jumped to his feet. "I have to get going. Duty calls," he said.

John grunted at him and leaned back in his chair, sliding his sunglasses back over his eyes. Ruby had pulled out her phone the second the queen left, and the king had picked up his newspaper.

He left them to their devices and hustled out of the room.

CHAPTER SEVEN

EMMA

"Why didn't you make something fancier?" Maya's nostrils flared, and the effect made her look even more like a dragon than usual.

Emma sputtered. Croquembouche was one of the most elegant recipes in her repertoire. It was usually only served at weddings.

She had been completely off-kilter since finding Leo seated with the rest of the royal family. Her dog had peed on a prince.

But the fucking *audacity* of this man. She had quite literally saved his life, and he couldn't even bother to mention that he was the prince of the whole damn country?

And that was small potatoes compared to the queen's criticism. This job was the reason she was here. If they couldn't pull off something spectacular, she'd never get the other half of the money, and she'd be right back at square one.

"Oh, I don't know, maybe because I had to do everything by myself in an unfamiliar kitchen with the bare minimum of equipment on zero hours of sleep?"

Her voice echoed in the long, elegant hallway. She didn't usually make a habit of yelling at her boss, asshole though she was. But the lack of sleep was culminating in a lack of self-control she hadn't experienced in a long time. If the royal family hadn't been thirty feet away, she probably would have been even louder.

"You embarrassed me in front of John," Maya said.

"What? Who?"

"John. The prince."

Oh, the older brother who said nothing and could barely bother to take his sunglasses off at breakfast. The dictionary definition of an ass-nugget.

"I highly doubt that my critically acclaimed espresso croissants *embarrassed* you."

Maya got up in her face, and Emma suppressed the urge to pin her between the cart and a tapestry of what appeared to be a bunch of grown men chasing a fox.

One manicured finger shook in Emma's direction. "You will not embarrass me again. I will fire you if I have to."

Emma crossed her arms. "Really? So you're planning to bake everything by yourself?"

"The baking is your job. This time, *I'm* going to come up with all the ideas for the meeting because you have no idea what royal tastes are like. Aesthetics are my job," Maya said.

Emma blinked. Beyond periodically redecorating the café, Maya had never volunteered to do any real work in the shop. Chances were she would dramatically overpromise or miss the mark. And maybe it was time to let her. Letting her fail in front of a royal audience would be deeply satisfying, even if their brand paid the price. What did she care if business tanked? If their doors closed, she would be free from her noncompete. But then she wouldn't get the second half of the money. Hmm.

"Sounds great," Emma said. "Now if you'll excuse me, I'm going to take a nap for the next two days."

"Ladies," a male voice interrupted.

Emma jumped like someone had just shot off a firework.

She turned around and nearly ran into Leo. Make that *Prince* Leo. Her hands balled into fists.

"Emma, could we chat?" His eyes stared earnestly into hers.

Maya narrowed her eyes. She was trapped between an angry boss and someone she wanted to punch in the throat but couldn't for diplomatic reasons. Which of the two evils would she accept?

Maybe it was the sleep deprivation, but a crazy idea began to form in her mind. She would let Maya pretend to take the reins on this project. She would let her present her ideas to the queen. But Emma was going to come up with her own idea, and it would blow Maya's away. She would pull it off, collect the second half of the money, and then she'd quit this job for good. And by the end of it, she would have a literal royal stamp of approval on her baking skills. She'd never need another celebrity endorsement to launch her own brand.

But in order to do that, she was going to need some insider information on the queen's likes and dislikes. And that meant talking to someone who knew her.

"Fine," she said to Leo.

His eyebrows shot up. He probably wasn't used to people speaking to him this way. Who cared if he was a prince? She wasn't going to kiss his ass because of the family he was born into. She would treat him just like any other person who had lied to her.

"Five minutes only," she added. "I'm going to bed."

She shoved the cart in the direction she was pretty sure

led to the kitchen she had borrowed it from. She caught a split-second sighting of Maya staring at her, open-mouthed. Ha.

"I wanted to apologize," Leo said, falling into stride with her.

She quickened her pace. The cart clattered over the marble tiles.

Servants curtsied and bowed as they careened down the hallway.

"Apologize for what?" she asked sharply. "Oh, for not telling me that you are not in fact a maintenance man but instead the crowned prince of the entire country I happen to be visiting?"

"Not the crowned prince. Just a regular one," he said. He had quickened his pace to match hers. They were almost jogging, which would have been funny if she hadn't been so tired.

"Where do you get off concealing your identity? Were you trying to trick me? Get me to say something that would get me fired?"

He pulled to a stop, and she blew past him. For a moment, she fantasized about riding the cart down the sloped hallway and crashing it into one of their precious tapestries. But she still needed to make a good impression on the queen, and splattering a castle wall with sticky croquembouche wasn't likely to help.

Suddenly, he appeared in front of the cart with his hands out. She pulled to a stop. It was just as well. She wasn't wearing the right shoes for cardio.

"Of course I wasn't trying to trick you." His voice was low, soothing. Like a crackling fire on a winter day. "I'm sorry, Emma. I'm just not used to having to...introduce myself."

Her lips pressed together. That was probably true.

"It was nice to speak to you when you didn't know who I was. You were so warm and funny. But you're right, I should have told you."

"Yes, you should have."

"Let me make it up to you," he said. His eyes were sincere. Something tingled deep in her. He may have been a sneaky fuck, but he was irresistibly charming.

"I promised I would go to the winter carnival tonight," he added. "Will you come with me? I'll give you a tour of the village. Maybe it'll help."

She crossed her arms and debated. Leo had grown up here, and he was the son of the person she was trying to impress. He was her best shot at getting this money and starting her new life. And he had apologized. Maybe he deserved a second chance. Or maybe his chiseled jawline was skewing her judgment.

"Fine."

He suppressed a laugh. "I'm sorry. I've never had anyone agree to plans so begrudgingly before."

"You've got a lot to learn, Your Highness." She wheeled the cart around him.

"Emma?" he called after her.

She stopped and looked over her shoulder. "What?"

"Where are you going?"

She pointed at the cart. "To the kitchen."

"Kitchen's that way," he said, then pointed. "I'd be happy to escort you there, but you'll have to downgrade the hostility a millimeter or so."

Emma's shoulders slumped. It was her turn to apologize. "I'm sorry. I'm incredibly sleep-deprived."

"Have you slept at all since you arrived?" the prince asked gently.

She shook her head.

He put his hand over hers on the cart, and electricity jolted her awake.

He gently tugged her hands off the handle. "I'm going to take this back. You need some rest."

Her lower lip quivered. Maya would be mortified if she knew Emma had let the prince take the cart back. But she was going to fall asleep leaning against this cast-iron sconce if she didn't find a bed in the next ten minutes.

"Do you need help finding your way to the apartment?"

She shook her head, even though she had no idea which direction it was. She would figure it out, even if she had to climb out a window to get to the outside.

"I'll pick you up at seven. You might want to wear a disguise."

A disguise? Did he think she had a carry-on full of fake mustaches and monocles or something?

"In case the paparazzi bothers us," he clarified. "They sometimes take an interest in who our family...spends time with."

Ah, shit. She didn't have time to invent a disguise and come up with a plan that would put Maya's to shame. But she also couldn't cancel on him—she needed insider information. A big hat and bulky coat would have to do. Besides, no one here knew who she was.

CHAPTER EIGHT

EMMA

"Hold on," Lola said on speakerphone. "You're telling me Cooper peed on a member of the royal family? And you weren't immediately extradited or imprisoned?"

Cooper raised his head from his reclined position on Emma's unmade bed. The gatehouse apartment had proven to be very cozy. The nap had done wonders for her emotional stability, but she was still tired. A responsible night of sleep would have to wait until after the winter carnival.

"Well," Emma said, rifling through her suitcase, "I did kind of make up for it by saving his life. It would be a bad look for them to deport me. Plus then Maya would be completely screwed. Maybe I *should* convince him to deport me."

"Holy shit," Lola said. "I am so jealous of your life right now. You know what Mateo and I did last night? We put together a thousand-piece puzzle of Big Ben. How are you peeing on princes in foreign countries while I'm stuck in Chicago doing puzzles and getting my ass blown into the river?"

"I'm not peeing on princes," Emma said. "Probably should have though, since he lied to me about who he was."

There was silence on the other end of the phone.

"Your problems are so much cooler than mine," Lola muttered. Her fingers clattered on a keyboard in the background.

"Really? You want to add a disabled mother and a terrifying career change to yours?"

"Point taken. How is your mom?"

Emma had spoken to her only half an hour ago, but now that she didn't have the distraction of five types of baked goods in process simultaneously, the distance was making her nervous.

"She's fine so far. I check the nanny cams every half hour at least."

"It's not going to happen again," Lola said firmly.

"One in four stroke survivors go on to have another one," Emma said flatly. "And once again, I'm not there."

Lola started to say something, but the conversation was interrupted by a knock at the door.

"Shit," Emma whispered. "I was supposed to have another hour. I have no clothes. What am I going to do?"

"Go naked. Bring home a royal baby."

"You're the worst. Love you. Bye." Emma hung up and swept a glance over her room. There was a dirty coffee mug in her kitchenette sink, and the few clothes she had brought were strewn all over the bed.

"Emma?" a female voice came from the other side of the door.

Oh, thank god. It wasn't Leo. She crossed the room and pulled the door open.

"Ruby! I mean, uh, Your Highness."

Shit. She still should have cleaned up.

Ruby smiled.

"What can I do for you?" Emma asked.

The young woman wandered into the apartment and settled on the bed next to Cooper. He laid his gigantic head in her lap and happily accepted her pets.

"I'm sorry about my mom," Ruby said.

Emma glanced around the room, but there was no way to tidy up without the princess noticing. At least it was a teenage girl and not the queen herself. She would have had to pitch herself out the second-story window if Eleanor had shown up.

Would it be super inappropriate for her to interrogate Ruby for information on her mother's likes and dislikes?

"I—uh—appreciate a good challenge," Emma said.

Ruby snorted at that. "You can be honest."

"I do wish there had been a bit more guidance. But Maya —my boss—is working on some ideas."

The princess straightened up. "She loved it, you know. That was by far the least amount of criticism I've ever seen her give a pastry. That's why I wanted you guys to come here. You're the best."

Emma's heart softened. "Thank you. Stop in when you get to New York for school, and I'll make you something special on the house."

Ruby glanced around the room. "Are you going somewhere?"

"Kind of. I was planning to go to the winter carnival to get a feel for the town, but I realized I don't have anything appropriate to wear."

She probably shouldn't mention the fact that she was going with her brother.

Ruby stood up and walked over to her, seeming to size

Emma up. "I think we're about the same size. Come with me," she said, heading for the door.

"Oh, I couldn't—"

"We can't have you freezing to death. Besides, it's nothing. The winter carnival vibe is very après-ski and casual."

Après what now?

"Even if you're—hypothetically—in the company of royalty?" Emma asked.

Ruby stopped in her tracks, and Emma almost ran into her. She whirled around. "You're not going with John?"

Emma shook her head.

Ruby seemed to be relieved. "Good. We do have to do a little bit more work, in that case. I assume you'd like to keep a low profile?"

"The lowest. Can you make me invisible?"

"I'll do my best."

Forty-five minutes later, Emma emerged from the princess's department-store-sized closet feeling a bit foolish. The girl had a keen eye for fashion—maybe a little too wild for Emma's taste, since she rarely wore anything but work and athleisure clothes. She hadn't been on a date in almost two years, and she had sold some of her going-out clothes to help make ends meet.

Ruby had grilled her on life in New York—what was her favorite Broadway show? Where were the best tacos? Had she ever run into celebrities? While the real highlight of Emma's career had been crafting a commissioned birthday cake for Alexandria Ocasio-Cortez, Princess Ruby was more excited by Timothee Chalamet's brief visit in the fall.

Emma had to talk her down from wearing faux fur head to toe, and instead they had settled on all-black attire. A black cashmere sweater beneath a black puffer jacket. Surprisingly warm leggings tapered into fur-lined snow boots. And a black beanie pulled low over her ears. Would it be insane to wear sunglasses at night? The less of her face that was recognizable, the better.

Maybe Leo was exaggerating the interest from the press and public. She could probably keep a few feet between them. No one had ever noticed her before—why would they start now?

"Thank you so much," she said to Ruby.

"It was nothing. Thank you for the croissants."

"I'll make them for you anytime." Emma checked her watch. "Crap, I better go." She took a step, then stopped. "Crap, I probably shouldn't say 'crap' around a princess."

The girl giggled. "Don't worry about it. Have fun tonight."

Emma started to leave the room, but Ruby stopped her once more.

"Cardamom," she said.

Emma turned around. "Pardon?"

"My mom loves cardamom. Use the information however you see fit."

She disappeared back into her closet with a wave.

Emma's mind spiraled with ideas. Maple cardamom sticky buns. Browned butter snickerdoodle cookies. Wait, shit. Not fancy enough. Maybe fig and cardamom macarons? There was time to worry about this later. Cardamom was a start, but right now she needed to pump Leo for more information—and try not to humiliate herself again.

Magnificent and regal was the official request, but the secret to Emma's success had always been identifying the client's unspoken underlying needs. Did the queen want to feel special? Powerful? What made her tick?

CHAPTER NINE

LEO

Leo knocked on Emma's door. His gut was a tangle of nerves, and he couldn't figure out if it was because of the project or because she might still be mad at him. And who could blame her? He had plenty of opportunity to tell her who he was, but he hadn't. Hopefully some carnival food would help mend things.

The door opened, and he smiled without meaning to. He was still getting used to how short Emma was. She didn't look mad, at least. Her apartment smelled like cinnamon and clove. It was warm and inviting, unlike the drafty halls of the castle.

Cooper leapt off the bed and trotted over to him.

"Hello," Leo said, handing over a bouquet of pink roses he had stolen from the greenhouse on his way over.

"Oh, they're beautiful. Thank you. How did you get roses in December? Wait, shit. Should I be curtsying?"

She started to bend, but he put a hand on her arm to stop her. "Please don't curtsy."

She couldn't be that mad if she was prepared to curtsy at him.

"Imagine what your mother would say," she said breezily as she opened half a dozen cabinets in the kitchenette before filling a pitcher with water.

Damn. He should have brought her a vase.

"I really am sorry. About earlier."

She shot a look at him as she trimmed the blooms and nestled them in the vase. "That really did suck. But I've never been in your shoes, so I can't fully understand what you go through on a daily basis. You get one mulligan."

"Mulligan? Is that some kind of punishment?"

She snorted. "No. It's like a do-over. But do not hide things from me again." She brandished a pair of scissors in his direction. "Especially gigantic secrets about your identity."

He raised his hands like she was holding him at gunpoint. "Never. I swear. I'll take the do-over."

He put his hands down, then stuck one out toward her. "Hi, I'm Leo. Technically, Leopold Chester Beaumont-Castillo, Prince of Lynoria."

Emma made a face. "Oof."

"I know. Anyway, I'm technically second in line for the throne, but I prefer getting my hands dirty over christening boats or whatever ceremonial bullshit my brother is always up to."

She smiled. "It's nice to meet you, Leopold. I'm Emma."

"Just Emma?"

"Were you expecting another outrageously long name? Emma Clark of New York, Artisan of Fine Confectioneries, Breaker of Bread, Mother of Scones?"

"Do you have children?" he blurted out.

For some reason, he hadn't even considered it. His gaze dipped to her finger, but there wasn't a wedding ring. Why did it matter? This was just an apology outing for a contracted service provider. There wasn't anything going on here.

She raised an arm and almost knocked the vase over before smoothing her hair. "No children. Just dogs."

"There's another one?"

"Arizona. My mom's service dog."

A beat of silence fell. "It must be hard to have so much responsibility on your shoulders," he said quietly.

A storm passed behind her eyes, but she shook it off. "Well, at least I'm not partially in charge of a whole country. Anyway, ready to go? Am I disguised enough?"

She spun in front of him, giving him permission to take her in.

Leo hesitated. More than one relationship had fallen apart because of the press hounding his partners. But they had been locals. And besides, he and Emma weren't dating. He was just being a good diplomat and showing her around.

And thanking her for saving his life.

"I think you look perfect."

She shuffled her feet and looked down.

"Are you sure you want to do this?" he asked.

"What? Yeah, it's fine. I'm not worried about the *Lynoria Tribunal* thinking I'm your secret American girlfriend or whatever. How are you feeling, by the way?"

"Feeling?" He raised his eyebrows.

She touched a hand to her throat. "From the whole... choking incident."

He shook his head. "I'm fine."

It was partially true. That moment had been on his mind all day. His throat was still raw from the effort of dislodging the pastry. The panic that accompanied the obstruction had been so visceral that he had gone to bed still shaky. If Emma hadn't been around, he would have been all alone, unable to alert a staff member. He could be dead.

She reached over as if she was about to touch him but stopped. "It's okay if you're not. It's terrifying."

Leo paused. He could count on one hand the number of times someone had told him that feelings and vulnerabilities were okay. He didn't know what to do with that information. He resolved to google how to self-Heimlich and filed the idea away for now.

"I'm fine," he repeated. "Ready to go?"

"Sure. Bye, Coop." She bent over to kiss the dog between the small brown dots of his eyebrows.

"He's a beautiful dog."

"Thank you." She shut the door behind them. "He's the sweetest."

"How long have you had him?"

They descended the stairs together and emerged into the frigid winter night. Massive snowflakes lazily drifted down.

"About three years. Someone abandoned him down by the docks in Brooklyn. I came across him on a walk and took him home with me. We've been together ever since. Do you have any pets?"

He shook his head. "My mother's allergic."

So she claimed, anyway.

"Oh, that's too bad," she said wistfully. "I would go crazy without Coop. He's the best company. And he's surprisingly invested in reality TV."

"Really?"

"Yes. I think he belonged to a Real Housewife in a past life."

Leo smiled. He had smiled more in twenty-four hours of

knowing Emma than he had in months. It was a refreshing distraction from the stress of his project.

He waved as they passed through the gates on foot. Alejandro, the security officer on gate duty for the night, nodded at him from behind the desk.

"Do you have Christmas festivals at home?" Leo asked.

Their boots crunched over the fresh blanket of snow.

"Oh, yes. They're so over-the-top and packed with the best food vendors. And incredibly crowded. My mom loves them. Or did love them, before her mobility challenges."

"How do you and your mom celebrate the holidays now?"

Emma bit her lip and hesitated, like she wanted to divulge something. "Christmas is really important to us. We make a big show of it every year and do a bunch of super embarrassing stuff. One activity every day of December leading up to the holiday."

Interesting. That was taking consumerism to a whole new level. And yet, he had to know more.

"Like what?" he asked as they descended the hill toward the glimmering lights of the village.

"I don't think you want to know. You might think of me differently."

"Tell me. Please. I'm curious what American Christmas is like."

She tugged on a strand of hair. "Well, we do the stereotypical stuff. Hallmark movie marathon, ugly sweaters. We set a theme for cookie decorating every year—dead celebrities, swear words, animal butts."

"Animal butts?" He raised his eyebrows.

She nodded. "I told you you didn't want to know. When things were...better, my favorite tradition was making care packages for the homeless. Warm socks and toothbrushes and things like that."

He tilted his head. Better? Meaning that things weren't so great now? His heart dropped at the idea.

"Mom used to propagate and sell mistletoe out of a rickety old wagon. But our most embarrassing tradition by far was playing this obscure dancing game on our decrepit Wii. There were like two Christmas songs on there, which automatically made it a holiday tradition. One time, my mom drank too many Santa's Revenges beforehand and accidentally punched a vase off an end table."

Leo laughed. It sounded warm, loving, and fun—the opposite of Christmas at the castle.

"Santa's Revenge?"

"A drink I made up when I was twenty-one. It's basically hot buttered rum with M&Ms. I didn't have good taste."

"It must have been hard for you to leave your traditions to come here. You don't have any other siblings?"

Emma shook her head as they passed a streetlamp. The tip of her nose had turned pink, and snow clung to her hair and eyelashes. He had to stop himself from reaching over to brush them away.

"No, it's just me and my mom."

Another question was starting to bother him.

"Your boyfriend doesn't mind you being away for the holidays?"

She snorted, then clapped a hand to her mouth. "Sorry. No boyfriend. There was, once. But he left me a few months after my mom's stroke. He didn't like the idea of marrying someone who was a required caregiver."

He straightened. "What an arsehole."

Emma's expression shifted from cloudy to delighted.

"Are you allowed to say arsehole? Is Beatrice going to pop out of a bush and smack you with a ruler?"

"They gave up on me a long time ago," he said.

"The people love a rebel," she said warmly. "What's Christmas like for you and your family?"

Leo kicked a rock down the road. Faint strains of music were audible, and the air was spiced with cinnamon. It smelled great, but not as good as whatever had been wafting out of Emma's apartment.

"We're not big on Christmas. We go into town and ring the bell, then have brunch and gifts."

She looked at him. "That's it? Do you decorate? Make cookies? Watch movies? Play games?"

"Ruby and I do on occasion. I always volunteer around the holidays, so there's not a lot of time for frivolity."

"Hmm. Sounds like your Christmas needs more vase-punching," she teased.

He shook his head. "It's just another day on the calendar."

She seemed to consider this in silence. "Are you planning to go to the ball?" she asked after a beat. "Five hundred years is a big deal."

"No. I usually volunteer at the community kitchen on Saturdays."

Was it his imagination, or did she look slightly disappointed?

"That's too bad. You'll miss the desserts," she said.

"I'll have Ruby save me some."

"Ruby's wonderful," Emma said. "So smart and kind. She loaned me this outfit."

Right. His eyes drifted down. She wasn't wearing her stitched-up jacket. Was there money trouble at home?

"She's the best," he agreed. "Definitely the family favorite."

She side-eyed him. "There must be a significant age gap between the two of you. Unless you're secretly a very wise and mature twenty-one-year-old."

"I was fifteen when she was born. John was sixteen. She was a surprise, but a welcome one. She's the only one who can convince my mother to do anything. Hence, you're here."

Emma nodded. "I'll be honest, I thought all of this was a scam. I was convinced we were going to touch down in Spain and get kidnapped and tossed in a trunk. Why pay room and board for a couple international randos when you could support a baker from your own country?"

Leo smiled. "I might have said something similar. But my mother's very concerned about image. She was impressed by your Instagram."

"Good," she said flatly.

"I'm sorry if she made you feel like your desserts weren't up to par," he said.

She paused like she was debating on saying something. "I do wish she had provided a little more direction."

Emma must have been crippled under the pressure, especially considering the queen's lukewarm reception.

"For what it's worth, I thought everything you made was more than spectacular enough on its own," he said.

She perked up. "Really? Which one was your favorite?"

"The raspberry tart. Even though it almost killed me. Honestly, worth it."

She looked pleased. "Can I quote you on that? A royal endorsement would be a boon to my future business."

"Future business? Are you not planning on staying with...what's her name?"

Emma bit her lip. "We have some...differences of opinion that make it challenging to work together. I do all the baking," she explained.

He could have guessed. Maya didn't even seem to know the name of half the things they had offered.

"Well, I'm so glad we caught you before you struck out on your own. Oh, careful—" he pointed to a patch of black ice, but it was too late.

Emma's boot hit it, and in a split second, she was falling backward.

He lunged sideways and caught her before she hit the ground. Her eyes were wide, mouth frozen in an O as he held her.

Even with the puffy coat in the way, the feeling of her in his arms was like a hot shower after a long day. They froze that way for a moment, snow falling on them. He had an absurd, almost irresistible urge to kiss her. The music, the snow, the beautiful woman in front of him. It was like one of those kitschy snow globes sold by shops in the village.

He was being weird.

He tugged her back to her feet and shoved his hands in his pockets.

"Thank you so much," she said. Her cheeks were flaming. "Maya would have killed me if I got a concussion."

Leo frowned. Maya seemed like a pill.

Emma stopped in her tracks and sniffed the air. "Oh, it smells amazing."

"Roasted nuts. They're my favorite."

They had reached the outskirts of the winter carnival. People teemed through the cobblestone streets, ducking into local businesses and perusing jewelry and wood-carving stands while shopkeepers stomped their feet to keep warm. The scent of onions and butter drifted over from the pierogi stand. A band was playing on the newly fixed stage at the park. At least the new boards were holding.

Emma started toward the elaborate wooden archway that marked the entrance to the market, but he grabbed her wrist.

"Are you sure you want to do this?"

She raised an eyebrow. "I'm sure that I'm going to push you into a snowbank if you prevent me from finding those nuts."

Another smile. Damn it, she was funny. "I just meant... people might assume things."

She waved a hand flippantly. "Let 'em talk. We both know exactly what this is."

"And what is this?" The question slipped out in a rush of condensation. Shit. He hadn't meant to say that.

CHAPTER TEN

EMMA

Her mouth went slack at Leo's question. What the hell was that supposed to mean? Surely he was joking. They both knew this was little more than an apology or maybe a business transaction. Right?

"This is a clandestine nut-fetching mission, obviously," Emma joked to break the sudden tension.

Leo smiled, but it didn't seem as genuine as the one he'd given her earlier. "Right. Nuts, which I will buy as a thank you for saving my life."

"I'll allow it." She crossed the threshold of the archway and stepped into the market. Her stomach growled. She hadn't really had a square meal since she got here, just bites of rejected pastries.

She swiveled to take in the hustle and bustle. It wasn't the larger-than-life extravaganza she found in every neighborhood in New York. Hollybrook's festivities were smaller, subtler. Almost illegally quaint. Instead of six-story projections timed to music, simple star lanterns hung from awnings. Red bows adorned lampposts, and storefronts were draped with garland. Vendors in booths sold everything from crafts to food to slightly creepy wooden puppets. A scatter of stars was visible over the vapor of their breath, and she stopped to take them in. Stars were an uncommon sight in the city.

The stupidly romantic atmosphere of the market had to be to blame for her lack of focus. The twinkling lights were like an Instagram filter, showcasing a romanticized version of Leo. The strength of his chin, the dimple in his right cheek when he smiled. His glasses from earlier were gone, and strong, dark brows showcased the deep brown of his eyes.

She hadn't given much thought to romance in a long time. Not since Douchey Dylan had dumped her by text three weeks after her mom's stroke. It wasn't a great loss. Even when they had been together, their relationship had been shallow. While the companionship—and the sex— had been nice, she had never let him below the surface where the dark things were. She had never been good at relationships.

Besides, there was no room for a relationship when a paper-thin wall separated her bedroom from her mom's. Her plan had always been the same since Lisa's accident: save enough money to quit Crumb and Get It, freelance for the duration of the noncompete year, open her own business, and find a way to get her mom better care. That was what she needed to focus on, not some broody Christmas-hating prince who hadn't mastered the art of chewing and swallowing.

"You know what else would be a great way to thank me?" she asked.

"What?"

"Some insider information on your mom. I interrogated poor Ruby, but all she said was your mom likes cardamom."

He put a hand on the small of her back, gently guiding her through the throng. Even though they were separated by a marshmallow-sized layer of jacket, her spine tingled.

"I suppose it's the least I could do," he said. "Do you drink wine?"

"Do raccoons have an insatiable hunger for deviled eggs?" she asked.

She was talking nonsense again. There was no reason to be nervous. It wasn't like this was a date.

He stopped to look at her. "I don't know how to answer that question."

They had arrived at the wine tent. "Two, please," he said.

The salesperson's eyes lit up. She curtsied, and he nodded at her. Her gaze shifted to Emma, who smiled.

There was something bizarre about accompanying a royal person. Was this what ordinary people who married celebrities felt like? She had a feeling she was going to be taking a lot of pictures for people.

Orange peels and mulling spices perfumed the air. She inhaled deeply before fishing for her wallet.

"No," he said, closing a hand over her wrist. "I'm paying tonight."

Not because it was a date. Because he was thanking her for saving his life.

"Well, thank you."

"So about the raccoons," he prompted as he pocketed his change.

Emma took a sip, and the warmth flooded her body all the way down to her toes. Citrus, spice, and red wine. "God, this is good. What's it called?"

"Glühwein." He smiled, maybe pleased that she was enjoying something from his hometown.

"I love it. You're not getting out of the racoon story," she said as he steered her in another direction.

She should have been annoyed that he was steering her all over the place like some kind of catamaran. But his touch was a lick of fire, even above the forty layers she had on.

"I should have realized that was not an anecdote that would make sense overseas. Last summer, my mom and I went to a block party. We brought some deviled eggs. Long story short, I looked over during the party and saw a raccoon perched on the buffet table, scooping as many deviled eggs as he could hold into his tiny little hands. We chased him away, but he came back twice, and only for deviled eggs."

Leo seemed to be considering this information. His lips were tight like he was trying not to laugh. "She hates fondant," he finally said.

Emma stared at him. How would he know?

"My mother, I mean. Not that specific raccoon. Probably."

"Oh. That helps, thank you."

Any cake features without fondant would be challenging. It was just as well, though. Fondant sucked.

They started walking again.

The town was impossibly adorable. Lampposts decorated with bows were connected by string lights and garland, and children pointed in wonder at the two-story Christmas tree in the center of it all. It felt a little bit like home. But cleaner.

"Are you rewarding my charming raccoon anecdotes with fun facts about your mom?" she asked to cover the silence.

"Maybe. How about you tell me a little more about yourself, and I'll tell you a little more about my mother."

"What else can you possibly want to know?"

"Anything. What made you want to be a baker?"

Emma considered in silence for a moment.

"My mom, I guess."

He nodded. "Does she bake as well?"

"No. But she is—was—a florist. She can grow anything, even in our minuscule backyard. She made incredible arrangements for high society weddings and events. Like she was born to do it. I didn't have a knack for flowers. I'm not even allowed to water the ones at home anymore. But she got me an Easy-Bake Oven when I was eight, and something just...clicked. There's something so powerful about turning a pile of ingredients into something delicious."

"You have a true gift."

She pulled her scarf up to hide her smile.

They joined the end of the line at the roasted nut stand. A couple people in front of them turned around and whispered.

She took a half step closer to him. "Do you not have a security detail?" she whispered.

It seemed awfully cavalier to allow members of the royal family out in the world with no protection. There could have been a dozen kidnappers in the crowd, ready to take him for ransom.

Leo snorted, then straightened like he was expecting to be reprimanded.

"In case it hasn't become abundantly clear yet, the monarchy doesn't really mean anything in Lynoria," he said.

"No?" she asked.

Interesting.

"No. About thirty-five years ago—after my parents got married—the country voted to transition to a constitutional monarchy."

"Oh. That must have been hard."

Leo nodded. He continued in a low voice, "Ever since then, my mother has been obsessed with reminding everyone that we're still here. Our duties are mostly ceremonial bullshit. Christening hospitals, holding fundraisers, that kind of thing. Technically, my dad is the commander of the armed forces, but our 'armed forces' is about two dozen people with day jobs and nightsticks."

Hmm. Finally, some useful information. That gave her a lot to think about.

"Sounds like that wasn't what your mom signed up for."

He gave a curt nod. "Correct. So now she compensates by trying to control every aspect of our lives and thrust us out into the public eye as much as she can. Fortunately for me, she's mostly focused on John and Ruby. They each have a security detail, but Ruby ditches hers all the time."

Something in Emma softened. Classic middle child syndrome. Even though he said it flippantly, she could sense a source of pain there.

"Excuse me," a woman said in front of them. "Your Highness?" She curtsied, and Leo stiffened for a moment before relaxing.

"Good evening," he said with a deep nod. "Miss Kent, right? From the tailor shop? I hope business is booming this season."

She nodded, and her cheeks flushed. Holy crap. Did he know the name of every citizen in the village?

"We're very fortunate, Your Highness. Thank you for thinking of us. I was wondering if we might get a picture?"

"Of course," Emma said on his behalf. The woman handed over her phone, and Emma stepped back to take the picture.

Leo looked pained, like he was suppressing a fart.

"Let's get a couple more," she said, shifting so that the Christmas tree was in view. "Say 'deviled egg.'"

Ha. She had bamboozled Leo into a genuine smile.

"Perfect. Gorgeous. Christmas-card worthy, if I say so myself," she said as she handed the phone back.

"Thank you, my lady," the woman said with another curtsy.

Oh, no. She hadn't signed up to be curtsied at.

Now that the ice had broken, more people were stepping up with sheepish smiles, bows, and curtsies.

After a dozen more pictures, the line parted in front of them. People ushered them to the front. Finally, a royal perk.

Leo graciously thanked everyone in line, and Emma could hardly take her eyes off him. Even though she was getting a strong sense that he wasn't happy in this role—a reluctant royal—he treated everyone with kindness. The people were enamored with him. Instead of dismissing them, he asked one about his wife's surgery, and another about their grandson's football game.

It was amazing to watch him work. If she was a painter or a royal photographer, she would have captured him there, clasping hands with people who made up the back-bone of the community. She had a feeling the scene wouldn't translate as powerfully to cake.

Long minutes later, they had escaped the crowd and ducked behind a booth to sample the candied nuts. They were rock-hard but tasted of a tantalizing blend of cinnamon and brown sugar.

"Sorry about that," he said.

"I'll bet you never go to the grocery store. A week would pass just trying to get to the chocolate milk."

He smiled again. "You're not wrong."

"For someone who claims to be an empty figurehead, you sure know a lot about your subjects." She twisted the neck of the bag and shoved it in her pocket, then set off toward the park.

He shrugged and followed her. "It's the least I can do."

"How many people live in the village, anyway?"

"A little over five thousand."

"Do most of them work at the castle?"

He shrugged. "Some do, but a lot own or work in small businesses right here. And the rest commute to the city for work. It's only twenty minutes away."

She glanced at the stage as they passed by. A band was standing on it, new wood gleaming brightly against the old. That must have been what Leo was doing when they met yesterday.

"Why is it that you do so much yourself? Aren't there maintenance staff to take care of things like broken boards on the stage?"

"I have certain privileges, access to some funds for community outreach. The least I can do is cut through the red tape when I can."

"You really care about the people," she observed.

"Of course I do. I wish I could do more," he said, scanning the festival. "I'm trying to do more."

"Oh?" She waited, but he didn't elaborate.

"We're supposed to be talking about you, not me," he said.

"I think technically we're here to thank me for saving your life. Which you could do by telling me more about your impossible-to-please mother's likes and dislikes," she said pointedly.

He nodded, and they pulled to a stop.

She swayed to the band's rendition of "O Come, All Ye

Faithful" while Leo pondered. Her stomach growled, apparently unsatisfied by the candied nuts, and he glanced at her.

"Come with me. Let's warm up a little."

Her eyes dropped from his face to his toes against her will. The hormones that had lain dormant seemed to be firing up again. Maybe it was the brisk walk in the frigid air. But she had a visceral mental image of Leo shedding his clothes next to a crackling fire. Desire stirred in her, and she bit the inside of her cheek.

Focus, idiot. He's a literal prince, and you're a girl who bakes cookies. He's just being polite.

"Sounds great."

He led her to a pub with a weathered sign over the door that read The Scarlet Hare.

It was welcoming and warm inside, which was great because her nipples were about to snap off.

The pub's interior was surprisingly modern and tasteful —almost industrial chic. Clean lines, rich leather booths. Glass globes dangled throughout, bathing the space in warm golden light.

"Leo!" someone exclaimed from behind the bar.

Leo slid onto a heavy iron barstool, and she claimed the one next to him. The barkeep didn't bow or even nod. They must have been friends. Unless he was royalty too?

"And who's this?" asked a man with amazing eyebrows.

"This is Emma. She's part of the baking team for the anniversary party."

"You're the girl with the dog," the man said. His eyebrows were perfectly manicured, and his teeth were incredibly straight and bright.

Right. Shit. He had been there when Cooper peed on Leo.

"Yes. I instruct Cooper to pee on heads of state everywhere I go. I have a punch card," she said with a serious face.

The man laughed. "I like her. She's funny. I'm Salvador. Everyone calls me Sal."

"Emma." She reached across the bar and shook his hand.

"What's your special tonight?" Leo asked.

"Pasta pancetta."

So that was the heavenly smell. Leo looked at her, and she nodded. "Two, please. And a couple pints."

Leo tugged his coat off and hung it over the back of his chair. His deep blue sweater stretched across his broad chest and clung to a surprising set of biceps. This was not helping her random surge of hormones.

They sat in the warmth of the restaurant, nursing their beers. She wasn't usually a beer girl, but if slamming down a couple pints of Guinness helped the prince spill all the dirty secrets about the queen, she would do a keg stand.

His knee brushed against hers under the bar, and her heart leapt into her throat. *Relax.* That was definitely an accident.

She busied her hands by shrugging off the borrowed jacket and pulling off her hat. Her hair was probably a hot, staticky mess. Not the most professional look for what was practically a business meeting, but at least it wasn't a Yankees sweatshirt covered in dog hair.

A few other patrons claimed booths, but no one seemed to be paying attention to them. Good.

Leo looked up at her, and his brow furrowed. "Here," he said, reaching for her. She turned to look at him, heart in her throat. Was she covered in cinnamon sugar dust?

His pinky grazed her cheek, and her underwear disintegrated. His hand moved to her hair.

"Leo! Your Highness!"

A flash popped, and Emma blinked in the sudden burst of light. Leo jerked away from her. A couple of men with cameras elbowed each other, trying to get a shot.

"Fuck," Leo grumbled next to her. "Get your coat."

She recovered Ruby's coat and hat, and Leo grabbed her hand. A burst of static electricity shocked her, and it was like a warning.

He pulled her across the room and through a set of double doors into the kitchen.

The chefs looked up and bowed at Leo as they ran through the kitchen and into a back storage room. He pressed her against a shelving unit and shielded her with his body.

CHAPTER ELEVEN

LEO

Leo stopped to listen, his heart pounding in his ears.

It fucking figured. The first time he had the audacity to take a woman out since Petra, and the paparazzi had been on them within minutes. Someone must have tipped them off.

The door to the kitchen opened, and Leo yanked the brim of Emma's beanie down over her eyes and shielded her with his arms. He had known this was a risk when he asked her to the carnival, and he had done it anyway. Selfish. Stupid and selfish.

"It's just me." Sal appeared holding two to-go containers. "Sorry about that. I kicked them out and told them there was a rumor John was throwing up behind the porta-potties at the park."

Emma slapped at Leo's arm and pulled the beanie off. She looked annoyed.

"I could set you up a nice little table back here if you wanted to stay," Sal added.

He turned to Sal and shook his head. "We'll take it to go. I've put her through enough tonight. Add it to my tab."

He had meant tonight's outing as a way to say thank you and make up for deceiving her, and instead she had spent the whole evening taking pictures of him and fleeing from the paparazzi.

"I'm so sorry about that," he said as they stepped back into the winter dark minutes later. A to-go bag dangled from one wrist. He peeked around the corner of the building, but the paparazzi had seemingly moved on.

"It's okay. You warned me. And that was pretty mild compared to the treatment some celebrities get," she added.

"Well, we are a small country. It doesn't make it less annoying, though."

Emma said nothing. A knot formed in his stomach. All he could do now was escort her back to the apartment...and give up everything he knew about his mother's tastes.

"My mother likes crunchy biscuits, not soft."

Emma, who had been staring forlornly back at the Christmas festival, snapped her attention back to him.

"Oh, great. Let me write this down." She pulled her phone out and opened a blank note. "Crunchy cookies, not soft. Cardamom. No fondant. What else?" she asked, looking up at him.

"She likes more essences than raw fruit, if that makes sense. Rose water, that kind of thing. And she prefers choco-late cake to vanilla."

She looked up from her phone. "And the king?"

"He likes everything. He also doesn't get to have an opinion about anything related to the ball."

"Huh. Okay." She tucked her phone away.

They settled into a companionable silence as they trudged back up the snow-covered road toward the castle. It glowed ahead of them, an intimidating structure.

"How does your mom feel about nuts?" she asked.

"Hates Brazil nuts, tolerates everything else."

She nodded and made another note. "What would you say are some traditional flavors in your country?"

"We have a little influence from everywhere. France, Spain, Germany, England. We have a version of crème brûlée called Crema Lynoria. And our chef would make coca masegada on holidays."

She straightened up. "I've heard of cocas." She jotted down another note, and he could practically see the wheels turning.

Their pace slowed as the castle appeared in the distance. Even though Leo had a thousand things to do, he wasn't ready to say goodnight. Something about Emma was comforting and warm, like a flannel blanket. If a flannel blanket was also incredibly good-looking and funny.

"Thank you for taking me to the festival," she said as they headed up the stairs to the second floor of the gatehouse. She pulled a heavy brass key out of her pocket and slid it into the keyhole. Cooper barked on the other side of the door.

"It was my pleasure. Here." He reached into the bag and pulled out one of the to-go boxes. He handed it to her.

"Are you sure you don't want to come in and eat with me? Give up some more closely guarded state secrets?" she asked. Her green eyes shone in the half-light. One hand rested on the doorknob.

He hesitated. Beyond that door, they'd be away from prying eyes. There was also a giant dog he really wanted to get to know. But she was only here for a few days. Getting attached was a bad idea.

"I think I've put you through enough today." He gently took her free hand in his and bent to press a kiss to it. Her fingers tensed under his touch. When he straightened, she looked a little disappointed. He was close enough to smell the vanilla notes of her perfume. It was making sticking to his convictions almost impossible.

"Thank you, Emma. That was the most fun I've had in some time."

Her hand was small in his. It was taking every bit of Leo's self-control not to pull her to him and press her against that doorframe.

"Even though I couldn't stop talking about raccoons with a penchant for picnic foods?" she quipped.

"Especially because of that. I'll see you around."

"See you," she said. She pulled her hand back and opened the door, disappearing behind it without another look behind her.

He leaned against the opposite wall and let out a long breath. What was he doing? Fraternizing with an American? His mother would die of a heart attack.

But did he care? The solid wood of the door beckoned to him. There was nothing wrong with having dinner with her. That had been the plan, after all, before the press interrupted. It was pasta, not a marriage proposal.

He raised a hand to knock on the door when it suddenly opened.

Emma shrieked, and her fist came flying out of nowhere. He jumped back.

"Shit, I'm sorry. I didn't think you'd still be there. Did I hit you?"

She put a hand on his cheek, and her eyes searched his. Cooper's leash was wrapped around her wrist. He circled the prince, sniffing at his shoes, before walking down the hall.

The leash tightened around them and pulled them

together until they were torso-to-torso and staggering toward the stairs like some kind of many-limbed monster.

Cooper paused to sniff at a doorway, and for a moment they were only a hair's breadth apart. Moonlight shone in her green eyes. His hand found her waist instinctively, and they looked at each other. A door shut down the hallway, and Leo snapped back to reality.

"Sorry, I didn't mean to scare you. The, uh, Wi-Fi is particularly good in this hallway." He extricated himself from the leash and took a step back.

What nonsense was he speaking?

"Right," she said with a small smile. "The Wi-Fi. Well, I need to let Cooper out. Have a good night...Your Highness," she added with a small curtsy.

"We talked about this," he called after her, and she looked over her shoulder to wink at him.

He confidently strode the opposite direction before remembering that it led to a dead end, then had to wait an extra minute to be sure she was outside before hustling out the exit.

He was in trouble.

CHAPTER TWELVE

EMMA

EMMA AWOKE TO HER PHONE RINGING. SHE STARED BLEARILY at it with one eye. Her mom. It must have been two a.m. at home.

She sat bolt upright in bed and answered. "Hello? Everything okay?"

Her heart pounded full-tilt like she had been woken up by a machete-wielding intruder instead of a phone call.

"No, everything's not okay," her mom said. "Why am I finding out from the internet that my daughter went on a date with a prince last night?

"A what?"

Oh, shit. The paparazzi had moved fast. How had they figured out who she was?

"A date. With a prince. You seriously weren't going to tell me about it? Here, I'm sending you the link."

Her phone dinged, and she pulled up the article. Oh, hell. There was a picture of the two of them sitting at the bar, and it looked like Leo was stroking her hair when he had really been on a fuzz-retrieving mission.

"'Prince Leo's Mystery Date'? Sources say she had an

American accent," she muttered to herself as she scanned the article.

Luckily, no one seemed to have put the pieces together and identified her. What a weird day.

"Well, first of all, it wasn't a date," she said to her mom. "I kind of saved his life, and then he lied to me about who he was but then felt bad. He took me to the winter carnival as an apology."

"I'm gonna need more details than that, sweetie."

Emma rehashed the story but skipped over the weird part where he had been lurking outside her door after she went inside. What had that meant? Was he reconsidering? Or was he secretly a mega creep who was going to watch her eat pasta through the keyhole?

"How did you even find this story?" Emma asked.

"I followed all the Lynorian tabloids the second you got on that plane. Just in case I spotted you in the background of a royal picture or something. I never imagined I'd find you on a date with one of them."

"Again, it wasn't a date."

"Whatever you say, sweetheart. It'll be totally worth losing the apartment for you to marry a prince. I better make sure my passport is still valid."

Emma sputtered and launched herself out of bed, digging through the clothes she'd hastily thrown into her suitcase. "I'm not falling in love, Mother. I've known him for twelve minutes, and I'm basically just using him to get information on the queen. Now if you'll excuse me, I have to go to the damn library because apparently Lynoria can't be bothered to put their history and customs on the internet. I love you. Go to bed."

She hung up the phone and let out a frustrated grunt. Her gaze fell on the bouquet of pink roses Leo had given her the day before. For someone who had made such a show about getting to know her, he acted like he'd rather be boiled alive than have dinner in her apartment.

The whole latter half of the evening had been fraught with tension. When Cooper wrapped them up in his leash, she had been seconds away from throwing caution to the wind and kissing him. She had made a fool of herself. She must have been imagining the frisson between them.

And what was she expecting, a tryst with a prince? She didn't need to be putting her energy into chasing after some guy from a different country who wouldn't even agree to dinner. He was a colleague. That was all. She would just have to avoid him for the rest of the trip.

———

Two hours later, after a rejuvenating shower and some breakfast snatched from the royal kitchen, Emma strolled down the road toward town. It was a beautiful morning. The sun was blindingly bright, glancing off the snow. They sometimes went all winter without seeing the sun in Brooklyn.

Hollybrook was stunning in the daytime, like it had been ripped from a calendar for European tourist destinations. She paused by a lamppost to turn and drink it all in. Even though she spent every waking moment worried about her mom, maybe coming to this beautiful little country had been worth it. She would probably never have another opportunity like this one.

An elderly couple passed by her, walking a poodle. They nodded and smiled at her. She glanced at her watch—10 a.m. The library was open by now.

She hustled that direction, edging around icy patches

and doing her best not to fall on her face. There was no Leo here to save her from a broken tailbone. Not that she was thinking about him.

She ducked into the library and unwound the scarf from her neck. Ruby's chic clothes had been returned, so she was back to hand-me-downs and thrift store finds.

A handful of other people were here, browsing shelves. Where would she even start? She looked at the stacks, but most of what was in front of her was fiction and children's literature. A checkout counter caught her eye.

Aha. Librarians were magic.

After a quick conversation, a librarian led her to the second floor and gave her a precarious stack of books about the history and culinary traditions of Lynoria. Emma sat at a table in the reference loft near the computer bay, with a view of the front door.

The library was outdated but cozy, and it smelled amazing. She could practically feel the knowledge saturating the air. It felt just like her local public library, where she had spent countless hours reading *Sweet Valley Twins* books in her youth.

The clock was ticking. She needed to come up with something amazing in the next few hours, especially if she was going to bake a test batch of something to wow the queen before tomorrow morning.

She busied herself leafing through books, tearing bits of paper from her notebook to mark important pages. Lynoria's culinary traditions were similar to the rest of this region in Europe. Nothing jumped out immediately, but maybe if she dug deeper. She needed to make some copies and start a plan, but the copier had an Out of Order sign on it. The queen expected an updated plan the very next day, and she hadn't even checked in with Maya to see what her ideas were. Not that it mattered—they were probably deranged.

Emma needed to dream up something incredible, majestic, breathtaking. Maybe even romantic. She turned back to another book, this one about the architect who designed the castle.

The front doors opened, and a deep male voice came from downstairs. She peered over the railing, and her stomach plummeted. Oh, fuck. Leo was down there, holding a sizable box. So much for avoiding him.

A book slid off the top of her pile and landed on the floor with a muffled thump. He looked up at her, and she had a split-second view of recognition flashing in his eyes before she pushed her chair away from the ledge as fast as she could. A horrible screech filled the air.

Great. Not only had she unwillingly run into Prince Sexy and drawn attention to herself, she had also disturbed the sacred peace of the library. Why the hell was he here, anyway? Checking out a book on sending mixed signals?

A faint voice came from downstairs. "Thank you so much, Your Highness."

That was Maria, the librarian who had helped her.

"It's Leo," he corrected. "Where do you want it?"

"On the second floor, if you don't mind."

Emma dropped her notebook. *She* was on the second floor. Should she run? But no, he had already seen her.

Footsteps padded up the stairs in front of her. Maybe he was just bringing a box of books. She probably wouldn't even see him.

"Over here," Maria said.

They emerged from the stacks. Emma's cheeks grew hot, and her grip tightened on the pen. She refused to look up as he walked by and pretended to be engrossed in a picture of the castle.

"I can't thank you enough. I thought we wouldn't see a new copier until sometime next year," the librarian said, sounding a little more flustered than when she had spoken to Emma earlier.

"If I had it my way, you'd have a new building, not just a new printer," he said. "The services you offer the community are so important. My sister loves it here, and your resume-building classes have helped so many people."

Her heart softened. Damn it. The universe delighted in her suffering.

Minutes passed while Leo unpacked the copier and set it up. She was still staring at the same spot on the page, every inch of her body on high alert and aware that Leo was six feet away. She felt his gaze on her a couple times, but he didn't say anything.

It was just as well. There was no telling how long it would take her to assemble this show-stopping dessert for the ball. If she could even find an idea for it.

The queen was obsessed with reminding people that the monarchy was still relevant. What would stroke her ego enough to gain her approval?

In an effort to distract herself and seem busy, Emma started a list of ideas with the information Leo had shared with her at the top.

The Lynorian flag made out of tarts.

A ski slope made of cake and macarons.

A crispy-rice-and-marshmallow portrait of the king and queen.

Stupid. Useless. None of these ideas were showstoppers fit for a royal ball.

Her gaze fell on the garland that was wrapped around a shelf, and she gasped.

The librarian and Leo looked at her, but she didn't care.

There it was. The perfect idea. She would recreate the most powerful symbol of the monarchy: the castle. And she would do it in festive, elaborately decorated gingerbread. In fact, she was certain she had once made cardamom rose gingersnaps for a past client. She could recreate all of the castle grounds—the gardens, the lake, the craggy peaks of the mountains, the turrets and spires. Everything captured in delicious miniature.

Possibilities flooded her mind. It would be insane. An almost impossible task. But if she did nothing else but plan and bake for the next seven days, it might work.

She slammed all the books shut and hefted them onto a return cart. Then she slid her notebook into her purse and ran out of the library without a backward glance.

CHAPTER THIRTEEN

LEO

Leo stormed down the castle hallway, mood as black as the night sky.

Sal had texted him late last night with a string of questions about Emma, none of which had real answers.

He shouldn't be bothered by the fact that Emma left the library without so much as a hello. She was perfectly free to do whatever she wanted. She didn't owe him anything. But even an acquaintance whose name he barely knew would greet him on sight.

Maybe it was an American thing. Or maybe she had seen that paparazzi article and shied away.

The night before, there had been an undeniable connection between them. It couldn't have been one-sided. Had he really misread the situation?

Maybe it was for the best. She lived on a different continent. While his brother was the king of one-night stands, Leo struggled to separate feelings from physicality. It was better to focus on his project.

The end of the year was approaching, and the presentation he was preparing was proving to be challenging.

He had to find a way to stroke his parents' egos to get their approval. Perhaps he could name the new complex after them? Maybe a statue of them in the community garden? Would it be enough?

He froze outside the door to the kitchen. That was Emma's voice beyond the door. What was she saying? He leaned closer.

"For the last time, it was not a date," Emma said.

"Uh-huh," an unfamiliar female voice said on the phone.

"I asked him to come in to eat with me after the paparazzi chased us, and he said no. He's not into me. And even if he was, there's nothing I can do about it."

Leo jerked back. His heart beat in his ears.

"I disagree," said the other voice. "You can bone his brains out and let your boring married friend live vicariously through you."

He pressed his lips together and suppressed a laugh.

He should leave. This was a private conversation. But he leaned closer.

"Whoa. First of all, I can't afford to be thrown in a foreign dungeon for sexually harassing a prince. And second of all, I don't have time to worry about romance."

"Not even a week-long fling? For me?"

"Do I need to explain consent to you again, Lo?"

"No, no. Fine. But if anything happens, you have to tell me immediately. Im-mee-dee-at-lee. Am I clear?"

"In the statistically impossible situation where I fall in love with a prince, abandon my disabled mother, and move to a foreign country, you'll be the first to know."

"How is your mom?" the other voice asked. Her tone had lost its playfulness.

"She claims to be fine, but she totally unplugged one of the nanny cams. If it happens again—"

"It won't," the caller said firmly. "And the first one wasn't your fault either. If anything, it was Maya's fault."

Emma breathed a deep sigh, like something that burbled up from the depths of her toes. "I have to go. If I don't impress the hell out of the queen tomorrow morning, I may never get the second half of the money, and I'll be right back to square one."

"Go do what you do best. Love you."

"Love you," Emma replied.

Leo paused. She seemed to be taking deep breaths on the other side of the door. He could practically feel her tension. He wanted to see her, to comfort her. But he hadn't gleaned much from her conversation with her friend—only that she wasn't looking to fall in love.

Which was good. Because he wasn't either. There was no time for romance when women and children were forced to flee to ramshackle shelters with poor water pressure and half-broken furniture.

But that didn't mean he couldn't try to help her. Abruptly making up his mind, he pushed the door open.

Emma shrieked and grabbed the object nearest her—a baking sheet. She wielded it like a shield for a moment before recognizing him. It clattered to the island.

"Do you always greet people this way?" he asked.

"Only when they sneak up on me."

A scatter of papers surrounded her. Hairs were escaping from her bun, and there was a frown line etched between her eyebrows.

"Is it really sneaking if I'm entering my own kitchen?"

She shot him a dirty look.

"Is everything okay?" he asked.

"What? Oh. Yes. I'm just working on something for tomorrow."

"You sound stressed."

"Stressed? Me? No, I'm only preparing a dessert that will decide my entire future." The tension in her voice was palpable, and it tugged at his heart.

Coming around the island to where she stood, Leo gently took both of her arms and jostled her until she looked at him.

"Everything's going to be fine."

She stared at him, tears forming. He stroked her cheek, and something changed in her eyes.

"Let's take a dinosaur breath, then you can tell me about it."

She stopped and looked confused. "A dinosaur breath?"

Idiot.

"Sorry. That was something I used to do with Ruby when she was upset."

The corners of her mouth twitched, and she obediently took a deep breath.

"Is this your idea or your boss's?" he asked when she looked a little calmer.

She scoffed, then briefly clamped her mouth shut. "It's mine."

He nodded. It was better that she wasn't wasting energy on what was sure to miss the mark.

"I could use a laugh. What did your boss come up with?"

The tension in her shoulders disappeared, and a smile appeared. "A ten-layer cake, which would collapse under its own weight and require us to find customized pans. A map of Lynoria made out of brownies. And an eight-foot macaron tower in the likeness of your brother."

Leo chuckled and then covered the sound with a cough.

"Well. Those are all certainly ideas. Now tell me about yours."

She bit her lip. "It's insane."

"The best ideas usually are."

"Okay, so your mom is all about reminding everyone that the monarchy exists, right?"

He nodded.

She pulled a piece of paper out of her stack and showed him a drawing dusted with flour. "I want to capture the festive spirit and make a model of the castle and grounds out of gingerbread. All the landscape will be edible—macarons and tarts and cookies and Lynorian candies. A croquembouche tower for the Christmas tree in the courtyard."

He could picture it in his mind's eye.

"I think it's amazing. She'd love it—in her own way. So what's the problem?"

She threw her hands up. The stress was back in her eyes. "I'm not a damn architect, that's the problem. I don't have any idea how to go about breaking down the castle architecture into something even remotely replicable."

"I know someone who can help with that."

"Do they accept payment in gingerbread, by chance?"

"My mother didn't set a budget. This consult falls under the budget purview."

She perked up. "Really?"

"Definitely. I'll talk to her tomorrow."

Emma threw herself on him.

He went rigid for a moment, while his nose filled with the scent of rose hips and vanilla. She pulled back to look at him. "Thank you so much. Oh, shit." Her expression changed, and she leapt back. "I'm sorry, I probably shouldn't be hugging you. That's a thing, right? Don't touch a royal unless they touch you first? I read it on Wikipedia."

Leo raised his arms to his side. "Consider this blanket, state-sanctioned permission to touch me."

Whoops. That sounded more sexual than he meant it. Or was it?

She smiled, and her gaze dipped for a second. Was she imagining touching him? He hardened at the thought.

Emma was beautiful in the muted light of the kitchen. His earlier annoyances were almost forgotten. Almost.

"You ignored me in the library today," he accused, leaning against the kitchen island.

She seemed to debate silently for a minute, then busied herself by shuffling papers into a neat stack. "I did. I was annoyed that you turned me down for dinner last night. So was Cooper."

Aha. So she was annoyed.

"I'll make it up to you. Let me plan something."

She grunted and turned back to the sheet of gingerbread in front of her, and her shoulders tensed. "I don't have time. This project is going to be my entire life for the next week."

He frowned. That wasn't exactly a yes. But now wasn't the right time to press her.

"Why don't you just make a super-simplified version for now? She'll get the idea and get to taste it."

She nodded, then her gaze snapped up to his. "I don't know how I'm going to sneak this in tomorrow. Maya doesn't exactly know that I'm coming in with my own idea."

"I'll take care of it. The maids will help. What's the deal with you two, anyway?" he asked.

Emma bit her lip. "I realize this is all going to sound extremely ungrateful."

He lowered his voice. "I promise you will never sound more ungrateful than the king-to-be."

It was true. John was probably the only person to ever complain about receiving a Bentley on his birthday.

"Go on," Leo encouraged.

"So when I was about to graduate from the Institute of Culinary Education, we had a senior showcase to show off our skills. I made entremets, and Maya attended the show. She wooed me and offered a job at Crumb and Get It, which was just starting to make its mark on the map. I accepted and neglected to read the employment contract thoroughly."

Leo frowned. He didn't like where this was going.

"It turns out the head baker had left, presumably because Maya is a nightmare who does nothing. Maya went to the senior showcase to find someone with talent who she could criminally underpay and take credit for all their ideas. She also trapped me with an ironclad noncompete. So I've been saving every possible cent while running the whole business. I do the baking, the ordering, the marketing. I even do onboarding for new hires and meet with the accountant."

She turned to look out the window. "In a way, I should probably thank her. I have all the tools and knowledge to start my own business now. That's why this trip is so life-changing for me. It'll put me two years ahead of my plan. If I wow your mom and take home the second half of the money, I can quit on New Year's Eve, then ride out the noncompete period freelancing in social media before starting my own business. At least, that's the plan."

Leo considered this in silence. "You've been doing all this and taking care of your mom?"

She turned back to him. "Yeah. Her disability payments aren't enough for groceries, let alone skilled care. I have to pay for a nurse while I'm at work, and then I take care of her at night. She's my mom, you know? It's hard, but she's worth it."

She might as well have thrust a five-kilo bag of flour directly into his gut.

This was insane. Good people didn't deserve to struggle like this. Emma and her mother were exactly the kind of people they could be helping here in Lynoria.

What could he even say to soothe her? Empty platitudes?

"I can't believe you've been shouldering this burden all on your own. You must be exhausted."

A single tear slipped down her cheek, and she brushed it away.

"It's fine. It'll all work out eventually. But not if I don't pull off this dessert."

He took her hand. "I'll help you. In any way I can."

He meant it. If he had to fly to New York and hide envelopes full of cash in her bushes twice a month, he would do it. There was a very palpable sense that Emma hadn't had anyone to take care of her in a very long time.

"Thank you."

As they stared at one another, time seemed to stretch and flex, simultaneously moving at lightning speed yet as slow as January.

He took a step closer. They were practically toe-to-toe. She looked up at him. He towered over her.

He had a deep urge to kiss her, to take her in his arms and hold her until they found a way to solve all her problems.

But he barely knew her. She didn't live here, and she would leave the country in a week. What was he thinking?

She was so remarkable. Funny, resilient, driven. Delightfully uncouth and relaxed around him. It was unlike any interaction he'd ever had with a woman. They were always on their best behavior around him, but Emma couldn't be bothered with formalities. She didn't care who his family was.

He lifted his free hand and gently touched her cheek. Her skin was soft and warm, her eyes clear and wide. Beckoning to him. Kindling something within him.

He leaned down and was a second away from kissing her when the door to the kitchen opened.

They sprang apart. Was it his mom? But no, it was just Flossie, one of the house managers.

"Oh," Flossie said, stopping in her tracks. A swift curtsy followed. "Your Highness. Pardon the intrusion. I was just fetching a glass of sherry for Her Majesty."

Emma's cheeks flushed, and her posture went rigid.

"You're not intruding, Flossie," he said. "I was just chatting with Miss Clark about the ball."

"Of course," Flossie said, fetching a bottle and a glass.

The servants were notorious gossips. Even though nothing had actually happened, news of this encounter would be all over the castle by the morning. It figured.

An awkward silence ensued, which was thankfully interrupted by Emma.

"Thank you so much for the advice," Emma said. "And for the listening ear."

"It was my pleasure. You're meeting with my mother tomorrow?"

"Yes, in the drawing room at ten."

Leo nodded. "It'll be great. Just leave your gingerbread on a shelf in the pantry. I'll arrange for one of the maids to bring it in."

He would be there. And he would make sure his mother picked Emma's idea. If it pissed off her boss, even better.

CHAPTER FOURTEEN

LEO

Leo walked into the drawing room at 9:45 the next morning.

The queen looked up from her desk. "What are you doing here?"

"I live here," Leo said.

"It's good that you stopped in," she said, ignoring his comment. "We need to chat. What's going on with you and the baker?"

Bollocks. Either the servants' gossiping had traveled fast, or she had actually paused to read the tabloids this week.

"I don't know what you mean."

She slid a paper across her desk. The picture of Leo stroking Emma's hair in the bar was on the front page of a gossip rag. Damn.

"Beatrice brought this to my attention, and then I overheard the servants gossiping. So, what's going on? And don't lie, I don't have time for it."

The truth couldn't hurt. At least part of it.

"Emma saved my life," he said.

The queen looked up at him like he was insane.

"What do you mean?"

"I choked on something in the kitchen. No one else was around. She gave me the Heimlich."

She leaned forward, continuing to look at him like he was crazy. "You almost died, and you didn't think that you should mention it to your own mother? Did you see the doctor?"

"I'm fine."

Not exactly the truth. He'd had more than one nightmare that he was suffocating since the incident.

The queen threw up her hands. "So she saved your life. Why were you out in public with her?"

"I took her to the carnival as a thank you."

She raised an eyebrow. "A nice fruit basket wouldn't suffice?"

"She's a guest in our country. Isn't it my diplomatic duty to show her around and make her feel comfortable here?"

"I know you. Don't get attached," the queen warned. "We do *not* need an American mucking up the bloodline. If you can't control yourself, I'll have to send her home. I'm sure Miss Farrell could handle it on her own with a couple of the sous chefs."

His temper flared. *Mucking up the bloodline?* Threatening to fire Emma? How *dare* she? He opened his mouth, ready to retort, when the door opened and Beatrice stepped in.

He would save the verbal lashing for after she chose Emma's idea. He came to stand behind his mother's desk. She would never send Emma home after seeing her idea. Her ego wouldn't allow it.

Beatrice curtsied. "Good morning, Your Majesty. Your Highness. Are you ready for your meeting with the bakers?"

Beatrice must have actively chosen to ignore the hostile vibes in the room.

The queen flipped the tabloid picture upside down on her desk and nodded. Maya and Emma entered the room. Maya strutted in and scanned the room, almost certainly looking for John. She pouted when she didn't see him. Emma looked at Leo, and he nodded. Clarissa, one of the maids, was guarding the gingerbread house in the hallway.

"Good morning, Your Majesty," Maya said, curtsying with a flourish. "We're excited to present our ideas."

Eleanor pressed her fingertips together. "Wonderful. What have you come up with?"

Maya pulled out a couple of clumsy drawings and laid them on the queen's desk. "You can't go wrong with a classic tiered cake. We can make a ten-layer cake that's half as tall as your ballroom. We could make it in the colors of Lynoria or airbrush it with edible silver-and-gold paint. People will talk about it forever."

The queen pressed her lips together. She wasn't impressed. "And this one?"

"A map of Lynoria with an edible base—our customers love our blondies. We could map the landmarks and rivers with icing." Maya seemed less sure of herself now that the cake idea hadn't been met with enthusiasm.

"I see. And your final idea?"

"We could make a life-sized replica of Prince John out of individual macarons. Or any member of the royal family," she added hurriedly.

The queen was silent for a moment. "Perhaps I was unclear," she began.

Maya's face fell.

"Oh, Your Majesty," Emma piped up, "forgive the interruption. We have one more idea. A visual aid might be more helpful."

Maya's nostrils flared, and she glared at Emma.

Emma darted into the hallway and returned with a small gingerbread house, elaborately decorated. It even had what looked like stained glass windows. How had she pulled it off?

She put it on the desk and offered the queen a separate square of iced gingerbread to taste. "To capture the festive season and honor the illustrious history of Lynoria, we thought we could do a gingerbread replica of the castle, complete with a variety of desserts for the grounds. Everything will be edible, and whatever you want—tarts, macarons, cook—uh, biscuits."

The queen leaned forward and looked at it. She nibbled on a corner of the gingerbread piece. The faintest hint of a smile appeared at the corner of her lips.

"Is that rosewater?"

Emma nodded.

"Very well. How big can you make it?"

"We can assemble it in the ballroom if necessary. I would estimate it could be at least a meter tall if we get the correct pans."

The queen nodded. "Send your requests to the kitchen. We'll source everything immediately. And you'll still incorporate the croissants? My Ruby loves them so."

"Of course. Anything you want," Emma said.

"Thank you, Your Majesty," Maya said with a frown.

Leo winked at Emma, and then they were gone.

A sense of victory filled him. That was as enthusiastic an affirmation as he'd ever seen his mother give. Emma would pull it off. And he would help her.

He had one foot out the door when his mother's voice stopped him.

"Leo?"

"Yes, Mother?"

"I meant what I said. Don't disappoint me."

He looked at her but didn't offer a reply. He shut the door rather roughly behind him and went to find Emma.

"Emma," he called. Maya turned to look at him and rolled her eyes. She kept walking, but Emma waited for him.

"I knew you'd pull it off. Believe it or not, that was a rave review from my mother."

"She could have fooled me."

"She's forever withholding with her praise. Except for Ruby. I'm about to head into town to meet with the architect. Would you like to accompany me?"

Emma perked up. "Um, yes. As long as we don't get chased by paparazzi again. Maybe I could disguise myself as a bush."

He laughed. "I don't think that'll be necessary. I'll meet you in the courtyard in half an hour."

———

"Emma, this is Kat. Kat, Emma," Leo said.

"I hear you're an architect," Emma said enthusiastically. "That must be such interesting work."

The community kitchen smelled like rich, savory stew. A winter storm was expected tonight, and he had just dropped off some fresh vegetables and an extra dozen loaves of bread. A pile of blankets was waiting in his truck to be taken to the homeless shelter next. Emma had insisted they stop to add a hundred pairs of clean socks and hygiene products to the care package.

Kat waved a hand. "Eh, it's a lot of banks and car dealerships. But I'm very excited about the prince's plans for the community," she said.

"What plans?" Emma turned to him.

"Nothing," he said quickly. When she raised an eyebrow, he yielded. "We'll talk about that later. Thanks for meeting us, Kat. I have an unusual request."

She smiled and leaned forward. "Go on. I'm intrigued."

"We need you to create a gingerbread-compatible blueprint for the castle and grounds. Something that's easy to replicate and similar enough to the castle to be recognizable, but not so intricate that it would take weeks to assemble."

"Okay," she said slowly.

"And we need them as quickly as possible. Tomorrow would be great."

"Well, I better make a trip to the library and scrounge up the official blueprints," Kat said. "I'll email them to you."

"Excellent. You can send the bill to the castle for this one. Feel free to include a hefty charge for the rush order."

"Any news on the other project?" she asked hesitantly, one hand on her purse.

Emma leaned forward in interest.

"I'll be making my presentation after the ball," he said.

She smiled and looked pleased. "Excellent. I'll get started on these right away."

Kat left, and Emma turned to him. "Okay, you have to spill the details. What are these plans for the community? Are you building a Cheesecake Factory?"

He scoffed. "No. We're building...well, I'll just show you after we stop at the shelter."

"Let's go." She grabbed his hand and dragged him out of the community kitchen with a wave at Gus.

Gus gave him a thumbs-up before they exited.

"Okay," Leo said after they had dropped off the supplies at the homeless shelter. The staff had been delighted to receive backups for what was sure to be a very cold night. "I'll take you by the site."

"I'm so intrigued. You're being very mysterious." Emma hopped in his truck, and they wound through the tight streets of Hollybrook.

They drove past the park, beyond a string of houses decorated with lights and snowflakes and inflatable Santas. Even the postboxes were topped with knitted scenes of Christmas trees and reindeer. So much fuss for one holiday.

They arrived at the edge of the village, where acres of empty snow-covered land butted up against the mountain that ringed the lake.

They got out and walked along the edge. She glanced at him, clearly waiting for him to speak.

He hadn't told many people about the project. There was always a decent chance his parents would say no. It was a massive undertaking, but the royal philanthropy fund would cover the bulk of it, and they could always do fundraising.

"I have a plan," he began. "I want to build a sort of complex with services for the community. A new library, a playground, a domestic violence shelter, a community garden. I'd like to relocate the community kitchen too, but I'm not sure if they'll go for that."

Some of the color had drained out of Emma's face. Had he said something to offend her?

But in a minute, she spoke as if nothing had happened. "Wow. Are there a lot of domestic violence survivors in the village?"

"Not exactly, but the existing shelters in Avolis, the capital, are woefully outdated. We need a new space to bring people so the others can be renovated."

"How awful."

Leo nodded.

"Can I make a suggestion?" she asked.

"Of course."

She averted her eyes and stared at the lot. "Make sure your shelter is pet-friendly. A lot of victims delay leaving when shelters don't accept animals. No one should have to leave their pet behind."

He stared for a moment. "I didn't realize that. I'll make sure it's in the plans."

"Good. Why were you so reluctant to talk about it?"

"I'm not sure it'll be approved. My parents are often... reluctant to greenlight pricier philanthropy projects because they don't provide income in the same way that tourism projects do. Most of our GDP comes from tourism," he explained.

Emma nodded and surveyed the lot. "I think it's beautiful. What a gift it would be to your community."

Leo shrugged. "It's the least we could do. We have a duty to protect and provide for our citizens, and sometimes I think they—we—forget."

A snowflake landed on the end of his nose. The storm would be upon them soon.

She turned her gaze to the sky. "You have such a beautiful country. I love it here. It feels a little bit magical."

"You should see it in the spring," he said. "The foothills are covered in wildflowers, and there's great hiking."

"Cooper loves to hike," Emma said, but it sounded like her mind was far away.

She wouldn't be here in the spring.

"I can threaten to withhold the gingerbread display unless your parents agree to your plans," she said with a cheeky smile.

"Then they'd have you tossed in the dungeon. We can't have that."

"Would you visit me? And slide baguettes through the bars?"

"Of course," he said with a smile. He glanced at his watch. Shit. "I'm going to have to take you back. I have a couple more appointments this afternoon before the storm hits."

She shook her head. "I'll walk back. I love to walk in the snow."

"You can't do that," he said. "It's like five kilometers, and the storm will be starting in earnest soon."

She scoffed. "I'm from New York. We walk that far in blizzards just to get to our preferred breakfast spot. Trust me, I'll be fine."

Something about the idea made him uneasy. But she was dressed warmly enough, and she was a grown woman. She wasn't even a citizen, so he couldn't order her to obey him even if he wanted to.

"If you're sure," he said. "Here—let me give you my phone number in case you run into any trouble."

Their fingers brushed as she handed over her phone, and a shockwave ran through him. Had she felt it too?

He entered his number and gave it back to her.

"Be safe," he said firmly.

"You too."

She turned on her heel and disappeared back toward town.

CHAPTER FIFTEEN

EMMA

EMMA STROLLED THE STREETS OF HOLLYBROOK AT A LEISURELY pace. A blanket of clouds had crept in, and snowflakes drifted lazily from the sky.

She spent an hour perusing the local stores. She ducked into a grocery shop and dodged around the people piling bread and milk into carts. There were flavors and spices she didn't recognize—mahleb, woodruff, cloudberry, blackcurrants and lingonberries. She pored over a counter of colorful desserts and bought several flavors of halvah and some carob cookies, neither of which she'd ever tried before.

Everything here was amazing. The spices were fragrant, the people were pleasant—well, except for the queen.

She glanced down at her phone. There was a freakin' prince's personal number in her phone right now. What alternate universe was she living in? Last week she had been experimenting with just how long she could stretch a packet of ramen, and now she was preparing a career-making dessert for a royal family.

Her thoughts turned to the night before as she sampled a fudge-like piece of halvah. Unless she was drastically misreading the signals—which was always possible—she could have sworn Leo was moving in for a kiss the night before. She'd lain awake in bed last night, wondering what might've happened had the house manager not walked in.

After a lot of googling and perusing gossip sites, she'd gleaned that Leo hadn't had a girlfriend for a number of years. The last one had left the country and moved back to Sweden. He also didn't have any social media to speak of, so there was no official register of his likes and dislikes. He was an anomaly. A mystery.

She had no intention of getting involved, but her attraction to him was becoming more unignorable by the minute. It wasn't because he was a prince. He had given her heart flutters from the second she saw him across the park, and now he was single-handedly helping her dream come to fruition. He was more help than Maya had ever been. Maybe that was just how he was with everyone, but he made her feel seen. It had been a long time since she'd felt seen.

Perhaps she should just go for it. No matter what she was telling herself, she was drawn to him. He was smart, kind, a great listener, sexy with his little Clark Kent glasses and surprisingly rugged physique. He cared about his community in a refreshingly authentic way. If he lived in New York, she would have thrown caution to the wind and started trying to bake her way into his heart.

She would have to keep it a secret if anything did happen, because her mom would never shut up about this. Her bingo friends would beg her to write a tell-all autobiography about the experience.

No matter what happened, Leo's privacy was always

going to be her priority. It must be hard living in the spot-light, especially in such a small country where there wasn't a lot going on. Luckily the paparazzi hadn't been stalking around today, or if they had, they at least hadn't recognized her.

Her stomach growled, and she glanced at her watch. It was five o'clock and almost dark out. She should probably get some dinner and head back to the castle before the worst of the storm hit. Cooper was obsessed with snow and would never want to come back inside.

She checked the nanny cam as she walked to Sal's pub. Her mom was chatting with the nurse, who was preparing lunch. She breathed a sigh of relief. In a week, she would be home, and their circumstances would be vastly changed. As long as they made it through the one-year lean period of her noncompete, very real change was on the horizon.

Her own business meant being her own boss. Only taking the orders she wanted to. Hours that were doable. Money for better physical and occupational therapy for her mom. Everything was in her grasp. All she had to do was knock it the hell out of the park.

She pushed the door of the pub open. Sal didn't seem to be working. She slid into a booth and accepted a menu from a server.

While she ate a succulent dinner of fish and chips, she watched people come and go. Many were picking up take-out orders, hurrying home to their families before the worst of the storm hit.

The bell over the door rang again, and a burst of cold air rushed in along with a group of young people.

Hang on...she knew that laugh.

A poorly disguised Princess Ruby stumbled across the

threshold, laughing with a bunch of kids who looked older than her.

Emma narrowed her eyes. Something wasn't right here.

Ruby slid into a stool, and one of the boys in the group stood behind her, arm over the back of her chair.

"Move, Paul," Ruby said. "My elbows need space."

He glowered but retreated a couple inches. Emma's hackles rose. She watched and waited. She didn't want to embarrass the princess if she was just out having fun with some of her friends. But judging by the cloud of vodka wafting over from them, they had been doing some day drinking.

Did Leo know? Ruby was seventeen. She didn't even know what the legal drinking age was here.

Ruby hopped off her barstool and tottered off to the toilets. Her leather miniskirt and tights were not at all suitable for a winter storm.

"Are you gonna hit that?" one of the boys muttered to Paul.

Oh *hell* no. Emma's fingers wrapped around her fork. She was going to end up in prison for stabbing a teenager in the neck.

Paul laughed. "I've always wanted to hook up with a princess. She doesn't seem into it, though."

Probably because Ruby was a woman of taste.

Talk turned to football, and Ruby made her way back from the bathroom. She stumbled over a chair leg and nearly went sprawling onto the floor, but Paul caught her.

"Thank you. You can let me go."

A couple seconds passed, but Paul didn't relinquish his grip. "Come on, Ruby. How about we go somewhere a little quieter?"

Ruby's eyes narrowed. "I said—"

Emma jumped up from her booth and stormed over. She jabbed a finger in his face. "Let her go, or so help me, I will pluck all of your nipple hairs out individually and make you eat them."

Paul was probably a foot taller than her. He looked down at her like she was an ant he was about to crush under a boot.

"Do you know who I am?" he asked.

"I don't give a fuck who you are," Emma said. "All I know is that you're harassing a member of the royal family, and I have her big brother on speed dial. So if you'd like to keep your organs inside your body, I suggest you let her go."

She held her phone up, and Paul let go of Ruby. Emma grabbed her arm and pulled the girl behind her.

"Don't *ever* let me catch you treating a woman like that again," she said with a jab of her finger. Pontificated fuck. The second that she got back to the castle, she was going to raise the alarm about him.

Emma threw some money on the table and yanked Ruby out of the pub.

"What the hell were you doing? And what are you wearing? Are you not aware that it's December and there's an apocalyptic snowstorm brewing?"

Ruby straightened indignantly. "I was just hanging out with some friends."

"Your friends suck. Come on, we're going home. Where's your jacket?"

"I didn't bring one."

Emma looked up at the sky and took a deep breath—or as Leo would say, a dinosaur breath. She had once been a drunk, foolish, scantily clad seventeen-year-old. And she hadn't grown up in the sterile environment of a castle where everyone was watching her at all times. She couldn't judge Ruby too harshly.

Emma shrugged her coat off and stuffed Ruby's arms into it despite her protests.

Ruby harrumphed but followed her up the winding road toward the castle.

Emma pulled her phone out with half a mind to call Leo. But she didn't want to stir up any drama for the princess. They could handle this alone.

"Are those really your friends?" Emma's teeth chattered as she asked the question again.

The no-coat thing was a mistake. The wind bit at her.

"Not really," Ruby admitted. "I don't really have any friends. People only want to get close to me because of my family, not because of who I am as a person."

"That sounds really hard," Emma said, even though she was dying to yell at her for doing something so dangerous. "Do you go to school?"

Ruby shook her head. "I have a governess. But soon I'll be at NYU."

That's right. Maybe that meant Leo would visit too.

"What will you major in?"

"International Relations, but only because I have to. I'm also going to get my teaching certificate, no matter what they say."

She tripped and almost careened into a ditch, but Emma righted her. The wind was picking up, and the snow pelted her from what felt like every direction. Her hands were ice blocks. She started to shiver. It was hard to see where they were going, but she could tell they were still going up.

"Leo says you have a soft spot for kids," she said.

Ruby nodded—at least that's what it looked like behind

the thick screen of snow. "I do. In a different world, I'd teach kindergarten."

"What's stopping you?"

"Princesses don't get to have normal jobs. My job is to make public appearances, christen yachts, organize charity events. None of it really makes a difference."

Emma smiled. "You sound so much like your brother."

"You've been getting awfully close with Leo," she accused.

"Hardly." Emma blew into the ice blocks that used to be her hands. "He's just helping me with something for the dessert."

"Sure. I've seen the way he looks at you. It's been a long time since he looked that way at someone."

What was she supposed to do with that information?

"He's great, but we're strictly platonic," she fibbed. "Is there anyone special in your life? Not Paul, I hope."

Ruby scowled. "Paul's an idiot. Never in a thousand years."

"Good choice. I bet you'll meet someone amazing at NYU. It's like a big, sexy melting pot. Did your governess give you a crash course on birth control?"

"Gross," Ruby slurred. "I won't need it."

Emma looked at her sternly. "I assure you, you will."

"I won't. Because I don't like men."

"Oh. Cool. But you still need to be aware of the dangers of STIs and—"

She stopped. Ruby was standing ten feet behind her, stock-still.

"What's wrong?" she called to her.

"I've never told anyone that before."

Emma's heart softened. She walked back and stood next to Ruby. "So your family doesn't know?"

Ruby shook her head.

Emma gripped her hand. A strong maternal instinct was kicking in. "Thank you for trusting me with this information. I can't imagine how difficult it's been for you to feel like you can't share your true self. How long have you known?"

"Forever."

Emma was silent for a moment. A gay princess. She couldn't know for sure, but she had suspicions about how the queen might react to the news.

"You can't tell them. Not even Leo," Ruby said with a hint of a plea in her voice.

"Oh, honey. I would never. That is your truth to share, and only you get to decide when to share it. Your secret is safe with me. I'll give you my phone number. Call me anytime. And if you ever feel like you're in danger, or you need somewhere to go, come to me. Especially when you're in New York. I'm just going to be a couple subway stops away."

"Thank you," Ruby said quietly, then resumed walking.

The lights of the castle flickered in front of them, barely visible through the whiteout. The wind ripped through her flimsy sweater. She was going to have to slip into a scorching tub to warm back up.

"So are there any girls in your life?" Emma asked.

Ruby wiggled one hand. "Sort of. Sammy."

"Does she treat you well?"

"She does. But we're not serious. For obvious reasons."

"Right."

Her legs burned and her toes were numb by the time they passed through the gatehouse and reached the courtyard. Emma opened the servant entrance to the kitchen and peeked in. There were too many people. Someone might notice Ruby was still drunk and tip off the queen.

"Is there another way in? A back way?"

Ruby nodded and went off in another direction. Emma followed her until they came to another door along the side of the castle. Some kind of scanner blinked red at them. As Ruby dug for something in her handbag, the door flew open and Leo ran out.

"There you are," he said, visibly relieved. "Roo, I've been looking all over for you. I called you nine times. Where the hell have you been?"

"Just down in town," Ruby slurred.

"Are—are you drunk? And wearing a miniskirt in the middle of a snowstorm? Did you do this?" he fired at Emma.

Her mouth fell open. "You think I got a teenager drunk in the middle of the day? Seriously?"

She pushed him back through the door and steered Ruby into the castle. She dropped her voice. "For your information, I found her like this and prevented her from getting assaulted. Get her some Gatorade and toast, and don't tell your mom."

She whirled around in a cloud of annoyance and marched back to the gatehouse. It was almost invisible thanks to the snow.

How dare he accuse her of getting Ruby drunk? The fuck?

She marched up the stairs and threw open the door to her apartment. Cooper was happy to see her, at least, and the apartment was invitingly warm. But she'd been gone all day and he needed to pee. The warm bath could wait.

She snapped a leash on him and walked him down the steps to the courtyard, still stewing about Leo's accusation.

Cooper lifted a leg, then sniffed around frantically. He was following something out of the courtyard and around the side of the castle grounds toward the lake. Hopefully it led to a poop spot. She walked behind him, wishing she had put on another sweater before coming back outside. She'd forgotten to get her coat back from Ruby.

Cooper's entire body perked up, and he stared into the distance. He lunged forward, and the leash ripped from her hand.

"Cooper, no!"

She ran after him, but he disappeared into the storm.

CHAPTER SIXTEEN

EMMA

"Cooper, you idiot," she called into the thick blanket of snow. She hadn't even thought to pocket a treat to tempt him with.

He must have seen a squirrel or something. She had been stupid not to wrap the leash around her wrist like she usually did.

Really, it was all Leo's fault. Or maybe Ruby's.

God, it was cold. She couldn't feel her hands or feet at all as she dashed through the snow, barely able to spot Cooper's gigantic tracks. That damn dog.

She called his name repeatedly through numb lips, but he didn't come bounding back. He could be halfway to Spain right now.

Anxiety settled in. Cooper wasn't just a dog. He was a soulmate. He had been there for her during her mom's diagnosis and hospital stay, when Dylan left. He had alerted her more than once when her mom had fallen getting out of bed. She couldn't lose him. She wouldn't. Snow be damned.

She screwed up her eyes against the blustery wind. Was that an inner tube dangling from that wooden structure?

Shit, she had walked all the way to the lake. She quickened her pace, heartbeat thudding in her ears.

Cooper wouldn't have gone out onto the lake. He was smarter than that. Right?

But the tracks ran alongside what seemed to be a dock and out beyond. Anxiety rose like a wave. She struggled against the snow that pelted against her exposed skin. Her entire body shook like a cat on a dryer.

The sound of splashing came from ahead. Oh, no. She struggled, slipping over the snow-covered ice.

There was Cooper, frantically paddling in a small circle of dark water.

Emma froze. Seconds crawled by as she calculated. There wasn't time to run back to the castle for help. Should she jump in? But how would she boost him up?

The life preserver.

"Hold on, Coop," she said. Her heart hammered in her ears as she scrambled back to the icy dock. She pulled the flotation device off and ran back to Cooper. As she approached, she dropped to her knees and crawled toward him, trying to spread her weight out on the ice.

"It's going to be okay, honey. Use this—"

She muscled the inner tube underneath him, hands dipping into the glacial water. His butt floated to the surface, and he thrashed his way out of the water and onto the ice.

"You're okay. You're o— Shit."

The ice spider-webbed under her palm, and in an instant, she plunged into the frigid lake.

The cold hit her like a fist to the gut. Knives pierced every inch of her flesh. Panic flared, and her muscles froze.

She was going to die. What would happen to her mom?

Cooper barked at her, snapping her out of her trance.

"No, Cooper. Stay," she ordered. If he came too close, he would just fall through the ice again.

Thankfully the inner tube was still within reach. She flung a numb arm onto it and used every last bit of her strength to hoist herself up and out of the ice.

She lay there for a moment, drawing shallow, painful breaths as the snow and ice pelted her. Her teeth chattered, but the shaking in her limbs was slowing down. In fact, she could barely feel anything anymore. This wasn't so bad. Maybe it was an unseasonably warm lake.

Cooper barked at her again, and she struggled to her hands and knees.

Was that a voice out there in the distance?

"Help," she called, as loud as she could.

There wasn't a response.

"Help," she called, a little louder.

Cooper's fur had frozen into spiky icicles. She needed to get him somewhere warm. But she was so tired. The ice was hard and impossibly slippery. The castle might as well have been on a different planet. Maybe she should just rest first.

"Emma?"

There was the voice again.

"Help," she called once more, then collapsed onto the ice.

CHAPTER SEVENTEEN

LEO

The heavy door creaked as Leo shut it behind him. Ruby was hydrated and safely in bed, and his parents were none the wiser.

Now that it was clear what had actually happened, guilt washed over him. He had been overcome with fear that something had happened to Ruby and had unfairly lashed out at Emma. She had saved Ruby from public humiliation —or worse. He owed her an apology.

Outside, he ducked his head against the bitter wind. There was no answer at her door and no greeting from Cooper. Surely she wouldn't have tried to walk the dog in a blizzard.

A creeping sense of alarm rose as he thundered down the steps to the courtyard. Large dog tracks and small human-sized ones cut through the courtyard. The edges of the prints were uneven, like they had been left in a hurry. He followed them as quickly as he could, kicking up snow and staggering against the harsh wind.

A niggling thought wormed its way to the forefront. Ruby had been wrapped in Emma's coat with the giant stitched hole when she returned her home. That meant Emma took Cooper out with no coat on. What if something had happened?

His stomach hardened into a knot, and he screwed his eyes up against the blistering winds. The tracks wound around the castle and headed in the direction of the lake. He quickened his pace, squinting against the punishing curtain of ice and snow.

"Emma?" he called. No answer.

He continued to follow the tracks. Shit. They broached the invisible edge of the lake.

"Emma?" he called again.

A low woof came from across the lake. Oh, no.

"Cooper, come."

A few seconds passed, then Cooper bounded across the ice and came skidding to a halt in front of him. Leo grabbed the frozen leash and knotted it around the post of the dock. Then he dashed across the ice, following the tracks.

There she was. A few inches away from a midnight circle of water, Emma lay prone on the ice.

Panic set in. He dropped to his knees and crawled over to her.

"Emma?"

"Leo?" she asked groggily. Her face was pale. Her lips were blue. Her hair was a mess of icicles, and her eyes were unfocused. He needed to get her warm. Now.

He grabbed her arm and tugged her away from the jagged edge. The ice beneath him groaned but didn't break. Slowly, he climbed to his feet. There was no time to lose.

He shrugged his coat off and zipped it around her. His foot slid and he nearly came crashing down as he picked her up and threw her over his shoulder.

She wasn't even shivering. This was bad.

He staggered across the lake, nearly slipping several times, until he reached the edge. He wound Cooper's leash around his wrist. Through the squall, he could make out the rough shape of the old caretaker shed he'd repurposed into his workshop.

He waded through the snow, which seemed to deepen by the minute.

"Stay with me," he said to Emma. She mumbled something, but the words were lost against the wind.

Finally, he reached the door to the shed. He squatted and fished around until he retrieved the key from under one of the rocks. He plunged it into the keyhole and muscled the door open. Cooper ran past them and collapsed on the floor.

Leo set Emma gently on the couch and ran to the fireplace. He grabbed some wood from the pile and threw it onto the firebox, then bolted to the cabinet in the corner for some matches. His hand shook as he lit a match and touched it to the kindling.

In minutes, a fire was sparking.

He turned back to Emma. The fire wasn't fast enough. He ripped his sweater off and threw it on the floor, his pants quickly following. Emma's eyes were closed, so he slapped her gently in the face until she opened one eye.

"Not the time for a boink," she mumbled. "Mad at you."

A boink?

He ripped his coat off of her, and she frowned.

"I need to get you warm. We have to take your wet clothes off." He yanked her sweater unceremoniously over her head and peeled off her jeans. He pressed her against his bare skin, jolting at the icy feel of her flesh, then wrapped his coat around her again.

She needed to see a doctor, but he had stupidly left his

phone in the castle. He needed to warm her up before he ran for help. His friend Joffrey had fallen through the ice when they were young, and he almost hadn't made it.

Leo ripped his hat off with one hand and covered her head. He pulled her off the couch and wrapped her legs around him. The logs had caught, and the fire was crackling in earnest as he walked them over to the hearth.

"Stay with me, Emma." He rubbed her arms beneath the coat, trying to encourage her circulation. She curled against him, head on his shoulder.

Cooper trotted over and sat next to them. The ice in his fur had already started to melt. He seemed largely unbothered by the incident, which was lucky because Leo knew exactly nothing about dog hypothermia.

Slowly, Emma's shallow breaths lengthened. Her limbs began to tremble, and color bloomed in her cheeks. Her skin went from icy, to frigid, to barely warm.

"Th-thank you," she said over chattering teeth.

"You scared the hell out of me," he said. "What were you thinking? Why didn't you call for help?"

"C-Coop doesn't kn-know how to swim. Wasn't thinking."

He sighed but resisted the urge to lecture her more. She had saved his sister not two hours before. He held her as she trembled, willing his body to lend her his warmth.

The fire crackled comfortingly. Cooper stood, and Leo shifted Emma just in time for the dog to shake and send a spray of water droplets at them.

"Damn it, Cooper."

"Don't swear at him. He's a good boy," she mumbled against his bare chest.

A flicker of relief was born in his gut. If she was forming whole sentences, her condition was improving.

"Sorry," he said. "How are you feeling?"

"Oh, fantastic. Like I had a brief vacation in a cryotherapy chamber."

His grip tightened around her. Even though the circumstances were dire, something felt incredibly right about holding her in front of a crackling fire.

"Thank you for looking after Ruby. She told me about Paul."

"I assume you have a spider-infested prison somewhere? Or maybe a guillotine for tiny, tiny penises?"

"He will be dealt with," he said firmly. Paul was the son of a lord, which meant his mother would insist on handling it privately. Leo didn't need to tell her that he was going to *privately* remind Paul to never come near his sister again.

"Good. Thank you for saving me," she said softly. Her shivering was starting to subside, but he didn't relax his grip on her.

"I came back to apologize. This isn't the first time Ruby's done something like this."

Emma shrugged. "She's a kid. Kids do dumb stuff."

"True. When I was seventeen, I climbed one of the castle spires and threw a frozen turkey into the courtyard. Decimated the roof of my dad's Rolls."

She pulled her head back and looked at him. "No, you didn't."

"I did."

"And they let you live? My mom would've drowned me in the Hudson."

"What's the Hudson?"

"A river."

"Oh. Well, no. I was grounded for like a year, but they didn't really enforce it. They didn't do a lot of...parenting."

Emma grunted and snuggled back into him. "Oh, sorry. I

was probably supposed to be shocked. That sounds like a hard way to grow up."

"It wasn't always easy. We've always kind of been accessories. Meant to be seen and not heard, perform for the crowd, that kind of thing. They didn't play with us. They rarely laughed with us."

Why was he blabbering about his childhood? He was a straight white male who'd grown up in a castle. He had all the privilege in the world.

"Did you feel loved? Safe?" she asked.

He was silent for a long time.

"No. They loved me in their own way, I suppose. But it's not the type of love I would give my own child."

Her fingertips pressed into his chest. "You still want kids after all that?"

It had always been a part of the plan. Like Ruby, he had a soft spot for children. Sometimes he went to the local daycare facility and read books to the toddlers. They were so curious, silly, and wonderful.

"I do. Someday. Call it breaking a generational curse, I guess. What about you?"

Though he could explain this conversation away as simply trying to keep her talking and conscious, he was genuinely curious.

Not that it mattered if they were compatible. She lived in a different country and had dreams that had nothing to do with him or moving to a small European country. She was used to the big city.

Emma hesitated, and her body tensed against his. Shit. He had said the wrong thing.

"Yes. At least two. But I don't know if I'll ever be financially stable enough to support a family. And then there's my mom to think about."

"What would you and your mom be doing today if you were home? Another holiday activity?"

She stared into the crackling fire. "Tonight would've been *It's a Wonderful Life*."

Leo leaned up and fumbled with a remote on the arm of the couch. A TV mounted above the workbench flickered to life. He scrolled through the channel guide—it had to be on somewhere. Finally, he found it and clicked.

Emma sighed happily, and her eyes closed. Should she be sleeping?

"Why is Christmas so important to you and your mom, anyway? Seems like a lot of fuss for a soulless corporate holiday."

Her eyes popped open, and she frowned. "It's just a special time of year for us."

"Why?" he probed.

She averted her gaze and seemed to be thinking. "It wasn't always. I grew up in an abusive household."

The breath caught in his chest.

"My dad would drink and just turn into this evil, unrecognizable person. He would yell and beat my mom over the smallest things—dishes in the sink, a surprise visit from her aunt, burned dinner. We walked on eggshells around him for years. She bought me a CD player when I was five so I could drown out the yelling. I would hide in my closet with our dog and blast the Spice Girls. But I only ever listened with one ear. Even back then, I was terrified that he was going to kill her, and I needed to know when to run. I had a little backpack with peanut butter crackers and clean underwear ready to go."

The words came slowly, like she had to dredge them up.

"Why didn't she leave him?" Leo whispered.

"It was complicated. She loved him. And it wasn't always

bad. I still remember hearing him apologize, swear it would never happen again. Sometimes he would even give up drinking for a week or two. But he always went back to it. He pressured her to stop talking to everyone—her parents, her friends. He controlled the finances. We were alone, with nowhere to go. She didn't leave him until he turned his hand on me."

His heart shattered, and he held her tighter.

"The day we finally left, we moved into a shelter in the city. We went out and bought our own Christmas tree, decorated it exactly how we wanted, and slept underneath it for a whole week. I can still remember waking up, panic in my chest, waiting for the front door to crash open, and seeing the twinkling of the Christmas lights. It was the first time in my entire childhood that I felt truly safe. It's wonderful that you're going to give your people a safe space."

Silence fell between them. Shock, grief, and shame warred in him.

"I can't believe I just complained about my two-parent household while being raised in a castle," Leo said. "I'm sorry."

Emma broke away from his chest to look at him. "We all have our own trauma. I was lucky to be loved so hard by my mom. One loving parent is infinitely better than two ambivalent ones. Don't cheapen your experience. You deserve to be loved."

The firelight brought out glints of amber in her green eyes. Her hair had thawed out and was drying in loose waves that hinted of summers on the beach. She had been so honest about something that caused her so much pain. Something deeply primal and protective had awoken in him. She didn't deserve this life. She was a caregiver, a hard worker, persisting even when the entire world conspired against her.

"So do you," he said.

Before he could second-guess it, he closed what little distance there was between them. Her lips were unbelievably soft and still had a touch of chill to them. She froze for a second under his touch, then snaked her arms around his neck.

Explosions rippled under his skin. A long, slow pull in his stomach had his fingers pressing into the bare skin over her vertebrae. He hadn't been kissed in an embarrassingly long time. Was it always this way—heat and ripples of need?

She pulled back a minute later, breathing hard. Her skin was warm beneath his fingertips. Finally.

"We should really get you to a doctor," he said to cover the silence, even though he'd give away his entire fortune to never leave this cabin again.

She shook her head. "Let's stay. Please."

"As you wish."

They descended into silence once more, but this time it was comfortable, almost necessary. Leo drifted into sleep with Cooper at his back and Emma clutched to his chest, the smell of lake water in her hair. For the first time in a long time, he felt at peace.

CHAPTER EIGHTEEN

EMMA

Emma awoke to the rough scrape of a doggie tongue on her cheek. She opened one eye blearily.

Her heart jumped in her chest. Where the hell was she? And why was she soaked in sweat and pressed into a very impressive set of naked pecs?

She elbowed the coat and blanket off her, and everything came rushing back.

Cooper. The lake. Leo coming to her rescue.

And now here he was, sprawled out mostly naked on a hard wooden floor, a beam of sunlight hitting him like he had been personally chosen by the heavens. He'd saved her life, and then—as long as her memory wasn't failing her— he had kissed the crap out of her.

That kiss. Holy shit. The velvety warmth of his lips pressed against her frozen ones. The scratch of his beard against her skin. A shower of sparks danced up her spine.

Maybe she had imagined it. She'd probably been closer to death than ever before.

But no. She could still feel the gentle press of his thumb against her pulse like it had been tattooed there.

So what did it mean?

Nothing. It had meant nothing. There wasn't going to be a fairytale ending here. He was a prince, and probably duty-bound to save the lives of dumb tourists who fell through the ice. Women probably threw themselves at him all day long. Who knew how many meaningless kisses he'd exchanged over the years?

But it hadn't felt meaningless—to her, at least. He had been unexpectedly honest and open about his childhood. Her heart ached for the little boy who felt forgotten and unloved. He deserved better, and he would find his own happiness in time. She was sure of it.

There wasn't time to dwell on it though. No matter what was—or wasn't—going on with Leo, she needed to get back to the castle and start plotting the parts of the dessert that she could without the blueprints. She needed to gather recipes, make a list of ingredients, and chat with the royal chef. Her future awaited, and she couldn't allow anything to distract her. Not even a half-naked prince who had saved her life.

She slowly climbed to her feet, knees cracking like kindling. There was a crick in her neck from sleeping on Leo, and the musky spice of his deodorant was on her cheek. Would it be weird if she never washed her face again?

To her relief, sensation had returned to her hands and feet, and they hadn't fallen off in the night. It would've been hard to bake with no hands.

She swiveled and took in the cabin, searching for her lost pants. She'd been too out of it to really inspect her surroundings the night before. Embers glowed in the fireplace. A workbench backed up to one wall. A variety of tools were scattered on top, wood shavings littering the floor. It smelled like sawdust and wet dog.

Cooper looked at her and whined. Damn, he probably had to pee.

She peered out the dusty window. Patches of blue sky peeked out behind gray clouds. It seemed like the storm was over, at least.

She swiveled to look back at Leo. What was she going to tell her mom about this?

Shit. Her mom. She hadn't checked in with her the night before, thanks to the whole almost-dying thing. She dropped to her knees and dug through the pile of slightly damp clothes. Would her phone even work?

Anxiety flared deep and hot, extinguishing all other thoughts.

Her phone slipped from the pile and clattered to the floor. Leo woke with a start.

"How are you doing?" he asked sleepily.

"I'm fine. I just..." She frantically pressed the power button on her phone. Nothing.

"Everything okay?"

"My phone's not working. I shouldn't be surprised." She tried to sound casual, but the words felt clawed from her throat.

What if her mom had fallen in the night and no one was around to help? What if she'd had another stroke and couldn't reach her phone?

Leo rose to his feet. His body didn't even have the audacity to crack like a sack full of marbles, and he didn't make any efforts to cover his bare chest and torso.

She only partially noticed, as she was stabbing at her phone, trying to get it to turn on. She didn't have access to the nanny cams. Anything could have happened.

"Hey," he said, approaching cautiously. "It's probably too

waterlogged to work. Let's go get it in a bowl of rice and put on some dry clothes."

"I need it to work," she said, clicking the power button over and over.

"Emma," he said softly. He laid his hand over hers. "Are you worried about your mom?"

She took a deep, shuddering breath and tried to banish the anxiety from her body. "Yeah. The last time—the last time I couldn't reach her, it was because she'd had her stroke. She called me, and I couldn't answer it because I was at work and there was a very strict no-cell-phone policy. She was having a medical emergency, and I didn't even know about it. I didn't find her until two hours later. It was all my fault. If I had answered the call, or if I would've found her earlier, things would be so much different now."

There it was. Her most shameful truth. The damage to her mother's body wouldn't have been nearly as bad if Emma had just caught it earlier. While Lisa's fiery spirit and sharp mind were still intact, her physical limitations had left her depressed and restless.

It was reason number three thousand why Emma needed this trip to go well. Her mom was trapped, a prisoner in her own body. With a little bit of money for better physical and occupational therapy, she could start to bring back some of that quality of life and independence.

Worry was written on Leo's face. He pulled a cordless phone off the wall and handed it to her. "Call her."

"Oh, I don't know if she'll answer. It's like, 2 a.m. her time."

He bent over and stepped into his jeans. "Just call her. I'm sure she's fine, but this way, you can know for sure."

Their eyes met, and the panic subsided just a little.

"Thank you." She turned her back to him and dialed her mom's phone number.

It rang three times before picking up.

"Hello?" a groggy voice called.

"Mom, it's me."

"Oh, sweetheart. Is everything okay?"

She sounded fine. Emma's panic dropped to a barely noticeable hum.

"I'm fine," she said. It was kind of the truth. "How are you?"

"I'm fine, honey. A little tired since I'm being woken up at—what time even is it?"

"It's late. I'm sorry. I had a problem with my phone, and I just wanted to make sure you were okay. Please stay in bed until Shante arrives. And if you need anything, call Beatrice so she can come find me, okay?"

"Ah, so that's why you're calling from an international number. I thought you were calling to ask about my car's extended warranty."

A startled laugh burst from Emma. "I'm so sorry for waking you up. Thank you for answering."

"I'll always answer for you, sweetheart. Wait, whose phone are you using?"

"Just a castle landline."

The last thing her mom needed was shocking news that her only child had almost died of hypothermia.

"Huh. I didn't know those existed anymore. Love you, dove."

"Love you too."

Emma hung up and handed the phone back to Leo. She took a deep breath and willed her hands to stop shaking. Everything was fine.

"Thank you," she said. "For everything. I really should

get back to the castle. Coop's going to gnaw my leg off if I don't get him some breakfast."

"We're going back to the castle, but you're going straight to the royal doctor. No arguments," he said when she opened her mouth. "What happened to you was really serious. I—we—need to make sure you're okay."

She shot him a look. "You can't just order me around, you know. I'm not a citizen."

"Consider it a favor. To me. And to my mom, because she'll be mad as a box of frogs if her star baker can't pull off this absurd dessert because her fingers fell off from hypothermia."

He must have seen something in her face, because his smile slipped off like royal icing on a cookie that was too hot.

"Are you sure you're okay?" he asked gingerly.

"I'm fine. I just need to get to work. I really need this to go well."

He walked over to stand in front of her and took both of her arms gently in his. The sweater she'd been clutching to hide her granny panties fell to the floor, and a sense of vulnerability she hadn't felt in a long time—maybe ever?—set in.

"What happened to your mom wasn't your fault."

Emma shook her head and averted her gaze. There was something too raw in Leo's dark chocolate eyes.

"It was. If I would have answered, her entire life would be different right now."

"She should have called emergency services, not you."

Emma took a deep breath, and her necklace glinted in the sunlight and cast a beam of light onto the far wall. She wasn't going to cry. She had cried over the incident what felt like a thousand times, and none of those times had she been standing half naked in front of a prince.

Her mom had said the same thing, but nothing was going to assuage her guilt.

"It doesn't change the fact that I failed her on that day, and everything is different now. I owe her a better life. That's why I need to put everything I have into this project."

Leo's dark eyebrows were knit together. "We'll get you up to the castle. Put my jacket on."

"No, you'll be—"

He silenced her with a look. "Put on the damn jacket."

The prickle of annoyance at being bossed around was almost a relief after the emotional flood of the last twelve hours.

If Leo hadn't found her, she'd be dead right now. Her mom would be childless and alone, Cooper would be without a mother. But Leo had given her a second chance at life. And she would give it all she had.

Minutes later, they waded out into the knee-high snow, blinking at the harsh sunlight.

Cooper plodded along happily, unbothered by what was probably eighteen undisturbed inches of snow.

Emma staggered along in the drifts with Leo's help. Her damn jeans clung to her. It was unpleasant, but nothing like the punishing freeze of the night before. Leo was silent on their walk back. She had trauma-dumped all over him. What was it about him that made her open up? She had never confided in a stranger this way.

Stranger wasn't the right word anymore. What was he? An acquaintance? A friend? Could someone really be your friend if you were never going to see them again?

Unless he came to visit Ruby in New York.

She banished the thoughts of the future from her mind.

Only five days remained before the ball. The timeline was almost impossible. There wasn't time to do anything crazy like fall in love with a prince who lived in a different country, even if she wanted to.

Leo took her past the courtyard and around to the same door she had almost gone through the night before. He cracked it open, and there was a rush of sound on the other side.

"How nice of you to join us."

Shit. That was the queen, and she didn't look happy to see them.

CHAPTER NINETEEN

LEO

"Where have you been all night?" the queen asked, looking at him in a way she usually reserved for servants who brought the wrong kind of tea. "And why are you with the baker?"

Leo bristled. "The baker has a name, Mother. Emma fell through the ice during the storm last night. I'm taking her to see the doctor."

Fewer details were better. She didn't need to know that they'd technically spent the night together.

The queen was silent for a moment. She turned to look behind her.

"Rosa, take Miss...Emma to see the royal physician."

Emma squeezed his arm before she and Cooper were swept away by the maid.

Silence fell as his mother looked at him. Her eyes were sharp, angry. "I explicitly told you not to get involved. You've left me with no choice. She'll have to go home."

Fuck. Leo's heart flew into his throat. He'd just destroyed her dreams. Why the hell hadn't they walked in separately?

"You can't send her home."

She looked at him disdainfully. "Watch me."

"Do you know what she's done for this family?"

"Yes, we're all very impressed that she knows the Heimlich," the queen said disdainfully.

Well. That showed how much she valued his life.

"Not for me," Leo said. "For Ruby."

The queen paused and looked at him.

He explained the situation from the night before but left out the drinking.

The queen's mouth dropped open. "Paul? He had the audacity to lay a finger on a member of the royal family? We won't stand for it. Beatrice, get Lord Axley on the phone immediately."

"So you won't be sending Emma home?" Leo interrupted.

The queen swiveled to look at him like she'd forgotten he was there. She probably had. Her expression was stormy, and she looked annoyed at the prospect of having to reconsider.

"In light of...recent revelations, I'll give her one more chance. As long as I have your word that there's nothing going on between the two of you."

He shook his head. "There's nothing going on between us."

It was a snap judgment, and it wasn't entirely the truth. Especially since he had kissed her and bared his soul to her last night. But this gig meant everything to Emma. He needed to protect her at all costs.

"She ran out into the storm without a coat on and fell into the lake. I pulled her out and helped her get warm. That's all," he added.

Another silence fell as she seemed to weigh his words. "Well. I do appreciate you avoiding an international scandal.

But you should have called security to handle it. You could have been hurt."

Leo bit back a retort. If she actually cared if he got hurt, she hid it well.

"Stay away from her," the queen commanded when he didn't say anything. "Trouble follows that girl, and we don't need to give the press anything more to talk about. They should be focused solely on the ball."

Leo nodded dutifully, but there was zero chance of him avoiding Emma until she left. He wasn't sure what his feelings were at the moment, but he knew he wanted to get to know her better. She was so refreshingly honest, funny, talented...and maybe a little bit stunningly beautiful.

This conversation needed to end before he lost his shit. "I'm headed into town to check on the shelter. Make sure everyone still has power."

"You're not driving," she ordered. "The roads aren't clear."

"No. I'll take a kick-sled."

The queen paused. "Thank you, Leo. Be safe. I don't want to have to send the guard to pull you out of a ditch."

Huh. That was probably the warmest thing his mother had said to him in a year.

He nodded at her and left. As he passed by the door to his suite, noises from John's drew his attention.

There was a lot of grunting, some exaggerated moaning.

"Oh, god," said a female voice. Definitely American. Well, that explained where Maya had disappeared to.

Two hours later, Leo pushed his kick-sled to the front door of their local representative of parliament and chained it to a bar outside.

He opened the door, and a receptionist curtsied and offered him a dozen kinds of tea before nervously dusting off a chair for him to sit on. Leo used the opportunity to glance over the gingerbread blueprints Kat had just handed over. It was totally doable, and with Emma's artistic flair, it would be magnificent. Her dreams would come true. He would make sure of it.

"Your Highness," a male voice interrupted.

"Henri." They shook hands. "Thanks for seeing me. I was hoping we could chat about an upcoming project."

Henri swept him into his office and closed the door.

"What do you have for me?"

Leo fired up a tablet and handed over the blueprints for the community charity project.

"I want to build this on the massive vacant lot over on the edge of town. The one that backs up to the mountain. But I know it's going to be a tough sell to my parents."

Henri swiped through the pictures, then leaned back in his chair. "You're right. Have you thought about how you're going to approach it?"

"The best-case scenario would be making them think it's their idea. But short of that, I'm going to have to convince them another way. May I speak frankly?"

"Of course." Henri looked a tad surprised.

"You've worked for them for a long time. What do I have to do to this project to make them say yes?"

Henri glanced at the tablet again. "I don't suppose there's any way to make this project generate income."

Leo shook his head. "It's a philanthropy project that the community needs. It'll create some jobs, but it's not about making money."

Henri pressed the tips of his fingers together and leaned back in his chair. "Okay, well. Then you'll need to appeal to their egos. Name one of the buildings after the queen, erect a statue, stage numerous groundbreaking and building and ribbon-cutting ceremonies. Lots of photo ops and positive press. That's the only way you'll pull it off."

Leo frowned. "I was afraid of that. Thanks for your time, Henri."

"Why don't you run for office?" Henri asked as Leo stood.

"What?" He paused mid-handshake.

"I've worked with you for a long time now. You have more than birthright. You're young, passionate, you have great ideas."

Leo shook his head. "I appreciate it, but I don't want to spend all my time arguing over semantics and getting tangled up in red tape. No offense."

Henri nodded. "None taken. Still, I'd consider it. You've got great potential."

"Thank you. I'll see you at the next town hall?"

"I'll be there."

Henri bowed, and Leo left.

Running for office. Ha. What, so he could propose changes and have them struck down and never get anywhere, never affect or change anything? No. Parliament wasn't the place for him. At least no one told him what he could or couldn't do as a prince. His hands would be totally bound in parliament—if he was even allowed to run.

His thoughts turned to Emma, and worry crept in. Had the doctor cleared her? Falling through the ice was no small thing. She seemed much improved this morning, but she could have drowned or succumbed to hypothermia in his own backyard.

Somehow, the baker from Brooklyn had become very important to him. And now his own mother had forbidden him from spending time with her. Ordinarily he couldn't care less about what his mother insisted on. But this time was different. He couldn't jeopardize Emma's dreams. Or his own.

But he also couldn't cut her off. Something about her called to him. It wasn't that she was a damsel in distress—despite the lake incident, she was fiercely smart and capable. She'd faced more hardship than he ever had in his life, and she did it with grace and dignity.

Maybe if he explained the circumstances, she would be willing to meet in secret. Waking up with her this morning had felt so incredibly right. He needed to taste her again, feel the quickening tick of her pulse beneath his palm. He also needed to change his train of thought before he spent the rest of the day kick-sledding around town with a raging erection.

The plows were out, the sun was shining. All the buildings in town still had power, and the shelter was well-stocked with volunteers and goods. He debated for a moment, then swung into a local electronics store.

Minutes later, a new phone for Emma was nestled in his pocket. Being unable to call her mom had almost sent her into a full-blown panic attack. She needed it. It was the least he could do. No one needed to know it had come from him.

And then there was the other package. It was foolish, impulsive, over-the-top. But he didn't care.

As he pushed his way through the castle gates, he subconsciously came to a stop outside the gatehouse. He really should check on her. Just to make sure she was doing okay.

He stowed his kick-sled behind a shrub and inspected the courtyard for prying eyes, but everything was quiet. With one last glance behind him, he darted up the steps and knocked on her door.

CHAPTER TWENTY

EMMA

Emma froze with one hand on the door. She had just showered, the oven was pre-heating for a test batch of macarons, and her hair was hanging all over like she had just climbed out of another frozen lake. To make matters worse, she was wearing her comfiest pair of sweatpants and an old I Heart NY T-shirt. Why did he always catch her looking like she had just fallen on the tracks of the G train?

"Leo! Oh, uh, I mean—"

"Don't you dare start with the 'Your Highness' bullshit," Leo chastised her.

He stood on her doorstep with a smile, and her heart did a full somersault. She needed to have a conversation with him, but she wasn't ready.

Her interaction with the queen this morning had proven one thing—Her Majesty did not like Emma, or at least did not like her spending time with Leo. And that was a problem, because she was in charge of the royal checkbook. If Emma kept getting caught with Leo, she risked getting fired. And that wasn't worth the risk—no matter how devastatingly handsome and kind and fascinating he was.

"Come in." She needed to get him out of the doorway before someone saw him and reported back to the queen.

Leo crossed the threshold, toeing his boots off when Cooper thundered over to put his paws on his chest. He gave him a pat on the head until the dog dropped to the floor.

"How are you?" Leo asked.

"I'm fine. Dr. Hastings looked me over and gave me the all clear—and a very stern lecture about running out onto frozen lakes. As if I hadn't already figured out the dangers for myself."

He nodded and seemed unsurprised. "Good. Here." He pulled a new phone out of his pocket and handed it to her.

"What's this?"

"A spare. Until yours resurrects." He glanced over her shoulder at the bowl of rice her phone was currently submerged in.

She bit her lip. Was he doing this out of obligation? "You didn't have to do that. I'll repay you."

"No, you won't. Again, you saved my life."

"And you saved mine," she said.

He tilted his head. "You're right. This is weird."

Emma tapped a finger on her chin. "I've never been in this situation before. Do the double life-savings just kind of cancel each other out?"

He laughed. "Maybe they do. I guess you won't want these blueprints, then," he said, pulling out a long paper tube.

She gasped. "Gimme," she ordered.

Once the plans were spread over the small dining room table, they bent over, shoulder-to-shoulder, to consult them together.

Her eyes were on the blueprints, but her mind kept honing in on Leo's warm presence. He smelled so good, like the outdoors and a spice she couldn't name. Something fluttered in her nether regions. She had hoped the next time she saw him she would be calm, put-together, and not falling into mortal peril. Stressed out, bedraggled, and buried waist-deep in recipes would have to do.

Not that there was anything going on here. Emma needed to stay away from him to keep her job. Besides, one kiss in a shack during a snowstorm didn't mean anything. Emotions were high. She had just almost died, and her brain wasn't working. If it had been, she certainly wouldn't have let him kiss her.

Would she? Shut up, brain.

"What do you think?" he asked as she leafed through the diagrams. He planted a hand on the table and leaned to look with her.

His sleeves were rolled up, exposing a very distracting set of forearms. *Focus, idiot.*

She blew out a long breath. "This is going to be a ton of work, and I only have a few days. It doesn't help that your mother will only let me in the kitchen after it's closed from dinner service."

Leo's gaze landed on her oven. "How much can you do in here during the day?"

Emma shrugged. "Some, but this oven is too small to bake the gingerbread pieces. Why is everything so small here? Your fridges are like half the size of an American fridge. What if you need to store more than four ingredients at the same time?"

"How can I help?" he asked. He reached over and brushed a hair away from her forehead.

Her skin tingled with goosebumps. She bit her lip.

"I don't think you should," she said.

He pulled back, looking surprised.

She reached over and laid a hand on his chest. Her heart danced. "Don't get me wrong. I'd love to have your help. But I'm pretty sure your mom hates me. I know there's nothing going on between us, but I can't risk her firing me because she can't handle her son consorting with an American. Or a poor nobody. Whatever she hates me for the most. I really need the rest of this trip to go well. So maybe we shouldn't… see each other anymore."

She lowered her gaze, unwilling to look him in the eye. The idea of not seeing him again smarted worse than a molten sugar burn. She would have to bury herself in work and try to forget about that kiss in the workshop.

"What if we met in secret?" Leo asked softly.

Secret?

Her heart thudded in her ears. She slowly lifted her gaze to meet his. There was an intensity in his eyes.

"And I wouldn't say there's *nothing* going on here," he added before she could say anything.

He pulled her to him, lowered his head until his lips were inches from hers. Or centimeters. Whatever they used here.

What was she doing? She was putting her future in jeopardy. But she had always done the right thing for her whole life, and it had gotten her nowhere—underemployed, taken advantage of, and alone in the world other than her mother. Maybe just this once, she could be a little selfish. She was worthy of adventure and excitement, especially since Leo was willing to keep it a secret.

His eyes smoldered as they searched hers. Fuck it.

Emma crushed her mouth to his before she could think better of it. He hesitated for a split second, then he gripped her by the hips roughly, powerfully—like she was anchoring him to the earth. Gone was the gentle Leo of yesterday.

There was a fire in him. His hands skated up her body, leaving a trail of goosebumps in their wake. He picked her up like she weighed nothing and put her down on the kitchen table. Right on top of the blueprints. She pulled back to protest, but he dragged her to him and kissed her again. All thoughts of work vanished as his lips moved lower, down her neck, his breath hot on her collarbone.

My god, the sensations flowing through her right now. Her synapses were firing, sensations screaming by like she was in the dark tunnel of a rollercoaster. His hands slid beneath her T-shirt and tugged it up and over her head.

She was normally a five-to-six dates kind of girl. But they were short on time, and Leo had awakened a visceral hunger in her.

She yanked his shirt off, savoring the shifting power in his back and shoulders. His mouth moved to the curve of her breasts, which she hadn't bothered to trap in a bra after her shower.

He teased a nipple with his teeth, and her fingers curled, head tipping back. She was totally at his mercy. He was made of marble, but warm and sexy and…okay, her brain had completely shut off now.

He leaned past her and made a sweeping motion with his arm. Paper rustled. She glanced at the floor, where the blueprints for the gingerbread house now rested. He returned to her mouth, investigating with his tongue. Thank god she had brushed her teeth.

He leaned her gently back onto the table, and she shuddered at the cold wood pressing into her spine.

His fingers slipped into the waistband of her sweatpants, and suddenly there was a knock at the door.

Fuck. She sat up abruptly, nearly cracking her skull into his.

He froze, shirtless and looking panicked.

"Hide," she mouthed to him.

"Where?" he mouthed back.

"Bathroom," she whispered, as though it was obvious.

"Who is it?" she called in a louder voice as she hopped off the table, lips still stinging from the intensity of their kiss.

"It's Beatrice, miss. The queen asked me to check on you."

"Oh. One second," Emma said.

Leo darted into the bathroom. Holy shit. She had nearly had sex with a prince. In a castle. And they had nearly been caught by the second-to-last person she would want to find them.

She struggled into her T-shirt and cast one last look around. The apartment wasn't neat, but at least Leo wasn't trying to hide behind the potted plant. Shit, his clothes. She plucked his T-shirt from the floor and tossed it into the comically small refrigerator, then threw his shoes in the oven.

Emma pulled the door open and put on her brightest smile. "It's so kind of you to check on me. I'm feeling well and ready to work."

Beatrice smiled, but it didn't quite reach her eyes. Cooper ran over to her, and she gave him a distracted pat as she looked past Emma and into the room.

"You haven't seen the prince, have you?"

Oh, shit. Did she know? Time to lie.

"John? No, why?"

"Not John. Leopold."

"Not since this morning," Emma said delicately. Her cheeks burned. Was she blushing? She wasn't used to lying. It didn't feel right, but if that two-minute preview was anything like the main event, she would lie to every employee in the castle to score more time with shirtless Leo. Principles be damned. "You guys should really consider putting an AirTag on him."

Beatrice smiled—a real smile this time—then pressed her lips together to hide it.

"Maybe so. He has a meeting, and I wanted to give him some talking points. Well, I'm very relieved you're feeling well. We're all excited to see what you and Miss Farrell come up with."

Emma bit her lip so she wouldn't laugh. As if Maya had contributed anything meaningful to this project.

"Did you prepare your shopping list?" Beatrice asked. "I'm happy to turn it in to the head of the kitchen."

"Yes," Emma said. She looked behind her, then remembered that it was buried under the blueprints Leo had just thrown on the floor.

"Whoops. Cooper must have knocked these off," she said, crouching down and digging through the mess.

Cooper whined, probably voicing his displeasure at being blamed for his mom's shenanigans.

"Here you are." Emma handed the list over.

"Great. Thank—do you smell something?" Beatrice paused with her nose in the air.

Emma sniffed. Oh, shit. What was that, rubber burning?

She had put Leo's shoes in the oven. Idiot.

"Oh, no. That must be my test batch of macarons," Emma said—despite the tray very clearly sitting on top of the oven. "I better get those. Thanks for stopping by."

"Have a good day," Beatrice said as Emma all but shoved her out the door.

"Fuck," Emma said. She ripped the oven door open and yanked the shoes out with a pair of tongs.

They hadn't actually caught on fire, though the soles looked a bit meltier than they had earlier. And now the apartment smelled like feet.

Leo poked his head out of the bathroom. "All clear?"

Emma nodded. "I may have burnt your shoes."

"You what?"

She pointed to the sink, where a curl of smoke rose above the boots. "Sorry. I panicked."

Leo laughed. He was all sex and sunshine, the darts of his hips visible above the waistband of his jeans. She went to reach for him when something changed in his expression, and he pulled his phone out.

"Damn, I *do* have a meeting."

Her heart fell, but it quickly righted itself when he crossed the room in two strides and delivered another searing kiss, pressing her against the door and cradling the back of her head in his hand.

"Have dinner with me. Tomorrow," he said breathlessly.

Another demand. But this one she didn't mind.

"Where?" she asked, pulling back to look at him. "We can't be seen together."

He paused for a moment. "Meet me in the greenhouse at six. I'll take care of everything."

She flushed with pleasure. She was playing with fire, but something about Leo was outweighing her capacity for logic. In less than a week, she would be back to her regular, monotonous life. Didn't she deserve to explore this connection while she could?

With one last breath-stealing kiss, he shrugged into his shirt, put on his toasty boots, and left. Things had escalated *very* quickly. Her life was unrecognizable from one week ago.

What was she getting herself into?

CHAPTER TWENTY-ONE

EMMA

"I wish you could see my face right now," Lola said through Emma's earbuds. "I am fully agog."

It was late, and the castle kitchen was awash in smells of cinnamon, nutmeg, and chocolate. It was now stocked to Emma's specifications—trays, piping bags and tips, a double boiler, candy thermometer, dozens of ingredients. The tools to achieve her dreams were spread around her. Now she just needed to figure out how to put all the pieces together.

"How are you feeling about everything?" Lola probed. "You don't seem as excited as you should be. You do realize that you're having a secret tryst with a prince, right? And you're the envy of millions of women on planet earth?"

"It's surreal. But it's also bringing up some feelings that I didn't expect," Emma admitted.

Leo's surprise make-out session had been on her mind all day, replaying over and over like a scene in a movie. It hadn't exactly made planning this elaborate dessert easy.

"What kind of feelings?" Lola asked.

Emma lowered her voice. "I'm scared. Remember how good things were with Dylan in the beginning? It was so exciting, so fresh. I fell head over heels for him, and he pulled the rug out from under me and then threw it—and me—into an incinerator the second things got difficult. And I know this isn't something serious. It can't be. But it's bringing back some of that fear."

"Vulnerability is scary," Lola said. "It's been a long time since you let anyone in. But Leo is not a Dylan. And even if he was, you'll be an ocean away before you find that out. I know this is hard for you, but try to just have fun. Treat it like a vacation hookup. No expectations, only fun. It's only a few more days. Enjoy them. And don't get caught."

"Right."

The ever-shortening timeline didn't bring her much comfort. As excited as she was to put this project behind her and celebrate the holidays with her mom, the prospect of never seeing Leo again filled her stomach with ceramic pie weights.

"I really hope that this sexy royal rendezvous is a palate cleanser for you. Your life has been nothing but stress and caregiving for over two years. It's about time you opened yourself to the possibility of love again. Or at least some banging. You deserve a bigger, more wonderful life."

"We'll see. If the queen finds out, I'm going to be— shit."

The door opened, and Emma stopped mid-sentence. Princess Ruby walked into the kitchen holding Emma's coat. Had she heard anything?

"Lo, I have to go. I'll talk to you later." Emma plucked her headphones out and stowed them in her pocket.

"Hi, Princess. How are you feeling?"

Ruby touched a hand to her head. "I'm fine. I wanted to bring this back to you and say thank you."

She handed over the coat.

Emma hung it from a peg by the door. "There's nothing to thank me for."

"You stepped in and protected me. Even against Paul."

Emma shrugged. "People keep saying that, but I have no idea who that little prick is. Nor do I care."

"Well," Ruby said, circling around the large central kitchen island and inspecting a tray of tarts, "I got a text from a friend saying he's unexpectedly spending his last semester of school in Italy."

"Good," Emma said flatly. Hopefully the women of Italy were well-equipped with tasers, mace, and large angry brothers.

Ruby looked hesitantly at the door and inched closer. "I also wanted to say thank you for your discretion."

"I've already forgotten it," Emma said. "Want one?" She offered the tray to Ruby.

"Uh, yes." The girl plucked a tart off the tray without finding a plate. Emma could only imagine what the queen would have to say about bare-handing a pastry.

"I'm going to miss your baking," Ruby said thoughtfully. "I wonder who Mother will hire next."

"Well, in the fall, you can come visit me, and I'll bake croissants for your whole dorm."

"I feel better knowing that you're going to be there," Ruby said with a small smile. "Anyway, thank you again."

She left. Emma had just settled back into her flow when the door swung open again. Her heart lifted for a second. Was it Leo?

But no, it was a far worse surprise.

The queen entered, still wearing a suit jacket and skirt even though it was nearly eleven p.m.

"Miss Clark," she said.

"Good evening, Your Majesty," Emma said, attempting a

curtsy as best as she could while her hands were covered in flour and her limbs were stiff from almost dying and then sleeping on a hardwood floor. Cradled in the arms of her son. Oops.

Speaking of whom, was she going to be visited by the entire royal family before Leo showed up? She hadn't seen or heard from him since their steamy moment in the gatehouse hours earlier. Not that she was keeping track or anything.

"I just wanted to see how things were coming along in light of your recent trauma."

"Oh, everything's fine. Your kitchen staff have been so helpful. I have everything I need, it'll just take time to get all the components put together. I think you'll be pleased with the results."

Assuming she could pull it all off completely on her own since Maya was A) useless, and B) apparently having a royal sex vacation.

"I trust you're right," she said, striding around the kitchen with her hands clasped behind her back like she owned the place. Which she did. "I also wanted to ask, if it's not too much trouble, could you make another batch of espresso croissants for Ruby before you leave? She really loves them."

"I would be happy to."

They were the pastry that had gotten her the job, after all. She owed the princess a lifetime of croissants.

"Thank you," the queen said, staring off into the distance. "I also wanted to thank you for what you did for Ruby."

Emma paused. Ruby hadn't mentioned that she told the queen about what happened. It was better to play dumb.

"It was nothing."

"That damn Paul," the queen said with a tsk. "He's as bad as his father. Lord Axley owns thirty luxury hotels between here, Italy, and Spain."

"Well, that does explain Paul's insufferable air of entitlement," Emma said without thinking. Yikes. She probably shouldn't have just said that to a queen.

Queen Eleanor had a ghost of a smile. "In a perfect world, we would dig out the stocks from the museum and make an example of him. But this isn't a perfect world, and sometimes things have to be handled a little more diplomatically."

Emma didn't comment. If someone had sexually harassed her little sister, she would've pushed them off the Brooklyn Bridge.

"Leo also mentioned that you saved him from choking," the queen said. "It seems our family has much to thank you for. As such, I've invited a representative from *Food Magazine* to come to the ball."

Emma froze. *Food Magazine* was the preeminent food publication of the twenty-first century.

"I'm sure you can expect a significant feature on your gingerbread castle," the queen added.

Great. Now the stakes were even higher. And worse, the journalist would probably assign all the credit to Maya.

"How kind. Thank you, Your Majesty," she added with a curtsy.

A silence settled, but the queen didn't leave. Emma sensed there was more than just the stress of the ball weighing on the queen's mind.

"Ruby's a wonderful girl," Emma said. "You must be so proud of your children."

"We're very blessed," she said quietly.

"It must be difficult for you, knowing that she's going off to college next year."

"Yes," the queen said, gripping the edges of the sink and staring out at the dark courtyard. "She's my baby. My last child. And soon she'll be thousands of miles away in a foreign place. She's always had a thirst for independence. Maybe it's my fault. Maybe I tried too hard to keep her here, keep her safe. She won't even be here for her next birthday. I've never missed any of my children's birthdays."

What an uncharacteristically maternal thing to say for someone who had apparently been withdrawn and uninterested in Leo's childhood.

"That sounds really hard," Emma said. "If it would bring you any comfort, I'd be happy to make a birthday cake for Ruby. I'll just be a few miles away when she's at school. She won't be alone."

The queen turned to her. "That's right. I'm grateful that she'll have a friendly face nearby. Watch out for her, won't you?"

"Of course."

"Don't let her fall in love with an unemployed musician."

Oh, a joke.

"I'll do my best, but New York's lousy with them."

The queen gifted her with another ghost of a smile before gliding out of the kitchen.

Had she just made some headway? Maybe she would be more open to Emma and Leo spending time together. Or maybe Emma could find a way to save John from embarrassment or harm and complete the trifecta, thereby earning a sizable bonus in the second half of her payment.

But for now, it was best to keep things under wraps. Her mind turned to her secret rendezvous with Leo the next night. Would he keep his word, or would she show up to a dark, disappointing greenhouse?

CHAPTER TWENTY-TWO

LEO

Leo's mind buzzed with details as he unfurled a white tablecloth and settled it over the round table he had commandeered from the garden. He had spent the bulk of the day fine-tuning his presentation for his parents. Every last ounce of his energy and creativity had gone into it.

His parents would see the need for it. They had to. There were women and children—like Emma and her mom—who were depending on them.

Roses perfumed the air around him. Rows upon rows of flowers in different colors bloomed in the glass enclosure. His mother insisted on having fresh flowers year-round. Luckily, the gardener only worked in the morning.

With the addition of a table and a couple dozen candles, the sprawling greenhouse had been transformed from plant farm to romantic first date material. It was warm, humid, and there were no interfering paparazzi to be found.

His parents were at a fundraising event and wouldn't be home for hours, and John and Ruby were having dinner, so as long as no one in the castle saw them and snitched, they were in for a lovely evening.

It had been a long time since his last date. He was rusty. Did this even count as a date? They weren't dating. Emma was only here for another few days.

The thought of the timeline twisted his stomach. They were in a weird situation. He was going to stay here and build something for his community that they desperately needed, and she was going to go back to New York to start her bakery empire. There was no future for them. They were from different worlds.

But maybe tonight they could pretend that none of that mattered.

He couldn't deny that he wanted to know everything about her. And physically, he wanted nothing more than to hold her in his arms, kiss her, and bring her to the edge of passion. He had lost control in her apartment the day before. Normally there would be days or weeks of courting, careful wooing. But his connection with Emma was instant —hot and fierce like a lightning strike. He couldn't help himself.

The curve of her lips when she saw him. The scatter of goosebumps and soft moan when he kissed her neck. She was mesmerizing.

He was getting hard just thinking about it.

The door opened, snapping him out of his thoughts.

"You have it so bad for this girl," Sal announced as he walked in holding bags. Ordinarily, Leo would have had the royal chef arrange a private dinner in the library at the castle, but it was better that no one from the staff knew. They were notoriously chatty, and he couldn't put Emma's job in jeopardy.

"I do not," he said defensively. "I'm just enjoying spending time with her while she's here."

"Whatever. Dibs on catering your wedding," Sal said, then ducked when Leo threw a spray bottle at his head.

"How's the presentation coming along?" he asked when he seemed to decide he was out of danger.

"It's as good as I can make it," Leo said. He arranged plates and candlesticks on top of the tablecloth.

"And what if they still say no?"

Leo straightened up and frowned at him. "Why are you being so negative?"

"I'm not. You know I like to play worst-case scenario."

Leo shook his head. "This is happening. I don't care what I have to do. If they say no, I'll find another way."

They wouldn't say no. You'd have to be a sadist to say no to building a domestic violence shelter in a lot that no one was even using.

"Good. That's what I wanted to hear. Do you need a pep talk before your date?"

"It's not a date."

Sal looked around very slowly at all the candles and flowers. "I'm sorry, did you drag an entire Christmas tree in here? You hate Christmas."

He gestured to the corner of the greenhouse, where an eight-foot tree had recently been decorated with lights and tinsel.

"It's—it doesn't matter what it is," Leo said. "Get out of here. Thanks for the food."

"As you wish, Your Highness," Sal said contritely. "Don't get caught," he called just before the door swung shut behind him.

Idiot.

Minutes later, the door inched open and Emma's head poked inside. His heart lifted at the sight of her, and some of the storm cloud of worry about his project receded.

"All clear?" she whispered.

"All clear."

"Good. It's cold as fuck." She stepped inside and shed her coat. "Oh, but so warm in here. How do you not spend every day in here?"

He blinked, and his brain went stupid for a second. A scarlet dress with a plunging neckline clung to her slender figure, which was incredibly sexy despite the fact that she had paired the outfit with massive snow boots.

"Sometimes I do," he said when his brain reentered his body. "It's a great place to hide from my family."

"Is that a Christmas tree?" She rushed over to investigate the tree and took an appreciative sniff.

"It's fake," he said apologetically.

"It's okay. I sniffed the one in the courtyard on my way here."

"Are you in the habit of sniffing trees?"

"Life's too short not to sniff the trees," she said.

He smiled. "You look beautiful."

"Thank you," she said with a small twirl. "Would you believe I found this in a thrift store in town today? Oh, shit," she said, looking down at the snow boots. "I meant to take these off and swap them with these." She pulled a pair of gold heels out of her bag.

"I'll pretend like I didn't see anything," he said, turning his back to her.

A minute later, she came to stand in front of him, now wearing the heels. "What do you think?"

He couldn't help himself. He wrapped his arm around her and dipped her, sliding his hand along her leg. Her arms slipped around his neck, and she tugged herself up to kiss him.

His heart beat furiously fast, and his grip tightened on

her. He could rip this dress straight off her and set her on the table, exploring with fingers and tongue and everything in him that screamed out to be closer to her, inside her, wrapped in her warmth.

"Sorry," she said breathlessly a minute later. "I was probably supposed to wait until the end of the date to do that. Not that this is a date," she said hurriedly.

"I don't mind," Leo said, leaning in to kiss her again, softer this time. "I would have done it anyway. You're a distraction."

"Me? I'm not the one setting up Christmas trees and making a gorgeous freakin' greenhouse wonderland. And is that dinner?"

"Of course."

She whimpered. "Thank you. I'm so hungry. I've been baking test batches of macarons all day. And while they are delicious, they're fairly devoid of substance."

Leo pulled a chair out for her, and she sat. His fingers brushed against her arm, which just made him want to dive back in. He'd never had to fight for control merely from brushing against someone.

"I hope you like it. It's one of Sal's specialties."

Emma leaned in and inhaled deeply. "Ooh, coq au vin? I love it."

Leo poured a hefty glass of wine for both of them. Maybe it would help distract him from the curve of her breast behind the daringly low neckline.

"I didn't hear from you this morning," she said after a long sip of wine. "I thought you were reconsidering our... agreement."

"Not at all. I had some meetings. And then I had to figure out the logistics of lugging a Christmas tree and a hundred candles to the greenhouse without being spotted."

"I don't know how you did it. It's stunning," she said, surveying the scene.

She was beautiful in the soft candlelight. Her blonde hair was out of the bun he normally saw it in, curling gently down her back. Lipstick the same shade as her dress was probably smeared on his face right now. It was going to be hard to focus on dinner.

"You didn't have to do all this for me," she added. "I'm low-maintenance."

She speared a mushroom on her fork and hummed appreciatively. He paused for an instant. It was customary to wait until the royal family took the first bite to eat. How refreshing that she either didn't know or didn't care about the tradition. It was a stupid one.

"Our time is short, and you're missing Christmas at home. I know it's not the same as ice skating at Rockefeller Center or window shopping on Fifth Avenue, but I wanted to bring some magic to you."

"Have you ever been to New York?"

"Not for many years," he admitted.

"You'll have to visit sometime. Maybe when Ruby goes to school. As long as you're not busy with construction on the new community project—or your royal duties. Whatever those are."

The idea of seeing her again was very enticing. Maybe their story didn't end in a few days when she went home. Maybe there was another chapter. Or a lot of them.

"I'd like that," he said.

Their eyes met over the tapered candles, and something lurched in his gut. Something he hadn't felt in a long time.

Things were getting more serious than he intended. Messier. He barely knew her. She had arrived less than a week ago.

The warning signs were flashing all around him, but for some reason, he didn't care.

"What's your favorite dessert?" she asked over the sensual croon of "Santa Baby." There was a shortage of sexy Christmas songs.

"My favorite dessert?" He was surprised by the question. The few women he had dated since Petra had seemed perpetually nervous and hadn't asked a lot of questions. "Cheesecake," he decided. They didn't have a lot of it in the castle, as his mother couldn't stand the texture of it. But when she went away, the previous royal baker would sneak it onto the menu.

"Oh my god," Emma said. "I have the best recipe. It will knock your socks all the way off. Into a different dimension, even. It's that good."

Leo raised his eyebrows. "Dimension-transcending cheesecake."

"That's what I call it. When's your birthday?" she asked.

"December thirteenth."

She put her fork down. "Are you kidding me?" she asked. "Were you even going to tell me?"

"Why would I tell you when my birthday is?"

"It's a week from now. And you've spent your entire life having your birthday overshadowed by Christmas."

He shrugged. Maybe that's where some of his resentment for the holiday had come from.

She shook her head and sat back in her seat. "That won't do. We'll have to celebrate your half birthday."

"A half birthday? What am I, twelve?"

She shook her head. "Anyone born between the months of November and January get a half birthday. With celebratory cheesecake. It's the law. Watch your PO box for a totally mangled cheesecake in the middle of June."

He smiled. "Totally mangled dimension-transcending cheesecake," he clarified.

"Exactly."

"I look forward to it. And when is your birthday?"

"January twelfth."

"Ah. I'm starting to understand why you're an expert in half birthdays."

She nodded. "The law may have been enacted by my own mother."

"Is she looking for another job? Maybe as a powerless figurehead for a small European country?"

"Sorry, but I think that position is about to be filled by my hopefully soon-to-be ex-boss who's banging your brother," Emma said.

Leo froze with a bite halfway to his mouth. "Wait, does that mean she could be my sister-in-law? I didn't agree to this."

It would never happen. The queen would arrange a marriage before allowing John to marry an American. The thought didn't bring him any joy, as he was bound by the same made-up rules.

"That's right," Emma said "She's yours now. Good luck. You know, I joked about this before coming here, but I never dreamed it would actually happen. Maybe I should actually stay at Crumb and Get It now," she said thoughtfully.

He shook his head. "Stay the course. You deserve to be your own boss."

"That's right. I do." She glanced at her watch. "Shit, I only have another hour. I really need to get the big pieces of the structure baked tonight. The oven in my kitchenette isn't big enough. And then there's the fact that it now smells like burnt shoes."

His heart fell. He wasn't ready to end the night.

"Dance with me," he said.

She raised her eyebrows. "Now? In here?"

"Normally a date would include dinner, dancing, and maybe a movie. But as we're short on time..." He held his hand out to her, and she took it.

"So you're saying this is a date?" she asked coyly.

"It's... I don't know what this is," he admitted.

She rose from the table, her hand in his. "Let's not worry about what it is or isn't. Let's dance."

CHAPTER TWENTY-THREE

EMMA

THE SPEAKER IN THE CORNER OF THE GREENHOUSE transitioned from "Grandma Got Run Over By a Reindeer" to "Fade Into You" by Mazzy Star.

A thrill ran down her spine. She had always loved this song, even though she could never quite figure out if it was a love song or a lament.

Leo pulled her close, one hand hot on her hip while the other clasped hers.

"Well, this is a little more romantic than patricide," she said.

"It felt right."

Everything about this night had been intoxicating. Maybe it was the glass of wine, or the humid warmth of the greenhouse. The smell of green everywhere. Or maybe it was just Leo.

He was a mystery. A masterpiece. A prince with all the room to be an entitled asshole in the world, but instead of playing polo and cashing in on brand deals, he spent his time on the ground, working tirelessly to make improvements for the country that he loved.

She couldn't take her eyes off him as they revolved slowly on the spot. Candlelight flickered in his brown eyes. A peculiar feeling flooded her, like she was sinking into a bathtub full of hot chocolate. They had learned more about each other in a week than people she had known for years. The desire to know everything about him was overwhelming. What food did he eat when sick? What was his favorite movie? Would she ever see him again? Were transatlantic friends with benefits a thing?

If she wasn't careful, this situation was going to get very out of hand.

The music flowed around them as they swayed together among flowers of every color. He spun her out and pulled her back in so that her back pressed against his chest. God, he smelled good. Like wood shavings and pine and fresh mountain air.

The heat of his breath reached her neck a moment before his lips. He pressed a gentle kiss to the spot just beneath her earlobe, sending a shiver down her spine. For a moment she just absorbed it all. Believed in the fantasy.

A slow dance in a greenhouse full of roses with a prince who had saved her life. It was really too bad that the end of this story would be here in a matter of days.

But she could breathe this secret meeting in and carry it with her always. One perfect moment full of promise and the trappings of love, even though it was all just a dream.

The song was coming to an end. She needed to get ready and plan the long evening of baking that lay ahead.

But just a little longer. She twisted in his arms so she could look at him and linked her hands behind his neck. She wanted to see him, commit to memory the grip of his capable hands, the taste of wine on her tongue, and the perfume of roses in the air.

The look in his eyes was indescribable but poignant. More intensity than you'd use to look at someone who was just a friend. Sultry, attentive, almost hungry.

As the last chord faded, she dragged him down to her and pressed her lips against his. If they only had one moment, she was going to make it one to remember.

Their tongues danced, and her hands went to his suit jacket. She slipped it off, let it drop to the floor. His shoulders were broad and strong under her grasp.

His hand came up to cup her breast, and her whole body stiffened and shuddered. It had been so long since she had been touched like this. The handful of Tinder dates she'd been on in two years didn't come close.

Her body yearned for his in a way that defied logic. It wasn't just the rush of early relationship butterflies. It was like a tenuous thread had connected them their whole lives, and unseen forces had snapped it taut the moment she had set foot in Lynoria.

Did he feel any of this, or was she completely delusional?

Shut up, Emma.

Her fingers went to the buttons on his collared shirt. Maybe if she kept her hands busy, she could quiet her damn mind and allow herself to just feel.

The shirt slipped away, falling to join the jacket. And now there was an undershirt. So many damn layers. What would she find next, a petticoat?

His fingers clawed at her back, probably searching for a zipper. When he didn't find one, he took her roughly by the hips and steered her toward the table. His hand left her side, and suddenly everything crashed to the floor—china, glasses, the remainder of the bottle of wine.

She flinched and pushed back from Leo, panic immediately flaring in her chest like a spark on a gas can. She stumbled backward and cried out when a thorn pinched the back of her arm in the exact spot of her long, thin scar.

Danger. Her body screamed at her. She needed to leave, hide. She scrambled toward the exit.

"Emma? What's wrong?" Leo called to her. His eyebrows contracted, and his arms were open, like he was trying to approach a fawn without startling it.

"Nothing, sorry. I—"

Her breath was coming in gasps, and she struggled to get the panic under control. Not now.

His gaze fell to the floor where the glass shards glittered, and his face crumpled.

"I wasn't thinking. I'm so sorry." He reached for her, but her hand closed into a fist, and he stopped.

"I should go," she said over numb lips. "The kitchen will be empty soon."

"Emma, I—"

She grabbed her snow boots and dashed out of the greenhouse before he could finish his sentence.

CHAPTER TWENTY-FOUR

LEO

Leo's footsteps thundered down the castle hallway. Broken china shifted in his backpack, an audible reminder of what an imbecile he was.

Fool. Bumbling idiot. There weren't enough insults in the dictionary to cover how asinine he had been.

Emma had told him that she'd been a victim of domestic violence—angry outbursts from an abusive father. And what did he do? Shattered a bunch of china in his haste to strip her bare.

What the hell was wrong with him?

This was a major screwup. There were only a few more days until the ball, and after that, she'd be on a plane bound for New York. He had fumbled the time they had left. He needed to apologize, but he didn't want to scare her.

He opened the door to his suite and dropped his bag inside to be dealt with later. His gaze landed on his sink. Maybe there was something he could do for Emma, a small way to apologize. With a little bit of help.

Twenty minutes later, a sharp tapping sound came from

his front door, and he opened it to find Ruby pushing a cart laden with dishes.

"Why the hell did you need twenty dirty baking sheets from the kitchen? You know Emma's going to need these."

"Shh. In here."

Leo ushered Ruby into his suite and ducked his head out into the hallway. It was empty. The door snapped shut, and he breathed a sigh of relief.

"You weren't seen?" he asked.

"No," she said slowly. "What is this about?"

He wheeled the cart into his kitchenette and turned on the faucet. He searched for the right words.

"You can't tell Mother and Father. Or John. I need to apologize to Emma. This is the only thing I could think of."

Ruby looked suspiciously at the pile of dishes.

"What did you do?"

He froze. While context would be helpful, he hadn't asked Emma if he could share her story.

"It's...not really my story to tell," he said. "But I was an idiot."

Ruby smiled. "Oh, man. Mom's going to be so pissed. You fell in love with an American."

Leo sputtered, and his heart rate ticked up a notch. "I'm not in love. I barely know her."

She scoffed. "Whatever you say. This is a start, but it's not enough."

He sighed. "Okay, then what do you think I should do?"

She seemed to consider for a moment. "Didn't you say she has like a million Christmas traditions with her mom?"

"Yes."

"And you have her mom's phone number?"

"I don't. But I'm sure Beatrice does."

"Call her. Then give Emma a piece of home." Ruby

crossed to the kitchen and grabbed the remote. The TV flickered on, and a Christmas movie started playing.

"What are you doing?" he asked.

"Helping." She rolled up her sleeves and ducked to peer into his cabinets. She reappeared a moment later with a bottle of dish detergent and a scrubbing sponge. "I'm not going to let you mess this up. Now go find Beatrice."

CHAPTER TWENTY-FIVE

EMMA

EMMA'S HEART WAS IN HER THROAT AS SHE STEPPED DOWN THE path to the village. Her toes were already numb, and her eyes were itchy with fatigue from staying up too late baking and checking the nanny cam the night before. Ziplock bags full of test croissants swung at her side.

Last night had been a disaster. Leo had given her the most romantic date of her entire life—a covert Christmas wonderland in a steamy greenhouse—and her past trauma had infiltrated as suddenly and as unexpectedly as a rock shattering a windshield.

It was yet another thing her father had taken away from her. She had no idea how to have a functional relationship. A profound hesitancy to open herself up. And now, the only time in years she found someone she felt a real connection with, her own brain had betrayed her.

She had made Leo feel awful. For hours last night, Ruby had scooped up her used pans and replaced them with clean ones. The first stack had arrived with a piece of Leo's stationery and a simple note.

I'm sorry.

How was she going to explain herself to him? Not even Dylan, her only long-term boyfriend, knew the details of what she and her mom had gone through. And should she really be dredging all these volatile memories up days before the biggest project of her entire career?

She needed to keep her head in the game and secure the money. The safest course of action would be to hide in her apartment and avoid Leo until she left. She had known all along that they were fundamentally incompatible. He was a European prince. She was a Brooklynite baker. But he deserved an explanation in person, no matter how inept she was at providing it.

She hesitated outside the doors of the community kitchen. Would they even allow donations? The bag of test croissants crinkled in her hands. There was no reason why they should go to waste. They were perfectly edible, and the people of Lynoria certainly deserved them more than the royal family, who wanted for nothing.

She shoved the door open with some difficulty and ducked inside to find Gus.

"Miss Emma," he said with a smile. "What brings you in this morning?"

"I don't know if you can take these, but I have some fresh donations." She slid the bags across the counter. "I'm Serv-Safe certified, and these were made in a clean environment, if it helps."

Gus opened the bag and sniffed. "These smell magnificent. We won't let them go to waste. Could you plate them and put them on that table over there?"

He rummaged under the counter and passed her a pair of tongs, gloves, and a serving platter.

The door opened, and a handful of people filtered in. Gus greeted them by name as Emma plated the baked goods. She made a quick detour to the bathroom and took a moment to breathe. The nerves were making her pee every ten minutes.

On her way out, a voice caught her ear.

"Did you make these, miss?"

A man in a frayed jacket lifted a croissant in her direction.

She nodded.

"I haven't had a croissant like this since I left France thirty years ago. Thank you."

Heat rushed into her cheeks. "I'm glad you like it."

All around them, early patrons were taking bites of pastry. She cast a glance over the other kitchen offerings. Cold cereal, a slow cooker full of what looked to be oatmeal, and hot water for tea. The croissants were almost gone. Any food was better than no food. But how long had it been since these citizens had had a treat? Gus tried his best, that was evident. But he was probably at the mercy of whatever government-sponsored food vats were sent down the pipeline.

She made a mental note to return with some of her homemade dinner rolls and left with a final wave to Gus. If she had more time, she would chat with Gus, learn about their donations process and supply coordination. But time was short, and she still needed to explain herself to Leo.

Minutes later, the doors of the community center rose before her. They were enormous, weatherworn, and heavy-looking. Every door she had encountered in this village was slightly irregular and had required an unusual amount of muscle to open, so she braced herself and pushed on the right one with all her might. The door opened effortlessly, slamming off the wall as she stumbled through the opening. Her hand caught the edge of a bench before she could fall face-first, but the damage was done. Everyone in the audience whipped around and stared at her. Warmth rushed into her cheeks.

Idiot.

Leo was at the front of the room, yellow legal pad in hand. His brow was furrowed, and it looked like he was frozen mid-step. When he caught her glance, a smile crinkled the corner of his eyes. Was it her imagination, or did he look relieved? It was probably only a millisecond, but an eternity passed as they looked at each other.

Something fluttered in her stomach, and she was suddenly hyperaware of her body. What the hell was that?

"All right?" Leo asked softly.

She nodded.

"Uh, next on the agenda," Leo said loudly, "the community kitchen needs a temporary sous chef for six weeks starting in February while Colette is on medical leave. Emergency funding was approved, so the short-term position will be compensated. Please spread the word."

A couple of the attendees whispered to each other and took an extra look before turning their attention back to Leo. Emma slid into the last row. Her heart was still pounding, and she wasn't sure if it was from making a damn fool of herself or from that snapshot of Leo that would live in her brain forever. Concern melding into joy, relief.

She tried to focus on what he was saying. He looked so at ease at the front of the room, listening attentively as citizens described struggles facing the kingdom.

The fire company needed to raise money for repairs to

one of their engines. Parliament was threatening to take away the free lunch program at elementary schools in the kingdom. And then there were a handful of smaller concerns.

"Yes, Mrs. DuPont. I will personally check on the feral kittens on Alpine Street," he said to an old woman wearing what looked to be six layers of clothing despite the fact that it must have been eighty degrees in the room.

His list grew longer by the minute, but he never looked stressed. He was calm, interested, and invested. Royal, even. It was fascinating to watch him work. He truly just wanted to help the kingdom. What a lasting legacy he was going to leave, even though he had no interest in his title.

His project was going to have such a profound, lasting impact on this community. Women and children would be safe, cared for. The library would educate the local children, while the garden would teach them about agriculture. It was amazing. A real impact that directly helped people. Much more impactful than making fancy desserts for rich assholes.

A burst of realization was unfurling deep inside her. She wanted to see all of Leo's expressions. Gratitude, annoyance, joy, pride. Whatever he looked like when she put a plate of freshly baked cinnamon rolls in front of him on an arctic February morning.

An image popped into her mind of Leo in a simple gray suit at the end of an aisle dotted with wildflowers grown by her mother. Cooper sat at his side, panting happily with a ring box strapped to his collar. The community garden bloomed in the background, sunlight glancing off the new library. A cozy reception in the town square with every villager.

What the fuck?

She sat back in her chair as if it could put some distance between her and the intrusive scene. Why the hell was she fantasizing about marrying Leo? She had never even considered the possibility of marriage before. The only example she had was that of her own parents, which had ended catastrophically. Her mom had never dated much after the divorce. The only successful relationship she'd witnessed was Lola and her husband, Mateo.

Now those two were meant to be. The universe had put them in the same English class at the same university at the same time. No complications, just an instantaneous spark across a crowded room. That's how it was meant to be. Not whatever tangled mess this was.

There was only one solution. She needed to shut this down now before she got hurt. Or fired. They needed the money more than she needed a boyfriend.

The meeting adjourned, and Emma fidgeted with the strap of her purse. She needed to turn off the tiny horny romantic running the controls behind her brain and apologize. Even though the two of them weren't meant to be, she still wanted to be on good terms with him.

Villagers filtered out, some of them nodding at Emma on their way. Eventually it was just her and Leo.

"Hi," he said.

"Hey. Um, I wanted to apologize for last night."

He shook his head. "You have nothing to apologize for. It was my fault. I was so consumed with need that I didn't stop to think." He reached forward like he was going to take her hand, then stopped. "I'm sorry."

She reached over and took his hand, even though she knew she shouldn't. "You couldn't have known because I didn't tell you specifics. I haven't dated in a long time, so I'm not used to...explaining myself. Especially this early on."

He squeezed her hand and stared straight into her eyes. "I will never do that to you again."

She hesitated. His words suggested a promise that didn't apply. Their story would careen to an end in seventy-two hours. Before she knew it, she'd be back to her everyday normal of working all day, then helping her mother to the toilet and cooking and cleaning all night. This entanglement of theirs—whatever it was—was going to be a mere blip on his radar, maybe a moment he looked back on fondly on his deathbed when he was married to a Queen-Eleanor-approved aristocrat and surrounded by a gaggle of grandchildren.

She bit her tongue. Why was this so hard to say? "This isn't going to work, Leo. We're from different worlds, and there's too much at stake. I think we should—"

"Wait," he interrupted with a voice of authority she had never heard before. She paused in spite of herself.

"Before you say anything else, let me try to make it up to you. I'll leave you alone tomorrow so you can focus. But what about Friday before you start the last push?"

She dropped her gaze. It was too hard to look into those brown eyes. "I don't think it's—"

"Please, Emma." He brushed a curl off her face, and his touch was like velvet. "I'm not ready to let you go."

Reason warred with desire. Standing in this drafty town hall with Leo had brought relief, comfort. His very presence gave her a profound sense of peace. Like sliding into flannel sheets after a double shift at the bakery.

Shit. She had caught feelings. It was her own fault. In a few days, she would be on a plane to New York, and she still had to pull off the biggest project of her career before that. The last thing she should do was put her entire future in jeopardy by having another date with Leo. She needed to turn him down and focus. Everyone was relying on her—her mom, the dogs, their crappy apartment in desperate need of repair.

But when she looked into his deep, warm eyes, her brain disconnected from her mouth.

"Okay."

CHAPTER TWENTY-SIX

EMMA

Emma stood in her kitchenette, eyeing the gatehouse apartment. Her back ached. Her hands were chapped from endless hand washing. And she was running out of room.

Cheesecakes and tarts were all but spilling out of her tiny refrigerator. Every inch of free space that was out of Cooper's reach was covered in containers of cookies, croissants, and breads.

Maya had reluctantly answered Emma's thirteenth phone call, and her apartment and refrigerator were also now full of baked goods.

Tomorrow night, Lynoria's elite would flood the halls of the castle and sample her desserts. Not to mention the critic from *Food Magazine*. This was her make-or-break moment.

She was pouring every ounce of her stress into this bake. Maybe it would help distract her from impending heartbreak. She had a date with Leo in less than an hour. It was a mistake. A reckless decision. But she couldn't deny the part of herself that deeply wanted one more night with him.

He wasn't going to the ball. He said he would spend it the same way he spent most Saturday nights—volunteering at the community kitchen. And even if he was going to the ball, she'd be manning the dessert table all night. Tonight was their last opportunity for a stolen moment. She may never see him again. And for some reason, that was outweighing the voice that screamed in her head about her future.

It didn't have to be a rational decision. It was just a few hours, and then she'd likely be up all night in the castle kitchen. While most of the pieces of the gingerbread castle had been painstakingly baked, measured, and cut, they still had to be decorated. That was going to be backbreaking, hand-cramping labor that would ruin her for a straight week. It was a good thing she'd brought along ibuprofen.

Tomorrow would be spent on the things that absolutely had to be prepared at the last minute—the croquembouche Christmas tree, preparing the tarts so they didn't become soggy, and assembling the massive beast of a gingerbread castle.

She had poured every ounce of her expertise into this project, pulling out methods she hadn't used since baking school. She'd shaped pieces of the castle's turret by cooling gingerbread sheets over wine bottles. At home, she would have had an entire team helping her. Someone on pastries, someone on cake, one on candy, another for assembly and final decor. But here, she was alone and exhausted. When this marathon sprint was over, she was going to sleep for a week.

Someone knocked at the door, and Cooper let out a low woof. A quick inspection through the peephole revealed someone who looked a lot like Leo, and she almost breathed a sigh of relief. If it had been another one of the queen's cronies checking to evaluate her state of preparedness, they would surely report her for her insane storage method.

She opened the door, and Leo rushed inside and closed the door. He paused, pressing his ear to the crack.

"What are you doing?" she whispered. "And why are you wearing a fake mustache and glasses?"

Cooper came over and licked his hand, whining until he pulled away from the door and committed to petting him.

"Just making sure I wasn't followed. My mother has spies everywhere."

"You live a super weird life," Emma said thoughtfully.

He grunted noncommittally.

"Sorry for all the subterfuge. Are you sure you have a couple hours? You must be exhausted." His gaze moved around the room, where baked goods were stacked haphazardly almost up to the ceiling.

She shrugged. "When am I ever going to have the opportunity to do this again? I can handle a few days of being tired."

"Oh, here." He handed over a box.

She stared at him, then opened it. A brown wig and a large pair of sunglasses fell out. "I'll be honest, I wasn't expecting role-play."

"We're going to have to split up," he explained. "So I can make sure the coast is clear. This way, if anyone does see you, they won't recognize you and report you to my mom."

She piled her hair on top of her head and slid the wig on. "So just to be clear, no one on the staff is going to be alarmed by the sudden appearance of Liza Minnelli in the royal family's personal living quarters?"

"You don't have to wear it," he said defensively. "I just wanted to keep your identity—"

"I'm just joking," she said quickly. "Yes, I'll wear it."

Whatever it took.

"Okay," he said, looking significantly calmer. "I'm going

to leave first. Wait two minutes for my text, then follow me to that doorway Ruby showed you before...you know."

"Before I almost died? Got it."

He nodded, then stuck his head out of the apartment. He looked side to side, then slipped into the hallway.

Emma took a moment to pet Cooper. She straightened her wig in the mirror, then watched her phone until two minutes had passed.

Leo sent a thumbs-up emoji, and she crept out of her apartment and closed the door behind her. She stopped to listen, but there was nothing but silence. She slunk down the stairs and out into the courtyard.

The guard in the gatehouse nodded at her despite the wig. Shit. Hopefully he wasn't a snitch. She popped the collar on her jacket and strode toward the castle, passing the magnificent Christmas tree and skirting the main double doors.

The grounds and exterior hallways were deserted, so she had impersonated an American treasure for nothing.

Leo met her at the door. He held his wallet up to some sort of scanner. The device beeped, and there was an audible click as the door unlocked.

He hurried through the door, and Emma hesitated behind him. He strode to the intersection of the hallway and glanced around in a way that wasn't very casual before turning around and nodding at her.

She slipped inside and followed him at a distance. Suddenly, a door opened down the hallway and the king stepped out. Emma leapt sideways and crashed through a random door, falling heavily onto the floor.

The room was beautifully decorated, with an intricate four-poster bed and blush-and-gold decor. And on the bed sat Ruby. Shit.

"Uhhhh, Emma?" Ruby sounded unsure.

"Oh, hey. I didn't know this was your room," Emma said, despite having been in it a few days earlier.

"Don't get me wrong," Ruby said. "I'm happy to see you. But why are you in my room? And dressed like Pete Wentz from Fall Out Boy?"

"Right? That's what I told him."

Ruby perked up. "Him? Ooh, you mean Leo."

"No—I—" Emma began, but Ruby had an amused expression.

"You can't tell anyone you saw me. Swear," Emma said with a pointed finger.

"Relax. I won't tell anyone you're having a secret relationship with my brother."

"It's not a relationship."

"No? So it's a normal part of your contract to wear wigs and sneak around with the children of your customers?"

"Shut up," Emma said, but couldn't hide her smile.

"I could have you tied to a turret for telling me to shut up." Ruby's teenage sass was unparalleled.

"And derail your mom's dream ball?" Emma asked. "You wouldn't dare."

"You have a point. Just promise me one thing."

"If I must."

"Don't hurt him," she said firmly.

Emma's heart lurched. "I would never. That's not what this is."

"Are you sure? I watched him drag like ninety-five bags of Christmas decorations to his room last night like he robbed Whoville."

"Maybe he's just feeling festive."

"He hates Christmas," Ruby said flatly.

"Can you go out in the hallway and see if your dad's still

out there?" This bickering was wasting time. Emma only had a few hours before she needed to get down to the kitchen for the final push.

Ruby hopped off her bed and strode boldly out into the hallway. "Coast is clear," she said over her shoulder.

"You didn't see me. And your boots are adorable," Emma said on her way out the door.

Ruby smiled before the door shut.

Shit. Leo had disappeared, and she didn't know which way his room was. She popped Ruby's door open.

"It's down the hall, second door on the left," Ruby reported without looking up.

"Thanks."

Emma hurried away, pausing to make sure the coast was clear. All of this was insane. Dangerous. Reckless. But one more night with Leo was worth it.

She paused outside the indicated door and listened. Faint strains of Christmas music were playing, so at least Ruby had told her the correct door instead of pranking her. She opened the door and slipped inside.

CHAPTER TWENTY-SEVEN

EMMA

An explosion of light and color greeted her. Leo's suite was as big as three of her apartments put together.

"Oh, wow. This is incredible."

"Sorry about that," he said. "My dad wanted to talk about the football match."

Emma didn't respond and found she could only stare. Every corner had been decorated. It looked like she had just entered a department store's Santa setup. Multicolored lights stretched around the room, and garland was hung from the mantle. Candles flickered warmly, and Bing Crosby's soulful voice melted out of the speakers.

"It's fine. Ruby's aware that something's going on though. I had to dive into her room, and she basically threatened to have me extradited if I hurt you."

He cleared his throat. "She can be protective."

"Hang on," she said, striding over to the small kitchen island. She sniffed the concoction simmering in the saucepan. "Is this Santa's Revenge?"

"I think so. Hot buttered rum plus M&Ms, right?"

"You're insane. And amazing. How did you know about all this?"

"I had a lovely chat with your mom yesterday."

No wonder she had been so inquisitive today.

"You called my mom?" she said softly.

"I hope that's not weird."

She bit her lip. No one had ever done anything like this for her before. "It's not weird. How did you have time to do all of this?" she asked.

"Who needs sleep when there's Christmas to be had?"

She tapped her chin with a finger. "Didn't you call it a soulless corporate holiday earlier this week?"

"Maybe somewhere along the way, I lost perspective. And I know you've been missing your mom and your traditions."

"This is wonderful. Thank you. Did you try this?" She handed him a mug of Santa's Revenge.

They clinked glasses, then sipped.

It was a little bit different than her usual batch—better, if she was being honest—but it still felt warm, familiar, and right. She couldn't have more than one, or she would be useless at baking and decorating later that evening.

"What do you think?"

"Honestly? Better than I expected," he said. There was a bit of cream on his lip, and she reached over to wipe it off. The movement brought them very close together, and a wave of heat washed over her.

She had made their perfect date awkward. He would probably be too afraid to cross that bridge with her again. And they only had tonight.

"There's one more thing," he added, taking her hand and guiding her into a living room.

She gasped. "Hold the fucking phone. Dance Your Face Off Four?"

He nodded.

"How did you even find this?" she asked.

"I had some time," he said.

"No, you didn't. You have a life-changing presentation to prepare for."

"I'm prepared," he said, but his eyes suggested otherwise.

Against her wishes, her heart was growing in her chest. This was problematic. This trip was supposed to be career-focused, no nonsense. She wasn't supposed to meet a man who washed her dishes and drove around all night to recreate a piece of home for her.

He shook his head. "Regardless, it's here. And I think tradition dictates a dance."

He handed her a controller, and she took it. It felt good, like being back five years ago when her mom could dance alongside her and, frankly, kick her ass. Even though she was thousands of miles away, this moment felt like home.

"I hope you're warmed up," she said, dropping her Liza Manelli wig on a chair.

"You didn't strike me as the competitive type."

"I'm not. Except for this game."

She pulled her phone out and took some pictures. Just so she could remember it always, exactly as it had been. She caught Leo in the last frame, eyes glimmering with Christmas lights and hands shoved into his boot-cut jeans.

She sent a couple pictures to her mom, who responded almost immediately.

Mom: Don't have too many Santa's
Revenges or your gingerbread house will
look like an abandoned asylum. Love
you xoxo

Leo had basically already met her mom. How strange.

"Shall we?" she asked in an attempt to ignore whatever emotional warfare was going on inside.

"I'm ready," Leo said. There was a peculiar expression on his face. Wistfulness, maybe? She might be imagining things. The Santa's Revenge was coursing through her veins after one measly sip.

She expertly flicked through the video game menu to the traditional songs and picked the first one.

"Santa's Sleighin'" blasted through the intimidating-looking soundbar, and Leo and Emma began to dance side by side, following the instructions that whizzed by at lightning speed.

Leo followed along beside her, better at it than he had any right to be. Had he practiced? She couldn't stop watching him out of the corner of her eye, and she nearly missed a couple of moves even though she knew all these songs by heart.

When the song ended, they were both out of breath.

"That used to be easier," she said. Not to mention she wasn't wearing the right bra for it.

God, it was hot in here. Especially with the fireplace on.

Without stopping to think, she stripped her sweater off and stood there in her bra and jeans.

Leo's gaze zeroed in on her chest, then snapped back to the TV. It looked like his grip tightened on his controller, and he cleared his throat.

"Another?" he asked, looking very determinedly at the screen.

"Aren't you hot?" she asked.

"A little," he admitted.

"I'll feel more comfortable if you're shirtless too. Your Highness," she added cheekily.

He considered for a moment, then stripped his sweater off. The candlelight contouring his abs was extremely distracting. Desire bloomed in her, hot and fast, like the evening primrose that opened at night in their garden back home.

"Loser of the next song loses their pants," she announced. The Santa's Revenge was making her bold. She raised an eyebrow, daring him to refute her.

"Deal. I hope you're not attached to yours because you're going to lose," he said.

"We'll see," she said.

They danced to the next song. He lost, and his pants slid down over muscular thighs and dropped to the floor.

"Again?" he asked, looking awfully cocky for someone who was down to a pair of silk boxers.

"Again."

They paused for another sip. Her guard had dropped so low it was probably somewhere in the basement.

They danced again, and her movements were getting less sharp. Her ass was sweating. At least he was sweating too.

The song ended, and Leo won.

Emma made a show of unbuttoning her jeans and sliding them off.

If Lola knew about this, her scream would be audible from Antarctica.

He was standing closer to her now. There was a hunger in his eyes.

"One more?" he asked, trailing his fingertips down the back of her arm.

Goosebumps developed despite the heat in the air.

"One more."

Time was running short. She needed to knock this song out of the park and figure out what was happening next. The kitchen awaited, and she really needed to get to work. Her entire future hung in the balance. But for some reason, she could only focus on Leo and the beads of sweat forming on his lower back.

His biceps bulged, and his deltoids rippled with strength as he followed the TV. Halfway through, the controller slipped through Emma's sweaty hand and bounced onto the rug. She bent to pick it up, and Leo's hand grazed her ass.

It was all she could do to not throw everything to the side and leap on him. She stopped trying so hard, flailing her arms at the wrong time and watching Leo even more intently.

"Don't throw the game, Emma," he said, nodding at the screen.

"I don't know what you're talking about."

The song ended, and the score tallied on-screen. Leo won.

Emma let her controller fall again, and she slowly and deliberately unclasped her bra. The straps skated down her arms, and it fell to the rug with a muffled thump.

There was a response in Leo's boxers.

She stepped closer to him, trailing a hand down his arm.

It didn't matter that it didn't make sense. It didn't matter that she was setting herself up for heartbreak, or that they might never see each other again after tomorrow night. For now, this was enough.

They looked at each other, and time stretched and

slowed like they were passing through some kind of personal wormhole. Every heartbeat was audible, and every part of her body screamed at her.

Now.

She wound her arms around his neck and pressed her mouth to his. He pulled her tightly against his chest and fisted a hand in her hair, kissing her deeply.

It stole the breath from her. All she could feel was Leo and heat. The slide of his damp skin along her nipples, the soft bite on her bottom lip that tore a moan from her throat. Even this was too far apart.

She shifted, and he pulled back.

"Are you sure this is okay?" His eyes searched hers.

"Yes," she said, then dove back in.

Christmas music still played in the background. Her body physically ached for his, delighting in the feel of strength and power and being held.

It had been so long since someone held her.

He reached around and grabbed her ass, lifting her until she wrapped her legs around his waist. The friction of his silk boxers against her underwear was too much. His erection was rock-hard and pressing into her belly button.

He carried her across the room and muscled a door open. She caught a glimpse of a regal-looking bed frame before he tossed her back onto a pile of pillows.

He took a second to look at her, and she automatically moved to cover herself.

"Don't," he commanded. "I want to see you."

Her hands fell helplessly to her sides, and he took in every bit of her frame before he came back to her mouth, kissing her tenderly.

His mouth was soft, his tongue warm and gentle as they explored each other.

She was probably sweating all over his comforter. Maybe she even smelled. But for once, she didn't care.

His hand glided down her torso and stopped at her underwear. He teased her through the cotton, stroking with strong and capable fingers.

Impatient, she slid her underwear off and flung it to lands unknown. She opened her legs wide, silently begging him to take her, to fill her.

He dipped his head to her nipples, and he sucked on them and blew. A shiver ripped through her. Her body went rigid under his touch, and she clawed at his back. It was a good thing she had to keep her nails short for the bakery.

She groped for the waistband of his boxers, but his hand wrapped around hers.

"I'm not done."

His head ducked between her legs, and he kissed her thighs tenderly, like she was a Michelin-star meal he was savoring every bit of.

A finger slipped gently inside her, and her back arched. Her teeth clamped down on the inside of her cheek, sending a jolt of pain that blended confusingly with the pleasure rippling through her. She hadn't been touched for a year, maybe longer. But her body responded like it had been primed and ready since the first moment she laid eyes on Leo.

His tongue joined the fray, every breath and stroke so precisely placed it was like he had taken a PhD-level course. In seconds, she was trembling, rigid with the sensations rising in her. She was completely at his mercy, powerless against his deft fingers and clever tongue.

"Breathe, Emma," he said between her legs, and she exhaled in a whoosh.

Almost in response, an orgasm ripped through her so

fiercely that her vision dimmed a little at the edges. She gripped his fingers tightly enough that they might snap right off. That would be a challenge to explain to the royal physician.

Dylan had never been one for oral sex. He had been a clumsy lover even at the best time, fumbling around in her pants for maybe ten seconds before rubbing his erection on her.

But this. This wasn't something she even knew was possible. Intimacy was so rarely on her radar, thanks to the crippling fatigue from her schedule of working and caretaking, an endless waltz that left her incapable of almost anything else.

But here, in Leo's bed, she could be someone else.

His face was half in shadow when he came back, hovering over her with a contented smile.

"Holy shit," she said.

"You're too kind," he said, kissing her just under her earlobe again. Her body responded with a fresh shower of sparks.

Finally, some feeling crept back into her limbs. She yanked at the hem of his boxers, and he planked above her to help.

His dick hovered between them, diamond-hard and irresistibly responsive to a gentle stroke from her fingers.

Overcome again, she rolled Leo onto his back and climbed on top of him. If this was their only moment, she would make sure he thought about it every night for the rest of his life.

She took him into her mouth, sliding as far back as she could manage without gagging. Throwing up on a prince's dick was not an experience she needed.

She pulled back and licked and stroked, swirling her tongue around his head before plunging him back in again.

His breath came in short gasps, and he was rigid beneath her.

She summoned every blowjob tip she had ever read and channeled all that energy into blowing his damn mind.

The power was intoxicating.

Within a couple minutes, he pulled her off him, and she leaned back on her knees.

"Condom?" she asked.

He rolled onto his side and rifled through his nightstand until he found one. She rolled it onto him slowly, deliberately.

She started to turn around to take him reverse cowgirl style so she wouldn't have the vulnerability of staring into his eyes, but he stopped her. She lifted her hips, and he lowered her onto him.

A sigh burst from both of them.

Her muscles stretched to accommodate him, and she raised and lowered herself slowly. But her knees weren't working right.

In a flash, he flipped her onto her back, still inside her.

His earthy brown eyes stared into her very soul as he pushed deeper, until she was certain he was ramming into an internal organ. Were vaginal extensions a thing?

He pumped gently, and the muted lights from the other room silhouetted him. He was impossibly beautiful, almost hard to look at.

But she couldn't look away. There was a tenderness in his eyes and in the way he cradled her head in his hand.

He leaned forward to kiss her, and a vortex of sensations and emotions swirled inside her. Fuck. She was definitely catching feelings for him.

And how could she not? They fit together like they had been specifically designed for each other, like every moment in their lives had led up to this one, in this castle, during the most magical time of the year.

She was screwed. But as he thrust, her mind quieted. She let the worries go and instead embraced the exhilaration of his rough hands on her, his powerful body surrounding her, making her feel so safe.

Another orgasm was rising, hot and fierce and as unstoppable as the sunrise. He must have sensed it because he went faster, bringing a hand to her to drive her ever closer.

His gaze burned into her, and they watched each other as they crashed over the peak together.

Finally, he released, twitching and pulsing inside her. His arms shook, and he partially collapsed onto her.

She held him like they were lovers of twenty years, and he rested his cheek against her breasts. Her hand went automatically to his hair, and she stroked it. It smelled like expensive shampoo—pears with a hint of sandalwood.

They stayed like that for a while, until their breathing returned to normal. He slipped out of her and rolled away, only to gather her into his chest and hold her there.

She would remember the sound of his heartbeat forever. She focused on the pulse of it beneath her cheek, the red-and-green lights casting a sheen on his damp skin. The feel of his fingertips resting on her hip.

How was she ever going to recover from this? And go back to New York like nothing had happened?

She could see everything as clear as if it was already happening. Birthday cheesecakes, family dinners with Ruby, mountain hikes with Cooper. A baby girl with Leo's dark eyes.

She could *not* be thinking this way, especially not about someone she had known for barely more than a week. This was insanity. Her brain needed to shut the fuck up, and she needed to get back to work before she ruined both their lives.

"I need to get to the kitchen," she said, voice barely more than a whisper.

His grip tightened on her. "No."

She slithered out of his grip. "I have to. Thank you for everything. This was the most perfect date I've ever had. I just wish it could last longer."

Forever, even.

He caught her hand. "Will I see you tomorrow?"

"Won't you be volunteering?"

"Not all night."

"Tomorrow, then."

He pulled her in for a last kiss, and she threw her clothes on and scurried away before she ruined everything.

CHAPTER TWENTY-EIGHT

LEO

Leo lay in the dark, staring at the Christmas lights shimmering on his ceiling.

His sheets still smelled like her, and her absence from his arms was like a vacuum.

This was a problem. He had never intended to get entangled with Emma. A week ago, he had been laser-focused on the community project, utterly certain of his path forward.

But now his priorities were muddied. He couldn't stop thinking about Emma. The twitch of her rosy lips when she smiled at one of his dumb jokes. Her waterfall of hair swinging around as she danced. The warmth in her green eyes when she talked about her mom. And the fact that she would be going home after the gala.

He was panicky at the very thought. Their connection had been so instantaneous, it stole his breath. They fit together like perfectly planed wooden joists placed by a master carpenter.

But she wasn't his.

His mother would never allow him to date an American. That had been the refrain in this house for his entire life.

But suddenly, he couldn't care less what she thought. Why did she get to tell him how to live his life? He was a grown man, and he would love whoever he wanted to.

Wait, what the fuck? Love? Why was that word even in his vocabulary? He had barely known Emma for more than a week. It was impossible.

But in that week, she had saved his life. Saved his sister. And wound her way into his heart with that irresistible smile and gentle fortitude.

Whatever was going on with Emma—whether it was love or just lust—it wasn't worth throwing away over some medieval idea about mixing blood.

He couldn't let her leave. He wouldn't.

He leapt out of bed like he was about to rush off and tell her all this. But he stopped with a hand on the doorknob.

Her dream. He hadn't ever been part of it. What was he going to do, demand that she uproot her entire life and move to Lynoria? And besides, he had a duty to the people of this country. He couldn't leave. And she couldn't stay.

And beyond that, she was fiercely strong, so independent. Thriving even under insurmountable pressure that would have made him crumple in an instant. She deserved to have what she had worked for her entire life. He couldn't do anything to compromise her plan. Even if he shattered his own heart in the process.

It didn't matter what he was feeling. This was bigger than he was. But maybe he could do something to help her, something to take some of the pressure off.

He threw some clothes on and sent a text to Emma's mom.

———

THREE HOURS LATER, HE SLUNK DOWN THE HALL TO THE kitchen. His parents had retired to their rooms, and most of the staff had finished their shifts and gone to bed.

Emma probably didn't need his help, and maybe she wouldn't even want him there. But he couldn't stand the thought of her all alone in the kitchen, slaving away with piping bags and gingerbread.

He pressed an ear to the door and heard nothing. He bumped it open an inch and saw Emma looking frazzled, staring at giant pieces of gingerbread on the island in front of her.

"Hey," he whispered, and she jumped. Flour dusted her cheek.

"All clear?" he asked.

She surveyed the kitchen and nodded. Her expression was still stormy, but it seemed to have softened a bit.

"What's wrong?" He sidled up next to her. She was like a radiant heater, exuding warmth. And stress.

"There's something wrong with my icing," she blurted. "It's not stabilizing enough to hold the big pieces. It's going to fall apart in the middle of the dinner, and your mom will never give me the second half of the money, and then I won't be able to afford my mom's medication and I'll have to run Maya's business for five more years. I'll never escape."

He took her by both arms and steered her away from the kitchen island.

"Take a deep breath. Now take another one," he said when she complied. "We're going to figure this out together. Are you sure the problem is the frosting?"

Emma waved a hand at a miniature version of the castle sitting on the drying rack. "It worked on the cardboard version."

"What if we make some supports to hold the pieces in place?"

"Supports? What kind of supports? I don't have time to measure and bake something that might not even turn out."

"No. Like wooden supports."

Emma bit her lip. "They're not edible. It's cheating."

He leaned closer to her. "Who in their right mind is going to dismantle this masterpiece? No one is going to eat this. It's too beautiful. That's why you made all the tarts and pastries and chocolates. No one will know. And no one would care."

She seemed to make up her mind. "Okay. How do we do it?"

"Let me get my tools." He kissed her on the cheek and hustled to his workshop.

Hours later, a partially constructed gingerbread castle stood before them. They had left it in pieces so it could fit through the door, but it was now considerably more stable. The walls and gatehouse stood sentry, waiting to surround the castle. The turrets were shaped, the roofs were affixed. Emma had insisted on obscuring the wooden supports with frosting—just in case.

"What now?" Leo asked.

Emma took a deep breath. "The pipework and decorating. Then the croquembouche tomorrow. It's going to take all night."

"I'll be here. I'm going to help you. We've got this."

"I've seen your handwriting. Put the piping bag down," she fired in warning.

He backed away with his hands in the air.

"I still can't believe you made this," he said, inspecting a curved piece of gingerbread that had candy glass windows. "How?"

"That's nothing. Check this one out." She pointed to another piece.

She had somehow exactly recreated the stained glass dome in the solarium. It was breathtaking.

"This is incredible. *You're* incredible."

"Thank you. And thank you for your help with the supports."

He brushed a hair off her face. He longed to kiss her, to convince her that everything was going to be okay. But that wasn't what she needed right now.

A survey of the kitchen revealed a sink full of dishes. "I think I figured out how I can help."

Hours passed while Emma decorated and he washed and dried dishes, minded the timer on the mixer for the royal icing, and gave ample hand massages. He also snuck out for provisions, including snacks and a Bluetooth speaker to play Christmas music.

They worked mostly in silence except for occasional instructions, and he watched her out of the corner of his eye.

Her lines were machine-straight. She hand-painted edible beads, piped red-and-green wreaths and garlands, accented each faux brick. Macarons made a dazzling roof for the turrets. She airbrushed, dusted with icing sugar, cut, and adjusted.

It was amazing to watch her work. She was so focused, and every movement seemed so natural. Like she was a human 3D printer, reaching inside herself for some cosmic directions to sculpt the most perfect gingerbread castle. It looked like it had taken years to make, not a week.

Finally, she set the piping bag down and surveyed her work. The sun was starting to creep up outside the window, sending a rosy hue into the midnight blue sky.

"I should go," he said, furrowing his brow. The staff would be up any minute to prepare breakfast. "How can I help?"

Emma shook her head. "Maya and some staff are supposed to come help me move the gingerbread pieces to the ballroom. I just have to work on the croquembouche in my apartment. Thank you. Seriously."

She grabbed him by the lapel to kiss him, then released him. "Now go. Before you get us both in trouble."

All of a sudden, time seemed very fleeting. Tomorrow morning, Emma would be on a plane to New York. She would be gone. And Lynoria would suddenly feel very empty.

It was best that he keep himself busy today. But he would see her tonight, even if he had to skip out early from the community kitchen.

It could be the last time he ever saw her.

CHAPTER TWENTY-NINE

EMMA

EMMA CHECKED HER HAIR SURREPTITIOUSLY IN A GILDED mirror by the gingerbread table in the ballroom. A string quartet in the corner was tuning, and smells of a magnificent feast were in the air. Round tables with golden charger plates and dramatic rose centerpieces were clustered toward the back.

The castle was exquisitely festive.

But if she were being honest, no part of the ball was as regal as the gingerbread castle. Against all odds and in a kitchen that ran on Celsius, the castle had come together. Nothing crumbled or collapsed. And it was—by far—the most magnificent thing she had ever made. All the castle staff had oohed and aahed over it as they helped Emma transport it to the ballroom.

Tarts, pastries, and cupcakes made up the grounds. And with the addition of the croquembouche Christmas tree in the nonpareil courtyard, it was as close to perfect as she could make it.

Guests would be arriving any moment. The royal family had provided her and Maya with black-and-gold chef's coats to wear, but Maya had disappeared in hers. She had looked teary-eyed all morning, so apparently things were not going to end well with Prince John. It figured.

The doors opened, and Emma straightened up. It was the queen.

Her anxiety spiked to eleven, and she held her breath as the queen approached.

Emma curtsied, and the queen greeted her with a casual "Miss Clark."

Slowly, the woman circled Emma's creation. She bent to inspect the tiny petals on an apple tart and the macaron-dotted pathway down to the greenhouse made of candy glass.

An eternity passed as she examined every part of it—pausing extra long on the stained glass solarium dome. Would it meet her expectations?

Finally, she clasped her hands in front of her.

"This is lovely. Beatrice will see that you receive the second half of your payment."

Relief flooded Emma so instantaneously that her knees almost collapsed.

"Thank you, Your Majesty. This project was fun. Stressful, but fun."

The queen looked surprised at her description, and the corners of her mouth twitched.

"Perhaps we'll collaborate again someday."

Emma nodded and curtsied again as the queen walked away.

Holy shit. She had done it. The money was hers. Now all she had to do was man the table and enjoy the party. She could probably even sneak a drink or a plate of food from a server.

This money was about to change everything. Her mom

could stay on her medication. She could tell Maya to kiss her ass on New Year's Eve. Or maybe she should wait until she lined up a couple of freelance social media gigs. Their following had increased by at least a third since their trip to Lynoria, and the video Emma had just posted of the gingerbread castle was already up to twenty-five thousand views.

Everything was perfectly on track. She should be euphoric, shouting from the rafters. But instead, there was a dark cloud inside her. In a matter of hours, she and Cooper would be on a train to Barcelona, then a plane to New York. And Leo would still be here, fighting for his dream.

And she probably wouldn't even see him before she left. He was busy with the community kitchen, serving his people as always.

Did he even care that she was leaving? The way he had made love to her the night before didn't feel like a casual, friendly thing. He had worshipped her, savoring every inch of her flesh like she was a gift he was unwrapping.

Shit. His gift. She had almost forgotten. She had baked a cheesecake for his birthday and left it in her fridge. She'd have to find a way to sneak it to his room without the queen seeing her.

A pang hit her heart. She would miss his birthday. It shouldn't matter, but for some reason, it did.

The doors opened again, and guests started filtering in. Ruby ran over to gawk at the castle, and Emma slid her an espresso croissant she had made just for her. A dozen more were in the freezer per the queen's request.

A couple members of the press had slunk in and were taking pictures. One approached her and held out her hand.

"Miss Farrell?"

"Clark. Emma Clark."

"Oh, great. I'm Sidney Mukherjee from *Food Magazine*."

That name was familiar. The nerves were back. Emma held her breath and fought the sudden strange urge to curtsy.

"It's wonderful to meet you. I love your travel pieces. The mochi ice cream feature you did in June? Inspired."

Sidney smiled and brushed her dark hair away from her face. "Thank you so much. Do you mind if I ask you a few questions? And take some pictures. I'll be honest, I've never seen a gingerbread on this scale."

They talked for forty minutes as the gala commenced. Maya was nowhere to be found, so Emma never bothered to mention her. She didn't deserve even an ounce of credit.

By the time Sidney left, Emma's heart was full. The magazine feature could change things for her.

Tons of people had stopped to take pictures with the castle, including the king and queen. Guests chattered excitedly, bending down to inspect the tiny windows and shingles.

For the next couple hours, people streamed up, asking questions about the castle and pulling cupcakes and macarons off the grounds. But no one touched the castle. It was just as well. Queen Eleanor would probably have them beheaded.

God, Emma was tired. Maybe she could catch a couple hours of sleep before her ride to the train station.

She searched the crowd continuously, hoping against hope that Leo would return. How selfish was she to hope that he left the food bank early?

A server slipped her a plate, and she ate it on the floor behind the gingerbread castle. Garlic mashed potatoes, cornish game hens, and buttery carrots. It was to die for. And within a year, she'd be able to afford better food for her and her mom. Her savings plan was complete. Now she just had to ride out the noncompete period and set up her own business. It was terrifying, but exhilarating.

"You did it," a familiar voice said behind her, breaking her out of her reflection.

"Leo," she said with what was probably a gigantic smile. "You made it."

He must have slunk through the back door behind the dessert table. He was dressed in jeans and a flannel, but he was sexier than any of the tuxedo-clad men in the ballroom.

"I told you I would. Emma, this is incredible. True art. Your mom must be so proud."

"I think she is," she said with a smile. They had video chatted earlier and Emma'd had to mute her exclamations as they echoed in the ballroom.

Leo glanced past her, nodded at someone across the room, and held out his hand.

She looked at him. What was he doing?

"You've been paid, right?" he asked.

She nodded. A wire transfer with the other half of the money and a sizable tip was pending.

"So dance with me."

He turned and made eye contact with the conductor. The string quartet started playing "Fade Into Me," and goosebumps raced up and down her arms.

"I can't. Your mom—"

"She wouldn't dare say no to the shelter. She'd have to have a lump of coal for a heart. Dance with me. Please."

There were a million reasons why she shouldn't. She didn't want to jeopardize his plans or piss off the queen. And yet another part of her—the much bigger part—wanted nothing more than to be enveloped in his arms just one more time.

"Outside," she said with a glance over her shoulder. The queen was chatting with Beatrice at a cocktail table.

He pulled her through the door behind them. Their footsteps echoed in a hallway she'd never been in. It was dark, and his hand was warm around hers. Together they passed through a doorway and the foyer.

The orchestra was still audible from the courtyard. She shivered, and Leo pulled her close. Her cheek pressed against his chest, and she breathed in the sharp mountain air. They swayed to the music, a sea of unspoken feelings swelling between them. The night was almost perfectly still, like the world was holding its breath.

It was so profoundly unfair that this wasn't the first chapter in their happily ever after. Tomorrow she would be on a plane to New York, and the distance would break whatever hope she had left for a future with him. Conversations would slow to a crawl, and Leo would forget about her. Someday he'd fall in love with someone else, and she'd have to read tabloid headlines about it.

She lifted her head to look at him. His expression was cloudy too. Was he feeling the same?

"Leopold." A sudden steely voice cut across the courtyard like the crack of a whip.

Emma and Leo sprang apart.

Oh, shit.

CHAPTER THIRTY

LEO

"You lied to me." His mother approached with one shaking finger pointed in his direction. "You said there was nothing going on, yet here you are. Ready to throw away your future. It's bad enough that you showed up late to the most important ball of your entire life. But then you had to dance with the help in dirty street clothes."

His temper flared.

"Emma is so much more than the 'help.' Need I remind you that this country was built by 'the help.'"

The audacity of his mother to even speak about the group of tireless workers who took care of everything in this stupid household on a daily basis. Every house manager worked ten times harder than anyone in the royal family, every single day.

The queen's backbone was ramrod-straight, and she seemed taller than she actually was. "She's a commoner, Leo. Not even European, and from a low-class family. I thought you were smarter than this."

Emma shrank behind him. His mother spoke like Emma wasn't even there, like she wasn't even a *person*.

His project proposal was in desperate danger. Pissing off his mom was a surefire way to get the whole thing canned. He should shut his mouth and apologize for the subterfuge for the sake of the kingdom, but something about the criticism of Emma had sparked a powder keg.

"Why does it matter who her family is?" His voice shook.

"Leo, you are a member of the royal family. You can't date just anyone. You know this. You've always known this."

He reached around and grabbed Emma's hand. "In case you've forgotten, I'm not the heir. It doesn't matter if I marry a Swedish princess or a bounty hunter from Alabama. I'm almost thirty-three years old. You don't get to tell me who I can and can't date. Why don't you focus on something more important? You're in a position to do so much good for our country. And yet, you put your entire focus on throwing these elaborate balls while our people are starving only a kilometer away." He pointed at the village.

She inhaled sharply. "How dare you."

There was a ringing silence, like he had just lobbed a grenade across the courtyard.

He had gone too far. He was going to pay for those words.

"We're here to serve the community, Mother," he said firmly.

"No," she said. "We're here to rule them. Beatrice, put a stop payment on Miss Clark's wire transfer. The crown doesn't work with liars."

Emma gasped, and something in him collapsed. He had done what he swore he would never do. He had irrevocably compromised her timeline and ruined her chance to quit her job. All because he couldn't shut his mouth.

The queen walked off, fury emanating from her like a cloak of darkness.

Fuck.

"Emma, I'm so sorry."

Tears streaked down her face, and he brushed them away. He pulled her in tightly. There was no point in hiding anymore. The secret was out, and they were both about to face the consequences.

"I'll get you the money." He'd have to sacrifice the next trust payout that he usually used for community work. But he had royally screwed things up for Emma. He needed to make it right.

She shook her head fervently. Her eyes were glazed, and the color had drained from her cheeks. "I don't want to take money from a family who can speak about people like that." She thrust a finger in the direction of his mother's retreating back. "Like I'm nothing, just because of where I was born. If she had any idea what my mother went through, what I went through. We have clawed our way to where we are with grit and determination. I'm not nothing. I am a *damn* good baker."

She straightened up suddenly and whirled around. "I should destroy it."

"No," he said quickly.

She stopped in her tracks.

"Let me talk to her," he said. "I've dealt with her my entire life. I can convince her to return the money to you. She just needs a day to cool off, and to bask in compliments about her wretched ball from the lords and ladies."

"She doesn't deserve to get away with treating me like I'm some kind of second-class citizen, Leo." Danger was in her voice.

"I know. But if you do this, the repercussions could affect you for years. Your professional reputation. Your future business. I can fix this. Just give me a chance."

Emma buried her hands in her hair and turned away from him with a frustrated groan. "I need to pack."

Relief flooded him. At least he had stopped her from making a huge mistake. He would find a way to fix the situation, no matter what it took. Emma wouldn't suffer because of his own selfish actions.

"I let myself believe it was almost over," Emma muttered as she trudged across the courtyard. "All the double shifts, running the entire business for a pauper's salary, Maya taking credit for everything I've done. I was so close to making a better life for my mom. Now I'm right back at square one."

"We will figure this out. I swear to you."

They climbed up the stone steps to the gatehouse apartment and opened the door.

There was a scream and a sudden flurry of movement in the dark room. Leo shoved Emma behind him and picked up the nearest object—a dirty baking sheet. Emma flicked the lights on to reveal Ruby, hair a mess and dress crooked, and a friend of hers he recognized from her clarinet lessons in a similar state of undress.

A shockwave flooded his whole body, and he froze.

Ruby liked girls?

"Oh, you must be Sammy," Emma said. "It's nice to meet you."

What the hell?

Sammy waved sheepishly, and Ruby pulled her out of the room. "Sorry, Emma. We thought you'd be gone all night. See you later."

Sammy and Ruby disappeared down the stairs.

"Awkward," Emma said with a watery smile.

Leo was still frozen in place, body pulsating with numbness.

"Are you okay?" she asked after a minute.

"You knew my sister was gay and you didn't tell me?"

"Uh—"

"How could she keep this from me? How could *you* keep this from me?"

Emma's eyebrows contracted. "It wasn't my secret to tell, Leo."

He turned to face the wall, hands shaking. He was closer to Ruby than any other member of his family. He couldn't care less that she was gay. Or bi. He didn't know the specifics. But how could his own sister have concealed something that was so deeply foundational to who she was as a person? And yet she trusted Emma, whom she had barely known more than a week?

"Does she think I'm some kind of bigot?" he spat.

"No," Emma said quickly. "I don't think it's that at all. I can't speak for her, but I think she might be worried about your mom finding out."

"It's not like I would tell her. We only talk about all the ways that I'm failing my family and my country."

Emma's eyes watered, and she turned away from him. She scanned the room, which was still covered in dirty baking sheets and bowls, and silence fell. A minute crawled by. Suddenly, her hands clenched into fists at her side, and her shoulders straightened.

"She's not going to get away with this."

"Emma, wait."

Before he could stop her, she dashed through the door and down the stairs toward the castle.

CHAPTER THIRTY-ONE

EMMA

"Emma, please. Think about this. If you do this, there's no going back." Leo's voice shook as she pushed the castle doors open.

Fury was coursing through her veins. "I've spent my entire life thinking before acting. And you know where it's gotten me? Trapped in a hole I can't dig myself out of. I'm at the mercy of Maya and our landlord and the freakin' health insurance companies who are canceling my mom's coverage of her medication. Which now I won't be able to afford."

She stopped next to the fireplace in the foyer and grabbed a fire poker from the basket of tools, then strode back into the hallway to a linen closet by the kitchen. Leo followed in her wake.

"Your mother has all the privilege in the world, and she uses it to make people fear her. Ruby's afraid to be honest about who she is. She's made you feel unloved for your entire life."

She pulled out a stack of tablecloths, then made a detour to the kitchen for a bottle of champagne and a stack of food storage containers. Then she was off again, marching toward the ballroom.

"And to top it all off, she didn't even pay for the fucking castle. We don't let customers get away with that in the city. If they don't pay, they don't get their product."

He bit his lip. "Are you—"

"Yes. This is Brooklyn justice."

She wasn't going to wait around for Leo to negotiate. His mother was an asshole iceberg, and she wouldn't be moved by logic or a plea from the child she treated like dirt. There was no chance Emma would ever see the second half of the payment.

She kicked the doors open, allowing light and music to spill into the foyer. She beelined for the dessert table, where a small crowd had gathered. The queen was standing in front of it, pointing at the intricate stained glass windows.

"Oh, is that the pastry chef? Did you do all this?" a fancy-looking lady in an emerald-green ball gown asked when Emma slid behind the table. She bowed when she noticed Leo.

"Yes, I did," Emma said brightly as she unfurled the tablecloths and laid them under the table.

Leo's mother looked very startled to see her. Her nostrils flared like a dragon's.

"It's magnificent. You're very talented," the fancy lady said.

"That's so kind of you. Thanks so much," Emma said, ripping the foil and cage off the bottle of champagne. She propped the bottle against her leg and wiggled the cork. "You should try the raspberry tart. Now."

"Uh—oh. Maybe I will." The Duchess plucked a tart from the table.

"Anyone else? I suggest grabbing them now because, unfortunately, the crown reneged on payment. So embarrassing, right?" she said as she stared dead into the queen's eyes. "As such, Crumb and Get It retains ownership of this project, and we'll be donating these baked goods."

The cork popped out of the bottle and flew across the room. The people who hadn't been staring before definitely were now.

Emma took a swig before holding the bottle out in front of her.

A dozen people scrambled to grab desserts, and a few more pulled out their phones and started filming.

"You wouldn't dare," the queen said with a voice that would curdle milk.

Emma leaned forward and made steady eye contact. "Watch me."

She swept the tarts and croissants into the food storage bins in the blink of an eye, then dumped champagne over the macaron courtyard.

"Merry Christmas, Your Majesty. Oh, and I fucked your son."

With that, she picked up the poker and smashed it into the gingerbread turret. The castle crumpled, chunks of gingerbread and sugar glass flying everywhere.

She brought the poker down again and again until it was nothing but crumbs.

"What the *hell* are you doing, Emma?" Maya, wearing a glittering black gown with a neckline cut to her navel, pushed through the crowd. "Your Majesty, I'm so sorry," she simpered to the queen. "Emma's not quite right mentally. You know it's her fault that her mom is disabled now."

Emma froze. A gasp rippled across the room.

"Get out." That was Leo.

Maya looked at him like he was a cockroach. "I'm sorry, who are you?"

"I'm the prince of the country you're currently trespassing in. Leave. Now."

"Hey, man," John began. Great, now the king-dipshit-to-be was here.

"Enough," the queen said. "All of you, out. Now. Guards—"

Maya raised a shaking finger and pointed it in Emma's direction. "You've embarrassed me for the last time. You're fired."

"Sounds great," Emma said in a strangled voice. "Good luck running the bakery on your own."

She marched toward the ballroom door, arms laden with food storage containers, but stopped next to a terrified-looking maid. "Gina, I'm so sorry about the mess. I tried to mitigate it with the tablecloths."

Gina shot a furtive look at the queen, then leaned forward. "Don't be. She deserves it."

Emma shot her a smile, then strode out through the foyer and out to the courtyard with her head held high. Leo jogged to catch up with her.

Panic was setting in. Everything had come crashing down in a matter of minutes. Her job and her healthcare were gone. She wasn't going to be able to afford rent, let alone her mother's medication. They were worse off than they had been before this horrible trip. If she had just kept her head down and done the work, avoided Leo, it would have been fine. But she'd lost control and ruined everything.

"Why did you do that? I told you I would handle it." His voice sliced like the tip of an arrow.

She whirled around. She didn't need his judgment. "I

did it because your mom's an asshole, Leo. I'm done being pushed around by assholes. I wish I had never come here." Her voice broke, and she ran up the gatehouse stairs to the apartment.

Leo didn't follow her. She would never see him again.

CHAPTER THIRTY-TWO

LEO

Leo stalked down the castle corridor with his laptop in hand. Fatigue clung to him like a winter coat. He hadn't slept a wink the night before and instead spent the night pacing his suite, marveling at how horrifically everything had spiraled out of control. Emma had left, and she hated him. By the time he had come to his senses and pounded on her apartment door, she and Cooper were already gone.

And of course his family wasn't about to console him. His sister had concealed who she really was. John was a certified wanker who had slept with the woman who degraded Emma. And his parents were probably on the brink of disowning him.

The community project was the only thing he had left. There were people counting on him. He couldn't let it die without trying.

The drawing room door squeaked as he opened it. He made half a mental note to grab the spray lubricant, then decided it wasn't his problem. He was greeted by the smell of sausage and a nasty look from his mother.

"I know you're angry at me," Leo said before his mother could speak. "But I need you to hear me."

"How—" the queen began.

"If any part of you has ever loved me, please listen to me now. This isn't about last night. This is about the people of our kingdom. They need us. They need *you*."

His parents exchanged a look, and he took the opportunity to open his laptop. A 3D picture of the new community center loaded, rotating on the screen. There were dozens of slides, but he had a feeling they weren't going to give him time to go through them. He needed to hit them with as much as possible, as quickly as possible.

"The domestic violence shelters in the city are woefully outdated. Peeling paint, flimsy doors, ancient wiring and plumbing. Women and children who are fleeing deserve to have a safe, welcoming space. Just like they deserve a new library, a community garden. A safe place to play. This village is our home, and we owe it to our citizens to invest in them. I have an architect, a contractor, a crew. All we need is the land and some support from the philanthropy fund."

"What land?" his mother asked icily.

"The lot off of Willow Street."

There was a pause.

The queen took a sip of tea and set the cup down. "We can't. Even if we wanted to, we can't."

"What do you mean, you can't? You're the monarch."

"The land is already under agreement, Leo."

"Under agreement? By whom?" he sputtered.

"A ski resort. We signed the documents last week. The lease starts in January. It'll do wonders for tourism. It'll bring a much-needed boost to the local economy. The village will benefit. More foot traffic to the restaurants, bookings at the inns."

Leo's mouth fell open. It couldn't be. The land was gone? This was worse than the worst-case scenario.

"We don't *need* another ski resort, Mother. You know what happened in Southbridge after the last resort was built. People—working-class people—got priced out of their own homes and had to leave in droves. Gentrification isn't going to help the village. Our people need our help. A shelter. A community garden. A library with books and toys from this century."

"The land is gone, Leopold. I need you to accept that." Her eyes were dark and cold, almost robotic.

His hands tightened into fists. This couldn't be happening. What now? Did he scout for a new location? Accept that the village was about to face its doom? Everything had hinged on that green space. Now they were on the cusp of destruction.

"Incidentally, since you're here," she continued, "your father and I do have something we need to discuss with you."

"It can wait," Leo said, picking up his laptop and storming off in the direction of the door.

"You'll want to hear this."

He stopped in his tracks. That didn't sound good.

"Your father and I have talked. Since you're unwilling to do what's required of you as a member of this family, we're cutting you off."

His heart dropped. He used his access to royal funds for repair work and community needs. He was the circumnavigator, bypassing things that could take weeks or months to repair or replace. If he lost access, it was their neighborhood that was going to suffer the most. Again.

He still had a trust, but it was structured to pay out only at the beginning of the month. He had investments, but nothing liquid. There had never been a need for a personal bank account.

In an instant, most of his money had been stripped away. He was powerless. And he hadn't even been allowed to make his presentation.

"Well, I guess it's time I moved out then. Merry Christmas."

He slammed the door behind him, then almost ran headlong into Ruby. Her hair was still sleep-tousled, and she yawned loudly.

"Watch where you're going, buttface," she said to him.

He took a second to breathe so he didn't snap at his baby sister.

"Why didn't you tell me?" Leo asked before he could think better of it.

Ruby's eyes darted left and right. "Not so loud."

"You don't trust me? You think I'm some kind of prejudiced asshole?" he asked.

"No, I know you marched in the Pride parade last year. It's not that."

"Okay, then what?"

She took a deep breath. "Telling you would make it real. And if I told you, then I have to tell the rest of them."

His anger deflated a centimeter.

"How do you think Mom's going to react when she finds out her precious princess likes girls? And what a scandal it's going to cause when the world finds out there's a gay princess in Lynoria?"

Leo stared at the drawing room door. Emma had been right. It was no wonder she didn't tell him. His mother had just disowned him merely for having a connection with an American. What would she do to her favorite child for not fitting the mold? He rubbed his temples.

"I'm sorry, kid. I understand why you didn't say anything. And I'm sorry you've been struggling with this secret." He turned to her and grabbed both her hands. "I love you, and I'm so proud of you for embracing who you are. The road ahead might be...challenging, but you'll always have me. No matter what."

Ruby's lip quivered, and she ran in for a hug. He squeezed her tight, wishing he could bottle up this moment while she was still his baby sister. Soon, she'd be in college an ocean away.

"And when or if you do decide to tell them, I'll be there."

"Thank you. You better not have been mean to Emma," Ruby said when she pulled back. "She only found out about it by accident. I blabbed while I was drunk."

Fuck.

"I...messed things up with Emma," he muttered. "Oh, and I'm moving out."

"What?" she looked confused.

"It's time. I'm leaving."

She narrowed her eyes. "Does this have something to do with Emma?"

"No. Well, inadvertently."

Ruby straightened. "Let me guess. Mom flipped out on you for what happened at the ball last night because now that's all anyone wants to talk about instead of what an amazing and royal triumph her ball was."

"Are the press really talking about it?"

She pulled out her phone and then scrolled through a series of videos of the altercation at the ball.

"Worse. It's all over TikTok. No wonder she's pissed."

Fuck. It was only a matter of time before someone identified Emma. Then her reputation really might be ruined.

"So you're really leaving?" Ruby asked.

"Yes."

"But what about Thursdays? Who's going to watch *Step-wives of Seacacus* with me?" Her voice was small.

"I'll still come. Or you can visit me at my new place."

"Which is where?" she asked.

"Great question. Haven't figured that out yet."

He had better check in with Sal to see if he could stay there for a few days.

"So you didn't get to make your pitch?" She gestured at his laptop.

Leo sighed. "It didn't matter. They're leasing the land to a ski resort."

The thought twisted his stomach. People were going to suffer, and it was largely his fault.

"Maybe I could bring it up to them?"

He shook his head. "This isn't your fight. I'll find a way."

"I know you will."

She gave him another hug.

"Your Christmas gift is in my room under the tree," he told her. "I need to go."

"Where are you going?"

"I don't know, but I can't...be here. I love you, kid."

"Love you back."

With a final squeeze, he released her and went back to his room.

The Christmas lights were still up, a dizzyingly cheerful display for such a melancholy morning.

Where could he go from here? He had squandered an opportunity to make a real difference in the lives of people in this community.

But he didn't regret dancing with Emma. Making love to Emma. He had seen firsthand what she knew to be true all along—his mother was immovable as marble. She never would have given Emma the money back.

He owed Emma a gigantic apology. And more than anything, he just wanted to see her again. Even if she slammed the door in his face.

With no real plan, he lugged a suitcase out of the closet and began checking flights.

CHAPTER THIRTY-THREE

EMMA

Everything was fucked.

Emma dragged her suitcase down the uneven sidewalk in Greenpoint. Even the tree roots were determined to ruin her day, tripping her up every couple of feet. Her body ached with fatigue and jet lag, and her eyes stung from crying. The couple hours of rest she'd had at the airport gate hadn't reinvigorated her.

She had torpedoed her career. Squandered her mom's best chance for a better future. And then Leo had scolded her. Against all odds, she was even worse off now than before she left.

Even Brooklyn matched her mood. Dirty snow was piled on every corner, and car horn blasts were everywhere as harried people crisscrossed the streets without waiting for pedestrian lights. It felt strangely alien after the small-town bustle of Hollybrook.

This was lower than low. She had taken a drill to rock bottom, mining straight to the hot, miserable core of the earth. No steady income. No health insurance. No money for food or heat. Merry freakin' Christmas.

And it was all her fault. She had almost fallen in love with a prince who lived thousands of miles away. She knew she should've stayed away from Leo. That's what she got for allowing herself to be distracted by a man. They weren't trustworthy. She was better off alone. Her mom needed her to be better, to do better. And now she had to go home and tell her she had lost her job and taken a crème brûlée torch to her future.

Tomorrow, there would be time to find a new way forward. But today, she was going to cry.

At least Cooper was still happy. His tail thumped back and forth, sweeping the curb they stood on.

They paused at an intersection. The woman next to her lifted her head and looked confused.

Emma offered a weak smile and turned away.

"Is—is this you?" The woman lifted her phone.

Emma tensed and moved her hand to her purse. Was this some new kind of scam? Distract people so a pickpocket could move in?

But no, it really was her. On TikTok. Screaming at the queen of Lynoria and smashing a gingerbread house. Great.

"Nope. But I'm sure that girl had a good reason," Emma said, then led Cooper across the street the second the light turned green.

Fuck.

Finally, she and the dog climbed the steps to her apartment. Back to reality. Her tiny apartment in Greenpoint with peeling paint, burned-out lightbulbs, and linoleum flooring that was so worn the subfloor was visible in some spots.

Cooper barged ahead into the living room.

"You're home!" Her mom's voice was like a salve.

Emma stepped inside and was greeted by glimmering

Christmas lights and the earthy warmth of a thousand meticulously kept house plants.

"Mom!" She released her suitcase and rushed into her mother's arms.

Lisa gave her a tight hug and rocked her like she hadn't since she was a little girl.

Emma pulled back and looked at her. She looked no worse for the wear—no drop in weight, no obvious bruises. At least there was one thing her trip hadn't ruined.

"What's wrong, sweetheart?"

"What do you mean?" Emma asked.

"You know I have a nose for drama. Something happened."

Emma paused and debated, but there was no point. Her mom always got the truth out of her eventually.

"I ruined everything."

The entire story came pouring out, from Leo's community plans to her sudden burst of feelings for Leo to the retaliation against the queen. Lisa sat there and listened until it was all on the table.

When it was over, she wheeled into the kitchen.

"Mom?" Emma asked. Was she immediately jumping into crisis mode?

The refrigerator opened, and Lisa came back. "I had a feeling we were going to need this. I kind of hoped we'd need it because you'd come home in love, but this works too."

A crisp bottle of champagne and some flutes rested in her lap.

"We're celebrating me getting fired?"

"We're celebrating your new freedom, sweetheart. I don't like to speak poorly of people. But that Maya was a real clown. I was this close to sourcing some dead mice to hide in her walls. I still might," Lisa muttered.

Her mom struggled with the bottle, and Emma took it from her. The cork popped out smoothly and instantly reminded her of her outburst not even twenty-four hours ago. Her eyes watered as she poured two glasses.

"This isn't the end, Emma. It's just a minor setback. We're going to be fine. And it's going to be hilarious to watch Maya try to run the business without you. I might make popcorn and park myself across the street tomorrow morning."

At least something good had come from her destroying her own life.

"And for what it's worth, I have a feeling you'll see Leo again," Lisa said softly.

"I don't even know if I want to. He couldn't understand why I did what I did."

And then there was the fact that her outburst had almost certainly endangered his project. She couldn't see outside of her own rage during the incident, and now Holly-brook could pay the price for her gingerbread-smashing home run.

Lisa shook her head. "I think he understands, sweet-heart. He probably just wanted to help you and feels partially responsible. He made the choice to pursue you just as much as you did. If he's willing to give up at the first road-block, he's not the man for that project, and he's not the man for you."

Emma sighed. She wasn't ready to analyze whatever was going on with Leo. His birthday was tomorrow, which made her insides feel squiggly. But she wasn't about to send a Harry & David basket after how things had ended. Would he even find the cheesecake she had convinced Ruby to stash in his freezer?

"Enough about me," she said, dabbing the end of her sleeve under her eyes. "Tell me everything you've been up to while I was away. What's going on in the neighborhood? Did the Keefers finally get evicted?"

"Well," Lisa said, pulling a legal pad off the table next to her. "I have a list. First, I'm pretty sure that guy with the fedora two doors down is having an affair. I'm gathering evidence. But that's not even the worst part. You remember Fabian? I used to work with him."

Emma relaxed into her mother's recounting of the neighborhood gossip. She took a sip of champagne and paused. How the hell had they afforded champagne? On a whim, she entered the kitchen and opened the refrigerator. An astonishing amount of food greeted her—vegetables, fruit, even a nice cheese. Far more supplies than she had ordered before her trip. She opened the pantry next to find a couple boxes of pasta and a variety of canned goods. Her mouth dropped open.

"Mom?"

Lisa stopped her storytelling and looked up. "Yes, honey?"

"Were we reverse robbed?" She gestured at the pantry.

"Oh, you mean the food? No, sweetie. A couple neighbors brought over some gifts. Mind Mr. Smith's fruitcake though. It tastes like ass."

"They brought over sun-dried tomatoes and whole wheat penne?" Emma asked with a raised eyebrow.

"No. It was the strangest thing. We got a package in my name with a slow cooker and five thousand dollars' worth of gift cards to Wegmans."

Emma clutched the refrigerator handle for support. "What? It didn't say who it was from?"

Lisa shook her head. "I assumed it was a local church but maybe it was...someone else."

Emma's heart warmed against her wishes. There was no chance it was anyone but Leo. She didn't want to owe him anything. Someday, she would find a way to pay him back. Even though the price of groceries was getting wildly out of hand, she was an expert at stretching. Five thousand dollars would keep them for months. If her mom hadn't already blown it all on sun-dried tomatoes, anyway.

Maybe everything wasn't lost. Tomorrow was another day.

CHAPTER THIRTY-FOUR

EMMA

Emma awoke with a start to the sun shining through her bedroom window. Her heart went into overdrive, pumping like she was running up a mountain. She had overslept. No one had opened the bakery. She was in so much trouble.

Wait.

She was fired. She wasn't late for anything. The sobering fact calmed her down for a millisecond before a host of realizations set in.

Her plan was in motion even though she wasn't ready for it. Coverage would lapse on her health insurance at the end of the month, and paying a premium out of pocket was going to be one more thing eating into her savings. It was time to take on as many freelance projects as she could handle.

One year from now, if the location scouting and brand building went well, she could launch her custom order bakery. Even if the worst happened and everything fell through, at least cottage food laws would allow her to bake at home and start selling at farmers' markets until she could try again.

She'd had a business plan for five years. She knew the market and how to run a bakery, thanks to Maya's colossal neglect. Except for finances, she was as prepared as she could be.

So much was up in the air, out of her control. It felt impossible. It was going to be a long, lean year. But hopefully five years down the road, things would be significantly better. It wasn't going to be easy, especially in one of the biggest cities in the world and while being her mother's full-time caretaker, but it was possible.

Shit. And speaking of caretaking, now she had to let her mom's nurse go. At least that would be one less monthly expense.

She got out of bed and caught a glimpse of the calendar on her way to the bathroom. Her stomach lurched. Today was Leo's birthday.

Their last interaction had been disastrous. Everything felt unfinished. Was he able to make his proposal to his parents? Would the community get the project it so desperately needed? She wanted to reach out, but she was afraid to learn what damage she might have done.

Her feelings for him had been so sudden and so strong, like a comet streaking across the sky. They had flamed out before even figuring out where anything could go.

It was better to leave him in the past.

She popped her mom's door open. "You want to go for a walk after breakfast? I need to clear my head."

———

It was windy and bitterly cold outside as Emma pushed her mother's wheelchair down the sidewalk, Arizona and Cooper trotting on either side like security guards.

They were out for some fresh air—as fresh as the air ever got in Brooklyn, anyway—and Emma willed the walk to distract her.

"What about Baked by Emma?" her mom mused. "It's classic, straightforward."

"Eh," Emma said. They'd been throwing around potential business names for the last four blocks, but nothing had felt right.

"You don't sound super thrilled to be starting your own business," Lisa said.

"I am. I'm just...distracted."

"Are you sure there isn't some other reason? Maybe a six-foot-tall European reason?"

"What? No. That chapter's over. It just all feels a little overwhelming. That's all. I'm fine."

Arizona tugged hard, and Emma pulled to a stop, her heart in her throat. Was it another stroke? A cardiac event?

But no. She had just nearly walked them all out into traffic.

"You don't sound fine," her mom prompted.

"It's just a big adjustment. Crumb and Get It was my whole life for years."

"I noticed some buzz on their Instagram this morning saying they were closed," Lisa said smugly.

Several people had posted the dark storefront of the bakery on their social media. It gave Emma a quiet pleasure that Maya was having a hard time reopening.

"Good," Emma said firmly.

Her phone had positively blown up with texts and calls from Maya, alternating between threats and pleading with her to come back. Emma had finally blocked her, and it was like a grown-woman-sized weight had been lifted from her shoulders.

She was never going back. That much she knew. It was everything else that was still unknown.

"What about Big Apple Bakes?" Lisa offered.

"Ugh, no. Respectfully."

A man on the opposite curb was staring at them. An expensive-looking camera was slung around his neck. He looked at something on his phone, then looked back at them.

Instinctively, Emma turned and went the other way.

"Aren't we going to the park?" Lisa asked. She shook a bag of oats meant for the ducks.

"Did you see that guy?" Emma said in a low voice.

"The one with the weird goatee?"

"Yes. He was looking at us. I knew I should have brought the pepper spray."

"We have two gigantic dogs. We're fine," Lisa said, but there was a note of concern in her voice.

Emma glanced over her shoulder. The man hadn't crossed the street and was now walking parallel to them. Her heart rate ticked up, and Arizona looked at her.

The guy was looking at his phone, seemingly distracted.

They hit another intersection and turned right, back in the direction of home. She glanced over her shoulder when they were a few yards down. No one was behind her. She blew out a long, slow breath.

She was being crazy. They weren't being followed. It was probably some street photographer or a tourist.

Suddenly, the stranger ran out of the alleyway in front of them and shoved a video camera in her face.

"Emma! Are you dating Prince Leo of Lynoria?"

"What?" she sputtered. A wave of lightheadedness swept over her. The paparazzi had actually tracked her down. Leo said it was a possibility, but how did they even know who she was? It wasn't like she'd worn a name tag at the ball.

Oh, shit. Maybe the article in *Food Magazine*? Had it come out already?

Her mind ran a mile a minute. On the off chance that Leo's project wasn't already dead in the water, her stirring up rumors would destroy whatever chance he had left.

"No, I'm not," she said firmly.

"Move aside." There was a note of authority in Lisa's voice.

Arizona tugged them forward, and Emma tried to sidle around the man, but he simply walked backward in front of them.

"Sources say the prince was spotted with you several times during your visit. Are you dating long distance?" he asked.

She averted her gaze and reminded herself to take deep breaths. What was he going to do, follow them all the way back to her apartment?

"Are the rumors about the royal family true? Was there an infidelity scandal?" he asked.

Infidelity scandal? That was news to her. Though it wouldn't particularly surprise her if the queen had taken a lover. Hypocrites were always the loudest protesters.

"Are you the reason your own mother is permanently disabled?" The question hit her like a water balloon filled with acid.

She stopped in her tracks, and the man stared cockily at her. His camera snapped repeatedly.

Cooper barked at him, and he flinched.

"How *dare* you?" Lisa asked. She put her hands on the

arms of the wheelchair and tried to stand, but Emma gently pushed her back down.

Emma put a finger in his face. "If you don't get out of my face immediately, I will call the police."

He walked away without another word, smirking.

Her hands shook. How did he know about the stroke? How did he know *any* of this? There was no way Leo or Lola had sold her out.

Could it have been Maya?

They hustled home as quickly as they could. Worst brainstorming walk ever.

Lisa rattled off an incalculable string of insults on their way back until the door was closed behind them.

"I'm going to buy more pepper spray," she said as Emma steered her up the ramp.

"Not a bad idea," Emma mused.

They had only been inside for a few minutes when there was an aggressive knock on the door. They both jumped, and Cooper barked like a bomb had gone off.

Lisa glared. "If that's a reporter, I'll happily tell them where they can shove their camera."

"It's probably a package," Emma said, but there was a tingle of anxiety in her belly. "You know how Roger knocks like our door has personally offended him."

"Maybe we should just ignore it," Lisa said.

Emma retrieved her baseball bat and tiptoed to the door to peer through the peephole. Complete darkness greeted her.

Panic flared. The last time this happened it had been—

"Open up, girls. Daddy's home."

The oily, gravelly voice of her father was a sound she had never quite been able to eradicate from her brain.

Lisa gasped. Emma's hands went numb. He was supposed to be in prison for another five months. She kept tabs on him so that they were able to anticipate when he might come around.

He always wanted something. Usually it was money. It was the only thing that would make him leave, and a big part of the reason why they were in this mess.

This time, there was no money to pay him off with. And they couldn't afford to move anywhere else. They were trapped in this apartment, where he knew he could find them.

Cooper appeared at her side, growling softly.

"Leave now, or I'm calling the police," Emma said through the door.

Every cell in her body screamed at her to run—hide. Like she had as a little girl.

"You're gonna leave your pop out in the cold?" he said, softer this time.

"Leave, Don," Lisa said. There was a tip-tap of dog toenails, and Emma glanced over her shoulder. Arizona planted herself in front of her mom, back bristling.

"Li-li," Donald said, and the sound of her mom's discarded nickname curled Emma's toes. Her heart was in her throat. He wasn't going to leave. But the police would take their sweet time getting here for a simple trespasser. What the hell were they going to do?

Emma ducked into the bathroom and hammered on the shared wall. Maybe Bob was home. Silence greeted her from the other side.

She shot a look at her mom and mouthed "Call 9-1-1."

Lisa nodded and picked up her phone with shaking hands.

"We both know you're going to let me in," Don said on

the other side of the wall. "It's been a long time since I've seen my girls, and it's almost Christmas."

"The police are on their way," Emma called. Hopefully it was true.

There was a sigh on the other side of the door. "Six grand and I'll leave right now." His voice was flat but dripping with a hint of malice.

"No," Emma said firmly.

"I'm gonna give you one more chance to reconsider."

"Get the fuck away from this door before I shoot you through it." Her voice shook.

"Come on, sweetheart. You and I both know you were never the gun type."

"Things have changed."

But they hadn't. Even if she wanted a gun, they couldn't afford it.

"I know you've got the money. You're dating a prince. My little girl's gonna be a princess. I have a feeling we'll be spending more time together."

Emma's heart fell into her butt. Of all the complications to come from her entanglement with Leo, she had never even considered that her dad would hear the news in prison.

"I'm giving you to the count of three to reconsider," her dad called through the door. His voice was different now. Darker. The way it had been after one too many drinks.

She exchanged a panicked look with her mom, then hefted the baseball bat. Her hands trembled.

"One. Two."

Suddenly, something hit the door with enough force that it wobbled a little. Cooper barked, a booming warning that was promptly ignored.

"Let me in, Emma."

Smash. Another hit, and a grunt of exertion from the

other side. The wood had definitely bowed. Cracks were starting to appear on the surface near the knob.

Their door wasn't going to hold. She retreated farther into the apartment, putting herself between her mom and the door. Adrenaline was firing in her veins, but she had nowhere to go. They couldn't go out the back—her mom couldn't get over the fence. And Emma couldn't—wouldn't—leave her behind.

"Are the cops coming?" she asked.

"Yes." Lisa wheeled herself backward into the kitchen and came back with a knife from the kitchen block. Arizona was her shadow.

They just had to make it until they showed up. But the last time this happened, it had taken them over twenty minutes to arrive. He'd never been so angry that he kicked the door down before. Last time, he had just hung around until Emma was forced to leave the apartment to go to work. What was different this time? Hard drugs?

A strange sense of doom had set in. Even with a baseball bat in hand, her father was six foot two. It wouldn't be hard to overpower her. But she was the only thing standing between her mom and him.

"I love you, Mom," Emma said.

"I love you, sweet girl." There were tears in Lisa's eyes as she gripped the kitchen knife.

Another hit landed on the door. The door groaned. The chain snapped. Splinters ricocheted off the wall, and blinding sunlight streamed in.

There he was. Older and grayer than the last time she had seen him, but there was no mistaking the manic glint in his black eyes.

"You little shit." He charged at her, hands outstretched.

Lisa shrieked, and Emma braced herself, ready to swing.

Crash.

Before she could move, her father crumpled to the ground, shaking the entire apartment. Oh, thank fuck. The police must have arrived.

"Emma?"

Hang on, that voice was familiar.

"Leo?"

CHAPTER THIRTY-FIVE

LEO

"Do you have something to bind his hands?" Leo drove his knee into the back of the bear-sized man beneath him.

Sirens sounded in the distance. His luggage now had a human-head-sized dent in it, and adrenaline and rage were charging through his veins. He had showed up on Emma's doorstep, ready to apologize, and instead found an intruder kicking the door down. How *dare* this man break into Emma's home? Who the hell was he?

The linoleum beneath his feet was scratched and thin, subfloor showing through in spots. The doorframe had splintered and given way, leaving Emma's apartment vulnerable.

There was a lot of work to do.

Emma returned with the sash from a bathrobe, and Leo quickly knotted the man's hands together.

He looked up at her. "Is this...?"

She nodded, and the knot in his stomach hardened. She hadn't mentioned her father was out of prison.

The sirens were getting closer.

Emma wheeled her mom into what must have been a

bedroom and slid the couch in front of the door. She ushered the dogs into crates somewhere he couldn't see, then returned to stand over her father's body with the baseball bat extended. Silence rang in the air. She didn't exactly seem surprised to see him, but she didn't take her eyes off her father.

His heart broke for her. How many times had she endured this man barreling back into her life? Trapped in an apartment he knew the address of? The urge to protect her was almost overwhelming. If he wasn't a man of discipline, he would beat the shit out of her father.

"I'm taking him outside," he announced. He grabbed the man's feet and dragged him out the door and down the shabby ramp to the sidewalk. A couple people side-eyed him on the street and gave him a wide berth, but no one stopped to ask what was going on.

Red-and-blue lights glanced off the windows of the rowhouses across the street. The police pulled up, and he took a deep breath.

———

It was impossible to tell if it had been minutes or hours since the police had arrived. They had taken statements, photographed the door, and provided Lisa and Emma with an incident number for their insurance.

The ambulance door slammed with finality, and the paramedics sped off in the direction of the hospital with Emma's father in tow.

Unfortunately, the blow hadn't killed him.

Leo watched until the ambulance was out of sight, then jogged up the ramp and nudged the mangled door open.

Emma was still in the hall, pressed against the wall like

it was the only thing keeping her on her feet. Her eyes were shrunken, hollow. Her knuckles were white around the baseball bat. He tugged it gently from her and set it on the ground.

"Are you all right?" he asked.

What a stupid question. Of course she wasn't. She'd just been intimidated and threatened by her own father, and Leo had a sneaking suspicion it was his fault.

"Come here, sweetheart. You're safe." He opened his arms, and she hesitated for a moment before rushing into them.

All at once, he felt at home. It didn't matter that he was on a different continent, or that his entire life had gone up in flames. With Emma in his arms, there was an overwhelming sense of peace. Maybe they could make a new beginning from the ashes of their old lives. Together.

"What are you doing here?" she finally asked in a shaky voice. She pulled back from his embrace to look at him, but she didn't put distance between them. Maybe there was hope.

"I came to apologize. I wasn't at my best in our last interaction. I was...frustrated that you didn't let me try to help. But I understand why you did it, and you're right. She wouldn't have listened. And she deserved it. She needed a wake-up call, no matter what it cost."

She snuggled back into him. "What did it cost?" Her voice was muffled against the lapel of his jacket.

Leo bit his lip. "Everything, I guess. But it wasn't your fault. The project's dead in the water. The land's going to another ski resort company. And then they cut me off."

"What?" She jerked away like she was going to storm over there and set them straight.

He smiled humorlessly.

"It's not your fault. This has been a long time coming. I've been disobeying her for years, slowly and increasingly pissing her off. Even if you'd never come to Lynoria, the outcome would've been the same. The worst part is that my people are the ones who are going to suffer the most. I used my salary for community needs. Tried to do something concrete and meaningful with my privilege. But now, I don't...I don't know where to go from here," he said. "When everything fell apart, all I knew was that I wanted to be with you."

Emma bit her lip, then pulled him into another hug.

"This is not the end," she said in a low voice. "We're going to figure this out."

A glimmer of hope stirred in his chest. He nudged her chin up so he could look her in the eyes. Her hand was small in his.

"I also wanted to say I'm sorry for the part I played in what happened to you. I was incredibly selfish. If I had simply left you alone, you would have the second half of the money."

She shook her head. "It's not your fault. I told myself time and again that I was going to stay away, and I just... couldn't."

"I know the feeling," he said softly.

A shiver ripped through her, and he tightened his grip. He ducked his head, aching to kiss her and take her in his arms again.

They were a centimeter apart when a voice came from down the hallway.

"Can someone let me out?"

"Oh, shit. Sorry," Emma called. She had re-barricaded the door after the police had taken her mother's statement.

Leo pushed the couch away, and Emma opened the door.

"Are you okay?" she asked in a low voice.

"I'm fine, sweetheart. Thanks to you two."

She pulled Emma down and wrapped her in a hug. When was the last time his parents had hugged him? His dad had once when Manchester United won. He had also sloshed a beer down his back.

Being with Emma was joyful, but seeing evidence of such a close family was confusing and melancholy in a way he didn't expect. The wheelchair creaked as Emma pushed her mother out, startling him out of his thoughts.

"You must be Leo." Lisa still looked pale and shaken, but she spoke with a smile. She held her hand out, and it was delicate and cool as a Fabergé egg. "It's so nice to meet you in person. Emma, dear, give him the tour while I prepare some refreshments. It's not every day we entertain royalty."

Emma froze, like she had forgotten she was in her own house. Her eyes darted to the ceiling, where a wispy spiderweb hung. Maybe she wasn't comfortable having him in her home. Which would be problematic because he was cut off and didn't get another trust payment until January 1.

"You don't have to do that. You've been through so much today," he said.

"No, it's not that, it's just—this isn't going to be what you're used to. We live on a very fixed income."

Something squeezed in his chest. "Technically speaking, I don't have a home right now. You're miles ahead of me."

Emma stared. "You have to move out too?"

"It was time," he muttered.

"So you have to find a real job and a new place to live," she said slowly. "What are you going to put on your resume?"

Shit. He hadn't even thought about that. Beyond his royal duties, he had never held a real nine-to-five job. Who was going to want an employee whose only life experience was being a prince for thirty-two years?

"I don't know. Maybe Sal will let me wash dishes or work in the kitchen. I'll figure it out."

"Damn. And I thought I'd messed *my* life up," she said.

They both looked at each other for a moment, then burst into laughter.

"Stay with us. For as long as you need. Come on." She tugged him forward.

Faded pictures of Emma as a little girl were framed all down the hallway—playing on a swing set, baking in an apron, smiling next to a Christmas tree. Her history was written on the walls. Were they a little shabby? Maybe, but the whole house felt lived in, loved. It couldn't have been more unlike the austere atmosphere of the castle where he had been scolded countless times for running down the hall, laughing, or just generally being a child.

A full blush had crept into Emma's cheeks. It pained his heart to see her so ashamed of her home.

Hardwood floors snapped and groaned as they passed a couple of closed doors and emerged into a small living room. It smelled like the color green. Plants were everywhere—every windowsill, on shelves. It was warm and full of energy.

She released his hand and bent over to open the dog crates. Cooper immediately bounded over and put his paws on Leo's shoulders.

Another smaller dog, a black lab, followed more cautiously.

"This is Arizona. My mom's service dog," Emma said.

He hesitated. "Am I allowed to pet her?"

Emma smiled. "Yes. She's not working right now. But thank you for asking."

He dropped to a knee, and Arizona immediately licked his face and put a rough paw on his knee.

"She's beautiful."

There was so much love and warmth contained in these four walls. He had never been allowed to have a pet. Maybe now he'd adopt one...once he found a place to live. But there would be time to worry about that tomorrow. For tonight, he was going to sink deeply into Emma's world and find out what magnificent melting pot had created the woman he loved.

Bollocks. There was that word again.

"Anyway, here's our living room and kitchen and—" She gasped, and Leo whirled around, half expecting to see another intruder trying to climb in their back door. But she was staring at the calendar on the wall.

"It's your birthday," she said.

"A birthday?" Lisa's head popped up. "We have so much to do. What's your favorite dinner, Leo?"

"Oh, you don't have to go to any trouble for me. And I don't want to derail your usual Christmas—" he started, but Emma threw a pillow at his face. It bounced off and landed on the floor.

"Don't make us drag it out of you. It'll help to have something to celebrate," she added.

He debated. "I quite like spaghetti. We almost never had it at home. My mother always said it was too 'pedestrian.'"

"Then I'm going to make you the best damn spaghetti you've ever had. Let me just run out and get a few—"

"No, please, let me," Leo interrupted. "I need to pick up a few things anyway. Just make me a list."

Emma jotted some things down, then handed it over. "Let me just get my coat—"

"I'll go. I'll come right back."

She had done enough.

"But you don't know where you're going."

Leo waved a hand. "I found my way here, didn't I? It's a grid system. It's not even possible to get lost."

"That's Manhattan—" she called as the door closed behind him.

CHAPTER THIRTY-SIX

LEO

Leo arrived back at the apartment laden with multiple shopping bags from the hardware and grocery store. It was a good thing he had pawned some old laptops and palace trinkets, since they couldn't very well wait for the insurance company to cover a fix for Emma's door.

He knocked, and Emma answered the door a minute later.

"I thought we were going to have to send a search party after you."

Maybe he had been a little cavalier about exploring a new country without an international phone plan.

"You know," Leo said as he stepped over the threshold, "I've always heard how rude New Yorkers are. But everyone I've met has been so kind."

Emma took some bags from him and walked down the hallway toward the kitchen. "Well, if a stupidly attractive six-foot-three European man asked me where the 'loo' was, I'd probably fall all over myself to help him too."

When he followed her into the dining area, Leo was greeted by the sight of purple-and-gold streamers—the national colors of Lynoria—and a birthday banner that looked like it had been cut out of a Diet Coke box.

No one had ever made him a birthday banner before.

"What's all this?" he asked. For some reason, he was having a hard time swallowing.

"It's not much, but we want to celebrate you. I'm really happy you were born. And I'm sorry your parents are being total dickbags right now, but I'm also selfishly glad it led you here."

He pulled her into his arms. "Me too."

The anxiety that had whirled in his chest since he left Lynoria finally quieted. This was all he needed. The girl of his dreams in his arms. The sweet smell of something delicious cooling on a rack. Car horns honking outside while Christmas lights glowed and streamers danced in the wake of the HVAC. It was foreign yet intimately homely all at the same time.

"Shouldn't you be doing your exercises?" Emma said pointedly.

He glanced into the living room, where Lisa was sitting on the couch with a smug look on her face.

"Yes, dear," she said, picking up a set of light dumbbells.

Leo released Emma and dropped the hardware bag on the kitchen table. Wood, screws, lightbulbs, and painting supplies spilled out.

"Oh, you didn't have to..." She gestured at the paint supplies.

He threw his hands up. "I'm freeloading here. Let me contribute the only way I know how. Though I can't believe you don't have a measuring tape. I had to get one that measures in *inches*." He said the last word like it was an epithet.

"How did you afford all this? Weren't you cut off?"

"I pawned some things," he admitted. "It's not a permanent solution, but hopefully it'll get me through to January. How can I help?" he asked when she pulled a can of San Marzano tomatoes from the bag.

"Just sit. Relax," she said. "It's a long flight. You must be exhausted."

"I'm fine. Got a pencil?" He picked up the hardware supplies, took the pencil Emma handed him, and set to work.

An hour later, the house smelled like rich marinara sauce. He set down a drill and pulled on the new doorframe with all his might. It didn't budge. Extra-long screws now kept everything in place, but even that didn't feel like enough. He couldn't keep her safe here. Especially if he didn't live here.

He was standing on a precipice. There was nothing for him at home anymore. Maybe he *could* move to New York. He could find a job, watch over Ruby while she was at NYU. This solution had the obvious bonus of more time with Emma. A real chance for the two of them, not just a holiday fling.

But who would hire him? He was a prince in name only (PINO?) with no real work history, whose only skills were fixing things by watching YouTube videos and holding town hall meetings.

His shoulders slumped. He was ignoring the bigger truth. The people of Lynoria needed help. Their need had to come before his want. He owed it to them to give it his best shot. He would find a way to greenlight this project with or without his family's support. Somehow.

"So, Leo, how long will you be staying with us?" Lisa broke him out of his self-reflection.

He tested the deadbolt for the third time. "Uh, well. I'm not entirely sure."

"Wonderful. You're welcome to stay as long as you need."

"Thank you," he said.

The visit was making him emotional in so many ways. He ached to be part of this tight-knit family. They had been a twosome for so long. Who knew if there was room for anyone else?

"Dinner's ready," Emma announced.

Leo vacuumed up the sawdust, then walked into the dining area to find a tablecloth, candlesticks, and the most beautiful pot of spaghetti he'd ever seen. His stomach growled. He had been so wound up from the day of travel and ass-kicking, he hadn't even noticed how hungry he was.

They sat around the table for almost two hours, talking, laughing, and devouring the spaghetti and homemade garlic bread Emma had whipped up.

"I didn't know you were such a good cook as well as a baker," he said as he collected their plates.

"Eh, I do okay."

"I'm completely useless," Leo mused. "I can barely boil an egg."

"I can teach you. Since you'll be without a royal kitchen soon."

"Right," he said. There was so much to think about, and everything was up in the air. He didn't want to think about it all right now. "So, what's the Christmas tradition this evening?"

Emma and Lisa looked at each other. "Christmas charades," she said. "I hope you stretched."

Though a cultural barrier prevented some of the charade success—he was too afraid to ask what a Grinch was—it was a lovely, warm evening full of laughter and holiday joy.

For the first time, he was beginning to see the appeal of Christmas. Here, in the confines of this tiny garden apartment in Brooklyn, Christmas wasn't about a sold-out toy or the latest tech device. It was about togetherness, family. Creating memories that would be cherished for a lifetime. It was something that stayed the same while everything else was up to the mercy of change. And maybe there was something a little magical about that.

The fatigue was wearing on him by the time Lisa mimed a snowball fight—a tradition that thankfully traversed the cultural continental divide. A yawn shook his entire body.

As if in response, Lisa yawned too. "Emma, I think I'm going to turn in early tonight."

"Oh, sure." Emma jumped up and fetched her mother's walker.

"Anything I can help with?" Leo asked.

"We're fine, thanks," Emma said.

"Good night, Leo. I'm so grateful you decided to drop in," Lisa said earnestly on her way down the hall.

With Lisa safely in bed and the dogs taken out for the last time, Leo slipped between Emma's sheets while she finished brushing her teeth. There was something so right about being in her bed, the scent of her all around him. She cracked the door open and tiptoed into the room, peeking at him. He opened his arms, and she slid into them like some cosmic jigsaw had designed her specifically to fit there.

Even though he'd been disowned by his parents, his entire life was in upheaval, and he'd had to knock Emma's father unconscious, it might have been the best birthday he'd ever had.

CHAPTER THIRTY-SEVEN

EMMA

Leo's side of the bed was cold when she awoke the next morning.

She sat up, and panic flared in her chest. He had left. He had flown to New York to have sex with her one last time and then just left. Had he even really been here the day before, or had she hallucinated everything?

But no. There was his banged-up suitcase, sitting in the corner of her room.

The luggage was an undeniable reminder of the horror they had faced the day before. If Leo hadn't arrived when he did, there was no telling what amount of damage her father would have done. He'd never kicked the door in before. He was escalating, and since they still lived in the same apartment, they were sitting ducks. At least Leo had reinforced the doorframe.

There was nothing she could do about it for the time being. Maybe as a thank you, she could start helping Leo stitch his life back together. This was just a temporary setback, she was sure of it. They would find a way to get his project off the ground. They didn't need the crown's jerk money anyway.

Unless he didn't *want* to go back. Maybe he had had enough of his mom's shenanigans and his father's blatant disinterest in anything not related to football. What if he moved here?

She ran a hand over his pillow. The night before they had clung to each other, speaking words their mouths were too afraid to say with every kiss. It was exciting, fooling around as quietly as they could with her mother and hypervigilant service dog in the next room. But more than that, it felt different from any sexual experience she had ever known.

Leo was gentle, patient, and generous. Almost worshipful of her body. There was an intensity that no other man had ever given her.

It was like they had known each other for years. Maybe even multiple lives.

But that was insane. He was honorable and duty-bound, and his people needed him. Even if he didn't realize it yet, there was no way he was going to move to New York.

To take her mind off the situation she was quickly losing control of, she let the dogs out and entered her mother's room. Lisa was awake and had her e-reader on.

"Morning," Emma said. "Sleep okay?"

"Don't tell anyone," her mom began as she heaved herself out of bed, "but I slept a lot better with a man in the house."

Emma smiled and supported Lisa's arm as she held on to her walker. "Me too."

"Is he here?" her mom whispered.

Emma shook her head.

"So, what's going on between the two of you?"

Emma looked over her shoulder. "I don't know. I'm afraid to ask."

"Do you want to be with him?"

"Are you kidding me? Of course I do. But it could never work. What would we do, a long-distance relationship? See each other twice a year? He's a whole-ass prince. And my life is here. Our life is here," she corrected.

"Sweetheart," her mom said. A shadow crossed over her face, and it seemed she was choosing her words carefully. "It's not your job to take care of me. I'm not going to allow you to limit yourself and make your life small because you think you have to carry the entire weight of our family on your shoulders. I've been looking into assisted living facilities."

"No," Emma said sharply. "I'm not putting you in a home. Are you crazy? You're only fifty-five."

"It would make your life so much simpler," Lisa said as they shuffled to the bathroom. "You could go anywhere, live anywhere without worrying about me falling or choking on a friggen noodle."

"I will always worry about you. That's my job." Emma lowered her mom onto the toilet, then left the room.

"No, that's *my* job," Lisa said through the door. "Emma, honey, you have such a beautiful future ahead of you. I've already held you back for too long."

"Why are you talking like I'm going somewhere? I'm not going anywhere."

"We'll see."

There was a knock at the front door, and Emma silently cursed before picking up the baseball bat again.

Leo stood on the stoop, shopping bags in hand and a concerned look on his face.

"Wow, you really do always answer the door with violence," he said.

"Do you blame me?"

"Of course not." He pulled her in for a hug.

She breathed in the scent of his leather jacket. How was this real? Two weeks ago, she was slaving away at Crumb and Get It with no end in sight. Now she was unemployed with a prince for a boyfriend. Well, not boyfriend. International booty call? Situationship? Whatever.

"What did you find?" she asked when she pulled back. She peered into his bags.

"Just some breakfast and a couple more things for the apartment. A thank you for the hospitality while I figure out what comes next."

The toilet flushed, and Emma returned to the bathroom.

"About that," she said as she walked her mother to the living room, "now that I have all this free time, I'm going to help you get your new post-royal life in order."

Leo raised his eyebrows and set a bakery bag on the kitchen table.

"New place to live, new bank account, an emergency budget, job hunting, whatever. We'll do it all today." She shook some pills out of the organizer on the kitchen countertop and brought them to Lisa with a glass of water.

"We should be working on *your* new job," he said. "Since I destroyed the last one."

She waved a hand. "I have a couple inquiries out to businesses I've worked with before."

"For what? Baking?"

"No, I'm not allowed to bake for profit for a year because of the damned noncompete. I managed all the social media for the bakery, so my plan is to freelance during the waiting period. And if that doesn't cut it, I'll look into serving at the diner down the street. Or start an OnlyFans," she joked.

Leo frowned, but he didn't say anything.

"Now, I assume I should be looking for apartments in Lynoria?" Her hands shook with nerves, even though she already knew the answer.

He hesitated. "I think so. For now, at least. I just don't think I can give up completely yet."

Emma squeezed his shoulder, then returned to the kitchen and turned on their ancient coffeepot. A rich earthiness flooded the space, and she breathed it in before stealing a glance at Leo as he cleared out the drying rack and set the table.

She had feelings. There was no use denying it. Leo probably had some too, or he wouldn't have chased her thousands of miles.

Where could they go from here? They were practically from different dimensions. Even if he formally left the royal family, his family's drama would always be in the background. And she would never be enough for them, all because of where she grew up.

It figured. The first time she caught feelings for a guy since Dylan, and it was an impossible situation.

After breakfast, Leo took all the paintings off the wall in the hallway and started sanding and spackling. Cooper supervised.

A couple hours passed as Leo painted and Emma hammered away at her laptop, browser filled with windows of apartments and jobs in Lynoria. Lisa regaled them all with fun facts from the bee documentary she'd recently watched and worked on her physical therapy plan.

Leo appeared in the kitchen, spackling dust dotting his T-shirt and paint splatters on his hand. The sight of him had awakened something in Emma's pants, but she couldn't do anything about it with her mom right there.

"I don't suppose you know anything about zookeeping?" she asked as he washed his hands.

"Not particularly," he said over his shoulder. "Is that a career option?"

"Yes. But it seems like a lot of the duties include shoveling excrement."

"Huh. It would be great exercise. And I'd love to know how enclosures are built. Keep it on the list."

"Great. How much is your monthly trust payment again?"

He told her, and she grimaced.

"You might need a roommate."

"That bad?" He looked scandalized.

"All the jobs are in Avolis. The city is expensive."

"So I'd have to leave the village?"

"Well, there is one apartment available in the village. But I don't know that it would suit your...needs."

She turned the laptop so that he could see it. A studio apartment with only the barest of amenities, but it was charming nonetheless. It would be an uncomfortable adjustment for someone coming from a two-thousand-square-foot suite in a castle though.

He clicked through a couple pictures, then pulled out his phone. He dialed a number and disappeared into the hallway.

Emma and Lisa made eye contact, and Emma shrugged.

He came back a moment later. "Right, that's settled."

"You took the apartment? Without going to see it first?" Emma raised her eyebrows.

"Of course. I'd like to still be near Ruby before she leaves for school. It's only a year lease."

"What's your mom going to say when she learns you're living in a studio apartment?"

"I don't care what she thinks. They've controlled everything for long enough. What I do, where I live, who I'm allowed to date. I don't want it. Any of it."

She sat up straight. "What are you going to do? Renounce your title? Is that a thing?"

"Maybe," he said thoughtfully.

"Can you run for parliament? Or local office?" Lisa asked from the living room. "I've been reading up on the Lynorian government. Really boring stuff."

He frowned. "I actually don't know. No member of the royal family has ever held a nonroyal office before."

"And who better to be the first than you? You don't need them," Emma said, pointing generally east toward Lynoria. "We can get your project built without the crown's money."

"How? I'm cut off, remember?"

She leaned back and pulled out her phone. "We call in the big guns."

"The big guns?"

In a moment, Lola was on-screen.

"Oh my god," Lola said. "Leo in the flesh. You're real. I can't believe it. I thought Emma was having wet fever dreams."

Leo smiled. "I'm real."

"Great," she said. "Now what's going on? Are you getting married? Because I will absolutely be your maid of honor. How's October?"

"Whoa," Emma said sternly. "We're just calling for some advice, because you're a brilliant genius grant writer and fundraiser."

Leo gave a brief overview of the project, and Lola considered for a moment.

"Okay," she said. "Give me twenty-four hours, and I'll get you a list of the biggest donors in Lynoria and a strategy. Emma said you have a presentation already?"

He nodded.

"Send it to me and I'll spruce it up. There is one other thing."

"What's that?" he asked.

"Trust me when I say you need to get your ass back to Lynoria and start knocking on doors. Big companies need to get all their charitable giving done before the end of the year for tax purposes. You don't have a lot of time, and you're going to have to be hella charming."

"He can handle that," Emma said.

"You think it's possible though?" he asked. For the first time since the queen's dismissal, he felt a glimmer of hope.

"It's possible. The goal is going to be to find big businesses with soft, squishy CEOs who actually give a shit about Lynoria. You're going to tug on a lot of heartstrings. You don't need those royal bastards. No offense," Lola added.

"About payment for your services—" Leo began, but Lola shook her head vehemently.

"It's Christmas. This is pro bono. Though I do expect a wing of the new library to be named after me. Kidding. Mostly," she added as an afterthought.

"I can't thank you enough."

"You can do this. You *will* do this," she said firmly. "One other thing. If you can get a survivor to share her story and how one of the shelters changed her life, it'll really make a difference. Donors remember stories, not statistics."

Lola straightened up and glanced over her shoulder. "Shit. I've gotta run, I think Mateo just set a pan on fire."

After the call ended, Leo turned to Emma. "I kind of feel

like I could do anything right now. No wonder you love her so much."

"Right? I always tell her she should've been a life coach."

He frowned and was silent for a moment. "I don't feel comfortable asking a victim to tell her story on camera. How would I even find someone willing to share? And what if their abusers are still out there and they use the video somehow to track them down?"

Emma sighed, then squared her shoulders. There was only one fast solution to this problem. "I'll help you."

"What do you mean?"

"I know I'm not from Lynoria, but I remember what it was like to grow up with an abusive father. The shelter that took us in could have been the difference between life and death for me and my mom."

"No. I would never ask you to relive that experience," he said. "There has to be another way."

She looked up at him. "If my story has the power to help even one other woman or child, I'll do it. And when I'm a little more financially stable and your shelter has been built —because it *will* be built—I'll help you organize donation drives."

"I would be honored to have your help."

She squeezed his hand, then stood up. Her stomach twisted with nerves. "I should take a shower if I'm going to be on camera."

CHAPTER THIRTY-EIGHT

EMMA

"Where do I start?" Emma said.

"Are you sure you want to do this?" Leo asked behind the phone they were using as a camera.

"Yes," she said firmly.

The prospect of reliving her trauma had her stomach in knots. But if it helped convince one stuffy banker to cough up the funds to build this shelter, she would reopen the wounds as many times as necessary.

"Okay. Start anywhere you want," Leo said behind the camera. "I'll have Ruby edit the video for me later."

They sat in the kitchen, a ring light Emma usually used for the bakery's social media perched in the corner.

She took a long, slow breath in and out, then opened her eyes. Her hands were clasped so tightly in her lap that her fingers ached. "Okay, well. I remember the first time I ever became aware of abuse in my home. I was three, and my mom was teaching me how to ride a bike. We were outside when my dad came home, and my mom took one look at him and told me to take the dog and get inside. I didn't know it then, but he almost always came home from work drunk. He always found a reason to yell at my mom and me —a dish in the sink, dog hair on the floor. Sometimes it was nothing at all. Like just seeing us brought out some kind of uncontrollable rage in him."

Her heart thudded in her ears. This was a memory that would never leave her, no matter how hard she tried. The sticky August heat, the plastic pedals under her Lisa Frank sandals. The sound of her bicycle clattering to the sidewalk as she ran for the house.

"The abuse started small. He would yell, tell us we were stupid and worthless. I believed it for a long time."

Leo's posture became more rigid the longer she talked.

"Eventually it escalated to throwing things. Glasses, plates, even the TV once. He cut us off from everyone who loved us. My grandparents, friends who were like family. One by one, he convinced her that they were toxic and poisoning her against him. There was just no one left."

Emma looked away from the camera for a moment and picked at a loose thread on her shirt. "Maybe you're wondering why we didn't leave. If things were so bad, why didn't my mom pack a bag and take me and the dog and run away into the night?"

She took another deep breath before plunging on. "There weren't as many resources back then. My dad controlled everything—the finances, in particular. My mom had to hand over her paycheck to him every week. He gave her an allowance for groceries and squandered the rest. She had to start a secret bank account and squirrel away loose change from trips to the store, tips from her clients. We used to make a game of finding quarters on the ground every-where we went."

"It was impossible to save enough for a new apartment. Rent was expensive even back then. Our only nearby relative that my dad hadn't been successful in cutting us off from was my great-aunt, who had cancer. My mom didn't want to burden her with two extra housemates. And my dad didn't allow her to see friends outside of work. We were stuck, imprisoned in this house of abuse."

She met Leo's concerned gaze, the story suddenly for him rather than a future audience. "The day I was talking about earlier, when I was riding my bike? I shut myself in my room, but I could still hear my dad walk up the steps and scream at my mom. It was something so arbitrary—he didn't like what we were having for dinner, or maybe there were dog toys in the living room.

"He dragged her inside and hit her so hard it rattled my door. She had an awful black eye and told her friends at work that she had tripped and fallen against the cabinets. Around that time, things started to escalate." She absently rubbed the back of her arm. "He was apologetic for a while, but a week later, he threw a glass at me when I asked if I could run out to the ice cream truck."

Leo's expression was somber, and he started to reach for her but stopped.

"It was...a lot. A living nightmare. Month after month of holding my breath, tiptoeing around. Never knowing what would set him off. Praying he would stop coming home. I remember the day we finally left. He came home drunk. Again. He argued with my mother because we'd had to spend some money on clothes. I'd outgrown everything I had. I was standing in the hallway, and he just...lunged at me."

Her voice shook, and she touched a hand to her throat. Sometimes that day resurfaced in nightmares, but she'd quickly lock the memories away again upon waking.

"He choked me. I couldn't breathe. The world started to

turn black at the edges. I was almost a little relieved—it was finally going to be over." Her voice shook, and she paused to gather her composure.

"My mom smashed a liquor bottle over his head. We grabbed the bag of school clothes she had just bought and left while he was unconscious."

She stared out the window at a solitary streetlight. She could vividly remember the chill in the air as they ran to the shelter. Her mom hadn't even paused to put on shoes. She had picked Emma up and run barefoot for eight blocks, the dog pacing them the whole way.

"The closest shelter wouldn't take us with Sadie. But they kept us warm and called around until they found one that would—over here, in Brooklyn. That place was our home. It was the first space I had ever felt truly safe. I could sleep without worrying that someone was going to break my door down and scream at me. I could play outside without fear of making him angry just by existing. That shelter saved our lives. Every woman and child who has suffered from abuse in their home deserves a safe place to run. Everyone. If we hadn't had access to one, we would both be dead."

Tears swam stubbornly in front of her eyes. It had been years since she had talked about this to anyone. She and her mom kind of pretended like it was an alternate universe that had never happened. She vaguely remembered the play therapy she attended for a year after the divorce—a nice older woman with glasses who sat on the floor with her.

Her mom had made up for Emma's lack of a dad a thousand times over. One time, she even wore a fake mustache and a suit and took her to the Daddy-Daughter dance at school.

But she'd seen the toll being a single parent had taken on her mom. If children were in her distant future, she wanted them to have two safe, loving parents. There would be laughter and dancing and rousing games of Scrabble. They would never live in a house of eggshells.

Leo stepped out from behind the camera and pulled her into his arms. He held her tight, like he thought she might crumble if he didn't hold her together.

"I won't use this," Leo said. "It's too personal. You shouldn't have to talk about this. I'll find another way."

She pulled back and looked at him. "You have to. People are counting on you. And besides, I want to help. I believe in you, and I believe in this project."

He didn't reply but kissed her firmly.

"So does this mean you're...leaving?" she asked hesitantly.

He took her hand with regret in his eyes. "I think I have to. I owe it to my people to try. And I have to find a way to stop them from building that ski resort."

Emma straightened. She was about to do something stupid. She could feel it in her bones.

"Time out?" she asked Leo.

He nodded, and she walked over to the couch where her mom was seated. Emma had asked her to put earbuds in so she couldn't hear them recording. There was no need to make her live through it again.

Her mom pulled the earbuds out. "All finished?"

"Is your passport still valid?" Emma asked in a low voice.

Lisa's eyes sparkled. "Why yes, it is."

"How do you feel about a fiscally irresponsible trip?"

Lisa let out a whoop. "I'll start packing now."

Emma returned to the kitchen. What was she doing? Dipping into her savings for the new business to go to Europe was foolish. Disastrous. Especially when she didn't have a steady income anymore.

When a floorboard creaked under her weight, Leo turned the full force of his gaze on her. Her heart staggered, and it nearly stole the breath from her lungs.

He had given her so much. The food in her fridge, hours of help in the kitchen at the castle. He had, in all likelihood, saved her life—again—only yesterday.

Leo needed her help. And she would give it to him, no matter the cost.

CHAPTER THIRTY-NINE

LEO

"*Fuck.*" Leo tossed his phone into the passenger seat of his truck. So much for the spirit of giving. Cytotech Corp had rejected his proposal barely an hour after he'd left. The petty part of him wanted to use his connections to make sure the royal family never did business with them again. But it wasn't their fault he'd waited until December to make a pitch.

Two meetings, two rejections. Greenfuture Industries sat across the parking lot from him. He closed his eyes and took a deep breath, trying to remember the words from Emma's pep talk earlier. Lola had sent an email with the top three donors in Lynoria, and he had blatantly used his royal connections to secure meetings with all three in a single day. This was the final one, and the business with the best track record for philanthropy.

He grabbed his laptop bag and started for the building. Emma and Lisa were arriving the following morning, and he was determined to have good news to share.

The receptionist led him into an intimidating room full of executives.

"Your Highness. We're honored to have you here in our humble office," a man in a suit said with a small bow. "I'm Robert."

Humble was not the right word. Greenfuture Industries had made a name for itself in clean energy and had branches all over Europe and North America. Everything about their office was modern, sleek, and seemingly recyclable.

"There's no need for formalities," Leo said with a wave. "It's just Leo. And thank you for seeing me. I know it's not an ideal time."

He handed over a box of pastries. They weren't Emma's, but they were better than showing up empty-handed.

"Thank you," Robert said as he took the box.

The other people in the room introduced themselves. The conference room was decorated for Christmas. Garland and bright red bows were everywhere, and multicolored lights were strung on a tree in the corner. He could only assume the tree was fake.

"We're interested to hear what you have to say. I have to be honest though, most of our funds earmarked for philanthropy have already been utilized this year."

Leo's stomach plummeted. "Well, I respect your time, so I'll make this as quick as possible."

He hooked his laptop up to the projector and went through the spiel as quickly as he could.

The last part of the presentation was Emma's video. He had seen it multiple times now, and it hadn't gotten any easier to watch.

When the video ended, there was silence in the conference room. This investor was his last hope. If they said no, they would be set back for another year while he applied for grants, and by then, the ski resort would already be built.

Was it enough?

They asked a few questions—when would the project start, was there an environmental impact assessment scheduled, would Leo be open to including a sponsored corner of the library where children could learn about clean energy.

"Honestly, if I had all the money in the world, I'd remodel the old library into a children's museum and devote a whole floor to clean energy," Leo said. "But I have to build the new one first."

Robert looked thoughtful. "We'll have an answer for you by the end of the day. Thank you for coming in, Your Highness."

Leo shook everyone's hands. "I really appreciate your time. I look forward to hearing from you."

With that, he was back out in the blustery cold. He had done all he could.

———

"So you still don't know what you're going to do about the ski resort," Sal said as he poured a glass of beer.

Whiskey swirled dark and warm in his glass. The atmosphere was festive, but his mood was not.

"Emma claims to have a plan."

Sal slid a Guinness down the bar and turned back to him. "I believe it. She's a smart girl. So she's coming in on the first morning train?"

Leo nodded. "You're sure you don't mind me staying for a few days? I know it's a big ask."

Sal shrugged. "Stay as long as you want. Cal's chuffed. Make sure you comment on the sheets in the guest bedroom though. He's been dying for someone to ask what the thread count is."

"Sheets. Got it."

His phone beeped, and his heart flew into his throat until he realized it was just a text, not an email.

Emma had sent her flight and train information. The fact that she—and her mom and the two dogs—would soon be here brought some quiet to the storm in his mind.

"Emma?" Sal nodded at Leo's phone.

Leo nodded.

Sal leaned forward. "When are you going to tell the girl you want a real relationship with her?"

Leo put his glass down for a refill. "What am I supposed to do, hold her hostage? She lives five thousand miles away. Her mom—and her dreams—are in New York."

Sal poured another finger of amber liquid. "Dreams can change."

"I'm not going to ask her to compromise the goal she's been working toward her entire life for some titled idiot she met two weeks ago. I've already gotten her fired. I've done enough damage."

"But you still want to," Sal said with authority. He had always been good at seeing through Leo's facade.

Leo lowered his voice. Sal had barred a member of the press from coming in earlier, but he couldn't be too careful. "She shouldn't have to change anything for me. She deserves to have her dream exactly as she imagined it. I'm not part of the equation."

"Have you talked to her about this?"

"Not exactly."

"Then how do you even know what she's thinking?"

Leo's phone vibrated, and they both jumped. Not a text. So did that mean—

He clicked his email app. There it was. A message from

Greenfuture Industries. His hands shook as he opened it and read.

"Dear Prince Leo," he muttered, then skimmed the rest of the text.

He slapped his phone down on the bar and buried his head in his hands.

"Should I put this away?" Sal asked.

Leo opened his eyes to spot a rather expensive-looking bottle of champagne. It mocked him.

"They were generous," he said carefully, "but it's only half of what we need. We won't have an answer on the grants until next year. The project is dead. I've failed. Again."

"Hey," Sal said, "you are not a failure. You've done more for this country than any member of parliament or even your own—in a *minute*, Tony, can't you see there's a man having a crisis here?" Sal called to a man who was banging his empty glass on the bar.

Leo pushed his chair back and stood. "I should go. Do some more research, maybe. I don't know."

CHAPTER FORTY

EMMA

THE FARTHER AWAY THEY GOT FROM NEW YORK, THE MORE Emma realized she had lost the damn plot. She was supposed to be preparing to start her business, sliding pieces into place. And instead, she was dipping into her painstakingly cultivated savings to board a plane to Lynoria for the second time in a month to help someone she barely knew.

It didn't make sense. But it was for a good cause. She wouldn't be putting her master plan on hold by spending a few days out of the country. And didn't she deserve a break, anyway?

"How are you doing, love?" her mom asked from the train seat next to her. The dark Spanish countryside whizzed by the window.

"I'm fine." It was mostly the truth. As anxious as she was about dipping into their savings and navigating a foreign country that might not be as wheelchair accessible as America, she was beyond relieved to be thousands of miles away from her abusive father.

"How are you?" she added.

"I'm so happy to be out of that damn apartment," her mom said with a laugh. Ever since Emma had made the rash decision to return to Lynoria, she had seen flickers of the old Lisa—the one who quietly yearned for excitement and adventure. Maybe the trip was irresponsible, but it was worth every penny to see wonder on her mother's face again.

Cooper was in the window seat across from them, and Arizona was curled at Lisa's feet. They had made quite the spectacle from the plane to the train.

"Don't get me wrong, I'm eternally grateful to your great-aunt Claudia for giving us the gift of rent control," Lisa said. "We would've been in real trouble without it. But there's a whole world out there, and I haven't really seen any of it."

Emma smiled and glanced at her watch. They would be arriving in twenty minutes. She checked her hair in the window and tossed a breath mint into her mouth.

"I really hope this protest plan works," she said. "Leo's going to hate it."

"It's for the greater good," her mom said. "And I'm looking forward to spending more time with the man who finally stole your heart."

Emma sputtered. "My heart? What are you talking about?"

"I've never seen you rearrange a date for a boy, let alone fly across the world at the drop of a hat. You love him."

"I couldn't love him. I barely know him."

Lisa looked at her skeptically.

"Okay, maybe there are *some* feelings. I would be insane not to feel something. You've seen him."

"Truth," Lisa said. "It's more than that though."

"He's amazing," Emma mused, staring out at the dark trees flashing by. "He's not even the heir, but he would do anything for his people. He's taken on the responsibility of the whole world when he doesn't even have to."

"Sounds like someone else I know," Lisa said pointedly.

Emma shook her head. "He's on another level."

Lisa folded her hands carefully in her lap. "Let me be the first to say I would happily relocate to Lynoria."

Emma shot her a dirty look. There was no way she was just going to move to a foreign country, and especially not for a boy that she had met two weeks ago. The idea was insane. And besides, his family hated her. Minus Ruby, anyway.

"That's so not even part of the equation," she said. "Again, I've known him for less than a month. And besides, my dream is in New York."

"Is it? I'm pretty sure you could bake anywhere."

"You and I both know there's no better market for my skillset than Manhattan. Besides, I sparked an international gingerbread scandal while I was here. And with the queen in charge, I'd never have a prayer of citizenship."

Lisa leaned back in her seat and seemed to consider this. "That's fair. But is this really what your heart wants? Making fancy desserts for rich assholes like the queen for the rest of your life?"

An image of the community kitchen patrons enjoying her croissants flashed in her mind, but she stamped it out.

"It doesn't matter what my heart wants, what matters is security. Stability. A better life for both of us," Emma said firmly.

A shadow passed across her mom's face. Great, now she was upsetting the woman who'd raised her. Her mother turned toward the window. Arizona nosed her hand, and they settled into silence as the dark shapes of trees flashed by.

Finally, the train pulled into the station. It was all she could do to stop from sprinting off the train and into Leo's arms. But she had to help her mother down the stairs and keep the dogs from tripping anyone.

When they finally disembarked, Leo was waiting with a wheelchair. His hair was slightly tousled, and he was wearing his glasses. She warmed from the inside out like she had suddenly stepped into sunshine.

Leo carefully helped her mother down into the wheelchair, then wrapped Emma in his arms so tightly she could barely breathe.

"I'm so glad you're here."

"Me too," she whispered. "Where did you get a wheelchair?"

"Had Ruby steal it from the castle."

She kissed him, and it brought out the same feeling she had the first time she smelled freshly baked bread. Curiosity, and a calling that she didn't quite understand.

Leo gave her mom and Cooper a hug and bowed at Arizona in her harness.

He took Cooper's leash from Emma and wrapped it around his wrist before ushering them to the parking lot. "I have some bad news."

She almost stopped in her tracks. "Oh no."

"We only got half the money."

Emma bit her lip. It was awful news. What would happen if he couldn't raise the rest? Would he give up? Consider moving to New York, even?

But no. She refused to put that into the universe. There was so much more at stake here than her own selfish wishes. She straightened her shoulders. "Okay. So we have no location and only half the money."

"When do you need the money by?" Lisa asked.

"Monday," he said darkly.

Oh. That was in four days.

"If we don't have the funds and the land by then, the contractors and project manager will have to move on," he added.

"Shit. Let me think," Emma muttered.

Her mind spun as they walked down the ramp outside and crossed the stony parking lot. Her current plan wasn't big enough. They needed to go bigger. This was their last shot.

"Okay, you're not going to like this. But we don't have a choice."

He shot her a look. "This sounds troubling. What are you thinking?"

"We need a multi-pronged plan. First, we need to get you on social media. Just for a little while."

His nose wrinkled like she had suggested he leap into an industrial-sized vat of sauerkraut.

"We need to stir up some buzz," she added. "Start a protest. Make it impossible for them to ignore you. Force them to go on record saying they would rather build a ski resort than a community center."

Leo was quiet as Cooper, Arizona, and Emma squeezed into the back seat of the truck. He handed Lisa into the passenger seat and helped buckle her in.

"It's not a terrible idea," he finally said. "But do you really think people will care?"

"I know they will," Emma said firmly. "It's really going to piss off your parents though."

"Even better."

Her body, which had just gotten used to Eastern Standard Time again, had no idea what time it was. She was simultaneously exhausted yet wired, ready to tackle this challenge.

Leading a public outrage against the royal family was definitely not going to score her any points with Leo's parents. But if he didn't care, then neither did she.

"Hopefully that will be enough to take care of the ski resort problem."

"And the money?"

"You need to call an emergency town hall meeting. Today. All the business owners. Everyone from the library. Your congressperson—or whatever elected officials are called here."

"And then what?"

"We have the biggest fundraiser this country's ever seen. An auction, bake sale, karaoke contest, holiday pet parade, storefront decoration contest, gift wrapping, ugly sweater contest, ornament decorating. As many low-cost ideas as possible, as quickly as possible."

"It sounds like we'll need a lot of volunteers." His tone was unsure.

She reached between the seats and squeezed his arm. "People are going to show up for you."

The truck rumbled to life, and he squared his shoulders. "One last try."

"One last try," Emma agreed.

CHAPTER FORTY-ONE

LEO

"You moved in already?" Emma leaned forward to peer out the windshield.

Tendrils of red crept up from the horizon as he pulled into his parking space.

Leo nodded. "The landlords agreed to let me move in early and gave me a line of credit until the first. One of the perks of being part of the royal family, I guess."

"That's a big step," she said.

"It's very small. But it's nice to have my own place," he said, staring off into the distance. "I'll be staying with Sal and Callum, so you'll have a bit more room. The dogs alone will take up the whole floor plan. You might have to sleep in the bathtub."

He had a sudden vivid mental picture of her in the bathtub, which did not help him focus on the matter at hand.

She laughed and clambered out with the dogs. "We're not afraid of small spaces," she said. "Thank you."

Smoke drifted up from the chimney, and a small electric candle flickered in the window. Hopefully it would be comfortable enough for them.

Leo ushered them inside. A chorus of mews greeted them, and Emma stopped in her tracks.

"When did you have time to get...four cats?"

Ah, bollocks. He had forgotten to tell her about the fosters.

The chubbiest of the lot, an orange kitten he had nicknamed Marmalade, clawed his way up his pantleg until he sat on Leo's shoulder. "Sorry, I forgot to mention it. I'm just fostering them," he explained. "The resident cat at their previous foster home couldn't tolerate them, and the shelter was out of space. You aren't allergic?"

"No," Emma said, holding one finger out for the smallest one—Dahlia—to sniff. "I love them. I'm just surprised."

The mama kitty had immediately claimed Lisa's lap, and the last kitten was booping noses with Cooper.

The apartment was small, charmingly out of date, and sparsely decorated with the only furniture he could ferret away from his suite in the castle—a bed, a couch, and a French press.

Lisa had ignored Emma's protests about jet lag and insisted on a nap before Leo's promised tour, so he and Emma left her in the company of the animals and strolled the still-empty streets.

"Let's walk toward the castle," she said.

He put an arm around her and drew her in. Her arrival had extinguished his anxiety. With her by his side, everything seemed possible. "Are you hoping to get another verbal lashing from my mother?"

"Don't get mad when I say this," she said slowly. "I know you're not interested in being seen as a royal."

"Correct," he said flatly.

"But it's part of who you are. Part of your brand. And it's going to get you a lot more attention than being some random guy who's mad about something. Leveraging your identity is going to help save the community center."

Leo's mouth opened, ready to refuse. But seconds later, he snapped it shut. "I don't like it. I'm not some attention-seeking sellout like John."

John had a very active Instagram account with twelve million followers. The vast majority were staged photos carefully taken by Beatrice or a royal photographer. Why would he want to be a part of something that celebrated that kind of vanity?

"I know," she said. "It's just for a little while. When we win, we can delete it. Or migrate it into an account for community news or something. Give me your phone."

He pressed his lips together but handed it over.

"Remember, this is for your people."

The sun was creeping into the sky, enchanting everything in a golden hue. How long had it been since he had slowed down enough to admire how beautiful the village was at the first light of dawn?

She pulled to a stop next to a wooden fence and seemed to be calculating a perfect shot with the castle and the lake in the background. The tips of her ears were pink from the cold, and she was still wearing her hand-stitched jacket. Someday he'd get her a new one.

"Stop scowling," she chastised.

"Do we have to do this?" he asked.

She looked up from the screen. "You asked me for help. Do you want to get this project built or not?"

"Fine."

She instructed him to turn this way, then that way. Glasses on, glasses off. He leaned against the fence, staring over his shoulder at the castle grounds and lake. He felt like an idiot.

Emma eventually gave him permission to relax and flicked through the pictures. "Oh, man. You are so stupidly hot. People are going to go feral over these. You're going to have so many groupies."

"I don't want groupies."

"Groupies will get this protest off the ground. Trust me."

He scowled and looked over his shoulder at the castle. Though he had lived there his entire life, it had never felt like home. It was a prison. An albatross. A reason for constant supervision and criticism. Everyone he met treated him differently because of the family he was born into. Everyone except for Emma.

"What's wrong?" she asked. She must have noticed his space-out.

"Thank you," he said.

"For what?"

"For coming here. For not treating me differently because of who I am. And for putting your life on hold. I know it wasn't part of your plan."

"Plans change. This is worth it," she said with a squeeze of his hand. "But you won't be thanking me in a minute."

"Oh, god. What now?"

She averted her eyes to stare out over the snow-capped mountains. The sun had just burst over them, bathing the village in brilliant light. "Making an account isn't going to be enough. We have to ask someone for help."

"Who?"

"What's your brother's schedule like today?"

<hr>

"ABSOLUTELY NOT," JOHN SAID AS THE THREE OF THEM STOOD in the castle library. He had a pickleball racket slung over his shoulder, and his scowl suggested he was being held up. John didn't seem surprised to see Emma, who was strolling the perimeter of the library, examining spines.

"Mother will kill me," John added. "I'm already on the outs because of the whole...you know."

"It's just a family picture. She'll love the warm fuzzies. Great publicity," Leo said.

John considered the flames cracking in the hearth. "She won't be happy about me tagging a social media account she didn't approve of. Especially if it's you. No offense."

Leo raised his eyebrows. "Need I remind you that you're going to be king someday? You don't need to be afraid of her. And beyond that, you're my brother. I've never asked you for anything. You know I wouldn't ask unless it was really important."

He could feel Emma's eyes on him from across the room. He didn't enjoy having her eavesdrop on his forced groveling to the king-dick-to-be.

John spun the head of his racket on a table for a moment and seemed to consider it.

"Why are you suddenly embracing social media? You've never wanted to be online before. Is this about the thing you're trying to build?" he asked.

Leo nodded. Sometimes his brother was more than a pair of testicles in a tuxedo. While he had told John that he needed to tag his new account to get the word out, he had left out the part that he was planning to use it to garner followers and start a protest. Against their own parents.

"I just need to raise a little support, that's all. This project is going to change lives, John. I need your help. Please."

John sighed and pulled out his phone. He tapped away for a minute or two, then slid it back into his pocket.

"Close your DMs. Trust me." He walked toward the door, then stopped. "By the way, whatever you're planning to do, you need to do it quickly. They're supposed to break ground on the ski resort on Monday."

"Great," Leo said. Another deadline.

They were going to have to work very fast. Would they pull it off, or would the project be pushed months or years down the road while they scouted a new location and rebuilt the entire crew while Hollybrook fell to gentrification? The women and children of Lynoria couldn't wait.

"Exactly. Emma?" John asked.

She whirled around looking surprised. "Yes?"

"You quit the bakery?"

"In a manner of speaking," she said.

"Good."

He left without another word.

"Well," Emma said after a beat, "I guess we know where things stand with him and Maya."

Leo nodded. "Whatever happened with the bakery anyway? Did they reopen?"

Emma suppressed a smile. "It's been closed all week. There are some rumors online it might be permanent."

"I was hoping a disgruntled former employee might have burned it down," he said. It was what Maya deserved.

Emma threw up her hands. "I don't mess with arson. So you didn't tell John about the whole trying-to-start-a-protest-to-save-the-lot thing?" she asked.

"I didn't think it was important."

"Right. Well, let's have a quick meeting and schedule some posts so we can warm people up to the idea. Then we can take Mom out on the town. And take some more pictures."

"No more pictures," he said sternly.

"Do you want to save this project or not?" she asked.

He threw up his hands. The things he did for his country.

————

"What are you doing?" Leo asked as they stood on a street corner.

"Looking for paparazzi," Emma said, scanning the streets.

"And why would we want to run into them?" he asked slowly.

"I told you. We need you to blow up. You've stirred up some interest since you're dating a crazy American ginger-bread-smasher. Unfortunately, right now all attention is good attention. We need to go make out in the square or something, get the press talking."

He stopped in the middle of the sidewalk. "Absolutely not. I don't need them hounding you. And if I'm going to kiss you, it's because I want to kiss you. Not because someone's watching. You're not a pawn."

She turned to look at him. "They're already hounding me, remember? We might as well do something good with the unsolicited attention. Maybe we could really stir things up and go publicly buy a pregnancy test. It could be good for my business too. If I had one. Or could think of a name for it."

"All that time preparing for your future business, and you never thought of a name for it?"

She shook her head. "Nothing ever felt right."

He reached for her hand. "Once things are underway, I'm going to help you too."

"There's no need. I can manage. I've been preparing for this for years."

He narrowed his eyes against the sun glancing off the snow. "I don't think you had factored in helping a particularly needy prince on a different continent. Let me help."

"Fine. Maybe," she said with a smile. "But first, the shelter."

His stomach twisted. The guilt he felt taking her away from setting her plan in motion was unreal. But maybe if she spent a little more time here, she would reconsider moving her business here. Or maybe they could split their time between Lynoria and New York.

But Leo still hadn't figured out a job for himself. He'd had to apply for the zoo position in person since they hadn't believed his initial application. He had an interview at the end of the first week of January. Having a real job meant a fixed schedule, no freedom.

Plus, Emma had never actually said she wanted to keep dating. She had come here at the drop of a hat, sure, but maybe she just thought they were friends.

Friends who had mind-blowing sex and crossed continents for each other. That was a thing, right?

She nudged him and startled him out of thoughts of international booty calls. "We should check your post."

He pulled out his phone and fumbled for a minute, trying to find the stupid app. When he opened it, his screen was a mess of red notifications.

She peeked over his shoulder. "Oh boy. One post and you've hit the big time."

For his first post, they had decided on the picture of Leo in front of the castle. It had felt grossly self-serving, but Emma assured him that it would gather attention.

And she had been right.

"What does this number mean?"

"That's your followers," Emma said. "Twelve thousand in less than an hour. That's impressive."

"You're humoring me. Didn't the bakery have like half a million?"

"Eight hundred thousand, but who's counting? Oh, here we are."

They stopped at the end of the street where the vacant lot waited. He could see every detail of it as if the buildings were already there. The community garden, the library with rows of windows and natural light. A new soup kitchen with its doors propped open in springtime, filling the block with the scent of homegrown garlic and rosemary.

"Okay, now just stand in front of it. Don't cross your arms. Hands in your pockets, neutral expression. You want to look approachable but still semi-serious."

He struggled to keep a straight face as he attempted to follow her litany of suggestions.

She backed up and took pictures from several angles. It would have been exhausting even if he hadn't been up since 4 a.m.

She flicked through the pictures and chose one. "Perfect. Okay, now the library."

"Should we get your mom first?"

"Great idea. She loves a library."

An hour later, the stolen wheelchair clattered over the threshold of the library.

"I love it," Lisa whispered.

"You've said that about everything we've seen," Emma said, but her tone was teasing.

"Because it's true. It's all so quaint and lovely. I feel so at home here. Don't you feel at home, Emma?"

"I do love a library," she said noncommittally.

Leo shot her a look. Unless he was mistaken, Lisa was heavily hinting that she would give up their apartment and move to Lynoria. What did Emma think about that?

Maybe he was misinterpreting and Lisa was just happy to travel outside the small radius she had been trapped in for two years. He shouldn't get his hopes up.

He really needed to just man up and ask Emma what she was thinking. But the thought of losing her friendship gave him a type of anxiety he had never experienced.

Besides, everything was up in the air right now. He wasn't in any position to be a good boyfriend when he was jobless and directionless.

"Okay," Emma said, "the library and the community garden need to be our main plugs. While our donors need to know what they're paying for, for safety reasons, we can't disclose the location of the shelter to the public."

"Right." He glanced back at Lisa, who had a far-off look in her eye as they traveled between the tomes. Was all this talk of shelters making her relive her experience? He should be more sensitive.

"Ah," Emma said, coming to a stop in the children's section. "This is perfect."

A woman and child were playing with some faded-looking toy cars on a battered table. The children's section really did need an upgrade.

The mother looked up, and her mouth popped open in surprise. She rose to her feet, tugging her son with her. He couldn't have been more than three.

"Your Highness." She sank into a curtsy. Her son bowed next to her, then hid behind her.

"Just Leo," he said. He was ninety-five percent sure this was the woman who worked the evening shift at the local grocery store. "It's Mary, right?"

"I—uh—yes, Your Highness," she said, visibly surprised. "I mean, Leo. No, that's not right. I can't do it, Your Highness. I'm sorry."

Her cheeks flushed.

Leo cracked a smile.

"I'm Emma." She stuck a hand out to Mary, who shook it. "I just love a library, don't you?"

"Oh, yes," Mary said. "We come for story time every Tuesday. The princess read *The Very Hungry Caterpillar* last week," she said.

"Isn't she the best? Children's literature is so important. You know, Prince Leo is actually trying to build a new library," Emma said.

"Really?" Mary said.

The son peeked out from behind his mother and inspected the group. "Why are you in a wheelchair?" he asked.

"Asher," Mary said harshly. "I'm so sorry."

Leo held his breath, but Lisa smiled.

She leaned forward to look at Asher. "Something happened to my body that made my legs not work so well. I can walk a little, but it's safer for me to stay in the wheelchair while we're out and about."

"I'm so sorry," Mary repeated. Her face had gone from scarlet to pale as a fresh cut of wood.

"There's no need to be sorry," Lisa said. "It's good to ask questions. And it's better than the alternative. People often avert their eyes around me, or they speak to me like I'm elderly and infirm. Do you want to touch the chair?"

Asher crouched down to tap a spoke, then smiled.

Leo's stomach hardened, and he resolved to remember this moment every time he met someone in a wheelchair.

He would personally make sure every part of the new project was accessible.

"So, Your Highness, you're building a new library?"

"Well, I'm trying to. A ski resort is trying to lease the lot we want to use."

Mary's face fell. She glanced at the worn blocks and a toy train that looked like it had been chewed on. "We don't need another ski resort."

"I agree."

She probably didn't even know the danger the town was in.

"But the prince is trying to change that," Emma said smoothly. "The crown maintains ownership of the land, so we're staging a peaceful protest outside the castle on Saturday, followed by a holiday extravaganza to raise money for the project."

"A protest?" Mary asked.

"Yes. We're fighting for what's best for this community. We'd love to have you and Asher fight alongside us. We're actually having an emergency town hall meeting to discuss it tonight at 6 p.m. if you're available. Here, take some flyers." Emma handed over a few of the pages they'd had printed before picking her mom up.

Mary stood tall. "We'll be there."

"Excellent. Tell your friends."

"This is how it starts," Lisa said with a musical quality in her voice.

Not with a whisper, but a throat punch.

CHAPTER FORTY-TWO

LEO

"What's this all about, Your Highness?" An older woman wearing what looked to be seven different scarves shivered in the front row of the auditorium.

"Yes, and what do these flyers mean?" A man with a rugged beard waved one of the purple-and-gold sheets they had been distributing around town all afternoon.

Leo's heart was ready to fly out of his chest. This wasn't what was supposed to happen at town hall meetings. *He* was supposed to help *them*. But now he needed to ask for help, and he wasn't sure how the news would be received.

He owed it to them to give it his all. And hopefully the rapport they'd built over the years would be enough.

Emma sat on the table at the front of the room next to Leo, legs crossed and Leo's customary notepad in her lap. The room was packed with curious business owners and townspeople. With any luck, they would be willing to help.

"Just Leo," he corrected. "Thank you all for coming on such short notice. I've gathered you all here today because I need your help. Urgently."

A whisper rippled through the auditorium.

Emma hit the projector, which turned on to reveal a picture of a blueprint.

"I know this isn't what we usually do here," Leo said. His voice shook slightly. "And I hope you know that I wouldn't ask this if I didn't believe to my very core that this will benefit everyone."

The audience was rapt with attention.

"I've been in the process of planning a new project for our community. A new library, where we can have literacy and after-school programming for children. A community garden and a playground, among other vital services. It would be built right here, on the edge of town."

Emma clicked to the next slide, which was a 3D model. The old woman who had spoken earlier polished her glasses and leaned forward.

"This project would create jobs for local Lynoria-based companies. And once it's finished, it will be an enduring testament to the strength of our people. A place to gather and celebrate this beautiful town we call home. But there's been a problem. The crown has leased the land to someone else."

Disgruntled murmurs arose.

"And they want to build a ski resort instead."

"On the edge of town?" someone cried in outrage.

"We've seen this before," Leo said. "It won't just be a strain on our infrastructure. We will face the very real risk of gentrification. When the last resort moved into Southbridge, property taxes and rents soared and sixty percent of working-class residents were displaced within five years. We can't let this happen to Hollybrook. This is our home, and I believe in investing in *you*."

"Yeah," a number of people in the audience said.

"That's why we need a multi-pronged plan. First, we

need to raise the second half of the money for this project. And second, we need to march on the castle in protest. Make the crown hear us. Shut down the lease of this land and reclaim it."

"Let's *do it*." A man in his twenties jumped to his feet, then sat back down. "Sorry, I got excited."

Leo smiled.

"What do you need? How can we help?" someone asked.

"Let me turn things over to my beautiful coconspirator, Emma."

Emma waved and cleared her throat. "Hi, everyone. This is going to be a huge endeavor, but I know we can do it. The current plan is to have a massive fundraising holiday extravaganza. We need donations from local businesses for an auction and volunteers for a slew of holiday activities, with the proceeds going to the community center fund."

She turned around and began writing on the whiteboard at the front of the room.

"Gift wrapping, a storefront decorating contest, bake sale, karaoke contest, ornament decorating. We're open to other ideas."

Gretchen from the library raised her hand. "What about a book sale?"

"Perfect." Emma added it to the list.

Sal raised his hand, and she pointed to him. "How about a wine and chocolate pairing?"

"Excellent. The more alcohol, the better."

"How about a polar plunge?" another man asked.

"No," Emma and Leo said hurriedly.

A number of other townspeople added suggestions, and by the end of the meeting, they had a date, an extensive list of volunteers, and a plan.

"Thank you all so much for coming. Please take some flyers with you on your way out. Tell everyone you see."

"I can't believe it's actually happening," Leo muttered to Emma.

"You were incredible. I know you've said a thousand times you have no interest in being a prince, but you were born for leadership. You're doing the right thing, even at great personal cost."

His cheeks warmed.

"I'm really glad you're here," he said with a squeeze of her hand.

Sal sidled up as people started to filter out. "Emma, so pleased to see you again." They hugged.

"I'm going to take a stack into the city tomorrow," he said as he slid a ream of paper off the desk. "I might even go to the outer provinces. I think we can go much bigger."

"That's not a bad idea," Leo mused.

Emma hopped down from the desk. "It's time to publish the post."

He sucked in a deep breath. There was no turning back now. The fate of this town was in his hands. He had already done irreparable damage to his relationship with his parents. He might as well pound the final nail into the coffin.

CHAPTER FORTY-THREE

LEO

News of the protest spread throughout Lynoria like wildfire. His social media following grew by the minute. People expressed support from across the globe. Thanks to Emma's interventions, a movement was building.

After a long Friday of canvassing the country, distributing flyers, and chatting with community leaders, Leo's back ached as he stood at the front of the community center.

People milled all around, hefting homemade signs and sharing markers. There were so many attendees that people had to wait outside on the street. There was a tangible energy in the air.

His stomach was in knots, and he hadn't slept at all the night before. Not even because of Sal's impressive snoring. He was about to enrage his parents and endanger what little hope remained for a future relationship with them. This event would sever his familial ties for good.

Did he even want a relationship with people who were so quick to cut him off? And for what, dating an American? It was medieval. He could make do with just Ruby as his family—and maybe John, at least on holidays.

Even though it was a sensible boundary, it still hurt. What if he and Emma beat the odds and worked everything out? Would his parents attend his wedding? Would they have a relationship with his future children?

There was no perfect solution. No matter what way he went about it, someone was going to get hurt. And he would rather the hurt party be his parents than innocent women and children fleeing untold horrors.

This was bigger than he was. Bigger than any of them. And he owed it to his country to do whatever it took to get this project off the ground.

A gentle hand landed on his back, and the scent of vanilla drifted in the air. Emma.

"Doing okay?" she asked gently, like she was trying to coax a cat down from a tree. She was wearing a T-shirt that said Growth, Not Greed, and she looked fresh as a poet's daffodil despite having baked in his tiny apartment for the last day and a half.

Just looking at her gave him peace.

"I'm a little nervous," he admitted.

"Totally understandable. You're doing what has to be done. Everything will be okay. I can feel it."

He pressed a kiss to the top of her head and breathed in her presence. How was it possible to feel so strongly about someone he had met less than a month ago?

He glanced at his watch. Just a few minutes till noon. First the protest, and then the Christmas extravaganza. Who knew that the holiday that filled him with so much disdain might just be the thing that saved his entire project?

"Want me to wrangle everyone?" she asked.

"Thank you."

"Okay, everyone, gather your materials and meet us outside. We march at noon," Emma called.

People drifted out into the street, chattering excitedly, and Leo followed with a knot in his stomach. There was no turning back now.

The local police had closed the road to accommodate the protesters and prepare for the fundraiser. People spilled out onto the cobblestones. There must have been hundreds. Citizens of all ages had turned up—young teenagers who were certainly not dressed for the cold, parents holding small children and waving Lynorian flags, and even some slope-shouldered elderly people with walking sticks. Many of them bowed, to his chagrin.

It was a good thing the province had donated the use of so many portable loos.

The sun was shining, and it was warmer than any December day that he could remember. Storefronts were decorated with holiday flair, some themed after Christmas movies and others dressed up like giant gifts.

Emma darted to the front of the crowd, where Sal was pushing her mom's wheelchair. Even Cooper and Arizona were wearing tiny Lynorian flag bandannas.

Was that the marching band from the local high school?

The response heartened him. People genuinely cared. They wanted what was best for the community, even if the king and queen didn't.

Sal handed over the bullhorn from the night before, and Leo took it with a clammy hand.

"People of Lynoria," he called. Everyone stopped talking and snapped to attention. "Thank you for joining me today. For those of you who I haven't met, I'm Leo. And I'm trying to build something for our country. Right down the road from here."

He pointed to where the new community hub would stand.

"A country has nothing more valuable than its people. I want to assure you I see you for who you are—hardworking, dedicated, family-oriented, fun-loving. I have such pride in this community. I want to give you what you deserve. We don't need another ski resort."

A chorus of cheers rang out, and his nerves dissipated slightly.

"We need a place for our people to gather. A new library for our children to learn about new worlds and new ideas. A community garden where we can grow and tend crops, or flowers, or whatever you want—well, short of anything illegal."

A chuckle rippled through the crowd. A young woman at the edge of the crowd caught his eye. Her hair was curly and the same shade as Ruby's. She pulled her giant sunglasses down and winked at him. It *was* her. His heart lifted.

"And let's not forget a new community kitchen where we can feed our hungry. The castle's going to tell you that a ski resort would create jobs. And sure, maybe there would be a few. But a resort would be the downfall of this beautiful village. We can't allow a corporation to gentrify our people out of their homes."

He took a deep breath as another cheer arose. Hopefully no one could tell that his hand was shaking.

"This is one of the biggest challenges our village has ever faced. And I'm going to fight for it. I'm going to fight for you. Now let's go."

The loudest cheer yet ripped through the crowd, and the marching band started playing behind him. People lifted their signs, and he felt a tiny glimmer of hope. Maybe it would be enough. Maybe it would force his parents' hands.

The castle loomed on the hillside. Ruby had assured

him that his parents were home and would be there to witness the protest. They'd surely stay walled up in the castle, hiding behind the gates. But now that the eyes of the world were on them, his parents would be forced to make a statement, take a stance. Hopefully it would be enough to make them crumble.

Emma reached over to squeeze his hand, and his fortitude doubled. He led the charge toward the castle.

They marched through the cold air, chanting and waving their signs. Lisa waved a flag as Emma pushed her wheelchair. She looked exhilarated as they trundled up the road.

A half dozen members of the press were there to cover the event. They snapped pictures and asked for statements as they walked. Only one asked him about his relationship with Emma.

Finally, they reached the castle gates. A couple of people from the community—one of the librarians, Gus from the soup kitchen, and a local teacher all spoke about the potential benefits of the project. Even Henri, their local member of parliament, showed up.

"Growth, not greed," echoed in the courtyard. A couple members of the castle guard showed up, nervously standing in front of the gates in riot gear. He nodded at them, and they bowed.

A curtain twitched in one of the windows upstairs. Someone was watching. But as predicted, no one came out to address the crowd.

Leo spoke one final time before the crowd began to disperse.

"Thank you, Your Highness," one of the reference clerks from the library said, cheeks flushed, before darting away.

"It's just Leo," he called after her with a smile.

"Leo, tell me more about this community garden," Lisa said as people started the walk back to the village. "I could prepare some suggestions and planting schedules as soon as I figure out what growing zone we're in and what native plants are in the area."

"Let me take you to the library tomorrow," he said.

Where was Emma?

Lisa looked at her phone. "Oh, Emma says she'll meet us back in town before the extravaganza."

"She didn't say why?"

Lisa shook her head.

"Okay." A knot formed in his stomach, but he dove back into the fray with Lisa and the dogs in tow.

CHAPTER FORTY-FOUR

EMMA

THE DOOR CREAKED SHUT AS EMMA DARTED INTO THE CASTLE hallway. Castle security had been so concerned about the mass of people at the gate that they had completely neglected security at other access points. She had lifted Leo's key card and snuck in through the family entrance Ruby had shown her when she was drunk. It was an incredibly stupid move—in fact, she wouldn't be surprised if the queen had her arrested the second she confronted her. She had destroyed a masterpiece in the castle only a week ago, after all. But if there was even a small chance that she could make Leo's mother see reason, it would be worth the risk.

Emma pulled a clipboard out of her bag and pretended to consult it as she walked down the hallway. A couple of the servants looked confused as she passed them, but no one stopped her.

Where would the queen be? She decided to start in the drawing room, which had windows that faced the courtyard. After taking a turn down an unfamiliar hallway and briefly getting lost, she pressed her ear to the double doors of the drawing room.

There was silence within, and she popped the doors open. The queen stood by the window, and she sprang back as if Emma had caught her doing something illicit.

"Miss Clark?" she asked, clearly confused. That was fair. Emma had just committed an egregious form of breaking and entering. Hopefully criminal records didn't transfer between countries. "What the hell are you doing here?"

Feisty words for a hoity-toity queen.

"Hello, Your Majesty," she said with a small curtsy. She stepped inside and shut the door. They were alone. "Before you call for security, I need to talk to you."

The queen twitched the thick velvet curtain back for one more look before turning her attention to Emma.

"Is this about my son?"

"It is. I just needed to make sure you know that Leo isn't doing this out of spite. The protest isn't a retaliation because you cut him off. It's not an elaborate ploy to get back on the royal bank accounts. He's doing this because he cares so deeply about this kingdom that he's willing to put them ahead of repairing his relationship with his family."

The queen opened her mouth, but Emma plowed on. "Building a new ski resort will irrevocably damage the people in your own backyard. Leo's plan is going to be a gift to them. Do you really want to deny the children of the village a new library? And abandon women and children in need?"

The queen's lips pressed together.

"There's a difference between doing what's profitable and doing what's right. I know you've said your hands are tied," Emma said. "But I know who you are. You are a badass bitch, and the most powerful woman in this country. If anyone can take a stand and stop that ski resort, it's you. Cancel the lease. Go medieval on their ass and reclaim the land through eminent domain. Pretend they found a nesting site for an endangered bird species. Just do something. There's always a way forward."

Had she just called the queen a badass bitch? Whoops.

The queen paused for a long minute, staring off toward the curtain again. "I'll take it under advisement."

"Thank you for considering it," Emma said. She crossed the room before the queen could call in the guards and paused with a hand on the door. "I see so much of you in Leo, you know? You're both a little stubborn, a little reactionary, but I know that you care deeply. Even if you're not able to show it. Leo loves you in spite of and because of everything. I hope that, in time, you'll be able to see that."

The queen averted her gaze.

It was time for Emma's Hail Mary.

"Oh, and one more thing. I sent a video to Beatrice. It's about my experience in a women's shelter. I know I'm not your favorite person, but please listen to it. And then reconsider. You're the only person who can stop this. Do the right thing."

"You love my son," the queen accused as Emma turned to leave.

What?

Emma froze. Love? Not this again. They barely knew each other. Love meant many scary things—figuring out how to make their bicontinental relationship work for the long haul, building their lives together, being vulnerable and taking each other into account when they made plans for the future. They couldn't be there yet. It was impossible.

And yet. She had never felt this strongly for anyone before, not even her last boyfriend of three years. Leo had saved her life. And Cooper's. If not him, then who? She couldn't even imagine dating someone else. No one would fill the Leo-sized hole in her heart.

"I know you wouldn't have come here if you didn't," the queen added. "It takes courage—or maybe a great deal of stupidity—to confront a monarch in her own home, especially after that display at the ball. Some might even say it's an offense that would land you in a very dark, spider-infested dungeon," she said coolly.

Oh, shit.

"But for what you've done for my children, I'll let it slide. This time."

Relief flooded her. "Thank you, Your Majesty."

She slipped out the back door and bustled back down the hill to town before the queen could change her mind. Protesters were still scattered about, resting their signs over their shoulders as they drifted toward the holiday extravaganza ramping up downtown.

Had they done enough? Or was the queen really immovable marble? Either way, it was time for the second part of their plan. Getting the land wouldn't mean anything if they didn't have money to build.

CHAPTER FORTY-FIVE

LEO

Downtown Hollybrook had transformed into an explosion of holiday lights and color. It was like the winter carnival on steroids. Garland, holly, mistletoe. The roads were closed, all the storefronts were decorated, booths lined the high street and sat all over the park. A 3D model of the proposed community center site was set up at the lot. Kat had made it herself.

It was the biggest holiday celebration Hollybrook had ever seen. Countless people had volunteered their time and declared all their proceeds would go to the community fund. But would it be enough?

Leo caught Emma's eye. She flashed him a smile, then turned back to the line in front of her booth. It must have been ten meters long. She had decided that the noncompete clause didn't apply across international lines or for charity events. After convincing Ruby to smuggle some baking materials out of the castle, she had baked dozens of Christmas cookies, cakes, and pies. She'd had a last-minute burst of inspiration and thrown together fifty premade gingerbread kits, which appeared to be already gone. Lisa sat next to her, taking money and chatting merrily with patrons.

He scanned the crowd, nodding at the townspeople, who blushed and curtsied at him. People spilled out of Sal's pub, cheeks pink from their flights of wine. Dorinda from the seamstress shop stood at the gift-wrapping station, looking in concern at a bicycle lying on her table. Children squealed in a Santa-themed bounce house. The ornament-decorating booth was inundated with its first round of decorators. Even Henri had stayed to emcee the auction.

And it wasn't all Christmas-themed. Food vendors from all over the country had turned up, and it had been a serious last-minute effort to find space and electricity for them all. The air was perfumed with a heavenly mix of roasted mutton, spiced curry, sharp cheeses, and herby soups.

Citizens had turned up in droves both to volunteer and to shop. There was something empowering about being surrounded by his countrymen, all united in support of this cause. Someone was even wearing a shirt with Leo's profile on it and the word "resist" below. Hopefully his mother didn't see it.

It was, in the best possible way, truly magical.

"Your Highness." Isabelle appeared at his elbow with a clipboard and a frazzled expression.

"What's wrong?"

"The wireless mics aren't working, and the auction's supposed to start in five minutes."

"Let me see them." They sped over to the stage he and Sal had fixed earlier that month. Cases lay open all around them, donated from one of the local churches.

In a flash, Leo had looked up the model and serial number on YouTube and found a troubleshooting video.

"Check, check." His voice boomed out from the monitors lining the stage. The crowd turned to stare. Shit. He hadn't planned on making another speech.

He rose to his feet. "Good evening, everyone."

The crowd rippled like a wave as people bowed.

"I can't thank you enough for showing up today. I've talked your ears off already, so I'll keep it short. You know what's at stake. Your generosity is going to be poured directly back into this community. You have my word. No matter what happens here tonight, I won't give up. Somehow, we'll find a way. Now I'm going to turn things over to Henri so we can get the auction party started."

The crowd cheered, and Leo handed the mic off and went in search of the next disaster. He ducked in to help wrap a basketball for a local schoolteacher, then handwashed some wine glasses for the next round of Sal's tastings.

The town was alive, buzzing. A million different pieces were in motion, and it was incredible to watch. An excavator parked at the lot caught his eye, and his stomach clenched. They were almost out of time. His countrymen had come together and taken ownership where his parents wouldn't. He couldn't let them down.

Henri's booming voice was audible across the whole market, so Leo was able to keep tabs as spa days, gift certificates, and baskets of goods were auctioned off.

They were inching closer, but still miles away from their goal. Would the money from the vendors be enough? The uncertainty was driving him mad.

"Doing okay?" Emma asked with a sweet smile as he approached. Her table was bare. She must have sold everything.

"I'm fine," he answered gruffly.

"Everything is going to work out." She laid a gentle hand

on his arm. Her fingers were red from the frigid night air, and he wrapped them in his own.

"We don't know that," he said. "What if I let everyone down again?"

"Then we'll find another way."

"We?" A hint of a smile appeared.

"Yes, I'm invested now. Is that what you want to hear?" There was a glint in her eyes.

"I'm happy for any good news."

"Well then, you should know that I also made a buttload of money." She hit a button on a borrowed cash register, and the drawer slid out. Notes and coins were overflowing.

He slid it back in, then pulled her in for a hug. "I can't thank you enough for everything you've done. For me and for Lynoria."

They pulled back to look at each other, and something immeasurable passed between them. A question hung in the air. What would come next? Their circumstances hadn't changed. Even if they failed today, Leo couldn't give up on the shelter. Emma was supposed to return to New York tomorrow to start planning her business in earnest. And when she was there, he wasn't going to be able to protect her from her dad.

They hadn't even had a real conversation about their relationship. Were they together? When would they see each other again? Was there even a way to make this work with an ocean between them?

"Leo, I—" Emma stopped. "Hold the fucking phone. Did someone just say fifty thousand euros?"

"What?" He whipped his head toward the park.

"Go," she said.

He took off, jogging through the market and dodging passersby. Had they heard correctly? He had seen the auction items. Unless someone had airlifted in a luxury SUV, none of them were worth anything close to 50k.

"Fifty thousand going once. Fifty thousand going twice. One meal with Prince Leopold of Lynoria, sold to the—uh—hooded figure in the back row. You guys can see her too, right?" Henri asked.

A couple people chuckled.

Leo rushed around the corner in time to see a mysterious figure in a floor-length emerald cloak that completely obscured their face. The figure stopped at the payment table, then left. Who in the hell had just bought an incredibly expensive dinner with him? Even their hands had been covered in gloves, so there were no distinguishing features to hazard a guess.

Everything in his body was tingling with energy. With the mysterious person's generous contribution, there was an excellent chance that they had just hit their goal. But there was only one way to find out.

Leo ducked into the community center, where volunteers were double-checking the amounts brought in by the booths. Cash machines whirred, and a hand-drawn thermometer was filling up on the whiteboard.

Someone snuck up behind him and looped their arm through his. Emma. She squeezed him, and they waited together.

The cash collector from the auction came in. Silence fell as they tallied checks and double-checked everything. They handed a piece of paper to Isabelle. She turned her back to the room, looked at it, and looked back with a poker face.

She looked him dead in the eyes and broke into a smile. "Congratulations, Your Highness. You've got yourself a community center fund."

CHAPTER FORTY-SIX

LEO

"You did it!" Sal clinked a glass with Leo at the bar. The atmosphere was festive and joyful, but Leo was still apprehensive. "I have to admit, I never thought you'd pull this off when you got cut off."

Leo shook his head. "We have the money, yes. But we still don't know about the land. We shouldn't celebrate yet."

Sal leaned over the bar. "Do you really think your mom is going to go on record saying she doesn't think the children of the village deserve a playground?"

Leo took a sip of his beer. "I don't know. She's capable of a lot of things I never thought."

"Get your negativity out of here," Sal said with a wag of his finger. "We're manifesting."

"I don't put much stock in manifestation," Leo muttered.

Sal rattled the ice in his glass. "That's because you're a fool. Like you're a fool for not telling Emma you want a relationship."

"Shh," Leo said, then shot a glance over his shoulder. Emma sat in a booth with her mom and Arizona, laughing and clinking together glasses of Santa's Revenge.

"You need to have this conversation. Doesn't she leave tomorrow?"

"Yes."

"Then put your big boy britches on and go talk to her."

"Fine."

His heart was galloping as he crossed the crowded bar. Everything was teetering on a precipice—the project, his career, his relationship with Emma. He was unmoored, anchorless. But Emma was a lighthouse in the shitstorm of his life. And she would still believe in him, even if he let everyone down.

She didn't care that he was a prince. She didn't even care that he was the worst kind of prince with no real job and virtually no money. Emma took him as he was, warts and all.

"There he is," Lisa said as he approached. "Congratulations, Your Highness."

"Let's not celebrate too early," he said with a grim smile. "Emma, can we have a chat?"

"Of course," she said. "You're okay?" she asked her mom before she got out of the booth.

"We're great." Lisa gestured to Arizona, who was wearing a new Christmas tree collar donated by a local pet store owner.

When Emma stood, Sal slid into the booth and started asking Lisa about gardenias. He and Cal had a garden every spring.

Leo closed his hand around Emma's, and he led her out into the wintry streets. It was late. The booths were vacant, ready to be moved back to storage the following day. And Emma was leaving in a matter of hours.

"You're quiet," she said with a nudge. "More quiet than usual, I mean."

"I'm trying to figure out how to say this. I'm not...good at talking about my feelings."

They pulled to a stop under a streetlight and faced each other.

"Really? Your mom wasn't a founding member of the gentle parenting movement?" she said with a smile. "Sorry. Not everything needs a joke. I'm just nervous. Talk to me."

He took a breath and was silent for a moment. "I know you live thousands of miles away."

"Right."

"And your family and work and whole life are in New York," he said.

She nodded.

"I think you're amazing. Strong, resilient, ridiculously talented. You deserve to have everything you've always dreamed of. I don't want to destroy the plan you've been working toward your entire life. But I think losing you forever would kill me."

She bit her lip and reached over to take his hand. "I don't want to lose you either, Leo. I'm having crazy strong feelings for you. You stood up for me even when it cost you everything. I've never seen anyone love something the way you love this country. It's even made me question some things about my own life..." She was quiet for a moment, then snapped back to attention. "But I don't know how to rectify these two realities. We live in different countries. I have my mom and my plan to worry about, and our apartment and— you're a *prince*, Leo."

"Barely," he said.

The words were on the tip of his tongue. He loved her. He had known it for a while now. But if he said it too soon, it could scare her away for good.

He reached over and touched a strand of her hair.

"These weeks that I've spent with you have completely changed my life. I don't want to date anyone else. I want you in my life forever."

She averted her gaze. There was another long pause. "What if my dad uses me to hurt you?"

A pang hit his heart. "I don't care about your dad, Emma. Your family doesn't define you. I'll find a way to keep you safe from him."

But what was he going to do from thousands of miles away? Buy her a doorbell camera when he got his first paycheck from the zoo? If they even hired him.

"So then what?" Emma asked. "We date long distance? That never works out."

Leo sighed and stared off into the distance. "I don't know. I'm not sure what's going to happen when I get a real job. Maybe I'll find something that requires travel to America," he said. "I don't want to let you go, but I've also never had fewer resources. I can't even afford to give you what you deserve."

Her hand closed over his. "I don't care what you have to 'offer.' This isn't the eighteen hundreds. It's not like I have a dowry full of gold pigeons waiting for you either."

"Gold pigeons? Is that an American thing?"

"No, it's—never mind." She huffed, visibly frustrated.

They were at an impasse. Again.

"Long distance is better than nothing," he said. "Maybe we could meet in the middle."

"Where, on a random island in the middle of the Atlantic?" she raised an eyebrow. "I just don't know that long distance is going to be enough for me, Leo," she said. "I want all of you, not just a couple texts a day and visits twice a year. That's not a partnership."

"Try. Please. For me," he said. His grip on her hand was ironlike. "I can't watch you get on that train tomorrow and disappear from my life forever."

She was biting her lip again and seemed to be considering. Instead of answering, she threw herself at him and kissed him hard. There was a desperation in it.

"Is that a yes, or a goodbye?" he asked when she pulled back.

She put a hand on his cheek. "It's a 'we'll try.'"

Relief flooded his body. No matter what happened with her job or his project, at least they had each other.

"I'll take it," he said. He dove back into the kiss, burying a hand in her hair. His heart was still beating too fast.

He would show her what a lifetime with him could look like.

The moon was high when he pulled back and grabbed her hand. He tugged her down the street toward his new apartment, his insides a tangled mess of desire, yearning, and fear.

The second he opened the door, he moved to pull Emma to him, but Cooper bounded over. Then the kittens meowed. Shit. He had woken up the entire menagerie.

Emma smiled and tossed Cooper a treat, then pulled Leo into the animal-free bathroom. She immediately removed her stitched-up coat. He did the same, and they came back together. Her mouth was warm against his, but she trembled in his arms.

"You're cold," he said.

"I'm fine," she said, but her teeth chattered.

"Let's warm you up."

He leaned past her to turn on the shower, then draped two towels over the heated towel rack. Hot water pumped out, filling the room with steam. He shed his sweater and tugged her to him. Their tongues danced, and her hands raked down his back and then went to her own clothes.

In a flash, they were both naked. He pulled back to look at her. Her hair tumbled down her bare back, acres of curves waiting to be touched. Claimed.

She was *his*, damn it.

He grabbed her more roughly than he intended, hoisted her up so she straddled his waist. Her bare breasts teased his collarbone, and her nipples stiffened in response. He bent to nip them, bottom lip dragging over her silken skin. She shivered again, and he carried her to the shower.

This was all he wanted. *She* was all he wanted. She was here, under his fingertips, a dream in the flesh. But in a matter of hours, she would be gone. Again. What if she never came back? What if the distance was too much?

The warm spray ran in rivulets down Emma's torso, and steam curled into the air. She kissed him with a hunger he'd never known, like she was trying to squash a lifetime of passion into this stolen moment.

She forced a hand between them and found purchase on his dick, which probably could have supported her weight all on its own by this point.

He met her hunger with heat, running a hand over the magnificent topography of her body, trying to memorize every peak and valley by touch. She unwound her legs and dropped to her feet, and he pushed her into the spray to keep her warm while he sampled every inch of her—neck, breasts, stomach, and bikini line—before trailing a finger over her delicate folds.

Her back arched in response, and she yanked him back to her. He ached to be inside her, but a previous shower escapade in college had ended in disaster when the water had washed away all the natural lubrication.

She deserved tenderness, patience, finesse. Something he would give her forever if only she'd let him. He left the shower running and led her gently out of the spray. The towels were warm, and he wrapped one around her before lifting her to perch on the edge of the vanity.

Her eyes were dark with need as he dropped to his knees and guided her legs apart and over him to rest on his shoulders. He was hard as steel as he buried his face between her thighs, tongue circling and swirling. She went rigid as a board, breaths coming in short, ragged gasps. He slipped a finger inside her, and her moan echoed in the small room.

The floor was hard and unforgiving on his knees, but he would have happily stayed there forever. Bringing pleasure to this remarkable woman was one of the most fulfilling duties he'd ever had.

She must have been at the edge, but she pushed him back with her legs. His eyes met hers.

"Condom. Now," she said.

He grabbed the other towel and dashed into the flat, dodging around the kittens, who seemed to have dragged a pizza box out of the trash.

He rolled on a condom, and in seconds, he was back. She still waited for him on the counter. Her towel had fallen open, revealing every centimeter of her beautiful figure. She reached for him, and they met like two seas, crashing together and coalescing until they were a nebulous vortex of heat and need.

He took her, claimed her. Filled her from within. She wrapped him with her legs and her warmth, and it was everything he could do to not lose control immediately.

Their damp skin slapped together as he moved, slowly at first, then more urgently.

Stay. Stay, he mentally pleaded with every thrust. As if he could transfer the idea to her via dick-induced osmosis.

He had never connected with someone on this level. It was so far beyond a mere physical yearning. He craved her laughter, her cheeky glance from across a room. She was fearsomely addictive, and being apart from her was misery.

Didn't he have a duty to himself as much as his people? There had to be a way to make this work. He would find it.

Her entire body went tense, and her chin tipped up like the sensation was growing and changing inside her. He allowed himself to get lost in the rich emerald of her eyes as she clung to him with shaking arms.

With a final thrust, he drove them both to the shuddering brink. Her legs went limp, and he gathered her to his chest, his nose in her wet hair. He draped the towel around her with one arm. His legs shook, and he breathed hard from the exertion.

"Leo?" she said softly.

"Yes?" He drew back to look at her, and his heart went haywire.

There was love in her eyes. He could see it. She was going to say it.

"I—"

Her phone rang in the front room, and she froze. Her lips pressed together in a grimace.

"I should get back to my mom," she said hurriedly.

His pulse evened out as a pit formed in his stomach. Hardly the profession of love that he was hoping for.

"Of course." He helped her off the counter.

They awkwardly got dressed and prepared to leave the apartment, but she stopped and looked back at him.

"What is it?" he asked.

She took both his hands. "I wish I didn't have to leave tomorrow. Promise to pass on the news as soon as you hear something? Even if it's the middle of the night."

"You have my word." He kissed her again and hoped against hope it wouldn't be the last time.

CHAPTER FORTY-SEVEN

EMMA

Every goodbye with Leo was harder than the last. New York had greeted them by pelting them with sleet the second they left the subway station. Emma's apartment felt empty, drafty, wrong. Even Lisa seemed bummed with their return to normalcy and had meticulously inspected the plants, cursed their neighbor for overwatering her string of pearls succulent, then retired to her room for a nap with Arizona.

Emma collapsed onto the sagging couch. She needed to get up, to start looking for freelance jobs. At the very least, she needed to come up with a damn name for her business. But something inside her was weighing her down like a fifty-pound bag of H&R flour.

Her phone vibrated, and she jumped. Was it Leo calling with news?

But no. It was Lola.

"Are you home?" her bestie said by way of greeting.

"Yeah, we just got back."

"You don't sound happy. Did something happen?"

"No, everything's fine. Actually, Leo and I are going to try long distance."

There was an ear-piercing shriek on the other end of the phone.

"And you decided to wait until *now* to tell me?"

"I know, I'm sorry. Things have been crazy here."

"What's actually going on?"

Emma bit her lip. "I'm a selfish asshole."

"What do you mean?"

"Let me be clear. I am so, so happy that Leo was able to raise the money and he's a huge step closer to building this shelter. I'm so proud of him. He's worked incredibly hard for this."

"Right," Lola said slowly.

Emma lowered her voice. "But a small, very horrible part of me was kind of hoping it wouldn't work."

"Ah. Because then he might have given up and left Lynoria and his toxic-ass family for good?"

"Exactly. I let myself imagine all the possibilities—what if he moved to New York? What if we really gave this a shot? We could have had a beautiful, simple life together here. But now there's no chance of that happening, and I feel like I'm in mourning for this alternate reality that was never meant to be. It's so selfish for me to even think this way."

"You are the least selfish person I know."

"Obviously not. And I knew this would happen if I helped him, but when he showed up here, I could tell how much he needed me. This is so much bigger than the two of us. And I think that's how it would always be, dating a prince. The needs of a whole country are always going to be more important than our wants."

Lola tutted. "Okay, I know that's not true. Didn't he basically call his mom a Marie Antoinette and knowingly destroy his own chances of getting the shelter built because she slighted you? Pump the brakes, honey. You are not dumping this man just because of something that *might* happen. You haven't even given it an honest shot. What if the opposite happens? What if this is your husband? Your soulmate? You're just going to give up because things are hard?"

"I know," Emma said with a grunt of frustration. "I almost told him I loved him last night. We snuck away from the celebration and had sex in the bathroom, and everything just felt so—so right. He's so warm and caring. Ugh, this sucks."

Her friend gasped. "Why didn't you tell him the truth?"

"I was afraid. It's too soon."

"I told Mateo I love him on our second date," Lola said pointedly.

Emma lowered her voice. "You were nineteen. I'm a grown woman with a borderline-insurmountable amount of responsibility. Saying those words means something needs to change. And I don't know how to make this work."

"You have to tell him. He deserves to know."

This conversation was making Emma even more confused and uncomfortable. "Did I tell you I confronted the queen?" she asked.

Lola gasped again and immediately moved on to the new topic, then had to hang up five minutes later when her dog threw up on the rug.

Emma jumped up and stretched. She needed to get her shit together. Her family was depending on her, and that was more important than her relationship drama right now. Finding some freelance jobs fast needed to be her priority.

Replacing what she had impulsively pulled out of her business savings to get to Lynoria was going to take time.

She opened her laptop at the kitchen table. While it booted up, she wiped down the kitchen and paused when she spotted a mug by the sink. The last one Leo had used. She touched the cool ceramic and brushed a thumb over where his lips would have been.

She could clean up later. With Cooper hot on her heels, she stormed back into the hallway to the basket of mail. Bill, bill, junk mail. She froze. Her heart thumped like she was sprinting. The last envelope looked ordinary, but her name and address were written in shaky handwriting. The return address was the Metropolitan Detention Center in Brooklyn.

A letter from her father. A reminder that she was never safe.

She ripped it open and scanned the contents.

See you soon, Princess.
-Daddy

Her stomach hardened. Great, another item on the to-do list. The police had mentioned filing for a new restraining order after the assault, but there hadn't been time before they left for Lynoria. And besides, they didn't have money for a lawyer or time to peruse whatever programs might be available for victims.

She ignored the sense of dread in her stomach and turned to her laptop to stare at job postings, then switched to a website with home security systems. Completely unaffordable. Same with guns. Plus, she didn't have time to take a safety course.

They were sitting ducks once he was released. She picked up her phone to call Leo but stopped. This was her own baggage. He was waiting on some of the most important news of his life.

She would figure it out herself. She always did.

CHAPTER FORTY-EIGHT

LEO

Someone knocked on the front door of Leo's apartment. He opened one bleary eye and sat up in bed. Emma had left hours ago, and he'd come back and crashed after dropping her off. Who even knew he lived here? It must have been Sal.

He tossed off a blanket and ambled over to the door. He was in sweatpants and no shirt, but who in town was likely to care?

He opened the door without looking and almost fell over in shock.

"Mom?"

There was the queen, arms crossed and cheeks pink, looking like she had just walked down from the castle. He hadn't seen her on foot in the village in forever. Years, maybe.

There was a ninety-five percent chance she was here to scream at him. But she had already cut him off—what more could she do?

"Good morning, Leopold," she said very formally, as

though he wasn't wearing sweatpants with an adobo sauce stain on them from last night's celebratory nachos.

"Come in," he said, standing back to allow her to enter.

She stared at the tiny flat and the gaggle of kittens before turning back to him. Her brows were knit together.

"What are you doing here?" he asked.

She stiffly held out a bakery bag. He opened it to reveal two muffins.

"I'm redeeming my auction item," she said. "A meal with Prince Leo."

"That was you?"

She nodded. "I have some things to say. And a birthday gift to give you."

A birthday gift? Apparently she hadn't forgotten after all.

She reached into her purse and pulled out an envelope. She handed it over, and he thanked her. It didn't feel like a wad of cash. So what was it?

"I've never missed one of my children's birthdays before," she said quietly. "I remember every minute of the day you were born. You were always so conscientious, even then. You waited until I had a restful night's sleep and a hearty breakfast before attempting to make your arrival."

He smiled. At least she wasn't screaming yet.

"Spending your birthday without you was something of a wake-up call for me. I haven't always been the best at showing it, but I hope you know I care about you. Very much. Your father does too."

Leo fiddled with the envelope. His mom had never expressed feelings to him before. Was she ill? Or maybe this was a dream. That made more sense. He surreptitiously pinched his own arm but didn't suddenly jolt into a different reality.

"It's not easy being born into royalty," the queen said.

"I've seen how it's affected your father and brother. I'm not proud of what I've done to you. It was an overreaction, cutting you off. I know you do a lot of good with the money."

He shook his head. "While what you're saying is valid, I need to apologize for what I said after the ball. It was needlessly cruel."

The queen sighed. "It may have been cruel, but you weren't wrong." She moved to stare out the window at the street, a tiny slice of her kingdom.

"Somewhere along the way, I think I lost sight of what it means to be queen. When the country voted to transition to a constitutional monarchy, I took it as a slight. Like they didn't trust me and your father enough to lead them. When, realistically, it was just what needed to happen. Monarchies are outdated, antiquated. I just wanted to remind them that we're...still here."

Leo came to stand next to her, and together they stared out the window. "You still have such power. You have so much capacity to do some good for this country."

"I know. That's why I'm meeting with parliament this morning."

He frowned. "Why?"

"To discuss the creation of a new office and a new position. The minister of charitable giving. They would maintain oversight of the nation's need for charity projects and be given access to funds to accomplish the necessary work. I think I know the perfect candidate for it. It's highly irregular for a member of the royal family to hold a traditional job, but I can't think of anyone better suited."

Leo turned to her. "You do mean me and not John, right?"

The queen let out a startled laugh, then quickly

composed herself. "Yes, Leopold. I meant you. I see what you do for our people, even if you think I don't."

He was silent for a moment as he considered this. It was the perfect job, a permanent solution to his ingrained need to help the people of this country. He wouldn't even have to do it on the down-low this time. No one could stand in his way or hold him back. He could do so much good. And he'd be more suited to that than taking care of elephants or working in a diner.

But there was the Emma part of it all. What would a permanent position here to do their relationship?

Leo bit his lip. "I do hope that the position will allow for remote work some of the time."

The queen turned away from the window and sat primly on the edge of the couch. "Things are getting serious with the baker."

He struggled to find the right words. "She's more than a baker, Mom."

"I know," she said quietly.

"But you're right. Things are getting more serious. And we need to have a conversation about what that means."

She turned toward him. "Go on."

"I can't have you making snide remarks about her being American or being from a poor family. Emma's background has nothing to do with her value and her worth as a human being. She's incredible. Kind and funny and so smart. I think in time you'll see that."

The queen stood and reached into her purse. "I already do."

The righteousness fell out of his sails. Considering she had cut him off for merely dancing with Emma, he had expected more of a fight.

"I won't expose Emma to a toxic environment," he

continued. There was no way to tell if this was a permanent attitude change. "If you want to be in our lives, I am setting a boundary—today—that you will be kind. Or at the very least, neutral. I won't have her treated like she's 'less than' because of where she grew up or what her family situation is. This whole 'keeping the royal bloodline pure' thing is archaic and creepy. And you need to start attending therapy. Like, tomorrow."

The queen pulled a face for a moment, then seemed to decide not to comment. She removed a small box from her purse and rose to her feet. She pressed it into his hand. "Fine. Emma's unprecedented arrival here opened my eyes to a lot of things I was too stubborn to see. You have my word."

"What's this?" he asked.

She gestured at it, and he opened the lid. A massive solitaire-cut diamond winked at him from the box.

The fuck?

"For when you're ready. It was your grandmother's. I was planning to give this to your brother but..."

Was this his mom's way of saying she approved of Emma? After cutting him off just for being seen with her? Maybe she had poisoned it.

"Well," he said slowly. "Thank you. I think it'll be a while till we get to that stage. We still have to figure out how to make this work."

"Yes. Well. She came to see me, you know. After the protest."

He froze. Was that where she had disappeared to?

"She explained a lot about your motives. And she shared her story with me." Her eyebrows contracted, and she went back to staring out the window. "You're right to be worried about the shelters in the kingdom. We need to do better. Incidentally, I have one more piece of news to share."

Leo's breath caught. This was either going to be really good or result in another royal shouting match. He carefully shut the door behind him and consciously tried to adopt a blank expression.

"There's been an unfortunate issue with the permits for the new ski resort. So it seems the lot is available, after all."

His mouth dropped open. "It is?"

"The deed is in your envelope. Your father's already signed off on the project," she said carefully.

His mind raced a thousand miles a minute. There was so much to do. He needed to call his project manager and the contractors and—

He stopped. First, he needed to be present in this moment with his mom. He had never seen her have a change of heart on anything. They should consider making it a national holiday.

Before he could think better of it, he ran in and hugged her tight. She was rigid under his grasp but relaxed enough to pat him awkwardly on the back.

"Thank you," he said. "You have no idea how much this means to me."

He had never thought she would crumble this quickly. Emma's plan had worked. Maybe public humiliation had been the right call, after all.

"Well," she said, "you didn't leave me much of a choice after you had half the country marching on the castle." She waved a hand as if there were still protesters ready to boo her on the streets outside.

Leo pulled back and put his hands in his pockets. "I'm sorry about the protest. I knew it would force your hand. I just needed you to see how important this project is. And the tremendous impact it could have on our citizens."

"Well, you succeeded." She turned away from the window. "I fear I was too hasty when I cut you off earlier. Your suite at the castle is still yours, if you want it. And your salary, of course. I know you usually use it to fix things around the village, but I'd implore you to consider putting it toward your future. Whatever that looks like."

Leo paused. Having access to that money again would be life-changing. He could help the village again, make sure Emma had everything she needed. But for some reason, it didn't feel right.

"I think collecting a royal salary could be a conflict of interest if I'm working for parliament," he said carefully.

The queen nodded. "Very well. I'll just have it funneled to the charity fund. I'm off to parliament. Make sure your resume is shipshape. And don't wear those pants to your interview. In fact, you should probably burn them."

She strode to the door, then paused and turned around. "You would have made a great king, you know."

His cheeks grew hot. "Well, it's too bad I was born second."

"Yes," she said softly.

The door closed behind her, and Leo was left standing in the middle of his studio apartment, body vibrating with energy like he had just slammed forty espressos.

He looked at the box in his hand and tucked it into a drawer. He didn't have the mental energy to process what that meant right now.

There were a thousand things to do, and he had to share the good news with Emma.

CHAPTER FORTY-NINE

EMMA

"So, what do you think?" The realtor with the artificially white smile tapped the stainless steel counter of the commissary kitchen. "A new shift will be available in June. It's the twelve a.m. to six-thirty slot. We could lock you in for a year. Hopefully by then, a day shift will open up."

Emma hesitated, gripping the handles of her mother's wheelchair. Days had passed, and everything had changed. Leo's project had been approved against all odds, and through some miracle of nepotism, he had gotten a new job as minister of charitable giving. Her unspoken dream of him living in New York was officially dead.

Emma had been slamming through freelance project after freelance project, willing the endless cascade of tasks to distract her from the aching absence that followed her like a ghost. No matter how busy he was, Leo had called her every night before he went to bed. The calls were the best part of her day.

His dreams were full speed ahead, but hers were floundering. Maybe it was the fact that the sun hadn't been out since she returned home, or the inherent unnerving nature of being on the verge of such a major change, but something felt wrong. Her business still didn't have a name, and her zest for elaborately decorated cakes had somehow evaporated. Her thoughts returned often to the soup kitchen in Lynoria and the townspeople who had been visibly grateful to sample her pastries.

What was the point of all this?

"What do you think, sweetheart?" her mother prompted.

Emma blinked. "Sorry."

Get it together. This was the plan, the only path forward. The only way to make a better life for her mom. She wasn't about to change it for a boy she had just met.

"Uh, the shift isn't ideal," she said. "Sometimes a decorating shift alone takes eight hours. And what about storage? Or if the shift before me doesn't clean adequately and I have to spend half of it cleaning and sanitizing?"

The realtor's smile dimmed by several watts. "There is some storage space available for an extra fee. You won't find a cheaper solution for your needs. We can look at turnkey units or private kitchen rentals, but that's easily going to be three to four times more expensive, and they're less likely to have the type of equipment you need. At this point in your business, a commissary is your best bet."

Emma sighed and took in the steel surroundings. While it felt good to be back in a proper kitchen again, it wasn't what she had imagined. A commissary was, theoretically, the perfect solution. It was only thirty minutes from her apartment. She didn't need to buy her own equipment. The night shift, however, was problematic. Her mom regularly needed to use the restroom at night, and she had fallen the last time she attempted it on her own. And Emma would have to sleep during the day, which would double the amount of danger. Then there was the fact that her dad could stop by at any point the next time he was released from prison.

"I'll need to think about it," she blurted. She wasn't in the correct headspace to make a year-long commitment.

"Okay, but the owners will need your answer before the new year or they'll look for someone else to fill the shift."

"I understand. Thank you."

The gray sky was fading to black, and the wind was bitterly cold when Emma ducked out the door onto the streets of downtown Brooklyn. The smell of urine was strong on the sidewalk, and her eyes watered as she kicked half a dozen pieces of trash on her way to the crosswalk. It couldn't have been more different than the curving cobblestone streets of Lynoria. She adjusted the blanket on her mother's lap and headed for the subway station.

This was supposed to be the most magical time of the year. Christmas Eve was in two days, and although she and her mom had resumed their daily celebrations, it didn't feel the same as it used to. Like someone had put a crappy sepia-toned filter on her world and the colors were stubbornly muted.

Leo's groundbreaking would be held on Christmas Eve. And she wouldn't even be there to see the start of the project that had nearly cost him everything.

"Let's take a detour," she said to her mom, who agreed.

Without a firm plan, they went down an elevator and boarded a train in the opposite direction from home. She could recapture the Christmas spirit.

They exited in Bay Ridge, and her mother gasped. "Dyker Heights? We haven't been in years."

"I thought it might be nice."

Emma's hands were frozen by the time the blaze of Christmas lights appeared on the horizon. The neighborhood decorated to the nines every year. They pushed their way through a throng of people shivering in the cold. Inflatable Santas bobbed on balconies. Trees drooped beneath nets of flashing red-and-green lights. Children stared in awe at glittering reindeer and ten-foot-tall nutcrackers. It was Christmas in New York at its merriest and most spectacular. It was beautiful and temporary, just like one of her cakes.

So why didn't it feel right?

New York had everything she needed.

You know what Lynoria didn't have? Korean food. Corn dogs. Broadway. The Met. The only feasible market for her business. Not to mention an expansive public transportation system, some of which was even ADA compliant.

Tension was building in her body, and it grew with each elaborately decorated house.

"Are you okay, sweetheart?" Lisa asked. "If we go any faster, we're going to mow down a Santa."

Emma pulled to a stop. "I...I don't know."

Her mom twisted to look at her. "It's okay if it doesn't feel like it used to. That's the thing about new experiences. They tend to reframe everything."

"What if I want to do more than just bake cakes?" she blurted. "I could do more. Be more. Help people. But I can't just abandon my plan."

Lisa smiled. "It's okay to change your mind. You should trust the part of you that wants to grow and change."

"But I'm scared, Mom."

"That's how you know it's the right decision. Growth is terrifying. Admitting you want more, deserve better. You know how hard it was for me to leave your father."

"I know."

"It was the hardest thing I've ever done. We lost our home, our family unit. But that decision, while it felt impossible, opened up the most wonderful years of my entire life. Watching you grow into this remarkable young woman despite everything I put you through as a child—"

Emma sniffed. "It wasn't you, Mom."

"But I didn't leave. Not soon enough. I'll carry that guilt around with me for the rest of my life." She stroked a hand over the part of the coat covering Emma's scar. "You are braver and more capable than you know. Don't wait to do the big, scary thing. Tell Leo how you're feeling."

"What if he doesn't feel the same way?"

"There's only one way to find out."

CHAPTER FIFTY

LEO

"Friends. Countrymen. I want to thank you all for joining me today as we dedicate this spot to a new chapter in Lynorian history."

Leo stood on a small platform in front of the vacant lot that would now—officially—become the site of the project of his dreams. He was joined by Kat and Pierre, the general contractor. A crowd surrounded them, far more people than he expected. It was over-the-top—the queen had insisted on providing a golden shovel—but for once, Leo didn't mind all the pomp and circumstance. This wasn't a new storefront for luxury handbags. And it certainly wasn't another ski resort that no one needed. It was going to be a cornerstone of their community, a safe haven in more ways than the public even realized.

How he wished Emma could see it. Over the last several days, an elaborate plan had begun to hatch.

"It's something that will uplift us and bring us together in new ways," he said. "The garden will grow food for the people in town and teach our children about agriculture. The library will educate our children, help our adults, and open doors to other worlds for people who just need to escape for a little while. The new soup kitchen will feed and shelter our hungry. All of this is only possible because you stood with me. You made your voices heard. I hope that you always do. Because together, as your new minister for charitable giving—or whatever my new title is"—a chuckle rippled through the crowd—"we can do some amazing things."

He scanned the audience. "I'm going to be setting up a website where you can leave suggestions for services or amenities you'd like to see in your community. I'm also going to be visiting each province this year to host some town hall meetings and see what matters most to you all. Thank you so much for your time and for your belief in this project. Now go spend the holidays with your families."

He put the microphone down, and the crowd whistled and cheered. Together with Kat and Pierre, he dug the golden shovel into the partially frozen earth and broke the ground. This was the moment he had been working toward for months. It was amazing—the culmination of a dream he had fought for with everything he had—but it didn't mean as much without Emma at his side.

When would he see her again? He was still onboarding as a new member of parliament. He didn't even have an office yet, let alone a staff. It would be difficult to get away to New York with everything so in flux. Would serving his country always mean such deeply personal sacrifice?

He tried to dismiss the thoughts as he shook hands and took pictures with a number of people in the crowd, but his heart wasn't in it.

He missed waking up and watching as she smiled and rolled away from him, hair tousled from a night of lovemaking. They had known each other for so short a time, but there was no denying the staggering depths of his feelings for her.

From the moment the project received the green light, he had been working on a new plan. There was no guarantee it would convince her, and he wasn't certain that he was understanding succession rights for rent-controlled apartments correctly. Why would Emma compromise her carefully curated goals to move here for six months out of the year?

But he had to try. As soon as he got his first paycheck from parliament, he was going to buy her a plane ticket and make his plea.

He shook the last hand and said goodbye to Kat and Pierre, who were examining the lot. He was almost back to his truck when he noticed someone was leaning against it. His hackles went up for an instant, anticipating the press wanting a comment on his personal life. But he broke into a smile when he recognized who stood there.

Emma.

"What are you doing here?" he gathered her into his arms and squeezed her tightly, lifting her into the air.

"I wanted to see the groundbreaking. You were amazing," she said into his lapel, slightly muffled by the fabric.

He pulled back just to look at her again. It was really her. The glow of the white Christmas lights strung above brought out the spun gold in her hair. She must have been exhausted, but she was unbelievably lovely.

Finally, finally, everything was perfect. Well, almost.

"I can't believe you came," he said. "You didn't have to do that. But I'm so glad you're here. I—I wanted to show you something."

The nerves had reemerged. It was now or never.

"Can we talk first?" she asked.

He froze. Did she come all this way to break up with him face to face? On Christmas Eve? The thought was unbearable. All of this would mean nothing without her. If it hadn't been for her and Lola, this project never would have gotten off the ground.

"Of course."

They set off toward the village green. Snow drifted down, big fat flakes that dusted her jacket and caught in her hair. House windows glowed with happy families crowded around fireplaces and sharing meals. A group was caroling down the street. It was the perfect Christmas Eve, if someone liked that sort of thing.

The silence was killing him.

"Did you want to go to my apartment to warm up and chat?"

"No, my mom's there and I don't really want to say this in front of her. I hope you don't mind that I used your spare key."

"Of course not." His heart rate inched up another notch. The unknown was killing him.

They stopped in the center of town, under a crisscross of brilliantly colored lights. The lone traffic light shifted to red, policing vehicles that weren't there.

Emma turned to him and took both of his hands. She was really here. No matter what she had to say, he was so happy to see her.

"This is going to sound insane," she began. She averted her gaze, glancing over her shoulder at the merry carolers, who had switched to "Silent Night."

"Go on," he said.

She turned back to him. "I'm in love with you."

A thousand feelings hit him at the same time—joy,

disbelief, a soaring sensation like he had just been catapulted into the air.

He opened his mouth to speak, to stutter, to scream that he loved her too. But she stopped him.

"I know it's only been a month. But that doesn't make it less true. You've unlocked something in me that I didn't know was there. I was in New York, trying to put this plan that I've been working toward for a decade into action. But it didn't feel right. None of it felt right. And it's because of you. You broke me," she said with an accusatory finger.

He raised his eyebrows.

"I don't even know if I want to bake anymore. I want to do more, be more. Help people. Find a way to make a difference in this world the way you do. But I don't know how to do that. I still need to take care of my mom, and I can't just pick up and—"

Leo dragged her close and kissed her hard. She melted into him, gripping his shoulders as their tongues danced.

He pulled back and looked into the brilliant green of her eyes. "First, let me say I love you. I think I've known it since the second you walked into that pole. You are so talented, thoughtful, stunningly beautiful, and you bring peace in a way I've only felt when I'm in my workshop with a crackling fire and a mug of spiced wine. Second, I would never ask you to give up your home, your dreams, anything for me."

"Then how do we make this work? I can't handle not knowing when I'm going to see you again. I want you for every holiday, every Tuesday, every wing night at Sal's bar." She waved a hand down the street.

He broke into a smile. "Come with me."

They came to a stop in front of the soup kitchen. Smells of roast turkey and herby mashed potatoes were drifting out, warming the street.

"Actually, can you close your eyes for a second?" he asked.

"Okay," she said with a hesitant smile.

He reached into his messenger bag and pulled out a sheet of paper. He scribbled something on it and plastered it to the window with a piece of tape. He had hoped for a much grander and more concrete display, but hopefully it would still get his point across.

"Okay, open."

She opened her eyes and looked around, then looked at him. He pointed to the sheet of paper.

"Petal and Pastry?" she asked. "What's this?"

"When the new community center is built, the soup kitchen's going to move over there," he said. "Which will leave this building vacant."

"Okay," she said slowly.

"I know your apartment is rent-controlled, and that it's an invaluable commodity in today's day and age."

She nodded, and he continued. "I did some digging into succession laws, and there are some exemptions for the residency requirements. For example, there's some flexibility if you're required to leave the home temporarily for employment purposes."

She tilted her head.

He took her hand. "What if you lived here for a few months out of the year? Maybe in the spring or summer? I can keep you safe from your dad. Felons aren't even allowed into the country, in the unlikely event that he cobbled together enough brain cells to apply for a passport."

She bit her lip, but he plowed on. "We can create a seasonal position for your mom to be in charge of the community garden, and we could contract you to bake for the community kitchen. Your noncompete shouldn't apply across international lines. You could have this space, and your mom could sell the flowers she grows in the garden, and you can still make your beautiful cakes. If you apply for dual citizenship, you and your mom will both be eligible for free national healthcare, and I'll use every last connection I have to find her the finest physical therapist in this country. And I know it'll be tricky to find a place to bake in New York, but I asked my mother, and it turns out we actually have a Lynorian consulate in Queens with a fully equipped kitchen, so the next time Lady Gaga needs—why are you crying?"

A tear streaked down her face, and he caught it with his thumb. Shit. He knew it was too much. Only an unbalanced person would plan an entire life out for someone else without even consulting them first.

"I'm sorry," she said. "I just didn't expect this. No one's ever done something like this for me."

He took her hand again. "I think you haven't had anyone to take care of you in a really long time. But you don't have to do this alone anymore. This is a partnership, Emma. You've helped me so much. Let me return the favor."

"What about my mom? And the dogs? We're a package deal."

Leo smiled. "Someday, hopefully, your family will be my family. Your traditions will be my traditions."

A blush crept into her cheeks.

"We'll get a wheelchair-accessible caravan. She can come with us on our tour of the provinces. We'll decorate the hell out of wherever we live every Christmas with animal butt ornaments or—what did you say you do again? I'll have to work on finding a home with an in-law suite," he muttered to himself. Another item for the to-do list. "Not that I expect you to move in with me. We'll find a place for you and your mom while you're here."

"And what about your family? They still hate me," she said.

Leo shook his head. "I think you'll be pleasantly surprised. I've already set very clear boundaries with my mother, and I've insisted she start attending therapy. She knows that the second we hear one snide comment, she's out of our lives. I won't allow her to control this. And I mean that. I will protect you—emotionally, physically, mentally. With everything I have."

"I see. And what do I bring to this elaborate table you've set?"

"Love. And patience. That's the only thing I'll ask of you. And, you know, if you wanted to throw in some cheesecakes."

She laughed, and her eyes sparkled.

"I know there's a lot to consider," he said. "You don't have to make a decision now. I just want a life with you, Emma. Whatever that looks like. I need you to know that loving me doesn't have to mean giving up who you are. But it might mean a compromise."

She was smiling. "You're worth compromising for."

She jumped into his arms, and he twirled her beneath the dizzying array of Christmas lights. They kissed again in the falling snow, surrounded by the delicate melody of "Silent Night" from the carolers down the road. It was their first Christmas Eve of hopefully dozens together. Maybe the holiday wasn't so bad after all.

BONUS EPILOGUE

"I can't believe my best friend, the girl who once spent two hours in a middle school dumpster with me when I accidentally threw away my retainer, is going to be the Princess of Lynoria." Lola adjusted the flower crown on Emma's head.

The sun was beaming down, and a gentle breeze brought the scent of flowers through the open window. They couldn't have asked for a more perfect wedding day. Emma had grown to love the village in every season, but there was something truly magical about spring and the way everything burst into life after a long winter.

"Barely," Emma said with a glance in the gilded floor-length mirror. As Leo always said, it was an empty title. She was only accepting it because it would give her the means to start her own charity work.

Emma shifted side to side, delighting in the way the lace A-line gown brushed the tops of her pearl-studded flats. Cooper lay at her feet, wearing a matching flower crown. Her belly was a flutter of nerves, but that had more to do with the almost two thousand people spectating outside than it had to do with marrying Leo.

It didn't feel real. Four years ago, she and her mom were barely scraping by. Now they had a bustling family business in a foreign country, right down the road from the women's shelter Leo had fought tooth and nail for.

Running into that pole had completely changed her life. While she still took on at least one artistic challenge a month to keep her baking skills up to snuff, nothing made her feel quite as fulfilled as whipping up a tray of fresh pastries or crusty bread for the community kitchen. She was making a difference, even though it was in a small way. Women and children from the new shelter often stopped in, and when a new family arrived, she dropped off care packages—massive donuts with sprinkles and cupcakes the size of her head.

Lynoria had come to feel like home, and the people, her family. She and Leo went to Sal and Callum's for game night every week. She'd joined a book club with several library patrons and had even started teaching baking classes at the new community center.

Her new life wasn't all fairy tales and slow dances. The paparazzi had come skulking around again after the announcement of their engagement. And like any couple, they had arguments—where they would go on vacation, would their children go to public or private school, how they would handle parents overstepping in their relationship. For someone who came from an emotionally repressed household, Leo was really coming into his own as a communicator.

Ruby narrowed her eyes and dabbed a makeup sponge on Emma's cheek. "And I can't believe you talked my mom down from a traditional royal wedding to this boho hobbit feast with the entire town."

"Hey, I made a lot of concessions for your mom." Emma

waved a hand toward the door of the inn. "There must be a hundred royals and dignitaries out there that I've never met. Do you know how insane that is? One hundred people that I've never met at my own wedding."

"You're lucky it wasn't three hundred. Last week at dinner, she was still moaning about offending some member of the Swedish royal family. But it took some of the heat off of me, so thank you for that."

"She's still being weird about Alicia?"

Alicia was Ruby's girlfriend at NYU. She was in the prelaw program and zero percent afraid of the king and queen.

"I weirdly think she respects Alicia after she shut down Lord Pemberly over landlord/tenant relationships at the New Year's ball. Mostly she's losing her mind over me moving to New York permanently. And becoming a teacher. Oops."

"Those kids are going to be so lucky to have you."

There was a knock, and Beatrice popped the door open. She was clutching a clipboard, and an earpiece was nestled in her ear. "Oh, Miss Clark. You look gorgeous."

"Thank you. Are we ready to get this show on the road?"

"Yes. The groomsmen are getting lined up. Next will be bridesmaids."

"Could you send my mother in? Just for a minute."

"Of course."

Ruby and Lola hugged her tightly and left in a flash of royal blue tulle.

Emma took a few slow, deep breaths and glanced at the vows she had wrapped around her bouquet. She had made it very clear from the outset that joining the royal family wasn't going to change anything fundamental—though she would fulfill certain newfound duties as a member of the royal family, especially for participation in charity events, she was also going to continue working. Her choices had caused some friction with her future mother-in-law, but Leo had backed her up at every turn.

There was another knock at the door, and her mother walked in. It still made Emma's heart race to see her standing upright, with only a cane for stability. Leo had pulled endless strings and gotten her mother the best physical and occupational therapists in the country. She had made remarkable strides, though she still grumbled about the intensity of the program.

Part of her progress could be credited to Eduardo, her former physical therapist, who had ignored her threats and swearing and pushed her to be better—right up to the point where they fell in love. The second his feelings had crossed into beyond-friendly territory, he had referred Lisa to a colleague. He was as patient and caring in their relationship as he was in his work.

"Oh, my darling girl." Tears formed in Lisa's eyes. She crossed the room confidently and gathered Emma in her arms. "You are the most beautiful bride."

"I can't believe it's really happening. I kind of thought it would never happen for me."

Lisa's grip tightened. "I know Maya was a real asshole, but I'm so glad all the suffering you went through eventually led to something amazing."

"Me too. Maybe I should write her a thank-you card."

"I wouldn't go that far."

Emma smiled. "You're right. Your flowers are stunning, Mom. Everyone's talking about them."

The high street was exploding with floral arrangements, like a May Day festival had thrown up on midsummer. But in a really elegant way.

Lisa pulled back with a watery smile. She glanced out the window, where the corner of Emma's entrance archway was visible, covered in her blooms. "Eleanor almost complimented them. She called them 'adequate.'"

Emma gasped. "Are you going to put that on the website? Petal and Pastry: Royally Adequate."

Lisa smiled and squeezed Emma's hand. "Five years ago, I never would have believed this was possible. I couldn't have done this, gotten back to this point, if it wasn't for you, sweetheart. You and Leo."

Emma frowned. "Mom."

"Yes?"

"What's on your hand?" She flipped her mother's hand over and gasped. There was a diamond ring on a very specific finger.

"Oh, shoot. I meant to take it off."

"You're getting married? And you concealed it from me?" Emma clarified.

Lisa smiled. "Ed proposed last weekend. We wanted to tell you together, and definitely not on your wedding day. But you know men and their timing."

"Mom, that's amazing. I'm so happy for you." Emma's eyes pooled with tears for the umpteenth time that day as she drew her mom in for another tight hug.

"Do you think I have to invite Eleanor?" Lisa asked when she pulled back.

"Unfortunately, yes. Maybe she'll politely decline. Can you make the ceremony somewhere really inconvenient? Like the middle of a potato field, or maybe a water park?"

"I'll look into it. There's one other thing we should probably talk about."

"Now?" Emma raised her eyebrows.

"So you have time to think about it. I think it's time to give up the apartment."

Emma bit her lip, then released it when she remembered the makeup artist's instructions.

If she was being honest, it had been on her heart too. Traipsing back to Brooklyn to satisfy the succession requirements of their apartment had begun to feel like a chore. Most of the time, Leo couldn't join her, and her trips had grown fewer and farther between.

"It's your home, too," Lisa continued, "so I want you to have a say. But now that Eduardo and I are engaged, I want to make a new home here. Where my grandchildren will be raised. I don't want to miss out on their childhoods because I'm constantly running back to our dumpy apartment in a different country just so we don't lose it."

Emma's thoughts turned to the four walls that had been her home for most of her life. It had been her safe place, her just-in-case. But she was getting married, starting a new family. She needed to give it her all. And with her new royal duties, she probably wouldn't have time to fulfill the requirements for succession anyway. Maybe it was time to say goodbye.

Emma smiled sadly. "I think you're right. It's time to put down real roots. I'll miss it though."

"Me too, sweetheart. But I think it's the right call. Are you ready?"

Emma hesitated. "I think I want to see Leo first. Do you think Beatrice will freak out? We still have a couple of minutes."

"What's she going to do? You'll be one of her bosses in half an hour. I'll take care of it."

Her mom started for the door, then stopped and turned back. "I'm so proud of you, sweetheart. I love you forever."

"Love you forever," Emma echoed.

A minute passed while Emma anxiously paced and tried not to think about the crowd.

A soft knock preceded Leo's entrance.

Her heart faltered at the sight of him. He was in a tuxedo and bowtie, which must have annoyed the hell out of him. But holy hell, he looked good in it. When they made eye contact, he clapped a hand over his heart.

He crossed the room in two strides and took her into his arms. All at once, the anxiety lifted.

"Emma. My god, you get more beautiful every single day." He pulled back to look at her, and the intensity in his eyes brought a flood of warmth to her cheeks.

"You flatter me."

"You know I mean it. Are you having second thoughts?" he asked. His brows contracted.

"Never. I just wanted to have a moment with you before all the craziness starts."

"I needed this too," he said. He kissed her, and her toes curled.

"Speaking of craziness," he added, "would you like to know what my parents are giving us as a wedding gift?"

"Oh god. What? Fifteen golden horses and a mega yacht?"

"Worse. An estate."

She pulled back. "Pardon?"

"You know that place with the small castle we passed by on our way to the food and wine festival?"

"The one that I said looked super haunted?"

"That's the one."

Her mind spiraled. "We can't live in an estate. How are we going to keep a whole damn castle clean? I'm not mowing a hundred acres of grass. Does Target even deliver to castles?"

She stopped and straightened up. "Wow, I sound like such an ungrateful asshole. I'm sorry."

He smiled. "We don't have to accept it. I haven't really evaluated the ethics of it. But maybe we should at least pay a visit. Our place is so tight as it is. Mother showed me pictures. The kitchen there is top-notch. Gorgeous grounds for our future children to explore. And there's a guest house for your mom. All one floor, with an outdoor terrace and a massive garden. We could grow more vegetables for the community kitchen."

"It would be really nice to not have to overhear her and Eduardo canoodling through the wall," Emma muttered.

They had definitely outgrown the two-bedroom apartment they had moved into two years ago.

"By the way, they're getting married. And we're giving up the apartment."

Leo sputtered. "What?"

"And speaking of future children," Emma said.

Leo's eyes lit up. It had been a hot topic of conversation over the last year. Leo hadn't even wanted to wait for the wedding, but Emma was still chasing a sense of stability.

"In light of the current circumstances, I think I've arrived at a compromise."

"Which is?"

"Two years. Let's take two years to get our feet underneath us as a married couple, and all the things that come with it. Let's have adventures. Travel. And then let's make a baby. Or foster. Or adopt. I'm open to all options."

"You're really going to make me wait two more years? I'll need an oxygen tank and cataract glasses to play with our kids."

She took his hand. "I want to experience every beautiful minute of being your wife before things change. Again."

He kissed her hand. "You've done so much for me. I'll do this for you. Now let's get married before you come to your senses."

"I love you, Leo."

"I love you, too...Your Highness."

She shook her head fervently. "Just Emma."

He leaned in and brushed a lock of hair away from her face. "You've never been 'just Emma.'"

Her toes curled in her shoes, and he left her with one last searing kiss.

Beatrice poked her head in the second Leo exited. "It's time."

When Emma stepped out into the sunshine under the blue Lynorian sky, everything felt right. Sure, there were almost two thousand people ready to stare at her as she and her mom made their way slowly to the altar at the center of town.

But there was also Leo. And her new siblings-in-law. And over a hundred cheesecakes that she had painstakingly handcrafted over the last week.

Maybe she didn't have the hotshot custom bakery in New York that she had originally planned. But she had found something better. Purpose. Family. And most of all, love.

ACKNOWLEDGMENTS

Mike for always being my hype man and for not getting mad that our Christmas trees keep multiplying.

Matt for all the orange crushes.

Lucy, Avery, and Jill for encouraging me to write this.

Michelle and Jason for taking a chance on a weirdo.

Alexis for being the best alpha reader.

Jess and HEA Author Services for fixing all my damn commas.

Luna for policing Gatsby.

October for being the most breathtakingly beautiful month.

ALSO BY MADISON SCORE

Standalone:

Love Among Vines

Royal Icing

Claire Hartley Accidental Mystery:

Book 1 - Bride or Die

Book 2 - Say Yes to the Death

Book 3 - Happily Never After